PI

"*Passion* certainly lives u

absorbing . . . That special book that mixes a sizzling romance with an intriguing story, and it's a real treat for readers."

—*The Romance Reader*

"Sensual and intriguing . . . Truly a memorable read."

—*The Romance Readers Connection*

"This erotic Victorian romance will elicit moans from the audience whenever the lead male makes his mark . . . Lisa Valdez heats up the era with a fine historical starring two ardent lovers defying society's norms."

—*The Best Reviews*

"It's quite a fix they're in, and how Mark pursues his pleasure and his passion is as irresistible to readers as it is to Passion. Valdez lets you indulge in a bit of sizzling fantasy that leaves you sighing with pleasure. Like Susan Johnson, she mixes history, colorful details, and a strong plot with a large dose of sensuality. Savor the satisfaction of a little *Passion*. Very sensual."

—*Romantic Times*

"Highly emotional and sexually breathtaking novel."

—*Fresh Fiction*

Berkley Sensation Titles by Lisa Valdez

PASSION
PATIENCE

Patience

Lisa Valdez

BERKLEY SENSATION, NEW YORK

THE BERKLEY PUBLISHING GROUP
Published by the Penguin Group
Penguin Group (USA) Inc.
375 Hudson Street, New York, New York 10014, USA
Penguin Group (Canada), 90 Eglinton Avenue East, Suite 700, Toronto, Ontario M4P 2Y3, Canada
(a division of Pearson Penguin Canada Inc.)
Penguin Books Ltd., 80 Strand, London WC2R 0RL, England
Penguin Group Ireland, 25 St. Stephen's Green, Dublin 2, Ireland (a division of Penguin Books Ltd.)
Penguin Group (Australia), 250 Camberwell Road, Camberwell, Victoria 3124, Australia
(a division of Pearson Australia Group Pty. Ltd.)
Penguin Books India Pvt. Ltd., 11 Community Centre, Panchsheel Park, New Delhi—110 017, India
Penguin Group (NZ), 67 Apollo Drive, Rosedale, North Shore 0632, New Zealand
(a division of Pearson New Zealand Ltd.)
Penguin Books (South Africa) (Pty.) Ltd., 24 Sturdee Avenue, Rosebank, Johannesburg 2196,
South Africa

Penguin Books Ltd., Registered Offices: 80 Strand, London WC2R 0RL, England

PATIENCE

A Berkley Sensation Book / published by arrangement with the author

PRINTING HISTORY
Berkley Sensation mass-market edition / April 2010

Cover art by Gregg Gulbronson.
Cover design by George Long.

For information, address: The Berkley Publishing Group,
a division of Penguin Group (USA) Inc.,
375 Hudson Street, New York, New York 10014.

ISBN: 978-0-425-21054-3

BERKLEY® SENSATION
Berkley Sensation Books are published by The Berkley Publishing Group,
a division of Penguin Group (USA) Inc.,
375 Hudson Street, New York, New York 10014.
BERKLEY® SENSATION and the "B" design are trademarks of Penguin Group (USA) Inc.

PRINTED IN THE UNITED STATES OF AMERICA

10 9 8 7 6 5 4 3 2 1

For my beautiful and loyal readers who,
despite intense anticipation and thwarted desire,
gracefully submitted to waiting for this story.
Thank you for staying.
You are patience personified.

For musical inspiration,
I thank George Michael for his sensual song "Father Figure,"
and George Frideric Handel for his "Sarabande,"
one of the most beautiful, reverent pieces of music I've ever heard.

A Letter of Little Consequence

June 13th, 1851

My Dear Henrietta,

You simply can't imagine all the scandalous goings-on! You're missing everything! Of all the times for you to be in Italy! I tell you, my dear, there isn't likely to be a grander entertainment than this in all our lifetimes. And wait until you hear who is at the center of it all. I daresay you shall never guess. For until his engagement, he was considered one of the most eligible bachelors in England. Have you guessed? It is none other than the very man who you had once hoped to match with your daughter. Yes, Mr. Matthew Morgan Hawkmore!

Oh, Henrietta, where shall I begin? Let me just say that once you have heard what's happened, you will be thankful that Mr. Hawkmore never took to your Amarantha. Had he, you would now be embroiled in a scandal from which you would never recover. Never, I tell you!

Are you ready, my dear? (You should sit down if you aren't already seated.)

It turns out that the rich, handsome, charming, and popular Mr. Hawkmore is a bastard! Yes! And to make matters ever so much worse, his real father was a gardener! It's really true! And the whole thing came to light in a most shocking and unseemly way.

You remember from my last letter that Mr. Hawkmore's brother (I must say half brother now, mustn't I?), the Earl of Langley, had become engaged to a commoner by the name of Charlotte Lawrence? Well, it turns out that the chit's mother was blackmailing the earl into marrying her daughter. The woman had in her possession some letters that revealed the truth of Mr. Hawkmore's parentage—letters written by none other than the earl and Mr. Hawkmore's mother, Lady Lucinda Hawkmore! Yes, she wrote the letters that damned her bastard son and herself!

Henrietta, how a mother—a lady—could write such disgusting letters, I'll never know. One was actually printed, my dear, and spread all over London. I saw it myself in Lady Winston's parlor, and it was perfectly awful. In it, the Countess gloated, and spoke of how it pleased her to see her little bastard in the Hawkmore linens. She even spoke of the possibility of him inheriting the earldom one day! Can you imagine?

Anyway, the whole blackmail scheme was revealed in the society pages of the Times. *Though no names were mentioned, everyone knows exactly who was being referred to. Oh, and it turns out that the revelation of the truth was very fortunate for Mr. Hawkmore's brother, the Earl of Langley. Who knew, but it seems that he really is in love with a commoner—only it isn't Miss Charlotte Lawrence. It's some widow from Lincolnshire! A Mrs. Passion Elizabeth Reddington (have you ever heard such an outrageous name?). Apparently he is head-over-heels for her, and is to marry her within the next fortnight. Some have the idea that she's a distant relation of this Miss Lawrence, but I don't have that on any authority. Anyway, it's all too romantic, and everyone is just dying to meet her.*

But as for the unfortunate Mr. Hawkmore—well, his fiancée, the Lady Rosalind Benchley, has broken with him. And her father, Lord Benchley, is in an absolute fury over the whole thing. He believes Mr. Hawkmore knew of his bastardy all along, which might be true. This, of course, would make Matthew Hawkmore not only a bastard, but a liar and a fraud as well.

God knows what the truth really is. Right now, opinions do seem to be split on the matter. Some agree with Benchley, some are uncertain, but everyone is striking Mr. Hawkmore from their guest lists, so I suppose it doesn't really matter. He is now persona non grata—an exile, an outcast.

If you come home now, Henrietta, you won't miss whatever is to come—for, surely, there is more to come. Who is this bride of the earl's? Does she have any family? Will the Lady Rosalind get engaged again? If so, to whom? And most interesting of all, what will become of Mr. Matthew Morgan Hawkmore?

Yours,
Augusta

Chapter One
PATIENCE

Behold, thou art fair, my love; behold, thou art fair, thou hast doves' eyes.
SONG OF SOLOMON 1:15

June 30, 1851
Wiltshire, England ~ Hawkmore House,
County Seat of the Earl and Countess of Langley

His cock throbbed and his blood coursed.

Clenching his jaw, Matthew Morgan Hawkmore drew in a slow, silent breath. He'd been seething beneath a deluge of fury and resentment. But then *she* had walked in, and her presence had pulled his passions in an entirely different direction.

He watched her pause just inside the broad entrance as moonlight, soft and pearlescent, filtered through the windows that lined one side of the long portrait gallery. She strolled slowly forward, her satin dressing gown glowing softly, as she stopped here and there to study the faces of the Hawkmores, to whom she was now related by marriage.

Patience Emmalina Dare, his new sister-in-law.

With his emotions already running high, his reaction to the beautiful sight of her moving in and out of the bright moonlight was strong and immediate. Avidly, he followed her slow walk through the gallery. His heart quickened and his cock swelled. Like a wolf watching a stray sheep, he sat quiet and tense in the shadows as she came closer and closer. He watched her glance up at the two life-sized portraits—his mother and the man he'd formerly called father.

A narrow table separated the two portraits, as if to keep them apart. He watched as Patience stepped forward, reaching for the paper he'd left there. Picking it up, she lifted it to the bright moonlight.

His shoulder cramped. He should stop her.

But he didn't. He said nothing as he watched her read the words that had been burned into his brain.

Mr. Hawkmore,

I resent the necessity for this letter. But as you refuse to accept my father's word regarding the dissolution of our engagement, I find myself in the unpleasant position of having to write to you myself. Please accept all that I shall say as my true and sincere sentiments.

It should be obvious to you that we will not suit. The shocking revelation of your parentage, the publication of your mother's disgusting letter in which she revels over your illegitimate birth, and the scandal which accompanied its disclosure have made a match between us utterly impossible. It should also be obvious to you that I could never, ever, marry the son of a gardener.

Now, while I once felt a measure of appreciation for you, I no longer harbor any such sentiment. Indeed, I believe you will come to realize that you always cared more for me than I for you. So, perhaps your disgrace is actually a blessing, as it has saved me—and you—from a marriage that would have proven unsatisfactory in time.

Finally, as my father has already told you, we find your protests of innocence in this matter to be completely unbelievable. Were you a man of honor you would admit that you knew all along of your bastardy, but clearly your ill breeding disallows such honesty.

Mr. Hawkmore, I demand that you do not write to me again, or attempt to visit. My father has already informed you that neither you nor your missives will be permitted past our threshold. Do not embarrass me with further attempts.

Sincerely,
Rosalind Benchley

Post Script ~ Your mother would do well to stay in Austria where I hear tell that she has fled. Perhaps you should join her there.

With a short exhalation, she lowered Rosalind Benchley's missive.

Why had he let her read it? "Now that you've had a look, I'll take that."

Patience started, whirled around, and stared into the shadows that hung heavy around him. Her head tilted, and he could tell the moment she saw him in the dimness. She took a step toward him.

His frown deepened. Accustomed to the shadows, he could see her well. But what did she see?

A bastard?

A gardener's son, posing as a gentleman?

A man forsaken by the women who had claimed to love him?

She took a step closer.

His shoulder pulled tighter. He should leave.

But as she took another step, he couldn't seem to move. As much as his mind urged him, his body had no will to go. Her moonlit skin called for his touch. Her lips, full and soft, beckoned kisses and more. And her thick red curls, falling down her back in wild disarray, begged the grip of his hand.

Her beauty was potent with an uncontainable sensuality. And yet—his cock pulsed as she drew closer—she was completely contained. Her eyes had told him that from the beginning—her deep, verdant eyes that reminded him of unsheared grass. Though he couldn't distinguish their color in the moonlight, they held him now, unflinching and unshakeable.

His heart beat faster as she closed the distance between them. Pausing before him, she held out the letter.

The fucking letter. Snatching it, he crushed it into the couch cushion beside him.

"Forgive me for reading your private correspondence, Matthew."

He stared at her and wondered at the calming effect her voice had upon him.

"Shouldn't I call you Matthew?" she asked. "I know we've never actually conversed. But, since your brother married my sister this morning, I think it not unseemly of me to use your Christian name." She spoke with such a casual tone, as if it weren't the least bit unusual for them to be alone together in the gallery in the middle of the night.

A muscle in his arm jumped as she stepped toward the settee. He watched her and his hands twitched. His ears registered the soft swish of her dressing gown. His mouth watered.

She sat down beside him. He couldn't pull his eyes from her. Little more than the span of a person separated them. He took a deep breath. God, she smelled of gardenias, sweet and heady.

She leaned against the high couch-back but didn't look at him. "It's a beautiful night, isn't it? One not made for sleeping."

Matthew gripped the arm of the couch. *No, not for sleeping.*

She tucked one of her curls behind her ear. "My younger sister always says nights like these are made for secrets and magic." She paused for a moment before finally turning her head to look at him. His heart pounded as he stared into the shadowy beauty of her face. "I don't know if she's right. But just in case she is, would you like to tell me a secret?"

At another time, he would have smiled. But not now. His cock was hard and ready and his body was tense with restraint. He wanted her. He'd wanted her since he first saw her, when he was still engaged to Rosalind. And now he was affianced to no one. Now, his heart was near to bursting, and his body was in agony.

Her head tilted. "Perhaps not then." She looked away.

His body trembled as she leaned forward to go.

"Stay, Patience." His voice sounded terse. He clasped her hand and drew a shallow breath. "Stay," he said more gently.

Patience stilled. She looked down at his hand on hers before lifting her eyes back to him. God, had he ever looked upon a more gorgeous face? "Stay," he murmured again.

Keeping her gaze fixed on him, she leaned back. Rather than release her hand, he curled his fingers over hers. He thought she might pull away, but she didn't.

He rested his head against the couch-back when she rested hers. They sat still and quiet, their eyes locked.

The silence drew out. His prick throbbed and his skin felt alive. "I have no more secrets." Though he tried to keep his voice calm, his fury lay as close to the surface as his desire, and it infected his words with a hard edge. "Everything that ought to be secret, or private to me, is fodder for public gossip."

A frown creased Patience's smooth brow. "I know." Her hand moved slightly beneath his. "But you mustn't concern yourself too much with gossip. It will pass. Gossip never sticks to good people."

He looked at her and something in his chest pulled tight. "How do you know I'm a good person?"

She stared at him for a long, quiet moment. Her eyes looked dark in the shadowy light. "I have a sense for people," she finally said. "Besides, my sister thinks the world of you." A brief smile turned her lips. "And if Passion believes you're good and decent, then you are."

Matthew's heart thumped. *So long as you think so.*

Pulling his eyes from her, he nodded toward the moonlit portrait of the man he'd always thought was his father. "You spoke of magic. Is there any magic that can make me that man's true son?"

Patience's beautiful, intelligent eyes never left him. "Is that what you want, Matthew? If you could have only one wish?"

Yes.

But then he thought of his brother's wedding. Mark and Passion would stand together through everything. Their love was absolute. "No. I would have wished for love—love and loyalty." He stroked his thumb over Patience's hand. Her skin was so soft. "I could have borne anything then."

"You 'would have wished'? You don't anymore?"

The ruthless sting of Rosalind's rejection coursed through him. "No, not anymore." He looked into Patience's tranquil gaze. His shoulders relaxed. *Right now, I only want you.* "Perhaps I would wish for revenge," he said more quietly.

"Revenge?" A small frown turned her brow. "But I say unto you, Love your enemies . . . pray for them which despitefully use you, and persecute you . . . Be ye therefore perfect, even as your Father which is in Heaven is perfect." She paused. "The Gospel according to St. Matthew."

Did she really think him capable of such beneficence? A calming warmth seeped through him. And did she know how beautiful she was—quoting the Gospels in her dressing gown? His prick felt full as he rolled onto his hip to face her. "I'm not St. Matthew, Patience." He sensed her tension at his sudden proximity, but she didn't move or look away. "I'm not St. Matthew, and I'm not perfect."

Her lashes fluttered. "None of us is. But we must aspire to perfection." She regarded him for a moment. "Tell me you won't seek revenge, Matthew. Revenge is never free."

Her hand felt warm beneath his and her expression held a gentle seriousness. He stared at her plump, luscious mouth. What would it feel like to kiss such beautiful lips? "Very well," he murmured. What would it feel like to taste her and hold her close?

"Good." She released a sigh then looked back across the gallery at the portraits. Matthew studied her moonlit profile while the silence drew out between them. Was her cheek as soft as it looked? He wanted to touch it.

Finally, she turned back to him. "You know, Matthew, I think one day Rosalind will regret her decision to break with you."

Matthew thought of the letter crushed beside him. "I doubt that," he replied, bitterness seeping into his tone.

"No, I think she will," Patience insisted softly. Her eyes looked past him as she continued, "One day, she will see you somewhere, perhaps even from a distance, and she will pause to watch you. Memories will flood through her. She will remember how it felt to be in your presence—how it felt to know your touch and your smile. She will yearn for you, and 'what if' will reverberate in her head. For she will know that she could have had you, had she not thrown you away."

Patience stared into the distance. Then her long lashes flickered and she seemed to return to him. She lifted her shoulders in a small shrug. "And you shall walk blithely on—unknowing, yet content in the life you have made without her."

Matthew regarded her intently and couldn't ease the frown from his brow. She spoke from experience. Who had hurt her? And who carried intimate memories of her—her touch and her smile? Did she yearn for him still? A ripple of jealousy moved through him.

His frown deepened. "Kiss me, Patience."

Her gaze swept over him and her lips parted. A soft sigh escaped her.

Matthew's blood rushed and his cock ached. He forced away his frown then repeated his command. "Come. Kiss me, Patience."

Her lovely eyes were dark with desire and uncertainty. Such a beautiful contrast. "I don't think that's a good idea."

"Why not?"

"Because you and I ought not do anything that might cause us strife in the future. You're my brother-in-law, Matthew. I want no regrets between us." She paused, and her eyes rested for a moment on his mouth. "Besides, even when I think I want kisses, I am invariably disappointed by them."

Matthew released her hand and slowly stretched his arm across the couch-back. "I don't want to speak of regrets right now. I just want a kiss, Patience." He fingered one of her thick curls. It was soft. "And if our kiss is disappointing . . . Well, we won't do it again, will we?"

She seemed to consider his words as she held him in her searching stare.

He sat tense and waiting. Would she reject him? "Kiss me," he whispered.

Her gaze flickered to his mouth. Then, slowly, she turned toward him and eased forward.

Matthew's heart thudded and his breathing grew shallow. She stopped only a few inches from him. He breathed the scent of gardenias that clung to her. Had it only been three weeks since he'd first laid eyes upon her? Why did it feel like he'd wanted her forever?

"What are you waiting for?" he managed.

She shook her head. "I don't know. Many men have asked to kiss me. Many men have kissed me without asking." She paused and a tiny frown creased her brow. "But none has ever demanded that I kiss him."

He stared into her lovely face and realized he'd stopped breathing. Demands were what she needed. He inhaled. "Do it now."

He saw her indecision weaken. Then her hand smoothed slowly over his shoulder and her lips parted. Matthew's heart hammered in his chest as her lashes lowered. Her warm fingers touched his nape, pulling him to her with a gentle pressure. And then her mouth touched his—not in a pursed-lipped peck, but completely, softly, and searchingly.

A burning heat surged through Matthew's body, igniting something deep inside him. Yet, he sat still as a statue as over and over, between breathy sighs, she pressed her soft, parted lips to his. With each kiss, she lingered longer. His eyes closed and her other arm came around him. He drew a sharp breath and his hands began to shake as she drew even closer. And closer . . .

With a moan he swept his arms around her, pulling her fully against him and capturing her tender mouth with his. Desire flamed through him, hot and fierce. Fueled by his suppressed longing for her, fueled by emotions he couldn't even name, it ravaged him. He thrust his tongue. Her lips parted and her embrace tightened. She tasted of tea and lemon—and want. His heart pounded. She was wearing her stays, but even so, he felt the press of her breasts and curves of her body. She was soft yet firm, and the scent of gardenias filled his head as he kissed her and kissed her, pushing his tongue a little deeper into her warm mouth with each thrust.

His blood rushed in his veins and his prick ached. He held her even tighter and stroked his hands over the curves of her bottom, gripping it as he surged against her. Her open mouth clung to his, and her fingers curled in his hair. She moaned and then gasped, but he couldn't stop kissing her. Couldn't stop . . .

For in that moment, she was the balance against everything he couldn't have—Rosalind, the man he'd always thought was his father, his so-called friends who had abruptly become so scarce, his old life. All were gone. But this kiss was his—this kiss, with Patience. He crushed her against him and pulled her down with him on the couch. He pressed his body to hers. If he could keep her, then maybe . . .

She groaned and shuddered. Tearing his mouth from hers, Matthew gazed down at her as he drew ragged breaths. He'd rolled her beneath him. Christ, her half-closed eyes glittered with passion and soft pants escaped her kiss-swollen lips. Though her hands gripped the sleeves of his shirt, she lay limp and breathless beneath him, her bright curls spilling everywhere. His cock throbbed hungrily against her thigh. She drew a deep breath and her eyelids fluttered.

He could take her now. Right on the couch.

A dark lust moved in him.

Do it! You're in control.

Take her and triumph.

With a groan, he bent close and threaded his fingers into her hair. But the moment he did, a sharp sting cut across his knuckle. He froze as the nasty little pain sliced through his desire. Pushing aside Patience's heavy curls, he stared at Rosalind's crumpled letter and the sharp corner that had cut him. Just above it, he could see her tight, perfect signature.

Bitch!

His anger boiled. He crushed his hand over the thing as he returned his gaze to Patience. Looking at her, his lust flared immediately. But that only served to anger him more. He wasn't in control. He was completely *out* of control. How the hell could he be so damned weak—so pathetically desperate for a woman's arms? His fist tightened around the letter. He'd learned nothing!

"I told you"—Patience's soft voice was almost a whisper—"we shouldn't have done it."

Matthew frowned into her gaze. He saw tension in her beautiful eyes, but no censure. His cock throbbed and he hated himself for wanting her so badly.

Her hands fell away from him. "Go."

Yes. Go.

Why wasn't he?

Patience's eyes never left him as he forced his muscles to move, forced himself to pull away. Had his body a voice, it would have groaned in protest and resentment as he peeled himself slowly apart from her. And the more he withdrew, the more those feelings escalated. Until, by the time he got to his feet, he was stiff with a bitter fury.

Turning slowly, he faced the portrait of his mother—the beautiful, deceitful woman who had always claimed to love him. She was the source of all his pain. He wanted to rip the picture off the wall. He wanted to tear it to shreds and throw the remnants out the window.

He hated her. And he'd *despised* being "loved" by her. For even before the scandal, her character had been well known. What had it said of *him* to be loved by such a woman?

Christ, he'd spent his whole fucking life trying to make up for the fact that he was loved by her. He'd been honest and honorable—gracious and good-humored. In school, he'd tended to his studies. Once out, he'd built a fortune. He'd moved in the highest of social circles. And, all the while, he'd searched for a love he never need apologize for—a decent love, a noble love. A loyal and unconditional love.

Lifting his fist, he squeezed Rosalind's crumpled letter into a tight airless lump. His entire bloody existence had been either a reaction against the love he'd had, or a search for the love he'd wanted. He'd allowed himself to be governed by love—to be controlled by his desire for it. How little that had served him.

He dropped his hand. Never again!

Drawing a deep breath, he caught the barest note of gardenia.

Not even for her?

Patience . . .

His heart paused and his body trembled with want.

Fuck! Just go. Go and don't look back.

Squaring his shoulders, he put one foot in front of the other until the gallery—and Patience—were far behind him.

Patience stared at the high ceiling. Her limbs were trembling and her quim was aching. Her nipples felt tight and her skin tingled. The feelings were familiar in their tenor, but completely unfamiliar in their intensity. She closed her eyes and lay completely still.

Everything is going to be fine. You're alone and everything is fine.

She clenched her hands into fists.

It was just a kiss. You've been kissed dozens of times. Just a kiss . . .

But no matter how she tried to reason with her racing heart, it would not slow. Her body seemed strangely unresponsive to her mind's commands.

Forcing herself to sit up, she pressed her shaking legs together as she rubbed her temples. She tried to delineate her feelings—to break them into understandable and recognizable parts—to separate the physical from the emotional.

But she couldn't.

With a frustrated gasp, she got to her feet and walked purposefully from the gallery. She registered that her thighs were wet and her stomach was quivering, but she forced herself to ignore the sensations. Passing the balconies that overlooked the silent ballroom, she strode to the stairs and descended two flights at an even pace. Once on the main floor, she walked down the hall and didn't pause until she had turned into the wide double doors that opened upon the music room.

Large Palladian windows allowed the moonlight to stream into the expansive chamber. She saw her cello clearly. Resting in the pearly light, its maple-wood shoulder gleamed. Just beside it sat her cello case.

Keeping her eyes diverted from the large portrait over the mantel, she crossed the room. Her slippers tapped softly against the parquet floor. Her dressing gown billowed as she dropped down and settled onto her heels. She opened the lid of her case. Inside, the buff-colored silk lining was old, but she had mended all the small tears that had come with age.

All but one.

Slipping her fingers behind the section of loose lining, she pulled out the folded paper that she had first put there seven years ago. She paused only briefly before unfolding the well-worn creases and lifting the letter to the light.

Her eyes fell over the words she'd read a thousand times.

Patience,

I caught you watching me yesterday, and I realized immediately why your performance of late has been so unpleasant. Though you tried to hide it, I saw love in your eyes. I was repulsed. Your love for me has infected your music. Your playing has become soft and insipid, and I can no longer endure listening to it.

I told you when you became my student that the pursuit of art and the pursuit of love are antithetical. I thought you understood this. Yet, look what you've done. You've ruined a fine talent, and you've stolen almost a year of my life, during which I might have taught someone more worthy.

I ought to have known better than to have placed my confidence in a fifteen-year-old girl. I made the mistake of believing that you were above the emotional responses so common to females. Clearly, I was wrong—you are all the same.

Since you have proven yourself incapable of perfection, and therefore greatness, you would do well to quit playing altogether and marry one of those eager-faced young men who are always running after you. Yes, give your love to one of them, and take your joys from the more simple pursuits allotted to your sex—marriage and breeding.

Henri Goutard

Patience stared at the scrawling script. Over the years, the pain of the letter had faded into nothingness. But tonight, she felt a brief stab of the old agony. And though it came and went in an instant, it worked upon her like a douse of cold water, dampening the heated emotions Matthew's kiss had inspired.

She drew a deep, calming breath, and slowly refolded the paper. As she returned it to its hiding place, she thought how similar Henri's letter was to Lady Benchley's. Matthew would hurt for some time.

She closed the lid of her case.

But eventually he would recover—just as she had.

And perhaps he would find love again. An image of Matthew embracing a faceless, dark-haired woman suddenly appeared in her mind. She frowned at the sour feeling the vision gave her. Pushing it from her thoughts, she looked at her cello.

Her instrument was her love. Getting to her feet, she stared at it for a moment. It was her comfort. Sitting, she placed it between her knees. It was late, but if she played quietly . . .

Drawing and releasing another deep breath, she banished Matthew from her mind and pictured the opening notes of Beethoven's *Emperor Concerto*. Carefully—exactly—she pressed the proper strings against the fingerboard, then drew her bow. Faultlessly executed, the first notes filled the empty room with sound. Patience proceeded from one note to the next—playing each in pure and perfect succession. She heard the music with her ear, but she also saw it in her head, almost as she would a series of mathematical equations—each to be solved with unerring exactness and, of course, in proper order.

As she played, Patience prevented any error, any miscalculation that might disturb the perfection of the piece. It gave her immense pleasure to play precisely. Indeed, every moment that she sat with her cello, her goal was to get closer to the perfection Henri had claimed her incapable of.

Letting the final notes fade into the still air, Patience sighed with satisfaction. *This* was what she loved—her music and the pursuit of perfection.

She gazed at her instrument. Romantic love wasn't for her.

Again, Matthew's beautiful, penetrating eyes flashed in her mind.

She shivered.

But what of desire?

Getting to her feet, she returned her cello to its stand. Desire served a physical need that she would not be able to avoid forever. And she desired Matthew more powerfully than she'd desired any man. There was something between them—something strong and inevitable.

Turning, she raised her eyes slowly to the life-sized portrait that she'd avoided looking at earlier. Matthew, seated with his cello, stared back at her. Her sister had told her that he played the instrument brilliantly. A warm flush heated Patience's skin as she looked at him.

His pose was open, with his right arm falling indolently over the back of the chair. His bow hung from lax fingers, and his other hand rested on the shoulder of his cello, which was tipped between his widely spread legs.

Patience moistened her lips as her blood quickened. Matthew stared directly out from the painting, his expression idle and sensual. The full curve of his mouth had been depicted well, but nothing could surpass the incredible beauty and intensity of his dark eyes. Tonight, they stared at her with a knowing regard. Tonight, they seemed to say, *you're mine*.

Patience drew in her breath as her lips tingled. She touched them lightly.

Not just a kiss.

No. Their breathless embrace had been a prelude . . .

. . . a prelude to something more.

Chapter Two
A MASQUE

My beloved spake, and said unto me, Rise up, my love, my fair one, and come away.

SONG OF SOLOMON 2:10

Three Months Later
Wiltshire, England ~ A Masked Ball at Hawkmore House,
County Seat of the Earl and Countess of Langley

They never left her alone. Like proud bucks pursuing a lone doe, her admirers pranced around her. Following wherever she went, they jostled and vied for her attention, each hoping to be the one to win her regard—however briefly. And all the while, though she smiled and nodded, and indulged them, he could sense her disinterest.

My poor Patience. How do you bear it?

Matthew crossed his arms over his chest. Leaning into a shadowed corner of the upper gallery, he kept his eyes trained on her. Though her beautiful face was half covered by a demi-mask, her magnificent red hair made her identity unmistakable. Falling down her back in thick curls, it was like a flaming lure in a mottled sea of dimmer shades. A crown of flowers rested atop her bright head, and more blooms decorated her costume of delicate white layers that swept low across her shoulders and belled out from her slim waist.

She was an incomparable beauty.

In the three months since their kiss, he'd been unable to keep her from his thoughts. Despite his troubles, images of her had filled his mind. He'd tried to resist them at first. But as the weeks had passed, he had resisted less and less, until it seemed that every morning and night, his first and last thoughts were of her. His dreams and fantasies were of her. And the more he had thought of her, the more he had wanted her. And the more he had wanted her, the more worthwhile it had seemed to defeat the scandal that was rushing to ruin him both socially and financially. The scandal that was being maliciously driven and escalated by Rosalind's father.

Fucking Benchley. Archibald Philip Benchley, The Right Honorable Earl of Benchley, whose line was so old that his title and his surname were still the same. Lord Benchley, whose earldom was too illustrious and pure to be besmirched by bastard blood.

Matthew narrowed his eyes upon the milling throng below. Though dressed in silks and satins, they were like a pack of wild animals. For the last three months, they had watched Benchley claw and tear at him. But he wasn't dead. And he was through licking his wounds. He would take back his place amongst them—not by fighting them all, but by tearing the throat from just one.

Yes. While the pack looked on, he would take Benchley down. And the more blood he drew doing it, the better it would be. For after the dust settled, no one would dare cut him again.

Matthew almost smiled. His spy had already been in the Benchley household for two weeks. He should be reporting in soon.

He let his gaze fall back upon Patience. Tonight, *she* was his primary goal. His gut tightened with anticipation. He and she had unfinished business—and he was hungry for her.

"By God, it really is you. You've risen."

Matthew looked into the sardonically arranged features of Roark Fitz Roy, youngest son of the Marquess of Waverley. Speaking of bastards—the marquess's ancestral branch sprouted from one of Charles II's bastard sons. "Fitz Roy."

Roark Fitz Roy raised one black brow. "I bet Hollingsworth a hundred pounds that rumors of your presence were pure fabrication."

Matthew shrugged as he turned his gaze back to the ballroom below. "Never bet on rumor."

"Yes, well . . . unfortunately for you and Grand West Railway, plenty of people *are* betting on rumor."

Matthew tensed. "That's their mistake."

"It'll be yours if you don't do something about it soon."

Matthew glared at Fitz Roy. The man was a favorite of the Queen, but Matthew had never been one for currying favor and he wasn't about to start. "I haven't seen you since my fall from grace, Fitz Roy, and right now you're interrupting the solitude I have become accustomed to. So, if there's something you want to say, why don't you just say it?"

Fitz Roy stood with his hands in his trouser pockets. His shoulders lifted in a small shrug. "Very well, but I'm afraid it's bad news."

Matthew raised his brows in mock surprise. "Really? Bad news, is it?" He wiped the expression from his face. "Copies of my mother's letter declaring her joy in my bastard birth can still be found floating down London's sewage-filled gutters. The newspaper article containing the blackmail plot against my brother, in which he almost lost his one and only love for my sake, is still being passed around the drawing rooms of my *former* peers. And should that not be enough, my former *fiancée* and her *father*," he ground the words out, "have made their total and complete rejection of me a matter for public mastication. As people chew up the delicious gossip of my fall"—his voice grew progressively harder—"Lord Benchley and his daughter continue to add salt and seasoning to the feast with their public declarations and lies against me." He leaned forward. "And while Benchley slanders my character publicly, he privately infects my business associates with his vile influence. I'd wager my last pound note that *he* is the one who is at the heart of the ill rumor you speak of." Matthew drew back. "Bad news? My whole bloody life is bad news."

A long silent moment followed, but Fitz Roy's supercilious expression didn't change. "Well, since you put it that way . . . Lord Wollby just informed me that he intends to sell all his shares in your company." His black brows lifted. "He heard a *rumor* that Grand West Railway—in other words, you—will soon not be permitted to buy a single lump of coal unless Grand West Railway—in other words, you—is willing to pay twice its worth."

Matthew felt his blood surge. He was already overpaying for what coal he could get, and teetering on the brink of financial disaster. Wollby's sellout could spur an unstoppable wave of share dumping. *Ruination.*

"He's not likely to do anything while he's here," Fitz Roy said. "You have some time to convince him to hold."

As his mind churned, Matthew stared down at the swirling mass of society below. He found Patience in the center of the dance floor. His cock twitched. "Convince him to hold? To what end?" The dance was the mazurka, and his frown deepened as he saw Patience's partner, the Viscount Montrose, come very close to touching her breast.

A sudden possessiveness heated his veins. He turned back to Fitz Roy. "No. I'm not going to convince Wollby of anything. *I* built Grand West Railway. She's mine, and I'll be damned if I'll get on bended knee to beg the forbearance of every bloody shareholder." He lifted his shoulder to ease his tension. "Either they believe in GWR—and me—or they don't." He turned his gaze back to Patience. His prick throbbed and the call to claim her filled him with urgent determination, especially as Montrose leaned close to say something near her ear. "Whatever the case, I'll take care of what's mine," he said quietly.

"Very well, then." Fitz Roy paused. "Oh, by the way, you'll never guess who approached me at the Cromley ball and posed discreet inquiries about you."

"I really don't care," Matthew murmured, keeping his eye on Montrose's hands while watching Patience move gracefully through the steps of the dance.

"Yes, well, it was Lady Rosalind."

Matthew stiffened as he turned to Fitz Roy. "Rosalind?" he growled. "*Lady* Rosalind can go to the devil."

"So I take it you don't want the sweet-smelling note she furtively bade me give you."

Matthew stared at Fitz Roy. "After everything that happened due to my mother's sordid letters, Rosalind was *not* stupid enough to pen a secret note."

"Actually, she was." Fitz Roy pulled a small folded paper from his breast pocket and held it out. "I put it down to desperation."

Matthew stared at the folded pink paper. He ought to take it, but it repelled him.

He glanced down at Patience. Her bright, beautiful curls gleamed in the light. His heartbeat quickened and his cods tightened as he watched her pass close beneath Montrose's arm. *She* was the one he wanted. *She* was the one he craved. Rosalind no longer mattered.

Yet, he knew only too well that letters could be powerful tools—tools that could be used against one's enemies.

Dragging his eyes from Patience, Matthew snatched the note before he could change his mind. He quickly opened it while Fitz Roy turned his back.

Matt, Darling, I know you must be angry with me, so perhaps it will please you to hear that I am suffering. But I want you to know that I think of you every day as Father parades suitor after suitor before me, none as handsome or as "bold" as you.

Darling, if you regret our parting as much as I, then send me word. I blush to say this, but just because we cannot marry, does not mean we cannot be together. Yours, R

Matthew snorted derisively as he shook his head. If he weren't staring at Rosalind's small, tight hand, he wouldn't have believed what he was reading. Oh, what a change the months had wrought. And, oh, what possibilities this unexpected missive raised. Folding the note, he slipped it securely in his breast pocket. He needed time to consider how to make best use of both the note and Rosalind, but—he looked down at Patience—now was *not* that time.

He watched her move off the dance floor with Montrose, who seemed unwilling to forfeit her hand. Immediately, a crowd of men encircled her. He knew them all, and his shoulders tensed as he saw the Earl of Danforth press far too closely against her back. Matthew's gut tightened. He'd known Danforth since Harrow, but he'd never liked him. He was a randy, arrogant ass, an inveterate gambler, and a poor loser. If he moved one slimy hand toward her . . .

Suddenly, the tall graceless man grimaced and, jumping back, lifted his foot. Patience turned and, with an oh-so-regretful shake of her head, mouthed what appeared to be an apology.

Fitz Roy chuckled. "Nothing like a hard stomp on the instep for deterring imbeciles."

Matthew frowned. He'd almost forgotten Fitz Roy was there.

"By the way"—Fitz Roy turned to him—"have you heard Danforth's news?"

Now what? "What news?"

"Well, I probably shouldn't say a word. Danforth is likely beside himself with excitement over the prospect of conveying it to you himself." Fitz Roy briefly examined his nails. "But, since I do so love dampening the glee of idiots, I'll tell you." He leaned his hip on the low gallery wall. "The impoverished Earl of Danforth has just become engaged to none other than the very lady whose sweet-smelling note is now tucked in your breast pocket."

Matthew froze for a moment and waited to feel something—anything. Nothing came. "When did this occur?"

"It was finalized this very day. Danforth is positively giddy over the whole arrangement because his future father-in-law has agreed to pay all his debts and renovate his crumbling manse."

"Is that so?" Matthew stared down at Danforth. The man was incapable of staying out of debt. He would be a huge liability for Benchley. Matthew scowled. And the son of a bitch was still standing too bloody close to Patience. "Then he will surely be at the gaming tables tonight," he said tightly.

Fitz Roy snorted. "Can you keep a hound from a hank of sausage? Of course he'll be at the gaming tables." He pushed away from the wall and straightened his cuff. "Well, I must be off. I'm partnering Miss Dunleigh and her two hundred yards of pink tulle for the next waltz."

Matthew nodded as he returned his gaze to Patience. His heart thumped and his prick throbbed eagerly. It was time for him to go as well.

"Oh"—Fitz Roy paused—"not that you care, but Lady Rosalind bade me tell you that she is at the Filberts' autumn hunt should you wish to arrange a private meeting with her."

Matthew swallowed his distaste and kept his eyes on Patience. He wanted no more thoughts of Rosalind. Only one woman mattered now, and she stood below him. "Good evening, Fitz Roy."

"Evening, Hawkmore."

Matthew watched Patience's red curls bounce around her bare shoulders as she turned to address one of her admirers. He traced the curves of her body with his eyes. Drawing a deep breath, he could feel his excitement shifting into the controlled containment that fed his dominant passions.

Tonight would be the beginning—a new beginning with Patience.

He wanted her. He'd come for her.

And though she didn't yet know it, she belonged to him.

"She does *not*!" exclaimed Lord Farnsby.

"I hear that she does."

"Just because you hear it, doesn't make it true, Danforth."

"A ten pound note says she does," offered Lord Asher.

"Done," replied Farnsby.

"A bet! A bet!" cried some of the other gentlemen.

Male laughter filled the circle.

"So," Lord Danforth silenced them, and all eyes turned to her. "I ask you again, Miss Dare. Is it true that you actually play the cello?"

From behind her demi-mask, Patience raised a smile for the crowd of gentlemen that encircled her. Some costumed, some not, they all wore masks. Yet, their masks were lifted now and all eyes were fixed upon her. In the light of the huge ballroom, she could observe them well. Several were harmless, but she also saw lechery cloaked as friendliness, conceit disguised as charm, insecurity posing as bravado and—she returned her gaze to Lord Danforth—a predator, undisguised.

"It happens, Lord Danforth, that you are correct. I do play the cello. In two weeks time, I shall begin training in London with the renowned Fernando Cavalli. I am proud to be the first female student to ever earn his tutelage."

As a chorus of "ahs" filled the circle and jokes about debts were tossed around, Lord Danforth bent close. "I knew you were the sort of woman who could hold a large instrument between her legs."

She'd only heard that one about a hundred times. Patience squelched the desire to roll her eyes and excuse herself. Clearly men were the same everywhere—even if they bore titles. Instead, she laughed lightly and lowered her voice. "If you mean to wound me, my lord, I'm afraid your small prick has missed the mark."

A slow frown turned Lord Danforth's brow. "I beg your pardon?"

Patience lifted her brows innocently. "No, I beg yours, my lord."

With a touch on her arm, Lord Farnsby, costumed as Napoleon, drew her attention from the odious Lord Danforth. "You must forgive my incredulity, Miss Dare. Your beauty alone would complement any musical experience." He pulled his vest down over his portly middle. "It is only that the cello is such a large and unwieldy instrument, and therefore not well suited to the delicate nature and gentle sensibility of ladies."

Patience nodded. She'd heard that before as well—all too many times. Heaven forbid that a woman should play the cello, or ride astride, or do anything that required the parting of her thighs. Never mind that every man standing there had been born from between a woman's legs. How did they think *that* affected a woman's delicate nature and gentle sensibilities?

She smiled. "I understand you completely, my lord. But at the young age I took up the cello, I had no notion of the delicacy of my nature, and my sensibilities were quite determined. You have only to ask my father."

As the men chuckled and made jests about their own determined boyhoods, Patience caught the thread of a conversation behind her.

"I can't believe Matthew Hawkmore is actually here tonight."

Patience stilled. Matthew was here, at the ball? The sudden memory of his heated kiss brought a warm flush to her cheeks.

"Matthew Hawkmore? Don't you mean Matthew *Gardener*?"

Patience tensed as the ladies tittered.

"Well, I can't believe it," the first continued. "Does he think he shall ever be accepted back into polite society? I mean, really . . . He ought, at least, to have had the decency to stay away—especially after lying to all of us."

"But, my dear, I hear he never knew of his illegitimacy."

"You hear wrongly. Lord Benchley informed *me* that Hawkmore knew all along. And I, for one, do not appreciate being duped, least of all by some lowbred gardener's whelp."

The incessant banter of Patience's admirers faded from her hearing as she listened, with growing indignation, to the women behind her. She knew from her sister that Matthew had been suffering socially. But this haughty, ill-mannered meanness was unconscionable. Was this the courtesy of the nobility?

"You know, I overheard my husband say that no one will do business with Hawkmore. He says he may sell his shares in Hawkmore's railway company."

"And why shouldn't your husband do so? Who wants to do business with a liar and an imposter? Mark my words, ladies. In no time at all, Matthew Hawkmore will be both a bastard and a pauper."

Patience clenched her hands in her skirts. By God, if there was anything she hated, it was cruelty and injustice. She started to turn in order to give the malicious women a piece of her mind, but just then a tall, thin gentleman, ill-garbed as the hearty King Henry the Eighth, pushed between the gentlemen before her and clasped her hand.

Patience drew back with a start.

"My dear Miss Dare, here you are! I have been looking everywhere for you. I do believe this is our dance."

Patience heard the overture to the waltz. She glanced over her shoulder only to find that three gentlemen had crowded into the space behind her. Where were the horrid women?

Barely able to hide her frustration, she smoothly withdrew her hand from the eager man before her and looked down at the dance card that hung from her waist. "Why yes, Lord Fenton, it is."

"Bloody rude, Fenton, taking the beautiful Miss Dare from us," Lord Farnsby complained.

"Indeed," said Lord Montrose.

"Yes, don't go far with her, Fenton," Lord Danforth warned as he brushed a speck of lint from his evening attire. "Her next dance is mine."

"And then mine," called Lord Asher.

The eager Lord Fenton merely smiled at her crookedly from beneath his mask as he led her from her circle of admirers and out onto the dance floor.

Patience sighed. Was Matthew truly there, amongst the dancers? Fleetingly, she searched the crowded floor, but in the next moment she chastised herself. He obviously hadn't sought her out, so what did it matter?

She managed a smile for Lord Fenton as the waltz began, but she was soon grimacing as he trod repeatedly upon her toes.

"I'm terribly sorry, Miss Dare. A thousand pardons."

The man was concentrating so hard upon her décolleté, he wasn't leading. So she did.

"There now," Lord Fenton grinned. "We've found the way of it now."

"We certainly have," Patience agreed.

"It may take me a moment, but I always find the way of it."

"Do you?" she replied absently.

Why try to fool herself? If Matthew was in attendance, she at least wanted to see him. Just for a moment.

The morning after their kiss, he had left Hawkmore House. Three days later, she had gone home to the vicarage with her father, younger sister, and cousin. She had resolved to put Matthew from her mind, but no matter how hard she had tried, he had persisted in invading her thoughts, especially in the quiet of the night. In fact, his handsome features had come to mind so often that his face had become engrained in her memory—the hard angle of his jaw and the soft curve of his mouth. And then, of course, there were his dark, soulful eyes.

Frowning, she reflected. Had a day gone by that she hadn't thought of him? She didn't think so.

Where was he? Lifting her chin, she scanned the crowd as she turned to the urgent strains of the waltz.

Masked faces filled her view. Half revealed, half hidden, they whirled around her in a kaleidoscope of color. More masked revelers surrounded the dance floor of the huge ballroom, moving in an ever-shifting tide. Even the liveried servants, adorned in black demi-masks, seemed to dance through the milling crowd as they swiveled their trays of sparkling champagne.

But where was Matthew?

The music swelled. A tingle of awareness shimmied down Patience's spine. Sudden anticipation coursed through her. She whirled.

Matthew.

He was striding purposefully across the dance floor, his dark, penetrating eyes fixed unwaveringly upon *her*.

Patience drew in a breath.

The sense of inevitability that had overcome her after their kiss flowed through her even more strongly now. And desire—warm, rushing desire.

She couldn't take her eyes off him. Was he leaner than since last she'd seen him? His tall frame was adorned in strict black evening attire. No mask covered his incredibly handsome features. That had been a calculated move, she was sure. In fact, the hard and unassailable expression he wore seemed to say: Damn you all, this is who I am and I shall not hide.

Deep in her body something pulsed. Was it pride?

He drew closer.

A couple danced in front of her, blocking him from her sight.

"I say, Miss Dare, I don't believe you've heard a word I've said."

Patience snapped her attention back to Lord Fenton. "Forgive me, my lord. Uh"—she blinked—"you were saying . . . ?"

"I was saying we dance so well together that perhaps we might consider partnering for other activities." He smiled in what she was sure was supposed to be an alluring fashion. "I'm quite certain that we are very well suited."

"And I'm certain that you're not." Matthew's deep voice drew them to a halt. Patience's blood surged as he took her hand in his and bent a cold eye upon Lord Fenton. "Now, if you'll excuse me, I'm cutting in."

Lord Fenton frowned. "I've been waiting half the night for this dance with Miss Dare, Hawkmore."

Matthew's fingers curved warm and possessive around hers. "Then you won't mind waiting longer."

Lord Fenton pushed back his mask, revealing a sudden and nasty glare. "Blast you, Hawkmore. I suppose *cutting* in should come as no shock from a gardener's son."

Patience gasped her anger and spoke from Matthew's side. "Is that supposed to be a pun, my lord? If so, it is a poor one. Now, if you will excuse us, I find I am in agreement with my brother-in-law. You and I will not suit."

Lord Fenton turned haughtily to Matthew as if he were the one who had spoken. "I never did like you, Hawkmore. I see I was right to petition for your dismissal at White's."

Ignoring the man, Matthew swept her into his arms and turned her into the waltzing throng. His features were hard with fury, so she lowered her eyes to give him a moment.

Despite the uncomfortable exchange, exhilaration and relief coursed through Patience's body. She found herself leaning into Matthew, both offering support and taking succor. He held her so closely that she could smell the vetiver, rich and woodsy, that clung to him. She could feel the press of his lower body and the brush of his legs. His shoulder was strong beneath her hand as he led her with unwavering surety. It all took her back to the last time she had felt the power of his arms around her and the press of his body against her.

She closed her eyes and wished she could just lay her head against his shoulder. God, she hadn't realized how tired she was—so very tired of the constant onslaught of male attention. The wrong male attention.

"Look at me, Patience."

Her body hummed with sensual appreciation at the sound of his voice. She lifted her gaze to his dark, heavily lashed eyes. What did she see now? Determination? Pride? Desire?

God, his eyes were more beautiful than she had remembered. *He* was more beautiful than she had remembered. Glints of gold lit his brown hair, which was cut short at his nape and left longer on top. It waved back from his brow and she suddenly longed to displace it—to see it falling forward against his temples, as it had been the night of their moonlit meeting.

"What took you so long?" she asked. "I've been waiting for you."

Though her words surprised her, she knew they were true.

Matthew's nostrils flared and his eyes seemed to darken. "I'm here now." His fingers pressed against her back. "Are you prepared to give me what I want?"

The deep, resonant tones of his voice stroked her like a caress.

"Well, I don't know," she replied. "The last time I gave you what you wanted, against my better judgment I might add, you left."

His beautiful brown eyes didn't waver from hers. "Not a day has passed that I haven't regretted leaving you that night. Give me what I want now, and you won't be sorry."

"What is it you want?"

He didn't answer. Instead, his gaze dropped to her low, flower-strewn décolletage. "Your gown is lovely. As whom are you costumed?"

Patience drew a shallow breath. "Persephone."

"Ah, how appropriate. Persephone, the herald of spring—the goddess." His low voice held her captive as he turned her to the music. "Then I am Pluto, god of the underworld, and I want you. I shall steal you away and hide you in my shadow. I shall chain you to my side and demand your submission. I shall take everything from you and, in the doing, give you everything you desire."

Something dark and hidden reverberated in Patience's heart. Like a strike upon a tuning fork, it flowed over her in waves, filling her womb, her quim, and the pulsing heart between her legs with a desperate but unrecognizable hunger. Her lips parted on a silent sigh.

His gaze dropped to her mouth. "And you—you shall light my dark world."

Patience remembered the women's cruel words and her heart tightened. "How shall I do that, Matthew?"

His eyes returned to hers and they were unfathomable. "I don't know, perhaps by speaking my name as you just did." A spark tumbled from her heart to her womb. His voice was so tender. "Perhaps I have lost my way." He paused then drew back a little as he turned her. "Does it really matter, as long as I give you what you desire?"

"It does to me." When he didn't respond, Patience sighed then gave him a small smile. "You speak of knowing my desires. Yet, how could you?" She shook her head. "We've only ever shared a kiss."

He didn't return her smile. "It was more than a kiss, and you know it."

Her blood rushed. "Yes," she admitted quietly. "But that doesn't mean you know my desires."

He held her with his gaze. "Oh, I've been watching you, Patience. You're the belle of the ball. Every man here wants you. They practically stumble over each other to get to you. Isn't that true?"

She stared into his long-lashed eyes. "Yes."

"And isn't it true that your fawning admirers crowd you, almost beyond bearing, in their urgency to impress you. Isn't it true that they drown you in continuous compliments that are meaningless to you? That they suffocate you with their innocuous but unending attention?" His dark eyes seemed to reach inside her. "Isn't that true, Patience? Hasn't it always been true?"

She frowned into his almost hypnotic gaze. "Yes." The word came on a whisper. Did he hear it?

He bent closer. "And though you smile and sweep them off their feet . . ."

She breathed in vetiver.

". . . I think none of them inspire your passion . . ."

His cheek touched her temple.

". . . let alone your love."

Patience trembled. *Love?* Love was not for her.

But what of passion? Her need for sensual fulfillment often rode her hard—and she grew weary of being her own lover.

She looked into Matthew's proud, handsome face. "You're right about almost everything. But I have no desire for romantic love, nor marriage either. I love my family, and I love my cello. That is quite enough for me."

"Really?" One dark eyebrow lifted. "Are you sure?"

Patience drew a breath but then paused. Why didn't "yes" burst from her lips? She frowned as she met Matthew's inquiring gaze. "The pursuit of love and the pursuit of art are antithetical. One cannot live in the face of the other."

"Who told you that?"

The man I loved. "A former music master of mine."

"And you believe it?"

"I know it."

"How do you know it?"

"Experience."

"You're being cryptic."

"Yes."

The corners of Matthew's mouth lifted just slightly. "Very well. I'll allow that for now."

A tingle moved over Patience's skin. She raised her brows. "You'll *allow* it?"

Matthew nodded. "Yes. For now." He continued before she

could make further comment. "Shame all your admirers don't know you've chosen your cello over them."

Patience shrugged as Matthew turned her with the music. "It wouldn't matter if I told them. They would never believe me."

"No, I don't suppose they would. Each wants to believe that he shall be the one to win your heart." His beautiful eyes delved into hers. "Hope springs eternal, Patience."

"Yes." He had such a sensual, kissable mouth. "Hope springs eternal."

"Poor souls, with their hopeless hope." His head tipped closer. "None of them will ever have you, will they?"

"No."

"No. Because they don't know what you need." Matthew's hand tightened around her waist as he whirled her amongst the dancers. "But I know what you need, Patience. I am the perfect foil for your needs."

Patience's heart quickened. She stared into his dark eyes—such deep, compelling eyes. He tempted her, almost beyond her endurance, for it seemed he knew something she didn't—something that touched her with a deep and inexplicable force.

And yet, she couldn't help but be reminded of their tense parting in the gallery. She had *no* desire to be a substitute for Rosalind. "It's never good to be the one who follows in the footsteps of lost love, Matthew. And as I've already said, I cannot offer you love. So, perhaps you should have a run at someone else."

The set of Matthew's mouth softened and his long lashes flickered with a slow blink. "That would be a complete waste of time, Patience. You're the only woman I want—the only woman who can satisfy me." His dark eyes held her as he leaned close. "You are meant to be mine. And I *will* have you."

Patience's mouth went dry, even as moisture wet her thighs. She had felt certain this day would come. But now that the moment was upon her, she didn't know if she could go through with it.

"I know you feel it," he said softly. "It's always been there, hovering between us. You felt it in the gallery the night we kissed. You feel it now."

"I see you. I feel you."

"Yes," he breathed. "But why me? Why not another? Why not

Montrose or Asher, or any of the other dozens of men who want you?"

Because you are the man who calls to me.

"Why can it only be me, Patience?"

His eyes were hypnotic. She couldn't look away from them. "I don't know why. I only know that it is so."

His hand moved on her waist, drawing her even closer. His voice came low and soft. "Give me tonight—only tonight—and I'll show you why."

Tonight! Heat flooded Patience's womb and her heart thudded in her breast as she tore her eyes from his. Lord, she wanted him—quite desperately. But . . . What if it proved a mistake?

"Patience."

She looked back into Matthew's penetrating gaze.

"One day you will relent," he said softly. "For I will pursue you until you do. So why put off the pleasure that can be yours tonight?" He spoke with such casual reason. "I'm not asking for your love, Patience. Nor your hand." His shoulders lifted in a small shrug. "I just want tonight." He bent close by her ear. "Give me tonight."

Patience drew a shaky breath. He was right. One day she would relent. Only she wished he didn't know it.

Matthew twirled her to the edge of the dance floor and then clasped her wrist. "Come."

She tensed and stalled. "Come where?"

Hidden in the folds of her skirt, his fingers stroked her palm. "Wherever I say."

Staring into his dark eyes, her breath quickened and a shiver ran down her back. It wasn't the answer she had expected. She wanted to go with him—yearned to go with him. It was as if there were an invisible string between them, and he was pulling it. But, God help her, where would it lead? She glanced at the couples that milled around them and breathed her last protest. "How can I?"

He bent close and his low voice was firm. "You can because you hunger for something you do not understand—something you're afraid to even recognize. But I am going to make it clear and simple for you, because what you need cannot be asked for; it can only be taken. And I am the one to do the taking. *I* am the one." He drew back. "Now, not another word." Then he pressed his hand against her waist and, pushing her ahead of him, guided her through the crowd with the simple pressure of his palm against the small of her back.

Patience's blood rushed in her veins. His calm commands were surprising. Yet, her reaction to them was more so. Part of her wanted to turn and refuse him. But the stronger part—or was it the weaker?—felt a hot thrill and an urgency to comply.

Pulling her arm through his, he led her in a leisurely fashion and they nodded to people as they passed. Raised eyebrows and speculative glances followed them. She thought of the horrid gossips and lifted her chin. She was not ashamed to be seen with him. Indeed, there was no man she would rather be with. And why shouldn't they be seen together? He was her brother-in-law, after all.

But the closer they came to the wide ballroom doors, the faster Patience's heart beat. Doubt and desire, uncertainty and trust, all struggled for preeminence. The doors loomed before her. Her step faltered.

Matthew glanced down at her and his dark eyes flashed. "Come, Patience."

No sweet-talking, no cajoling. He tightened his arm on hers and a heavy throb pulsed between her legs. His firm command sublimated her resistance in a way that no amount of coaxing would have. Hot and flustered, she stepped over the threshold.

They crossed the wide hall and climbed the stairs leading to the third floor. Masked guests ascended and descended around them, moving to and from the upper gallery that overlooked the ballroom. As the strains of another waltz floated from the musicians' gallery, they mounted the landing and moved toward the corridor that led to the family's wing. There they paused.

Matthew released her arm and, while keeping his expression casual, spoke low. "Just down the hall from your sister's private parlor is a table with a large urn of flowers on it. Do you know whereof I speak?"

"Yes."

"Good. Go there and wait for me." Then he bowed his head as if he were bidding her good night.

Flushing, Patience nodded and turned down the corridor.

Sconces lit her way with a flickering light, and the noise of the ball receded. The quieter it grew, the more her nervousness grew. She considered turning back, but it seemed lily-livered to do it now. Besides, her desire for him overrode her nervousness, so she passed the hall that led to her room and continued onward. She had trod the path many a time in order to visit with her sister. But tonight, her final destination was . . . where?

She passed the parlor and no sooner had she reached the table with the urn, than Matthew stepped from a door just behind her. She barely had time to draw a surprised breath before he took her hand and pulled her with him. Her pulse quickened as he turned her down a second corridor leading away from familiar pathways. She had never been in this part of the house. It was empty and quiet. She could hear almost nothing of the ball and her breathing sounded loud.

She glanced at Matthew. One of the longer pieces of his wavy hair had fallen forward. However, his strong profile revealed nothing but a purposeful intent. He said nothing. And then, as they turned another corner, he pulled her in front of him and released her. Patience stared at a large tapestry. Only two doors faced the short hall.

She turned around.

Pulling off his gloves, Matthew looked at her with dark, hooded eyes. His sensual mouth was parted but unsmiling. "Remove your gloves, Patience."

As she undid the small button on the inside of her wrist, it occurred to her that she hadn't even stopped to consider whether she would comply—she just had. Gently pulling the white kid leather from her fingers, she eased one arm and then the other from the long gloves. Holding them in one hand, she suddenly felt a little naked with her arms bare. She stood, rooted to the spot, as he regarded her. But her fingers began to tremble as he slowly approached.

She saw that his trousers were tented by a formidable erection. A wash of desire sluiced through her. She swallowed the moisture that pooled in her mouth and tried to calm her nerves as he paused before her. He said nothing, but rather held out his hand, palm up. Uncertain, Patience laid her gloves there. He folded them and put them in his pocket. Then he stepped closer and his hands lifted.

She thought he was going to embrace her, but instead he slipped the ribbons of her mask and pulled it away.

Patience drew shallow breaths as his intense gaze shifted slowly over her features. Lord, did he miss any detail of her? The air felt static. Was he going to kiss her, embrace her? She stood, tense.

But when he finally moved, it was only to lean against the doorjamb to her left. Reaching for the handle, he pushed it down and let the door swing open. She looked into his dark eyes and then into the dark room. Some flickering light sent dim shadows dancing upon the wall. But standing in the illuminated corridor, she could see little else.

She remembered his words below. *I shall hide you in my shadow . . . chain you to my side . . . give you everything you desire*. Her clitoris throbbed hungrily.

She looked back down the well-lit hall. This was it—her last chance to change her mind. But to what would she be returning? To endless dances with men who were too busy gawking at her to partner her properly? To ceaseless talk with men who were more interested in telling her their opinions than discovering hers? To trifling associations with men who only wanted to get between her legs?

She glanced up at Matthew. Of course, *he* wanted to get between her legs, too. How could she give him that? She thought of her sister. Dressed as Aphrodite, her sister's gusseted gown didn't quite conceal her five-month pregnancy. This ball and hunt would be her last social event before her confinement.

Patience put her hand over her flat stomach. She couldn't risk a child for one night. She looked back at Matthew. His beautiful eyes seemed to dare her. But she didn't know if the dare was to flee or to stay. She spoke on a rush of breath. "I'm a virgin. And I intend to stay that way."

He raised his brows. "Forever?"

"For now."

He lowered his eyes and seemed to consider for all of two seconds before nodding. "Very well. Until you tell me otherwise, I agree to leave you intact."

Patience nodded, even as she thought of her other concern. "And if I walk through that door, can you really assure me that whatever happens will be between us? You won't be thinking of Rosalind?"

Matthew didn't even blink. "Rosalind who?"

"That's very amusing, but I'm serious."

"So am I."

Patience looked into his unwavering gaze, but she saw not the least bit of humor there. She turned her eyes back to the darkened chamber. She had refused so many and trusted so few.

Go. Discover the secret he claims to keep.

It's only one night . . .

Closing her eyes, she took a deep breath. *God and St. Matthew keep me.* Then, with open-eyed determination, she walked past him and crossed the final threshold.

Chapter Three

Everything She Desires

His left hand is under my head, and his right hand doth embrace me.

Song of Solomon 2:6

As the door slammed behind her, darkening the room, Patience turned with a start. Suddenly Matthew emerged, like a dark phantom, from the shadows.

"Welcome to my underworld, Persephone."

Patience gasped as he pulled her against him, his arm sweeping tightly around her waist and his hand slipping into her hair. She barely drew a breath before his mouth swooped down upon hers. Her eyes closed and her blood rushed as his tongue thrust between her parted lips. His hand, cradling the back of her head, allowed no withdrawal from his demanding kiss.

Retreat was not an option. That moment had passed.

She moaned and held him tighter. His body was hard against hers and his tongue was stroking the roof of her mouth and skimming her teeth. She tasted a hint of brandy, while the smell of vetiver, rich and amber, filled her senses. His arms supported her and his powerful presence seemed to surround her.

Moisture trickled onto her damp thighs, and she could draw only short breaths as his tongue drove more deeply into her open mouth. Like a river, all sensation seemed to course from his mouth into hers, then surge, with unstoppable force, to the pulsing well of her woman's body.

Wild with desire, she surged against him, giving him kiss for kiss. Nothing mattered but this endless embrace. Not even breath. Her head spun and, despite the drumming that had started in her ears, she heard his groan, low and deep. His hand tightened in her hair and then his other was gripping her chin. He urged her mouth wider as he drove his tongue deeper, seeming to test the depths of her. Blood rushed to her pulsing clitoris and her air grew thin. Patience moaned then gasped as he tore his lips from hers.

Their warm, panting breaths touched as he traced his fingers across her trembling mouth. "I never should have walked away from you before," he murmured roughly. "Never." He kissed the curve of her jaw.

Patience's heart skipped a beat and then raced when he slipped his finger between her parted lips. Instinctively, she curled her tongue and sucked in a sensual exploration.

"Oh, Patience, that's good," Matthew whispered, slipping in another finger. "Show me how warm and wet your mouth can be." His hips tilted against her.

Patience trembled with excitement and her clitoris pulsed while she sucked hungrily upon his long fingers. She remembered the many times she and her sisters had spied upon Wilson, their butler, as he had delivered his daily dose of ejaculate into the mouth of Mary, their upstairs maid. It had fascinated and excited them, but it was she who had been most entranced. It was she who had actually spoken of daring to take the maid's place. It was she who had started sneaking young cucumbers from the kitchen garden into their room, where they had laughingly practiced the act they so avidly watched.

Now, as Matthew pushed his fingers into the moist recesses of her mouth, she sucked them and her breathless excitement flared into an even more urgent need.

He lifted his long-lashed eyes to hers and they reflected her fierce desire. "You understand what I want, don't you? In fact, you're hungry for it, aren't you?"

Yes! Patience blinked slowly.

His voice was a low, soft contradiction to the hard gaze he bent upon her. "That's good. But I wonder"—he slipped his fingers deeper—"how a virginal vicar's daughter knows of such things?" He brought his mouth close to hers. "What have you been up to, my little virgin? Are you more Impatience than Patience?"

She answered him with a slow swath of her tongue along the length of his fingers as he withdrew them. His mouth, so close, covered hers in a deep, breathtaking kiss. The throbbing between her legs increased. Her knees grew weak.

And just when she thought she might collapse at his feet, he broke the kiss, and spoke against her gasping mouth. "You have the sort of beauty that makes men hard, Patience. Tell me, just how many cocks have you tasted?" The fire in his eyes belied the calm of his voice.

Her cunt tightened. With as many enthusiastic suitors as she'd had, the opportunity had arisen many times, but she'd never taken it. She'd never taken it because no one had made her feel like this. "None," she breathed. "None, ever."

His features hardened angrily and his hand tightened in her hair. "Don't lie to me. Whatever occurs between us, never lie to me."

She met his dark gaze. "I'm not lying." She felt her cheeks flushing. "But I've seen it done, many times. Our butler . . . and the upstairs maid . . ."

Matthew's expression softened in an instant. "Ah, the servants. They're invaluable teachers, are they not?" He kissed the corner of her mouth. "Tell me, did it excite you to watch them?" he murmured against her lips.

"Yes." Her hips tilted as he filled her mouth with another probing kiss that was over almost as soon as it began.

"Did you dream of doing it?" he demanded. "Did you think of it while you stroked your sweet cunt? Did you come as you imagined what it might be like to have a nice hard cock between your lips?"

Patience moaned. The bud of flesh between her legs felt like it was going to explode.

"Did you?"

She stared into Matthew's dark eyes. "Yes," she admitted on a whisper. "Yes—so many times."

"Good." His jaw tightened and, taking her hand, he drew it between them. "You think you can get your pretty mouth around this?"

Patience gasped as Matthew pressed her hand to his erection. His penis was hard and heavy, and oh so thick. Thicker than Wilson, surely—thicker even than Jeremy Snap, the potter's son, whose great joy in life was flashing glimpses of his formidable prick at all the young ladies of Lincolnshire. No, neither of those hearty male organs compared to what she was feeling now. Sudden moisture filled her mouth and more trickled from her cunt as she eagerly explored him.

Matthew's jaw tightened and his hips flexed against her. "Do you want it?"

"Yes." Patience pressed an urgent kiss to his lips. "Yes, please."

He gently slipped the crown of flowers from her head while his other hand moved soothingly against her scalp. "How politely you reply," he murmured. "But, alas, I will not oblige you."

"What?" Patience drew back in confusion. "But I . . . But I want to . . ."

"You want?" His dark brows lifted. "My sweet Patience, we are not here for what *you* want. We are here for what *I* want."

Patience blinked and tried to think past the barrage of heady sensations that coursed through her. "But you spoke of knowing my desires . . ."

The softest, most beautiful smile turned his lips. "Yes, I did." He brushed his mouth against hers. "That's quite a puzzle, isn't it?"

Patience gazed into his handsome face and felt her nipples tingle. "I don't understand."

He drew her before the warmth of the hearth. "That's all right. You will," he murmured gently. He placed her crown of flowers on the mantel then put her gloves there as well. When he turned back to her, something flickered in his hand. "In time, everything will become clear to you. It's so simple, really." He stepped close.

She tipped up her mouth for his kiss. But no kiss came. Instead, she felt a firm downward tug upon the front of her gown. She gasped as her low bodice suddenly loosened and slipped from her shoulders. Clutching it, she looked down and saw that Matthew had cut the laces of her provincial-style costume.

His arms came around her. She felt another quick tug at her waist, and before she could grab them, her skirts fell to the floor in a frothy heap.

Taking a step back, he closed a slim knife and put it in his coat pocket. Then he held out his hand to her. "Give me your gown," he ordered quietly.

Stunned, Patience looked down at her sagging bodice and the

circle of fabric at her feet. She thought of refusing, but what point was there to that? As it was, the gown was of no use to her. Indeed, she would have to contrive some repairs in order to leave the chamber.

Shaking, she slipped out of her bodice and scooped up her skirts. At least she still wore her undergarments. She handed the pile of discarded gown to him and then nearly leapt out of her skin when he tossed everything into the fire.

A small cry escaped her. The room immediately darkened. She could hear only her own rapid breathing. And then the fire flared, higher than before, and Matthew was there. His hands reached for her and, with one hard pull, he ripped the fragile fabric of her corset cover. It, too, fed the greedy fire.

She stood, both shocked and enthralled, as she watched her beautiful gown blister into ashes. But when he reached for her pantalets, she grabbed at them. "No," she gasped.

His brows lifted. "No?" He met and held her gaze. "You will not say 'no' to me, Patience. If there is something that you truly cannot abide, and I mean *truly*, then you may say, with due regret, '*I cannot oblige you at this time*.' Is that clear?"

"Yes," she breathed, and then frowned at the immediacy of her response. Shouldn't she have considered before answering?

"That's good," he said softly. Then, moving his hands to the slit in her pantalets, he sundered the fabric at the center seam.

He muffled her startled gasp with a soothing kiss. It was so soft, so gentle. It seemed in complete contradiction to what he was doing, and yet it seemed completely right. Patience moaned, and her arms went around him. Without the layers of her skirts, his erection pressed hard and firm against her.

"There, you see?" he murmured against her lips. "Everything is fine." Pulling back, he stared down at her and stroked his fingers across her cheek. "Isn't it?"

Somehow it was. "Yes," Patience admitted.

A small, brief smile turned his lips. "Yes, of course it is." Then, with the aid of the knife, he ripped her pantalets to shreds.

Patience stood in mute amazement, throwing her hands over the triangle of red curls between her legs as the last of her undergarment was torn away. Nothing remained but a few points of fabric peeking from beneath her corset. She raised wide eyes to

Matthew when he cut the straps of her chemise so that the high mounds of her breasts were exposed.

As she stared at him, she couldn't keep back a wondering frown. Though the heat from the fire warmed her bare skin, she shivered—not with cold, but with want. It seemed every shocking thing he did only wound her desires tighter and tighter, until she quivered like a coiled spring.

Matthew stood back to look at her. His handsome face was tense with desire, and his dark eyes reflected the firelight, making them seem to burn from within. "Move your hands," he ordered.

Patience felt her blood rising to her cheeks and descending to her already swollen clitoris. Her fingers trembled protectively above the nub of pulsing flesh. She couldn't bring herself to put her arms at her sides. No one had even dared dishevel her, let alone expose her like this.

That's why you need him. He dares what others will not.

And yet . . .

"I cannot." Her voice cracked. She didn't want to speak the absolute refusal, but she couldn't move either.

He looked at her and his gaze softened. "I'm afraid you must, Patience, or I will make you."

Patience squeezed her eyes shut. She should scream at him in righteous indignation. Where was her indignation? She tried to summon it, but found only a hot, undeniable passion in its stead. And yet—she looked down at her hands—she could not move. She shook as body and mind, passion and pride, battled inside her.

Matthew stepped close. "Is it so difficult?" he whispered.

Patience felt sudden tears well. God, she never cried! But she was half naked and vulnerable. It shouldn't feel good.

And yet it did.

It felt perfect and thrilling.

"Yes." She lifted her gaze to his and forced back her tears. "Yes, it is difficult."

A low moan seemed to catch in his throat, and his beautiful eyes locked on to her face with such rapt adoration. It took her breath away. "Ah, my sweet Patience, I worship the struggle in your eyes, and the tears you won't allow—for I value most that which is not easily given." He gripped his cock through his trousers and slowly stroked himself. Her womb quivered at the sight, but she raised her eyes back to his as he continued. "Every emotion you feel in the suffering of my commands honors me. I cherish each one. But ultimately"—he let go of himself and lay a gentle kiss upon her brow—"your struggle must always be toward obedience. Now, move your hands."

Patience's cunt throbbed with a deep, almost painful, craving; the pulsing bud of flesh that always brought her pleasure tortured her now with its burning desire for release. Every word he uttered enflamed her more, made her want him more.

What was wrong with her? And why must she obey? Why did she *want* to obey? Her emotions warred within her but, somehow, the battle only served to heighten her excitement.

She looked down at her hands again and, with the greatest effort, forced her arms to her sides. Her muscles stiff and rigid with tension, she pressed her fingers against her thighs.

"There," he whispered. "That's very good."

His praise, so quietly spoken, calmed and warmed her. But in the next moment, her eyes stung again at the realization that his simple words could affect her so. What power did he wield over her?

She lowered her head.

"No, Patience. Hide nothing from me." He tipped up her face and pressed a soft kiss against her lips. "Don't you see? I covet your every response. Each lovely reaction you experience is a gift to me." His dark eyes moved over her face with an intensity she had never seen. No one had ever looked at her with such passionate concentration. "Do you begin to see what I want from you?" His warm hands moved up her arms in a soft caress that sent a shiver down her spine. "I want you to give me all that I demand. And I want you to hide nothing from me as you do."

A rush of desire coursed through Patience's body, leaving behind a yearning that was tinged with both exhilaration and trepidation.

He stroked his fingers along the tops of her shoulders, then traced them up the sides of her neck to her jaw, tilting it up to him. "I want to see every struggle and every victory. I want to see each precious tear and each magnificent smile." Lowering his hands, he walked slowly behind her. She shuddered as his fingers curved over her bare bottom, squeezing gently. "I want all of you, every bit of you, for myself." Patience sighed and closed her eyes as he kissed the tender skin behind her ear. "Do you know why I want this, my sweet Patience?"

She moaned as he wrapped his arms around her and pressed his whole body against her back.

"Do you?"

Yes . . .

She leaned back against him as his fingers slid into the red curls over her mount. His erection was hard and strong against her bottom.

"Tell me, Patience." His fingers slipped lower. Her cunt throbbed. "Tell me, and I'll touch you as you long to be touched."

A soft, mewling sound escaped her and her hips bucked.

"Tell me," he demanded.

Patience drew a gasping breath. "Because it is what *I* want. It is what *I* desire."

"Yes," he breathed by her ear. "And what is it you desire?"

God, she tilted her hips but he didn't move. Why must he torment her?

"What do you long for, Patience? Tell me the secret I already know. Say it out loud."

Patience bit her lip. Her hips twisted with desire. Say the words. She need only say the words. But what words? "I long to feel more," she whispered. "I—I long to—to . . ." *To what?*

"Submit." Matthew whispered the word into her ear, but it grew and echoed in her mind.

He came around to face her. "The word is *submit*," he said firmly.

Yes. She stared into his eyes as she blinked the sting from her own. She didn't understand all the ramifications, but that was exactly the word. "Yes," she breathed.

"Say it."

"Submit." Her voice shook. "I long to submit."

A hot fire illuminated Matthew's dark gaze. His arms swept around her, and she gasped as he kissed her deeply and hungrily. She tasted him and clung to him. Then her body leapt as, at last, she felt his fingers touching the throbbing, distended nub of flesh that fed her rampant desire.

He pulled his mouth from hers. "God, your clitoris is so full, and your cunt is so wet."

He held her tightly around her waist while once, twice, a third time he slid his fingers over her sodden folds. And then he was rubbing her. In tight, firm circles he plied her tender bud.

Scorching pleasure shot through Patience's body. She moaned as she stared into Matthew's unrelenting gaze. Her fingers curled in the short hair at his nape. She bit her lip as her hips began to rock.

"There. There you are," he urged. "Come for me." The thick column of his cock was thrusting against her, short and tight. His jaw clenched as she began to shudder. "That's my beauty. Come for me—come."

"Yes," she panted. "Matthew!" *God! Oh, God!* Her chest heaved and her cunt clenched. Matthew's body pressed against her. His fingers stroked her. Everything drew up tight within her. Her muscles flexed. She gasped for air. And then her passions broke.

On a sharp cry, her head fell back—and as her hips jerked convulsively against the press of his fingers, she burst into a thousand tiny fragments. Shards of brilliant bliss imbedded themselves in her shattered nerves, where they pulsed and flared with a searing heat. Gasping and shuddering, she heaved against him as he seemed to draw out each smoldering ember and snuff it with his touch—until there was nothing left.

Collapsing against him, she would have fallen were it not for his strong arm about her waist.

Matthew held her for a moment, until her breathing began to slow. Then, bending, he scooped her up into his arms. Patience laid her head against his shoulder as they moved across the room. She felt wonder and amazement. "Thank you, Matthew."

He stared into her eyes as he laid her against the pillows on his bed. He braced his hands on either side of her. "You're welcome, Patience." His jaw was tight, but his voice soft.

He bent to kiss her, and the kiss was as full of passion as their first. Patience curled her arms around him as his tongue plunged deeply. Her heart pounded and she moaned as he bit down on her lower lip and sucked it. Then, as quickly as it had begun, it ended. He pulled away, leaving her wanting more.

She rolled onto her side to watch him cross the room. How gracefully he walked. Opening a door, he disappeared for a moment.

Patience waited. It appeared to be his dressing room. Was he undressing? Her pulse started to race again.

He reentered the room wearing a long, dark robe. White scarves or cravats hung from his hand. He walked purposefully over to her and sat beside her on the edge of the bed.

"Give me your hands," he ordered gently.

Her eyes widened and her tender clitoris pulsed painfully. Did he mean to tie her? She froze.

A small frown turned his brow. "Give me your hands," he said again, this time more firmly.

Patience sat up and her heart hammered in her breast. She'd trusted him thus far. Why withdraw her trust now? Slowly, she put her hands together before him.

His frown eased and he pressed a kiss into her palms. "Good girl."

He quickly tied her hands. She began to tremble as she felt the snugness.

"You're doing very well," he murmured.

When he drew her bound hands over her head, she fell back against the pillows and watched him tie her to the bedpost in such a way that left considerable slack.

Patience's body tensed and her nipples hardened against her corset. God, what was he going to do?

She sucked in her breath and almost screamed as she saw the flicker of the blade. But then she gasped as he imbedded it in the same bedpost she was tied to. Without a word, he moved to her ankles and tied first one and then the other to the opposing bedposts. Again, he left considerable slack. But as he stood back to look at her, his gaze hot and intent, she squirmed at the helpless desire that suffused her.

He stood there for a moment, observing her distress, before coming to sit with her. He smoothed his hand down her heaving side and over her hip, and then let it rest upon her patch of red curls. "A beautiful angel once told me that nights such as these are made for secrets and magic. Shall I tell you a secret?"

Patience's breath stilled. "Yes."

His dark eyes glittered in the dim firelight. "You are a wonder and a beauty, and there is something profound in you that calls to me. I've never wanted any woman more than I want you." A small frown furrowed his brow. "Do you hear me? Never."

Patience's heart quickened.

He leaned closer. "Even when I was engaged to another, I wanted you. Even as I tried to stay away from you, I wanted you." He paused and traced his finger slowly over her eyebrow. "You are the only woman I see. You are the only woman I want." He leaned low and spoke against her lips. "And your submission is powerful. Don't fear it."

With a soft moan, Patience kissed him and thrust her tongue into his warm mouth. His words were like a sensual touch and her body thrilled as both delight and desire tore through her.

She sighed into his mouth and arched against him as his hand began to stroke the moist folds between her legs. The press of his fingers, slick with her wetness, made her throb and quiver.

He broke their kiss but his dark eyes stared into hers as he continued to ply her, faster and faster. "You see, Patience. This is where you belong. Panting and wet in my bed."

His words spurred her passions. Pulling at her bonds, she lifted her hips as he worked her. She gasped and thrust against his hand. His eyes never left her. Then, just as she felt her cunt begin to pull, he stopped.

Patience watched, speechless, as he stood and crossed to the chamber door. She squirmed as her clitoris and cunt throbbed with aborted need. Then she blanched when he removed his robe and tossed it over a chair. He was fully dressed!

"Where are you going?" she cried.

He looked over at her and adjusted his cuffs. "I'm going downstairs to play cards. You will submit to my leisure and await me."

Patience gasped as he pulled on his gloves.

"When I return," he said casually, "I shall expect you to satisfy me in the manner your maid satisfies your butler."

Before she could respond, he was gone.

The lock clicked behind him.

Chapter Four
To Stay or To Go

Whither is thy beloved gone . . .

Song of Solomon 6:1

Matthew managed only a few steps before he had to pause and brace himself against the wall. Christ, his heart was pounding and his whole body was shaking. His breath came as though he'd been running, and he was so hard, he hurt. He winced as his straining prick throbbed.

He wanted to rush back to Patience, tear off his clothes, and throw himself on her. He wanted to breathe the scent of gardenias that clung to her and sink his cock into her warm, wet mouth.

But he couldn't do that. Not yet. He had to be sure of her. He had to give her the opportunity to reject what he offered—to reject him.

He straightened and shoved his hand through his hair. It might take her some time to realize it, but he had left her the means to leave. If she were gone when he returned, then . . .

His chest tightened uncomfortably. *Then, what?*

She would stay. She had to stay.

He straightened his shoulders and started down the hall. Patience needed his strong hand, and he needed her surrender. More than with any woman ever, he needed her surrender. For she was like a crystal prism that broke his desires into separate, distinct, and beautiful delineation. He saw, in a moment, all the ways that he wanted her. And he saw the totality of that want—complete possession.

He allowed a small, confident smile as he pictured her tied to his bed. God, but she was stunning. Her thick red curls felt like silk in his hand and her vivid green eyes—her beautiful, intelligent green eyes—held him captive with their shifting expressions.

She was far more beautiful than he had formed her in his dreams. He turned into the main corridor. More beautiful than . . . *Bloody hell.* He drew up short as he stared into the inquiring gaze of his half brother. "Mark."

His brother's eyes tipped briefly to Matthew's still prominent erection. "Matt." Crossing his arms over his chest, Mark leaned his shoulder against the wall. "I saw you leave with Patience. Where is she?"

Matt shoved his hands in his pockets and leaned against the wall as well. "I took her to bed."

"To her bed, or yours?"

"That's none of your business."

Mark shook his head. "This is unwise, Matt."

"And why is that?"

"Because Patience isn't just any woman."

"I know she isn't just any woman. That's why I want her, because she isn't just any woman." Matthew felt an indefinable anger rising. "Christ, must I defend myself even to you?"

Mark frowned. "I'm not asking you to defend yourself. I'm merely speaking with you, brother to brother, as we always have."

Matthew rubbed the furrow from his brow before looking at Mark. "I've wanted her since I first laid eyes on her—even before the scandal. I've wanted her with an undeniable certainty."

"Yes."

"But I couldn't have her then, could I?" A muscle jumped in his shoulder. His whole body felt tight. "So I stayed away from her, because I feared that if I spoke to her, if I even drew near her, I would do something that would cause me to shame Rosalind." Hot resentment churned in him. He looked at Mark. "But then Rosalind shamed me." His hands shook with his pent-up emotions. "Yet still I stayed away. And you have no idea what it took. On the night of your wedding, I could have had her, but I walked away."

"Why? Why did you walk away?"

Matthew paused before meeting Mark's blue gaze. "Because I couldn't stand the thought of wanting her that badly. Because I didn't want to want any woman that badly."

Mark nodded slowly. "Yet, here you are—wanting her as badly as ever."

Matthew's scowl deepened. "That's right, because for the past three months, while you have been living in passionate, conjugal bliss with the woman who adores you, I've lived like a damned eunuch. I'm done with that. Patience is here, and I am here. And there is no Rosalind to keep me from her. Don't *you* try to." He clenched his fists in his pockets. "My life as I knew it may be over, but I'm not dead. A man has needs. *I* have needs."

Mark raised his brows. "Yes, I know the direction of your needs. Are you sure she suits your needs?"

Matthew pictured Patience's beautiful, moist eyes—the sweet struggle in her face, and then the lovely bliss of her orgasm. "Oh, she is the personification of my needs."

"Really?"

Matthew frowned. "Yes, really. And if I'm right about her, she needs me as much as I need her. So you leave us alone."

"I can't do that, Matt. She's Passion's sister."

Matthew felt the reins on his anger slip a notch. "Yes, and I thought you were still my brother."

"I am your brother."

"Then why don't you bloody act like it, and show me a little goddamned trust."

"I would, but you haven't been acting yourself."

Matthew's body tensed with the effort it took not to lash out. "How can I act myself, when no one is treating me like myself—not even *you*," he sneered.

Mark studied him for a long moment. "All right, Matt. Just remember, Patience is under my roof. That means she's my responsibility. And despite how well suited to each other you say you are, she is not one of Mr. Stone's ladies. Nor is she a woman of experience."

If he weren't so angry, Matthew might have laughed. "Christ, listen to you. You, who not five months ago, were completely incapable of resisting Passion."

"I'm still completely incapable of resisting Passion." Mark paused, and his brows lifted. "But then, I don't have to resist her anymore, do I?"

Matthew pushed away from the wall. "If you'll excuse me, I'm going downstairs to play cards."

His brother stepped into his path. "I'm trusting you, Matt. I'm trusting you because, despite everything, *I* know you're the same man as always."

No. He wasn't the same man, nor would he ever be. He was a bastard, and a social pariah with a quickly dwindling purse. The latter two problems he would fix. But the former was forever. He clenched his jaw. "Just know that my pursuit of Patience will be on my own terms." He glared at his brother. "So don't start pushing me."

Mark stepped out of his way but then shoved his shoulder. "I'm still your older brother. I'll push you if I want."

Matthew shoved his brother back, harder, and then strode down the hall.

"By the way," Mark called after him, "I thought you'd sworn off love."

Matthew didn't pause or turn. "I have."

It took a while for Patience to fathom that Matthew had actually left. She kept thinking he was only testing her and would quickly return. But he did not. And as the minutes ticked away on the bedside clock, it seemed more and more likely he had spoken with complete truth—she must submit to his leisure and await him.

But how could she bear it? Her clitoris throbbed with excruciating tenacity. And the more she squirmed the more it tortured her. She wanted him back and she wanted him back now! How dare he leave her like this?

She tossed on the bed and pulled at her bonds. With a growl of frustration, she threw back her head to look again at the knots. They would be impossible. She lifted her gaze to the knife. It was far out of her reach.

She stared at it. Or was it? Did she have enough slack? If she scooted up against the headboard . . .

Shifting her body back as far as possible, she reached for it. She had to stretch completely, her arms and legs pulling hard against the bonds, but her fingers just brushed the handle. She could do it. She need only pull it out and she could be free.

She let her hands drop as she stared at the gleaming blade. But why had he left it? Did he want her to escape? She looked around the room. His black velvet robe lay over the chair. Left there for her to put on?

And what of the lock? She strained her eyes in the dim light and, just when she thought she'd never be able to tell, the fire flared. In the brief illumination, she saw the gleam of an inside latch.

She frowned. Was it so simple? Why had he made it so easy?

A painful disappointment flooded her. He wanted her to leave.

She felt tears well again. What in heaven's name was the matter with her? She was no stranger to disappointment. And she was perfectly capable of taking care of her own needs. Compelling back her tears, she began to reach for the knife. But as she moved, her swollen clitoris pulsed urgently. She squeezed her eyes shut and waited for the aching pleasure to pass. God, it was such sweet torment!

Her eyes flew open. Sweet torment—that was what he wanted. He had said he valued most that which was not easily given. To escape was easy. It was staying that would try her. She glanced at the knife and the robe. They weren't tools for her escape; they were tests of her obedience.

Relief blotted out her disappointment. He wanted her to stay. The question was did *she* want to?

Ah, perhaps that had been the question all along. She looked again at the knife. If she wanted to go, he had left her the way.

She stared at the slim blade. If she cut herself free, she could put on the robe and disappear into her own room, where she could please herself and then go promptly to sleep. All would be well, and life would return to normal.

But if she stayed, nothing was certain—nothing but the promise of Matthew's thick organ in her mouth. Her cunt clenched with excitement. And who knew what else he might show her? A shiver of anticipation tightened her nipples. Whatever he had in store wouldn't be easy.

No. If it was easy she wanted, that path was laid from the knife, to the robe, to the door. She need only follow it.

* * *

Matthew hated the way people's eyes followed him. As he passed amongst the guests on his way to the card room, he was distinctly aware of their reactions to his presence. Many looked away, perhaps fearing he might engage them in conversation—a risk of which they were in no danger. But many also met his gaze, either openly or tentatively, and exchanged a brief nod or greeting. Regardless, he could feel the curious and speculative glances that followed him.

He frowned. Once, his friendship, his presence—hell, even his name on a guest list—had been valued. What a difference a father made.

As he passed three young ladies, he heard the wind of their whispers behind him. His frown deepened. He hated being talked about. It was almost worse than the outright snubs.

He lifted his chin and rolled his shoulders as he approached the card room. But since he couldn't stop the relentless tide of gossip, he would turn it to his advantage. He'd really give them something to talk about—and he didn't even need Benchley's presence in order to deal his first blow. He stretched his fingers, and exhilaration flooded his veins when he heard Danforth's snorting laughter. Ah, the vile prig was right where he was supposed to be.

Striding into the card room, the first face Matthew saw was Danforth's. Seated at the center table, the tall, narrow-shouldered earl was balancing on his rear chair legs. Upon seeing Matthew, he sat forward as an arrogant, condescending expression came over his florid features.

"Well, if it isn't the infamous Mr. Hawkmore," he said, loudly enough to claim the attention of the entire room.

It seemed all eyes turned to him. Matthew settled his expression into lines of bland indifference as he moved to the center table. "Danforth." He nodded to the other men at the table. "Gentlemen." He was in his brother's house. They wouldn't dare decline him a seat. "May I join you?"

Lord Hillsborough nodded.

The aging Lord Rivers indicated the open chair across from Danforth. "Of course. Take a seat, my boy. The game is *vingt et un*."

"Very well. Ten thousand, then," Matthew said, taking his

place. His balance sheet could little afford such a withdrawal, but he must show no sign of financial weakness. He would just have to bloody win.

As Lord Rivers gave him his chips and made an accounting in the betting book, Danforth tipped back in his chair again and stroked his long moustache. "Tell me, Hawkmore, whatever did you do with Miss Dare? You infuriated Fenton when you cut in on him, and then you infuriated every man in the room when you led her off the floor. And now you're back." He leaned forward as the cards were dealt. "But is she?"

Matthew flipped a chip onto the table then took a moment to examine his cards. Finally, he glanced up blankly. "I'm sorry, what was that, Danforth?"

The earl's eyes narrowed. "I said, where is Miss Dare?"

A vision of soft full lips, swollen from his kisses, flashed in Matthew's mind. Would she stay or flee? He indicated he would take another card, and then shrugged. "I don't know where Miss Dare is at the moment. She complained of a headache, so I escorted her to the family wing." He placed his opening bet then met Danforth's cold stare. "Perhaps she had a little too much of your good company."

Danforth upped the bet without even looking at his cards. "Perhaps she did not understand what *low* company she had entered into when she allowed you to escort her from the floor."

The room quieted and Matthew's body stiffened with anger. He clenched his jaw and moved a tall stack of chips into the middle of the table. "Perhaps she preferred my low company to your boorish manners." He frowned for a moment. "In fact, if memory serves, even when we were boys at school, the girls didn't favor you."

Danforth leaned forward as the crowd surrounding the table thickened. His lip curled. "You thought you were such the golden boy then, didn't you? But look at you now," he sneered. "Now you can't even get an invitation to clear the plates in the dining rooms you used to preside over, and no gentlemen of honor will do business with you." He threw a stack of chips upon the growing pile. "So who is the favored one now?"

"Good lord, Danforth, at least look at your damned cards!" one of the onlookers exclaimed as Lord Rivers and Lord Hillsborough bowed out of the game.

It was just the two of them now.

The earl swept up his cards and cast a cursory glance over them.

Matthew watched him carefully then pushed forward another stack of chips. "I don't know who the favored one is, but it can't be you, for you have neither charm, nor talent. Your lack of the former makes you ill suited to the ladies. And your lack of the latter makes you ill suited for cards." He raised a brow. "Why don't you quit, and admit defeat to me."

"Damn you, Hawkmore! If I'm so ill suited to the ladies, then how is that I have become engaged to *your* former fiancée?" A hush fell over the room. "That's right," Danforth said victoriously, his moustache quivering, "the lovely Lady Rosalind is to be mine."

Matthew thought of the note tucked in his pocket. Danforth could have her. A vision of brilliant green eyes swam in his mind. Patience. He need only have Patience.

Danforth positively beamed in the face of Matthew's silence. "So"—he shoved the last of his chips into the pile—"why don't *you* admit defeat to me?"

Matthew allowed a mock scowl to briefly crease his brow. "Why ever would I do that?" He moved another stack of chips to the center of the table. "Oh, and I already heard about your betrothal." He moved another stack. "Forgive me for not mentioning it earlier," he said idly as he moved another stack of chips and then another. Finally, he sat back and leveled his eyes on Danforth. "Congratulations. I'm certain you deserve each other."

Danforth's forehead gleamed with a sudden sheen of sweat as he stared at the huge pile of chips. Murmurs filled the room, and Lord Rivers leaned forward. "You were already rather deep in before this hand, Lord Danforth. I fear that you are overextended." He laid his aging hands upon the table. "I believe that passions have overruled common sense this evening. Why not ask Mr. Hawkmore for a draw? The hands shall remain private."

All eyes turned to Danforth. His chest puffed up and his expression hardened. "I will not! He's bluffing." Reaching into his breast pocket, Danforth pulled out a folded sheet of paper and tossed it atop the huge pile of chips. "That is a coal mine in Gwenellyn that I just acquired from Lord Benchley, my future father-in-law." Danforth managed a grin, but his face was flushed. "Now show us your cards, Hawkmore, and let's have an end to this."

"You must sign that deed over to the table before the cards are shown, my lord," Rivers said calmly.

Danforth paused but then hurriedly signed the deed and the betting book. Tossing down the pen, he raised his chin as many in the crowd regarded him doubtfully. "Doesn't matter," he said dismissively. "I'll have it back in a moment."

Matthew stared at him and then at the piece of paper. He sat completely still as the beautiful irony of the moment overcame him. How often was one gifted with both a shield and a sword simultaneously? And how often did such a gift come from the very hands of one's enemies? Clearly the angels were favoring him tonight, for such a boon, coming from as unlikely a quarter as the Earl of Danforth, could only be heaven-sent.

Maybe his life wasn't entirely bad news after all. First Patience and now this. Indeed, if he hadn't come to the ball to claim her, he wouldn't be sitting at this table now. *She* was his lucky angel.

A wide grin had spread across Danforth's face at Matthew's silence. He threw confident looks of victory to the crowd of onlookers. Finally, he leaned forward casually. "Well, Hawkmore? Put your damned cards on the table."

With a steady hand, Matthew laid the ten of clubs, the eight of hearts and the three of diamonds upon the table. "*Vingt et un*," he said quietly.

All eyes turned to Danforth. His face became a red mask. Matthew barely glimpsed a ten and a face card as the earl leapt up. "You bloody bastard!"

Come on! Matthew threw back his chair as Danforth rounded the table.

"I ought to have known better than to play with the likes of you," the earl raged. "You're nothing but the cheating bastard of a cheating slut. You're noth—"

Matthew's fist connecting with Danforth's jaw interrupted whatever insult would have come next. The tall man reeled back, but no one seemed inclined to catch him. He fell against a marble column topped with a bronze statue of Athena. The goddess of war tipped then hit the ground with a clanging cacophony.

In the brief silence that followed, Matthew clenched his fists. Then pandemonium broke out as Danforth lunged forward, swinging wildly. Matthew pushed the startled Lord Rivers out of the way, but caught a glancing blow against his chin for his effort. Whirling around, he managed to sink his fist into Danforth's gut before he was leapt upon and restrained by several of the gentlemen in the room. Danforth was held back as well, wheezing while he glared defiantly.

"What the hell is going on here?" Mark drew up short when he saw Matthew. The men holding him let him go.

Matthew rotated his shoulders and straightened his coat. "Ask him," he said as he swept the deed from the floor.

Mark frowned at Danforth. "Well?"

Danforth looked up with watery eyes and a flushed face. "Your half brother has cheated me, Langley." He yanked away from the men who were supporting him and pushed back his hair. "I demand that my bet be returned to me."

Matthew recognized the angry set of his brother's jaw. "My *brother* doesn't cheat, Danforth," Mark said tightly. "Your demand is denied."

Matthew slipped the deed into his breast pocket and watched a flicker of panic light Danforth's eyes.

"I tell you, he cheated me!"

"And I tell you, that's impossible."

"You take the word of a gardener's son over the word of an earl?"

"I take the word of my brother over the word of an ass."

That was good. Matthew almost smiled.

"I ought to have known you would stand with him," Danforth sneered. "Any man who would allow his wife to cavort about in costume whilst with child is no gentleman."

"Cavort? Are you speaking of my lady?" Mark growled. "My lady wife, who has not once taken the dance floor this eve? My gentle wife, who is an angel of virtue and decency?"

Uh-oh. Matthew looked at his brother and saw all the warning signs—angry tic in the cheek, raised shoulders, and two twitches of the right hand. "You know, Danforth, I don't even like you. Why are you here? I didn't invite you." Mark turned to Matthew. "Did you invite him?"

Matthew shook his head. "No. No, I didn't invite him."

"Well, I didn't invite him." Mark strolled over to Danforth, who was sweating profusely. Even the man's moustache looked damp. "Ah, yes. It must have been my wife who invited you. My beautiful, gracious wife, who *I* insisted should enjoy this last event before her confinement." He leaned into Danforth's glistening face. "The woman I vowed to God I would protect, you son of a bitch."

Danforth didn't have a chance. In the next moment, he was being dragged across the room by his lapels. A noisy crowd followed as Mark yanked the man from the card room and hauled him down the stairs to the main floor.

Matthew leaned upon the landing rail to watch Danforth be thrown out. He smoothed his hand over his breast pocket where the deed had joined the note from Rosalind. He felt exuberant. The night had gone far better than he'd expected.

A light touch upon his arm drew his attention. He smiled into the beautiful face of his brother's wife and turned her gently from the scene below. "Hello, Passion."

She glanced over her shoulder as he pulled her away. "What's going on, Matt?"

He pulled her arm through his and escorted her from the crowd of onlookers. "Everything is fine. Your husband is just throwing out a little vermin."

"Oh, dear. I didn't realize we had invited any vermin." Passion smiled and, for a moment, it was as if he were looking at a vague reflection of Patience.

He wanted to go to her. He glanced at the stairs. Surely he had waited long enough.

"Matt?"

He returned his attention to Passion. They had paused in a quiet spot outside the grand salon. "Yes?"

"I saw my sister leave with you."

He regarded her intently as his neck stiffened. "Yes. I escorted her to the family wing."

"I see." Passion regarded him with her gentle eyes. "You know, I've always sensed that there was something between you two."

"So have I."

Her hazel eyes held his. "Matt, though Patience is very assured and capable, and has held innumerable beaux at bay, her heart is not unbreakable. She hides a deep and passionate nature—one that has suffered loss and disappointment. So, be careful with her. Be careful with my sister."

Matthew frowned. "What loss? What disappointment? Did someone hurt her?"

"Yes."

Matthew's frown deepened. "Who? What happened?"

Passion's gaze softened and she seemed to study him for a moment. "I won't say more. Patience wouldn't like it."

Matthew tensed and leaned close. "Who was he, Passion? It was her former music master, wasn't it?"

"That is not for me to tell you, Matt." Passion lifted one auburn brow. "But, if Patience tells you, then you may be sure that you have won her trust."

Matthew pulled back. He wanted to know everything—right now.

Passion put her hand on his arm. "Just take care of her, Matt. She needs to be taken care of."

Remembering the feel of Patience's straining body, his prick stirred. He looked into Passion's gentle eyes. "Marmalade or jam?"

Passion's brow creased. "What?"

"Does your sister take marmalade or jam on her scones?"

Passion smiled softly. "Marmalade."

"There you are, Hawkmore." Lord Rivers approached on his cane and bent to place a kiss over Passion's hand. "Lady Langley, you are Aphrodite incarnate."

Passion smiled at the aging lord. "My thanks, Lord Rivers. Are you enjoying yourself? Is there anything I can have brought for you?"

"Not at all, my lady. I merely came to thank Hawkmore, here, for taking care of me in the card room."

Passion glanced at Matthew. "I believe my brother-in-law may be particularly well suited to taking care of people, Lord Rivers."

"Well, he did a fine job of it by me. Were it not for you, Hawkmore, I would likely be sprawled in several pieces upon the card room floor."

"Oh dear, was there a scuffle over cards?"

Lord Rivers put out a reassuring hand. "Only a small one."

Passion frowned and looked the elderly man over. "Well, gracious, are you all right?"

"Yes, yes. I'm quite well. You should have no concerns. Your husband has deftly removed the troublesome influence."

"Ah"—Passion turned to Matthew—"the vermin?"

Matthew nodded and glanced again at the stairs. "The very vermin."

Lord Rivers chuckled. "That's quite funny. The very vermin. He *is* rather verminlike, after all." He wiggled his arthritic fingers by his cheek to indicate whiskers. "What with that moustache of his."

Passion's brow creased curiously as she laughed.

"The Earl of Danforth," Matthew informed her. "I'm certain your husband will request that you strike him from your guest list."

"Oh! Well, if you'll both excuse me, I should go distract our guests from the situation. Good evening."

As Passion left, Lord Rivers turned to Matthew. "Such a lovely lady. But listen, my boy. That was a fair game, and I want to be sure your winnings are accounted for. There are several lords willing to sign as witnesses to the legitimacy of the game and the bets. Why don't you come with me and we shall note everything in the book so that nothing is forgotten."

Matthew looked into the man's watery blue eyes. If memory served he had been a widower for a very long time. His son had been killed in a riding accident or a carriage accident. Matthew couldn't remember which.

With a sigh, he took one last look at the stairs. If Patience had gone, it didn't matter how long he took. If she'd stayed, it also didn't matter. For she must learn to await him, however long his business pressed him. And he must learn to attend to his business, no matter the temptation she presented.

Matthew turned back to Lord Rivers. "Let's go, my lord."

Perhaps she should go.

Patience turned onto her side and leaned against the pillows she had managed to push up against the headboard. As she moved, her clitoris quavered softly. Where she had suffered its sharp pulsations earlier and tried to restrain her movements, now she moved and shifted in order that she would feel it. Even dimmed, it was a persuasive reminder of why she should stay.

Besides, the truth was she wanted to stay. So why entertain thoughts of leaving? Simply because she thought she should? Who determined "should," anyway?

She sighed. The slack in the scarves allowed her to bend her arms and legs. Her arms rested on the pillow before her. She stared at her bound wrists. The white silk was snug, but not uncomfortable. Her hands lay relaxed, one atop the other. She suddenly realized that she found her bonds beautiful, and the longer she stared the more beautiful they appeared to her. But why?

She rocked her hips and closed her eyes as the gentle thrum of her clitoris whispered the answer. Because they contained her. Because they removed all decisions. Because she need do nothing but await the man who had put them there.

Matthew.

Her heart fluttered as she thought of the way he looked at her. Dark and intense, his eyes seemed to capture her every emotion. He watched her carefully as he issued his demands. He studied her with rapt attention as he touched her body. He made her feel as if each response she experienced were important and essential to him.

Her clitoris throbbed.

It was almost as if . . .

. . . as if he needed her.

She stared at her lovely bonds, and a sensual languor enveloped her.

Where was he? What was he doing? Could he still be at the card tables?

She felt no anxiety for his return, no envy for his freedom. Indeed, as she pictured him moving through the crowded ballroom, she pulled her hands close and snuggled gratefully against the pillow. She need not dance with Lords Farnsby, Asher, and Danforth, and the endless list of other lords and gentlemen that had filled her dance card. She need not answer their questions or respond to their compliments. She need not smile. She need not laugh. She need not address them at all.

She closed her eyes and listened to the quiet stillness of the room.

She need only stay—stay and wait—for the one man who mattered.

Chapter Five
First Submission

I sat down under his shadow with great delight, and his fruit was sweet to my taste.

Song of Solomon 2:3

Matthew walked purposefully toward the stairs.

Once he'd finished with Rivers, he'd been waylaid by Hillsborough, who had engaged him in an interesting but lengthy conversation about horse breeding. Because the man was a shareholder and a regular parliamentary vote for the railway, Matthew had exercised vigorous control over himself and let the conversation run its course.

Now, he was past his endurance. He wanted to go to Patience.

Had she stayed?

"I say, Hawkmore, good show at the gaming table this evening," Farnsby called.

Matthew drew up short. He'd almost made it. *Patience.* He must have Patience.

"Blasted Danforth has owed me twenty pounds since June," Farnsby said as he extended his hand. Matthew paused then extended his own. It was the first handshake he'd been offered since his fall. "I'll be damned if I can get it out of him, though," Farnsby continued.

Matthew flexed his sore knuckles. "Then I suppose I can expect trouble collecting the five thousand pounds he lost to me tonight."

Farnsby raised his brows. "Well, yes. Quite right."

"I'll tell you what, Farnsby." Matthew pulled out his watch. It was almost two in the morning. "When I collect my money, I'll try to get yours as well."

"Why, that's bloody stand-upish of you, Hawkmore. Say, why don't you join Asher and me for the hunt?"

Matthew paused. Farnsby was a considerable comedown from his old crowd. But it was the first invitation he'd received in a long while. "My thanks, Farnsby, but I'm uncertain if I shall attend."

"Well, I hope you do. Evening, Hawkmore."

Matthew nodded. "Good evening."

He waited only a moment before turning for the stairs. Though his pulse quickened and his cock throbbed, he forced himself not to hurry. The discipline was for him. For mastering Patience would take immeasurable restraint.

So he took one step at a time—slowly and deliberately. And as he ascended, he summoned the feel of Patience's lush red hair, the sight of her verdant eyes, and the smell of gardenias that clung to her. He thought of her long shapely legs and the feel of her wet, swollen clitoris.

Each new thought urged him to hurry. Each new thought made him harder. But, still, he kept a strict control over his pace, neither quickening nor slowing. The press of his trousers against his erection tortured the sensitive head of his cock, but he suffered it.

He must suffer it—for she would need him to be strong and unassailable.

He followed the path to his room, flexing his sore hand along the way as he thought of all the ways he would bring her into submission.

When he finally approached his door, a rush of unstoppable anxiety surged through him. He squelched it angrily. She would be there, obedient and waiting. *She must be.*

Rather than try the handle, he shoved the key in the lock and turned the latch. He didn't pause to register whether it clicked or not. He simply opened the door.

She was there.

Leaning on her side against a bolster of pillows, her back was to him—but she was there.

As he took several deep breaths, his anger was replaced with a fierce, yet calm supremacy. He'd been right about her.

Closing the door quietly, he removed his jacket before crossing to put another log carefully upon the grate. Untying his cravat, he approached the bed. Her thick red hair fell down her back in a mass of curls. In the flickering light, it looked like liquid fire, and her skin glowed with pale luminosity.

Slipping off his shoes and shrugging out of his vest, he let his eye follow the line of her body from her smooth shoulder, to her corseted waist and hip, and then down her long bare leg. He paused to appreciate her rounded bottom, and his cock throbbed as he remembered the firm, resilient feel of it. How incredibly beautiful it would look reddened by a hard spanking.

Removing the studs from his shirt, he walked around the bed and lit the bedside lamp. His chest tightened as the soft glow encompassed Patience. A taut little curl fell over her brow and her long lashes fluttered in her sleep. Her cheeks were pale, but her full, lovely lips were pink and parted. And resting before her lay her hands, one upon the other and still bound tightly together.

Matthew shook his head. She was so exquisite that it almost hurt to look at her.

He stroked the tips of his fingers gently against hers. What kind of idiot could ever reject her? And what the hell had happened to make her forego love and marriage altogether? He wanted to know everything. But first he must prove himself worthy of her trust—her complete trust.

Picking up the decanter from the table, he poured a healthy draught of brandy into a snifter. He sipped it as he continued to study her. In repose, there was a tender vulnerability to her beauty that was absent when she was animated. Though, earlier, he'd glimpsed a brief show of it in her tear-filled eyes.

His cock pulsed as he sat carefully beside her. He would unveil that vulnerability, and then he would teach her to embrace it. His heart thumped. Once he accomplished that, he would have her trust—and more.

Bending slowly, he brushed his lips against hers before slipping his tongue into her mouth.

He could tell the moment she awoke. She stiffened briefly and then she relaxed with a gasp. Her mouth opened wider and her body leaned against him. Matthew moaned as he pushed his tongue deeper and drew upon her breath. She tasted so sweet.

He swept his tongue along her lower lip then spoke against her mouth. "Wake, my sleeping beauty. You awaited me, just as I instructed, and I am very pleased with you." He kissed her again then withdrew to look at her.

Her large green eyes reflected want. That was good.

He offered her a sip of the brandy and watched her throat move as she swallowed. He took a sip himself before slipping his fingers over her mount to rub her. "Was it difficult—waiting?"

She squirmed a little and a flush rose to her cheeks as he explored her soft folds. "Yes," she breathed. "And no."

Earlier, he'd noticed that her clitoris had felt slightly larger than those of most of the women he'd "known." Now it seemed smaller, but as he drew moisture from between her legs and rubbed it, it seemed to grow again. "How yes? And how no?"

Patience gasped and tilted her hips. "Yes, because I couldn't touch myself. And because, at first, I was angry with you for leaving me." Her hips rocked.

He rubbed more firmly. "And no?"

She shuddered. "And no, because . . . Because, I wanted to stay—and after a while, I was grateful."

"Ah." Her clitoris felt plump and full. Matthew's cock throbbed. Such a juicy bud would be impossible for her to hide, either from pleasure or punishment. "It's very good that you felt gratitude. That's an excellent beginning. Now," he said, continuing to rub her slowly, "just as earlier, you must always strive to do exactly as I tell you."

A flicker of pride flashed behind the desire in her eyes. "Why?"

He immediately removed his hand from between her legs. It was a small punishment, and only the beginning. "Because that will please me. And if I am pleased, then you shall be pleased."

Patience glanced at his hand and her hips lifted toward him.

He moved his hand to his cock and began to stroke himself through his trousers. His blood surged but he kept his voice even. "Does that sound unfair to you?"

She bit her lip and rocked onto her side for a moment as she watched him. A frown creased her brow. "Yes. Yes, it does."

"I'll tell you why it isn't." He allowed himself a short exhalation of air as he squeezed the tip of his aching prick. Patience pulled at her bonds and lifted her hips, but he ignored her silent plea. "It isn't unfair because everything I do, including deny you, shall be for your benefit. I *will* exert my authority over you. But that authority exists to serve you, and you must remember that when submitting becomes difficult." He could see the battle that raged between her pride and her desire. "Tell me what you're thinking."

"When you were gone, it seemed easy. I wanted to submit." She looked at him so earnestly, so honestly. His heart thumped. "Only now that you're here and the moment is upon me, I feel uncertain. I feel as if I should resent what you say. But for some reason, I don't. This troubles me." Her eyes glistened. "And despite these emotions, I feel like I might die if you don't touch me. In fact, I'm sure that I would do almost anything to win your touch. Yet, knowing that only tortures me all the more."

He swept his fingers over her cheek. "But it's a beautiful torture, isn't it?"

A small frown creased her brow. "Yes," she breathed.

His cock pulsed with excitement. "And you will endure it, for it pleases me."

Her eyes looked like wet grass. He wanted to bury his face between her legs while he pushed his cock between her full, moist lips.

Instead, he stood at the side of the bed and positioned himself near her hands. "Open the front of my trousers, but leave the waist closed," he ordered quietly.

Patience paused only briefly before doing as he bid her. Matthew sipped his brandy and watched a blush tint her cheeks while she worked at his buttons. He clenched his jaw as she pressed against his erection in her efforts. Then he held back a groan of relief as his cock popped through the front of his undergarment and out the opening of his trousers.

Patience drew in her breath. Freed from its confines, his prick swelled to its full size. Broad and heavy, it stretched its reddened head toward her.

She stared at it unwaveringly and licked her lips as she shifted closer. Just the proximity of her face to his cock made his cum churn in his balls.

Reaching down, he lifted out his tight, swollen cods. "Do you like it?"

"Yes." She looked up at him with a glowing admiration in her eyes. "It's so thick." She returned her gaze to it. "I didn't know it could be so thick."

Matthew's blood rushed at her enthusiasm, and pre-cum spilled over the aching head of his cock. Putting down his brandy, he pushed his hips forward and placed his hand over her bound ones so that she wouldn't touch him. "It weeps," he said. "Lick it."

Patience looked up at him and her eyes darkened.

"Do it," he ordered softly.

Patience lowered her gaze, and then, sticking out her pink tongue, she lapped up the rivulet of fluid with the sort of slow zeal one might expect of one who had long awaited the opportunity to taste a great delicacy.

Matthew tensed at the warm, soft stroke, and watched her as she registered the taste of him. He waited for any sign of dislike, but instead her eyes closed for a moment and she licked her lips. When she looked up at him again, her eyes were shining and hungry.

Matthew drew in his breath and another salty spill immediately welled and dripped down his shaft. "There's more. Lick it all." As she complied—this time without pause—he held his breath. The long, soft swipe of her tongue against his swollen flesh was heaven. And each stroke coaxed more fluid from his burning glans, which she lapped up without pause. God—his whole body tightened—she was like a thirsty kitten at a bowl of cream. "That's good," he choked. "Now suck it from the top."

He clenched his teeth as he watched Patience slip her full lips over the enflamed head of his prick. Her eyes fell closed as her tongue swirled over his knob. He drew in his breath and his blood drummed in his ears. But when she began to draw upon him, he knew he'd gone too far.

He groaned and jerked back, but it was too late. Grabbing the base of his cock, he squeezed it hard as he thrust his hips forward again. "Open!"

Patience quickly took him into her warm mouth and, pushing down a little, began suckling greedily upon him.

"No," he gasped, "be still!" He grunted and squeezed harder as Patience froze, her lips snug around his knob. He felt his seed rolling up his shaft. Then a ragged moan escaped him as he ejaculated a single, heavenly spurt of cum into Patience's mouth. She flinched in surprise, but didn't pull away.

Shaking, he waited. But nothing more came. He'd held back the rest.

Drawing deep breaths, he stared down at Patience. Her eyes were closed, but she looked beautiful with the head of his cock in her mouth. Again, he waited for a sign of distaste, but none came. He touched her throat. "Swallow," he whispered. He felt her throat move against his fingers, and then she began to swirl her tongue over the tender head of his prick. Christ, surely he'd died and gone to heaven.

"That's good, Patience," he murmured, stroking back her hair. "That's so good."

She raised her eyes to his, and they were so rampant with want that a fresh jolt of lust rocked him. The muscles in his hips and thighs twitched with the effort it took to remain still. Slowly, he drew in air through his nose. He should withdraw, but he couldn't seem to make himself move. "You like it, don't you?" he found himself asking. "Show me how you like it."

Patience closed her eyes and opened her mouth to take more of him. Matthew tensed as he watched her lips close around him. Then he flinched and gasped when she pushed deeper, stroking the underside of his prick with her tongue.

Christ! He jerked away from her. Patience released a soft whimper.

Grabbing the brandy snifter, Matthew took three huge swallows. Where the hell was his control? He needed to slow down.

He looked at Patience. So did she! He slipped his hand behind her head and, putting the snifter to her lips, he tipped the remainder of the brandy into her mouth. "Drink," he said firmly.

Patience stared into Matthew's dark eyes as she swallowed all that remained of the brandy. She felt it warming her instantly. Her eyes fell closed when Matthew turned to set the glass on the bedside table.

Infused with a voluptuous sensuality, she slipped her tongue slowly over her lower lip. Beneath the warm flavor of the brandy, she still tasted the tangy essence of Matthew's seed. It tasted nothing like she had expected—salty and slightly bitter. Mary, the upstairs maid at the vicarage, had once told her it was an acquired taste. Perhaps, but as she'd swallowed, she'd felt filled with an erotic power. It was as if she'd swallowed liquid lust. Her clitoris throbbed. She wanted more.

Opening her eyes, she found Matthew regarding her intently. His breathing had slowed. "There," he said, gently. "You've pleased me well already."

Before she could think, her clitoris pulsed at his praise. But she didn't have time to ponder this for he was reaching for the knife.

Only a small tremor of nervousness touched her. But when he used the blade to cut all her bonds, she suddenly and inexplicably felt alarm. She wanted them back!

Matthew must have seen the dread in her eyes. "Don't worry." He drove the knife into the top of the headboard. "I'm going to retie you."

Patience almost gasped with relief. She watched with true pleasure as he twisted the silk around her wrist.

"The bonds make everything easier, don't they?" he said.

"Yes." Patience met his dark gaze. "Why is that?"

"They hold you—support you, in a way. Move to the middle of the bed and recline against the pillows," Matthew directed gently.

Patience's clitoris throbbed as she obeyed.

"The bonds also remove the burden of complete capitulation," he said, tying the fabric to the bedpost so that her arm was stretched out from her side. "Once you have more mastery over your submission, you won't need them. But for now, they keep your hands out of my way and give you something physical to struggle against when you feel the need."

Yes. Earlier, when he had demanded she stand with her hands at her sides, it had been almost impossible; for the reflex to resist was strong, despite her desire to submit. And if she hadn't been tied up to now, she didn't know what she would have done.

"There." Matthew tied the last knot.

Patience looked at her outstretched arm and then at him. "Are you going to tie my other arm the same way?"

"Yes."

"And my legs?"

His dark gaze held her as he moved around to the other side of the bed, his thick, ponderous cock swaying before him. "I ought to draw them up by your knees and tie them to your arms."

Patience's eyes widened.

He smiled softly. "But, as it's your first time, I'll allow your legs to remain free."

She released a relieved breath as he picked up what looked like his discarded cravat. As he tied it around her wrist, she admired his prick. Though the head protruding from its sheath was comparatively slick and narrow, just beneath the swollen rim his prick broadened quickly, widening all the way down to a truly incredible breadth at the base. More broad than round, she realized that, despite its thickness, his cock was much easier to suck than a cucumber—and it was far more delicious as well. She licked her lips and felt moisture trickle from her cunt. He was splendid.

Pressing a tender kiss into her palm, he secured her wrist. Then he walked around to the foot of the bed, his eyes never leaving her.

Her arms spread wide, Patience felt her vulnerability.

"You're so damned beautiful." He unbuttoned the top of his trousers and pushed them down with his undergarment. His cock bobbed from between his long shirttails. "I love to see you bound."

Patience moistened her lips and felt herself blushing. "You do?"

"Of course." He removed the studs from his cuffs. "The bonds are a symbol of who and what you are."

She tilted her head. "Who and what am I?"

He regarded her as he undid his shirt. "One day you will know."

One day?

"You're being cryptic," she said softly.

Matthew smiled as he shrugged out of his shirt. "Yes."

At the vision of his naked body, Patience released a slow breath. She didn't know where to look for he was beautiful everywhere—like some magnificent archangel. Broad shouldered and with depth of chest, his torso narrowed at the waist and hip, but not so much that he looked thin. He had weight and mass, yet no fat. Lean muscle covered every part of him—shoulder to arm, chest to abdomen, pelvis to thigh. Hair grew lightly on his chest, but was thick at his groin. And from the mass of dark curls, his penis rose broad and heavy—heavier looking than when it was protruding from his trousers. Veins laced down its length and, beneath, his cods looked tight and full.

As she stared, he gripped himself. One hand stroked firmly as the other rubbed his sac.

Patience swallowed and her womb felt heavy when she lifted her gaze back to Matthew's.

His eyes were pinned on her. "Your mouth is sweet and warm, and it feels like heaven on my cock." He still worked himself.

Patience shivered and pulled against her bonds. "Then let me taste it again."

His jaw tensed and he released himself. "When I say so."

Kneeling on the bed, he came to her. His brown hair dropped into a part and fell forward against his temples. His dark eyes captivated her. She shuddered with excitement then arched against him as he grasped her chin and took her mouth in a deep, probing kiss. God, if only she could get closer to him—she could feel his cock against her thigh. She moaned as he thrust his tongue deeper, but then she gasped as he broke the kiss.

He spoke against her lips. "When next I take your lovely mouth, I'm going to thrust."

Patience panted. She remembered Wilson humping wildly into Mary's mouth.

"When I do, you must relax. The more you relax, the easier it will be for you to breathe. If I go too far, and I likely will, tap my leg with yours and I'll pull back. Is that clear?"

Patience swallowed. "Yes."

"And very important, Patience—no teeth."

She nodded. Mary had told her, and she had become quite expert at not scoring the green skin of the garden cucumbers.

"Good." Matthew pulled back and yanked the knife out of the headboard. "Now, be still."

Patience trembled as he swiftly cut the laces of her corset. Once done, he closed the sharp edge, and tossed it on the bedside table. She sucked in her breath as he pulled away her corset and then ripped off the remnants of her chemise.

She felt her cheeks warm with an instant flush of discomfort. She had the family trait of thick, distended nipples. They could only be hidden behind the heavy stays of her corset. Now, in her excitement, they stuck out to an embarrassing degree. She squirmed as he stared.

But then he swallowed convulsively and raised his dark eyes to hers. "Is there no part of you, Patience, that God did not bless with beauty?"

A warm thrill passed through her, then she shivered as he swept his fingers along the outer curves of her breasts.

"Is there no part of you," he murmured, "that God did not make to suit my passions?"

A sharp tingle seeped beneath Patience's skin as he brushed his fingers firmly over her stiffened nipples. Then he swooped down and, covering one with his warm mouth, began sucking firmly. Gasping and moaning, her back arched at the intense, pulsing pleasure. It was as if he were pulling it from somewhere deep inside her. And the more he drew upon her, the more she was filled with it. She shivered and strained against him, yet, still, he fed upon her—laving her nipple and then sucking it more before finally letting it slip from his mouth. It was thicker and larger than ever. Lifting her other breast, he quickly brought her other nipple to the same state of excitement.

Patience moaned and pulled against her bonds. Her cunt clenched tightly. The feeling was wonderful. His devouring mouth made her wish that he could, somehow, truly consume her. She sucked in her breath as, in seeming answer to her thoughts, he bit down firmly upon her, pinching her other enlarged nipple as he did so. The slight pain sent a shock of delicious sensation directly to her aching clitoris. Patience's eyes widened and her hips jerked.

Drawing back, Matthew rubbed his heavy sac against her thigh. Large and distended, her nipples throbbed.

"Look at them." Matthew licked his lips and then raised his eyes to her. "They beckon punishment, don't they?" And then he delivered a light downward slap with his fingers to one nipple and then the other.

Patience expelled a soft cry. The sharp contact was like a hot shock of lightning. Her nipples felt warm and her skin tingled.

Matthew slapped each one again. Patience gasped yet her back arched, lifting her breasts to him. Her nipples felt as if they were swelling. "Please," she entreated, struggling against her bonds and lifting her chest as much as she could. The feeling was wonderful and incomprehensible.

"Yes." His voice was tight. "Because you beg so sweetly."

Lifting her breast, he spanked his fingers against the distended nub. Patience gasped as he did it again and once again. Then he lifted her other breast. The sound of each light spank excited her more than the one before, because each one sent a more powerful jolt of pleasure flashing through her body. Her hips jerked uncontrollably and she felt a heavy wetness, slick and hot, between her legs.

She heard herself panting as Matthew paused. His eyes seemed to glow and moisture spilled liberally from the engorged head of his prick onto her thigh.

"That's enough for now," he said. But then he gave both swollen nipples a long, hard pinch.

Patience groaned at the sensation of the stiff, dilated nubs being compressed. She strained and struggled beneath him. Her darkened nipples felt hot and huge. Her clitoris began to throb for release. "Please, Matthew . . ."

He rubbed the trunk of his meaty cock against her leg. "Beg me better."

Her heart thumped and her hips twisted. "Please! Please, Matthew—I'll do anything. I promise! Just touch me—touch my cunt—I beg you!"

"That's better."

Then his fingers were between her legs. She groaned and her hips jerked up. She was soaking wet. Had she ever craved release more?

"God, your desire is pouring out of you. You see, Patience? Submission suits you." His eyes burned into her. "I told you I knew what you desired. I'm the one, Patience. I'm the only one for you."

Patience's heart raced. She moaned and her hips lifted, as he rubbed his whole hand over her slick flesh. She drew up her free leg and pulled at her bonds. Then he pressed the heel of his palm against her tortured clitoris, and slipping his fingers past her outer folds, he rubbed the opening of her quim. Hot, pulsating passion scorched her. She surged against him. "Matthew! Please!"

Something dark and fierce radiated in his eyes. "Why? Why should I?"

Because she wanted it! No, that was wrong. She couldn't think. What was the answer? "I—I don't know!"

He snatched his hand away, and she almost wept.

"Yes, you do," he said, tipping his hips and zealously stroking his weeping cock.

Her hips undulated and she couldn't seem to stop them. She squeezed her eyes shut against sudden tears. *What was the answer?* God, she would do anything, just let him give her release!

"Whose pleasure do you serve, Patience?"

Her eyes flew open and she looked directly into his fierce gaze. "Yours!"

"And what do you get by serving my pleasure?"

"*My* pleasure!"

"Yes," he moaned. And falling prone between her legs, he opened his mouth over her slick, wet folds.

Patience gasped and flinched back in surprise and shock. But he pressed forward, and a ragged cry was wrenched from her as his tongue lapped ravenously—his lips, nose, and chin rubbing against her heated sex. Patience stared, even as her hips jerked and her body trembled. She couldn't get away. A beautiful and bewitching defenselessness flooded her mind and filled her heart.

And then Matthew's mouth latched directly onto her clitoris. She gasped and her toes lifted from the bed as more blood surged into the heart of her sex. She shuddered and shook, and, as he laved her relentlessly, he pushed his fingers just inside her wet cunt.

All thought caved in upon itself. Her hips heaved up. She pulled at her bonds. Her head spun and her body tightened. And still he laved her and rubbed her, and her body drew tighter and tighter. Taut as a bowstring, she bucked faster and faster. She panted and gasped.

Nothing mattered but release.

Nothing mattered but Matthew.

Her bottom lifted from the bed as she pulled upon her bonds and rubbed shamelessly against him.

And then everything he'd done to her—the stroking and withdrawing, the sharp and brilliant spanks upon her nipples, the delicious pinches, and his firm and unyielding control—all fused between her legs in a hot, glorious jubilation. Like a crack of thunder, she exploded.

Eyes squeezed shut and teeth clenched, her blood roared in her ears as fissure after fissure of blinding euphoria wracked her. And then it sundered her nerves into infinitesimal specks of bliss that floated into the nether reaches of her body.

Her legs dropped slowly and weakly upon the bed, and—finally—her tears fell. Tears of relief, elation, and frightening realization.

Matthew stayed between her legs, sucking upon her inner thigh for a long moment before crawling over her. As he looked into her eyes, his features hard and handsome, she saw the face of her domination. But rather than recoiling, her heart filled with joy. And this made her cry all the more, for she feared emotions that should not be.

Matthew stared at her, pulling hard upon his dripping prick as her tears fell. "Yes, Patience. That's beautiful. Let your tears come." A dark glow seemed to ignite in his eyes. "Don't fight them. For it's only through tears that you'll find your way down the path I'm leading you."

Held in his fierce regard, Patience couldn't look away. His words both confounded and thrilled her, and caused more tears to well up from deep inside her. And as they spilled, she felt as if something profound were occurring—something she didn't yet understand, but wanted.

"Yes. Let them fall," Matthew breathed. Crouching over her, he lifted her higher against the headboard and wrapped her in his embrace. Arms and legs holding her, he pressed kisses into her hair as he thrust his cock sensually against her belly.

She could not return his embrace; she could only receive—his comfort, his kisses, his hunched body covering hers both possessively and protectively. She was powerless, yet somehow she was safe—completely and entirely safe.

Moaning, she opened her mouth against his neck and sucked and tongued his taut skin.

He groaned and held her tighter. But then he pulled back, his eyes blazing with lust. "You make my heart ache and my cock throb."

He sucked a deep kiss from her mouth as he scooped his fingers into the wet opening of her quim. Patience gasped and her hips jerked, but then he stood on the bed, drawing his wet fingers over his tongue as he straddled her. "It's time for what I promised."

Patience's blood raced in her veins as he thrust his hands into her hair and, lowering himself, rubbed his meaty cock and swollen balls against her tear-streaked face.

A shudder wracked her body, and, in its wake, an animal-like passion seized her—one without shame or inhibition. She luxuriated in feeling the veiny column of his hard prick and the soft press of his cods against her cheeks, her nose, her chin. She smelled him and tasted him as she opened her mouth.

"That's right, use your tongue," Matthew rasped.

Patience obeyed immediately and drew a wet swath against the whole length of him. Again and again she stroked, wild for the taste of the salty fluid that ran down his shaft, and desperate to wrap her lips around the source.

But Matthew did not indulge her. Instead, he freed one of his hands from her hair, and scooping up his sac he lifted it to her mouth. "Lick my cods."

Patience's clitoris pulsed at his tensely voiced order. Without pause, she lapped and tongued him.

Matthew watched her, a hard glitter in his eyes. "That's good, now suck them."

God! Patience's cunt tightened as she opened and drew one tender testicle into her mouth. She moaned and felt him quiver.

Matthew held his dripping cock to his body and looked down at her as she tongued his flesh. Gasping, his hand moved vigorously on his cock.

Patience's clitoris burned as blood rushed into it. Letting him slip from her mouth, she drew in his other testicle. She caressed it with her tongue and then sucked it deeper, for the sight of his thick organ, dripping above her, made her dizzy with desire.

"That's good," he praised, never taking his eyes from her. "That's so good."

She laved him with firm passes of her tongue. Her cunt felt

hot and wet. He shifted his hips forward and pressed her to the headboard as he pumped his hand over his cock. A warm droplet of pre-cum splashed upon her brow. Her hips twitched. But what she really wanted reared above her, red and weeping.

"I know what you desire, Patience," Matthew rasped. "And I'm going to give it to you." His hand tightened in her hair. "Now, remember what I told you." Then he pulled free his sac, and she barely drew a breath before he swiftly pushed the whole dark red knob of his prick into her mouth.

Patience closed her eyes in sensual appreciation as she sucked the juicy head with an eagerness fueled by years of anticipation. It was so soft and velvety smooth. She loved the feel of it against her tongue. She loved the hardness beneath the softness. And she loved the salty fluid that she sucked from the dilated opening at the tip.

Matthew groaned. She felt his hands twist in her hair then he began to move in short thrusts. Just as she had seen Mary do with Wilson, just as she had practiced with the young garden cucumbers, she held him tightly with her lips.

"Look at me, Patience."

Patience lifted her gaze. Her cunt clenched anxiously, for his eyes held a fierce fire. He thrust then withdrew, only to thrust again more deeply and stay.

Patience moaned at the feel of him in her mouth and her clitoris pulsed with a hot, dry need.

"That's good," he gasped. "Now open for me. Open more."

His words and the sound of his voice worked upon her like an aphrodisiac. She blinked in complete and sensual obedience and opened her mouth wider.

Matthew grimaced as he pushed slowly into her. Patience shuddered and her hips tensed as she felt more of his thick flesh pushing into her mouth. Just when she thought she couldn't take anymore, he withdrew. She gasped for breath but then he pushed in again. Over and over he did this, and with each new press she felt her mouth moistening and her jaw relaxing. With each new press, she felt him sliding deeper. And then the smooth head touched the back of her throat, and this time he did not withdraw.

Patience drew her breath through her nose. Her lips were tight around his corpulent cock, and she could feel the thick passage that brought his cum depressing her tongue. Her mouth was full of him, yet she wanted more.

He pulled out and his cock swayed as he tipped her face up. His eyes looked black with lust, and his expression, stern and powerful, made her heart quake and her cunt rush. "That's good, Patience." His fingers slipped into her mouth, then over her lips. "That's so good. Now just a little more."

Gripping her chin, he lifted it, extending the column of her throat. Then with one hand in her hair and one hand around his cock, he pushed back into her, pressing and pressing until his knob was pushing against the back of her throat.

Patience groaned and her eyes watered, whilst her clitoris burned and her cunt wept.

Matthew held her in place, murmuring, "Yes, yes." Then he began to rock his hips, just slightly, causing the head of his cock to rub firmly against the sensitive area. Saliva trickled down her throat, but the more he rubbed, the more accustomed she grew to the feeling.

"That's my beauty," he said thickly. "Now remember my instructions." And then he ground hard against her, forcing his thick flesh into the turn of her throat.

Patience's body leapt and her hips heaved with uncontrollable lust as he thrust short and tight.

Moaning, Matthew withdrew completely, but only long enough for her to take a gasping breath. Then he sank deep and thrust again.

Her mouth was stretched and full of him. Her hips tilted and gyrated, and her clitoris flamed with the need to be possessed.

Faster and deeper he plunged, his loud panting the only sound above her own short breaths. She did not hold him back. And with each fury of thrusts, his cock seemed to sink deeper, filling and stretching the entirety of her throat. Her splayed knees pressed down and her hips jerked up. It was merciless and exquisite.

Then his breathing deepened to grunts and feral growls. His fingers tightened in her hair, and crouching like some fallen angel, he shuddered over her, thrusting his organ of dominion into her with a wild and unrelenting ferocity. And beneath him, she writhed and undulated as he stole her resistance, her inhibition, and her pride, and fed her obedience, carnality, and subservience.

Matthew's savage cry split the air. And in her mouth, Patience felt his cum pulse up his cock before it spewed down her throat. And like the fiery waters of the river Styx, his cum was a fierce and flowing tide.

But it didn't matter, for she was already his creature. As he ejaculated his hot, glutinous seed, her blood roared and her heart thundered. And, though he gave no touch to her straining clitoris, she found her rapture while drinking voraciously of the virile communion he fed her.

Chapter Six

The Opinions of Siblings

I sleep, but my heart waketh: it is the voice of my beloved . . .

Song of Solomon 5:2

An angel tore her from the grasping hands of her admirers who pulled at her clothes and her hair in order to keep her by them. Their rolling eyes and loud cries of frustration frightened her, so she clung to the angel as he flew away with her. High into the heavens he carried her, his mighty wings beating the air, until all she could see were planets and moons and bright starlight.

Then his voice came from all around her and inside her. "I have taken you. Now whom do you serve?"

"I serve you," she replied.

He drew her closer into his embrace. "And who am I?"

"Matthew." Lifting her head, she looked into his dark eyes.

"Yes." He pressed his lips softly to hers. "And if you serve me well, I shall heal you."

"Heal me?"

His gaze was tender. "It may hurt at times, but you will see that the pain is for your own good."

"But I am not injured."

"You're bleeding from your heart, Patience."

She felt a deep and sudden pain in her chest. Or, was it sudden? For in the next moment, she felt she recognized it. Yes, the pain was always with her.

"You see," Matthew said. "If it isn't stopped, you'll wither away."

Patience shivered in his warm embrace, but she held his gaze.

A small frown turned his brow. "Just because you refuse to look at it, doesn't mean it isn't bleeding. Look at it."

She wouldn't look. She couldn't.

His frown eased. "That's all right." He touched her cheek. "Leave everything to me. I will make you look."

Then he threw her over his arm, and she was falling . . .

Patience woke with a start. It was as if she'd fallen straight from her dream to her bed.

Her bed? Thoughts of her dream scattered as she sat up and glanced around her room. She'd fallen asleep in Matthew's arms, and in *his* bed. Now she was here—and alone.

She sighed. When had Matthew returned her to her room? Though the window curtains were drawn, she could see gray daylight peeking from between them. The clock chimed. It was eleven thirty in the morning. She looked at the other side of her bed. The linens were undisturbed. She wished he'd stayed with her, even if only for a while.

Falling back against her pillows, she stretched as a sensual languor came over her. Why hadn't he stayed, so that he might bind her and take her again? She shivered as she remembered the way he had forced orgasm after orgasm from her—with his hand, with his tongue, and with the vigorous thrusting of his cock in her mouth. Tilting her head back, she touched her throat. Her mouth watered just at the thought. There was something about the feel of his firm flesh filling her mouth that set her on fire.

But it was the control he exerted that made everything poignant and perfect.

With a long sigh, she turned on her side and stared at the thread of light between the curtains.

She felt awakened. As if she suddenly held the key to a chamber of secret and unthought-of pleasures—a chamber that had always resided within her, but was only accessible through Matthew.

Her heart quivered.

Lord, how could one night—one man—inspire such yearning?

One night?

She frowned. He had only asked for one night. Yet his words had implied, over and over, that last night was only the beginning.

She sat up again and, shoving her hands through her curls, closed her eyes for a moment. One night—or two or three—what did it matter? Nothing, after all, was forever.

Nothing.

Throwing back her sheets, she rose from bed. As she slipped her arms into the sleeves of her dressing gown, her gaze fell upon her cello. Leaning in its stand in preparation for her practice, it faced her, its upper sound holes looking at her like two unblinking eyes. For a moment, she was struck with the odd notion that it had been watching her. It was a silly thought, but the flutter of disquiet that moved through her was palpable.

Normally, she would have been practicing by now, especially since she was due to play that evening. She bit her lower lip. Only, she felt no urgency to play. In fact, as she continued to stare into the blank face of her instrument, her only emotion was a sort of dull resentment.

Shoving aside her odd feelings, she glanced again at the clock. Though the hour was late, she could still practice for a full two hours before her visit with her sister. "Don't worry," she murmured to her cello. "I shall be with you soon enough."

Turning away from her instrument, Patience worked the tiny buttons of her dressing gown as she crossed to the hearth. She'd noticed that her comfortable reading chair had been pulled before the fire, and she wondered if the maid had moved it. But as she rounded the big chair, she drew to a sudden halt.

Sitting on a table beside the freshly fed fire sat a tea tray laden with a small china teapot and teacup. A demure little sugar bowl and pitcher of cream sat beside a cut glass dish of marmalade and butter. And next to a tea plate topped with two golden scones, was a steepled slip of paper.

For P ~ From M

Unmoving, Patience stared at the tray while a succession of emotions tumbled through her—first happiness, but then a quick and growing discomfort. Why had he done such a thing? It was completely unnecessary. Just because he had served her passions didn't mean he needed to serve her breakfast. She was perfectly capable of taking care of such things herself.

Indeed, she preferred to take care of such things herself.

The fire crackled.

She pushed a loose curl behind her ear and then sighed.

Her thoughts were ungracious.

She ought to be pleased. Wouldn't most people be pleased? She'd been pleased for a moment.

Drawing closer to the table, she saw that a delicate *P*, scripted exactly as the one in the note, had been carved into the top of the butter.

Her chest tightened and her eyes stung.

Lord, she hadn't realized she was so close to crying.

Tipping her head back to prevent her tears from falling, she forced a slow, deep breath into her lungs. When she exhaled, her stomach growled. She pressed her hand over the rumbling spot and blinked to clear her eyes.

Whatever was the matter with her? She returned her gaze to the table. Everything looked delicious and she was hungry.

She sat down slowly.

Anyway, it was just breakfast. It didn't mean anything.

Picking up her napkin, she opened it carefully onto her lap. Then, clasping her hands, she leaned forward and let her eye wander again over the little tray.

Hmm.

No one had ever monogrammed her butter before.

And how did he know she preferred marmalade to jam?

'So"—Matthew spread jam on his toast—"tell me what you've discovered from mingling belowstairs at Benchley Manor. Tell me the Benchleys have a secret I can exploit—preferably a deep, dark one."

Mickey Wilkes grinned. "Oh, they 'as a secret—prolly more 'n one—I kin feel it. I jus' 'ave t' uncov'r 'em. Which'll take a bit o' time, fer they're no' very chat'y o'er there."

Matthew frowned. Though winning the coal mine was a blow to Benchley and a great boon for him, he couldn't rely on it being enough. Victory and some semblance of his former place in society would only come through Benchley's complete destruction—and, unfortunately, the state of Matthew's accounts disallowed any delay. He tossed down his toast and leaned his elbows on his desk. "Time is not something I have to spare."

"Yeah, well, I said a bit o' time, not a lot o' time. I's a'ready got me eye on a pret'y gel. She ain't th'one what's got th' mos' t'tell, mind ye, but she be real close wit' th'one what does."

Matthew steepled his fingers before him. "And who is 'the one what does'?"

"Tha' be Mrs. Biddlewick, the 'ead baker. See, nineteen year 'go—th' same year what th' 'ol earl died—Benchley changed o'er th' 'ole 'ousehold, 'ceptin' Mrs. Biddlewick. An' 'e did it kinda slow like, only no' *so* slow. Which says t' me, tha' 'e were actu'lly in a real 'urry an' were jus' tryin' t' 'ide it."

Matthew frowned. "Did this Mrs. Biddlewick tell you this?"

"O' course not." Mickey looked indignant. "I've chat'ed, real casu'l like, wit' e'ery servant in tha' 'ouse. I figgered all this out on me own, mat'matics an' all."

Matthew raised his brows. "Forgive me. Go on."

"Yeah, well, turns out th' only one Benchley kep' be Mrs. Biddlewick. Kep' 'er cause o' 'ow she makes 'is fav'rite strawb'y tarts." Mickey leaned back in his chair confidently and steepled his fingers in seemingly unconscious imitation of Matthew. "Course, Benchley 'ad to 'ave some reason, didn' 'e—some secret reason—fer bringin' in a 'ole new staff so no'chalant-like." He paused and narrowed his eyes. "Right? I mean, i's a lot o' work that, an' good 'elp's 'ard to find."

Matthew nodded. It *was* strange. While there might, at any given time, be a change or two in the servant roster of a noble house, most families cultivated their staff. Many even employed generations of servants from the same families.

Matthew pushed a bowl of stewed fruit across his desk for Mickey, and then leaned back in his chair and sipped his coffee. So why had Benchley done it? What had happened nineteen years ago? The old earl had died, but of what possible import could that be? Insofar as Matthew knew, the man had led an unremarkable life. There had to be something else. "You're sure it was nineteen years ago that this occurred?"

Mickey looked up from his bowl. "Yeah, I's sure. 'E go' rid o' e'eryone, 'ceptin' Mrs. Biddlewick, 'twixt the months o' April an' August 1832."

Matthew frowned. "Lady Rosalind was born in 1832—October 5th, 1832." He looked at Mickey, who had paused mid-chew with a cheekful of fruit. "Which means that Benchley rid himself of his old staff whilst the late Lady Benchley was with child. That's an awfully inconvenient time to do such an inconvenient thing."

Mickey nodded as he chewed then swallowed. "T'is that. Don' know much 'bout th' late Lady Benchley yet. Did find out, tho, that Benchley's daugh'er be a real flirt."

Matthew's frown deepened. "Really?" How had he never seen that?

"Yeah, 'paren'ly she likes teasin' th' footmen wit' views o' 'er fem'nin charms. Bit o' leg here, bit o' bosom there."

Matthew's brows shot up in surprise.

"Yeah, she per'tens i' all 'appens by accident. But the footmens tells me she be accident'ly showin' 'erself all th' time."

Matthew chuckled bitterly as he set down his coffee cup. Christ, had he only interviewed the servants of Benchley Manor before proposing to Rosalind, he might have saved himself much. He shoved his fingers through his hair. But he hadn't, and now he must defend himself against the villainy of the man he would have called father.

Glancing at the number at the bottom of his open ledger, his shoulders tensed. He looked across his desk at Mickey. "Find out everything you can. Then bring me something I can use that will force the Earl of Benchley to his knees. Do you understand me? Find his weaknesses—all of them—even if they lie with his daughter. For, somewhere, I must find one fatal flaw."

Mickey nodded. "I'll find it, Mr. 'Awkmore. I will."

A brief knock sounded on the door, and Mark poked his head in. "Ah, I knew I smelled bacon. And where there's bacon, there's my brother." He entered, closing the door behind him. "And if it isn't Mr. Wilkes. You're looking very well," he said as he crossed to the coffee tray.

With his bowl still in his hand, the lad stood and bowed his head. "Thank ye, m'lord."

Matthew watched Mickey polish off the last of his stewed fruit. Mark was right. Were it not for the clanking of his spoon, and his loud lip-smacking, the tall seventeen-year-old would have looked entirely respectable. Sporting a haircut, a new suit, and new boots, it was no wonder he'd been employed so quickly at Benchley Manor. It was a very different appearance from the one he had presented six months ago when he'd arrived fresh off the rough streets of Seven Dials. It was different even from how he had looked a mere four months ago, when Mark had employed him as a spy in the Lawrence household.

Then, he had still had the quickly shifting eyes of one who is accustomed to being surrounded by thieves and cutthroats. But now, he stood with his shoulders a bit straighter and he looked at Matthew with a steady eye. It was good.

Mark crossed to them and, sitting on the edge of Matthew's desk, looked at Mickey. "Mr. Pinter misses you in the stables. He says you have a way with the horses."

Mickey grinned as he put down his bowl. "Yeah, guess I do. I'll be back jus' as soon as I finishes up me job fer Mr. 'Awkmore 'ere."

Mark sipped his coffee. "Very well."

"A'right, then." Mickey looked at Matthew. "I'll be leavin' 'gain t'morrow."

"See me before you go."

Mickey nodded and, yanking his cap out of his jacket pocket, made a hasty exit.

Mark looked at the closed door and then at Matthew. "Tell me what you're doing."

"No."

"Goddamn it, tell me."

Matthew frowned. "I said, no."

Mark set down his coffee. "For Christ's sake, Matt, I'm your brother. Let me help you."

Matthew's frown deepened. "You're my half brother, and I don't want your help." He stabbed a sausage with his fork. *Damn it!* That was rude. He met Mark's angry frown. "Thank you, but I'll handle this on my own."

"Really?" Mark crossed his arms over his chest. "Benchley's already made it almost impossible for you to obtain coal. You're paying almost double for the coal you can get. You've got engines backing up and goods arriving late. And anyone who needs to ship goods to or from the west is doing it with Marchford Rails. How long can you last under these circumstances?"

His shoulders tense, Matthew tightened his grip on his fork. Mark had a damned annoying way of putting his thumb on mul tiple bruises at once. "I'll last. I'll last, and I'll win," he ground out.

Mark shook his head. "You can't continue to make up GWR's losses all on your own. Are you prepared to sell Angel's Manor if it comes to that? And what if your shareholders dump? Do you think the board is going to support you if these issues aren't resolved? What if they vote to remove you as chairman? What if they force your resignation from GWR altogether?"

"Bloody hell!" Matthew leaned forward as a muscle cramped painfully in his neck. "And what if *all* my investments fail? And what if my estate burns to the ground? And what if Benchley is having me slowly poisoned? Jesus Christ, are there any other menacing possibilities for my destruction that you'd like me to consider?"

Mark shrugged as he dropped into the chair Mickey had vacated. "I'm sure I could come up with several."

"Don't bother." Matthew slammed down his fork. "Just know that I'll do whatever it takes to keep Grand West Railway." He wouldn't be forced to heel by Benchley or anyone. "Whatever it takes . . ."

Mark nodded as he picked up his coffee. "Good. I take it you have a plan—one which utilizes the skills of our young Mr. Wilkes."

Matthew paused. In the past, he would have told Mark everything. But this was his own fight and he wanted to wage it alone—indeed, he *needed* to wage it alone. Besides, since discovering his illegitimacy, he felt as if there were an invisible barrier between his half brother and him.

He reached into his breast pocket. Of course, there were some things he couldn't keep a secret. He pulled out the deed to the mine and slid it across the table. "If no one will sell me coal, I'll mine my own."

A small smile turned Mark's lips as he reached for the deed. "I've been waiting for you to say something. Everyone was talking about your winnings at the card table last night."

Matthew sat back in his chair. *Good.* The more talk there was the better.

Shaking his head, Mark glanced over the deed, and then he grinned at Matthew. "Can you imagine the look on Benchley's face when he hears of this? Don't be surprised if tomorrow the *Times* announces Danforth's murder."

Matthew raised his brows. "That would be pleasant news."

Mark folded the deed and slid it back across the desk. "I hear six good men put their signatures on the legitimacy of the card game."

"Yes." Matthew returned the deed to his pocket. He counted each of the signatures as victories. "And speaking of the *Times*, I sent a messenger to London early this morning. He's carrying one letter to my solicitor and another to the *Times*, announcing that I've acquired the mine. While Mr. Banks begins the paperwork for recording the acquisition of Gwenellyn, I'm expecting that the announcement in the paper will forestall any selling of shares."

Mark nodded. "You know Benchley will contest your ownership."

Matthew stiffened. "He'll have to sue me for it then, and he'd better hurry. I sent a third letter to Mr. Penworthy, one of GWR's managers. I've instructed him to go to Gwenellyn to take hold of the books, and to see to the immediate loading of coal onto GWR engines."

Mark smiled as he studied him for a moment. "You said you don't want my help. But if you need an investor for your mine, I'm here."

Matthew nodded and forced his shoulders to relax. "Thank you. I know little about it, other than it's large enough to support a village. I'll know more when I see the ledgers."

Picking up his knife and fork, Matthew returned to his meal. He couldn't help feeling a measure of excitement over the prospects before him. Rail owners had been at the mercy of mine owners for too long. He was going to change that.

Chewing his sausage, Matthew watched Mark sip his coffee. Since marrying Passion, his brother's face had lost its hard edge and perpetual frown. He looked at ease, and—happy. Passion's love was good for him.

Matthew shoved down the swell of envy that rose in him. "How's the library coming?"

"They're clearing the site. Building will begin in the spring."

"How does it feel to be the architect of the next National Library?"

"Superb. Especially since my presence on-site will not be required until after the baby is born." Mark's eyes softened. "I want to be with Passion as her time approaches."

"Ah, yes." Matthew speared another piece of sausage. His brother had everything a man could want—his good name, his honor, his place in the world, and a woman who made it all worthwhile—a woman who loved him, and cherished him, and carried his child.

Matthew stared down at his plate. He suddenly had a vision of Patience with her belly full and round. His heart skipped. He'd always wanted children—children of his own, and a wife of his own. Before the scandal, the role of husband and father had been a huge part of how he'd envisioned his life. But what now—when the only name he had to offer was a stolen one?

"She looked beautiful last night, did she not?" Mark asked softly.

Yes. Matthew glanced up. "Passion? Yes. Yes she did." He dropped his napkin on the table. "My lovely sister-in-law seems to be faring beautifully."

"That she is." Mark cocked his brow. "But tell me, how is *my* lovely sister-in-law faring?"

Matthew pictured Patience as he'd left her—sound asleep, with her bright curls spilling across her pillow and one graceful arm curved sensually above her head. His chest tightened. He wanted her. "She's faring magnificently."

Mark curved his hands around his cup and propped his heels on Matthew's desk. "She's a great beauty. Montrose is head over heels for her. But, frankly, there are many who want her."

Matthew looked at his brother and a strong possessiveness fueled his desire. "None can have her."

"None but you?"

Matthew nodded. "That's right."

"Where will this lead?"

Matthew picked up his coffee. "To the possession of Patience."

"And will this possession lead to a proposal?"

Yes.

Matthew paused and put his cup back down.

Yes. Marry her.

Taking a deep breath, he felt his shoulders relax.

Marry her and make her yours forever.

Matthew looked at his brother then shrugged. "Perhaps. But she has no desire for marriage."

Mark was quiet for a moment as he held Matthew with his level gaze. Finally, he spoke. "Passion says that you'll have to win Patience's love if you ever hope to marry her."

Patience's love. Matthew sat back in his chair. Just the thought of it made his heart pound and his blood rush. God, what would it be like to have her love?

"She also says that winning her love won't be easy."

Can I do it?

Matthew tightened his fingers around the arms of his chair. He shouldn't think of it. "Neither of us is seeking love."

"That doesn't mean you won't find it."

Matthew frowned. "*If* I find it, that doesn't mean I need return it."

Mark's brows lowered as he dropped his feet and leaned forward. "If you find it, and you don't return it, Patience will be hurt." His brother's jaw tightened. "And if you hurt Patience, Passion will be hurt. I'm telling you now—do *not* hurt my wife."

Though Matthew was not surprised by Mark's warning, it angered him nonetheless. "Funny you should be warning me. If memory serves, it was only a few short months ago, that I was warning *you* against hurting Passion."

"And you were right to warn me." Mark sat back. "Just as I am right to warn you."

Matthew sat forward. "When you took Passion behind the screen at the Crystal Palace, with no idea of who she was or where it would lead—why did you do it? You'd never done anything like that before."

"Because . . ." Mark's gaze turned inward. "Because the moment I touched her—the moment I smelled her and felt her, I wanted her—more than I'd ever wanted anyone." He paused. "I couldn't even see her face at first. But then she looked at me, and it was as if the world stopped turning." He was quiet for a long moment before looking at Matthew. "I tried to walk away. I *did* walk away. But I couldn't stay away." He shook his head. "I had to have her."

"Exactly." Matthew tossed his napkin on the desk as he stood. "Now, if you'll excuse me."

He'd almost made it to the door when his brother's voice stayed him. "I know you want her love, Matt. Perhaps, you even know how to get it. But you'll only keep it if you love her in return."

Love. Matthew tensed. He hated that the word still called to him—more powerfully than ever.

Turning on his heel, he stared at his brother as angry resentment coursed through him. "You know, despite the fact that the Benchleys' desertion fueled my social ruin, I'm not sorry Rosalind broke with me. In fact, I'm grateful to her—to her and to her hateful father. Her abandonment saved me from a marriage that I would have grown to loathe. And her cold rejection showed me what a miserable fool the illusion of love had made of me." His jaw clenched. "Love? Love is not for me." *No matter how Patience tempts me!* "Do *not* speak of it." He turned back to the door.

"Why? Don't you think you're worthy of it?"

Matthew froze and a boiling rage seared him as he slowly faced his brother. "Fuck you."

Mark raised a dark brow. "Ah, I see I've touched the truth."

Matthew's body began to shake, and he stared at his brother through a wash of red fury. "How dare you speak of worthiness! You, who have everything—your name, your fortune, your place in society. You, who always disdained love, but now have so much you could drown in it!" Matthew gritted his teeth as a sharp pain stabbed at his gut and left an ugly bitterness in its wake. "You, who, even when we were boys, had the love of the good and noble parent in our home. You know what the truth is, Mark? The truth is that you've *always* been the one who had everything worth having."

Mark stood, a deep frown creasing his brow. "Worthiness is not measured by name or fortune, Matt. Worthiness is measured by character—honesty, decency, nobility, and the willingness to love. You taught me that—you and Passion."

Matthew clenched his hands into fists. "Yes, well that was easy for me to say when I still had my name and my fortune. And it's easy for you to say now, isn't it?—still being in possession of your own."

Mark stared at him. "Yes. But that doesn't make it any less true." He took a step forward. "I want you to be happy, Matt. If Patience is right for you, I want you to have her and be happy." He shook his head. "But if you refuse to love her, eventually you'll lose her."

"Enough!" Matthew turned and yanked the door open. "I don't need to love her to master her. And I *will* master her!"

The slam of the door shook the paintings on the walls.

" 'The disciple is not above his master, nor the servant above his lord. It is enough for the disciple that he be as his master, and the servant as his lord.' " Patience tensed and skipped to verse twenty-six. " 'Fear them not, therefore: for there is nothing covered, that shall not be revealed; and hid, that shall not be known.' " She looked at her sister as she closed the Bible. "The Gospel according to Saint Matthew."

As she drew upon her canvas, Passion glanced at her. "As with Christ's disciples, we should not fear the disdain and persecution of others who do not understand what we do. We must simply obey our Master and serve Him as He bids us. Therein lies salvation—not only our own, but the salvation of others."

Patience studied her sister. Half sitting upon a high stool as she worked, Passion's long auburn hair fell down her back over her pale green dressing gown. She looked beautiful and at ease. She couldn't possibly know the many places her words touched.

"Why did you choose this chapter for today?" Patience asked.

Passion kept drawing. "I saw you leave the ball with Matthew."

Patience's heart suddenly raced. Would her sister forbid her Matthew's attentions? "Yes."

"And, late into the night, your room was empty."

"Yes," Patience breathed.

Passion looked at her with her warm hazel eyes. "He's a good man, Patience. And if he's the one, I'm glad. Would you mind taking up your cello, now? I want to decide upon a pose."

Patience pushed down the layers of her petticoats beneath her violet gown, and set her instrument between her knees. She looked warily at Passion. "But . . . ?"

Passion met her gaze then lowered her pencil. "I trust Matthew. And I trust you. That's why I chose that reading for today. I sense that there is some purpose each of you has for the other, and only God knows what that purpose is."

Patience waited. "I hear the caveat in your voice. When is it coming?"

Passion sighed as she looked at her. "It's just that I fear you're wandering into dangerous territory—territory neither one of you can predict." She shook her head. "The sharing of intimacies changes things between people, Patience. And I don't want to see you hurt again."

Patience lowered her eyes and tapped her bow idly on the strings of her instrument. Passion was the only person who knew about Henri. And while Patience periodically felt the necessity to remind herself of her past weakness, she didn't like her sister reminding her. "This is completely different from before," she said quietly. "I'm a grown woman now and I know my mind."

"You've always known your mind, darling. It's your heart I fear for."

Patience frowned as she remembered her dream and the pain she'd felt in her heart. She plucked a few notes. "You know my heart belongs to my instrument."

"Oh, Patience, do you really think you can give your body to a man such as Matthew and not have your heart follow?"

Patience stiffened. Her heart was her own. She had rescued it and mended it from its earlier ill use. She met her sister's eyes. "Do you really think that I am incapable of keeping my own heart? That just because I finally enjoy some fulfillment of my body, my heart must follow, like some blind beggar?"

Passion didn't flinch. "No. I think you've built a tall and solid wall of protection around your heart. But what if Matthew is strong enough to tear that wall to rubble? Are you prepared for that possibility?"

Patience frowned. "Wait. What do you mean I've built a wall?" Her chest tightened and her fingers clenched around the neck of her cello. "Just because I've chosen a different path in life, means my heart is closed?"

"It's just that after Henri—"

"After Henri," Patience interrupted, "I still left myself open to love. You know I did. Lord, how many suitors and marriage proposals did I entertain?" She shook her head. "There comes a time when one must realize that one is on the wrong quest. And once I gave up that quest, I felt free. I've been able to give my whole self to my instrument, and I have been content and happy in my decision."

"Have you been happy? Are you still?" A small frown creased Passion's brow. "Because you never tell me so."

"Yes, I do."

"No." Passion shook her head. "No, you don't."

"Well, what is there to say? If I weren't happy with my decision, I wouldn't have made it. And if I weren't happy with my life, I'd be living it differently."

Passion regarded her for a long moment. "It's just that you haven't seemed happy—not truly. Not in a very long time. And I blame Henri for that."

Patience stared at her sister. "Do you?" *He's not the only one to blame.* Her eyes suddenly stung and she lowered them as she put aside her cello and bow. A deep pain throbbed in her heart—the same pain from her dream.

She hated this discussion. She hated the feelings it was inspiring. And she hated thoughts of her own adolescent foolishness. She stared down at the violet silk of her skirt. "Why must we keep speaking of Henri? I thought this conversation was about Matthew."

"Oh, darling, I'm sorry." Passion moved toward her, and then Patience was forced to look into her sister's eyes as Passion tipped up her chin. "I know you're accustomed to making your own path in life, and to following it alone. I know you're strong, and I know you can make your own decisions." The pad of her sister's thumb felt soft against Patience's cheek. "I just—I love you—and I don't want anything to go wrong. And you know what Father always says, 'When God's laws are broken—' "

" '—the world suffers.' " Patience finished the sentence that was their father's regular refrain. She clasped Passion's hand and lowered her eyes. She felt sad, and she didn't even know why. She wished Matthew were near. Where was he?

She traced the bones on the back of her sister's hand. "I know this affaire seems ill advised. It seemed so to me, too. But I can also tell you that it was inevitable. As you said, there is something between Matthew and me—something that cannot be avoided or denied."

"Is that what this is, an affaire?"

Suddenly the word sounded wrong. Patience searched for another, but none came to mind. All she could think of were dark lust-filled eyes, strong, unyielding hands—and engraved butter, and marmalade. She looked at her sister. "I don't know what this is." She shook her head. "But what would you have us do? Marry for the sole purpose of finding out? I do not love him, nor he me. And I would rather commit the sin of fornication than defile the sacrament of marriage with a lie."

Passion studied her for a long moment then smoothed her hand over her own rounded stomach. "You know, Father will never forgive me if you return home looking like me."

Patience touched her sister's belly and, for the briefest of moments, wished she hadn't denied Matthew her virginity. But as quickly as she registered the thought, she pushed it away. "I'm not going to let that happen." She allowed a small smile. "As you are aware, there are other roads to pleasure."

Passion's smile was soft. "He pleases you then?"

Patience flushed at Passion's choice of words. Her skin tingled as she thought of Matthew—the taste of him, the wild lust in his gaze as he'd forced her second release. She felt warm as she raised her eyes to her sister. "He pleases me wonderfully."

Passion pushed a stray curl back from Patience's forehead. "Then obey your heart, be as your Lord intends you, and do not be deterred by the doubts of others." Passion pulled her close.

Patience rested her cheek against her sister's full belly and sighed as her tensions eased.

"I love you, darling." Passion's soft voice stroked Patience's heart. "I'm here if you need me."

Patience's eyes stung again, so she closed them. It was so rare that she availed herself of her older sister's embrace. There had been a time when they'd been inseparable. But that had been a long, long time ago. Before—

"Girls! Wherever are you?" The familiar but inharmonious voice of their aunt sang out from the adjoining room.

Patience drew back from her sister with surprise.

Passion smiled. "She arrived this morning—a day early, as usual. Will you still be leaving with her in two weeks?"

London and her new music training would take her far from Matthew. She shoved down the regret that reared up in her. "Of course I'm still leaving with her." Getting to her feet, she hurried to the door. "Aunt Matty!"

Patience smiled as her father's older sister, Mathilda Dare, rushed forward with arms extended. Her lace cap fluttered and her plump cheeks jiggled. She took Patience in her embrace with a strength that was always a little unexpected from a woman of her years.

"Look at you!" Aunt Matty exclaimed, holding her at arm's length. "Good Lord, the gentlemen must be running over each other to get to you, my dear." She looked to Passion. "Isn't it so, Passion? They must be just wild for her."

Passion smiled ruefully as she poured a cup of tea for their aunt. "I'm afraid it's true." She looked at Patience. "At the ball, a number of gentlemen and lords inquired after you, darling. And Lord Montrose seems particularly enamored."

Aunt Matty grinned excitedly and patted Patience's arm as they crossed the room. "There, you see!"

"Of course," Passion continued, "I told them all that you were completely devoted to spinsterhood, and that they needn't bother you with useless proposals."

Aunt Matty pressed her hand to her breast with a gasp. "Good grief, you didn't really?"

Patience exchanged a broad grin with her sister. "And why shouldn't she, Aunt Matty? It is the truth, after all."

"Oh!" Aunt Matty took a seat at the tea table. "Don't start, Patience. I've only just arrived. It's far too soon for you to begin vexing me."

Patience held back her smile and dropped a kiss on her aunt's forehead.

"And don't try to butter me up with affection." Aunt Matty stirred her tea vigorously as Patience and Passion took their seats. "Tell her, Passion. Someone's simply got to tell her. Oh, very well, I'll tell her." She stopped stirring and turned to Patience. "Patience, my dear, you're getting rather high on the shelf."

"Am I?" Patience sipped her tea.

"Yes, I'm afraid you are. And if something isn't done about it soon, you're going to turn into—well, you're going to turn into rotten peaches."

Patience choked on her tea as Passion laughed behind her hand.

Aunt Matty drew back. "This is no laughing matter. Do you want to turn into rotten peaches?"

Patience gasped and tried not to laugh. "Well, no. But . . . well . . . you never married, Aunt Matty. And you don't look anything like rotten peaches to me."

Passion made a muffled noise as her eyes shifted to their aunt.

Aunt Matty's eyes narrowed. "Don't try to divert attention away from yourself, Patience. Of course I'm not rotten peaches." She wagged her finger. "But that's because I never was a peach to start with. You, on the other hand, are a peach through and through." She nodded as if to say *so there* and then sipped her tea.

Patience exchanged a bewildered glance with Passion, who just raised her brows and shook her head.

"Besides," Aunt Matty continued as she put down her cup, "you have a responsibility to our great nation to bear children."

"I do?"

Aunt Matty shot a whatever-is-the-matter-with-her look at Passion, and then turned back to Patience. "Well, of course you do, my dear. You owe it to Queen and country to pass your beauty to the next generation. Will you allow one of the most perfect compilations of British features ever born to pass into dust? Shocking, that's what that is. No, traitorous!"

Patience leaned her chin in her hand and looked at her aunt. She had no notion of what to say to her. A brief silence ensued. "So"—she raised her brows—"how was your trip from London?"

"Oh!" Aunt Matty clapped her hands together. "I must say that the accommodations on the train were a wonder. I told Mr. Hawkmore so myself."

Patience sat a little straighter. "Mr. Hawkmore?"

"Well, yes, my dear. We rode all the way from the station together. Quite coincidentally, he was there forwarding several letters with a young messenger. He was kind enough to offer me a ride in his coach so that I might have some reprieve from my luggage and my maid. You know how Frannie taxes me with her incessant silence."

"Yes, Frannie's silence would wrack anyone's nerves," Passion commented with a smile.

Aunt Matty nodded. "It's true. But I did so enjoy my time with Mr. Hawkmore." She smiled almost tenderly. "I like him, I really do. Such a shame about his father not being his father." She shook her head but then lifted her shoulders in a small shrug. "Oh well. We don't care about that anyway, do we?"

"Certainly not," Passion agreed.

"You know," Aunt Matty continued, "I hear from the Misses Swittley that he is one of the richest men in the realm. Not that we care about that either, mind you."

"Oh, no," Patience quipped, "*we* don't care about that at all."

Aunt Matty shot Patience a disdainful glare, and then her expression turned adoring. "He's so handsome and charming. And, you know, he really listens. He does." Aunt Matty nibbled her cucumber sandwich. "A more delightful companion I could not have had. We talked and talked"—her eyes shifted briefly toward Patience—"and talked."

Patience gulped her tea. God forbid that her aunt had spoken to Matthew about her. "And what did you and Mr. Hawkmore talk about?"

Aunt Matty leveled her gray eyes upon Patience. "Why, we talked about you, my dear."

Oh, no. Patience cringed inwardly. "What about me?"

Aunt Matty beamed. "I sang your praises, my dear. I catalogued your beauty, I remarked casually upon your culinary talent with scones, and I informed him of your truly remarkable penmanship. Oh, and I let drop the fact that while you had rejected a vast number of marriage proposals, that now that your sister was a countess you would, no doubt, be deluged with requests more worthy of your consideration."

Patience felt her face flaming. "Is that all, I hope?"

"Well, no. I suggested that if he were looking for a wife, he should ask you immediately before he lost his chance."

Patience groaned and dropped her face into her hands.

"Well don't worry, my dear"—Aunt Matty patted her arm—"I didn't say a word—not one word—about rotten peaches."

Chapter Seven

Training

I am my beloved's, and his desire is toward me.

Song of Solomon 7:10

Patience pulled on her dressing gown and hurried from the bathing chamber that adjoined her room. A startled gasp escaped her, and she clutched her gown closed as she registered a dark figure in the chair before the fire. *Matthew!*

Relaxed and with his legs set wide apart, he leaned against one arm of the chair, his head supported in his hand. A snifter of brandy dangled from the fingers of his other hand. His beautiful dark eyes captivated her. She saw admiration in them—and desire.

Her heart tripped and then began to pound.

"Send your maid away." His voice was low but firm.

Patience's skin warmed. "But I need to dress for . . ." Her voice faded at the lowering of his brows.

"Send your maid away." He repeated his command slowly, enunciating each word.

Patience shivered even though she wasn't cold. Moving quickly to the door, she opened it only partway and released her maid. After the girl had bobbed a curtsy and moved off, Patience closed the door and locked it. She turned to face Matthew. Her skin tingled as she leaned against the door and met his dark, beautiful gaze.

"How did you get in here?" she asked. "The door was locked."

He set his brandy on the small table beside the chair. "Does my presence offend you?"

"No." She'd been waiting for him all day!

"There is a hidden panel in the wall just behind me. It lets out behind the tapestry in front of my room. If you don't want me to use it, you may lock it by pressing the cupid carved into the fireplace mantel." He paused. "*Will* you be locking it?"

Would she? Whatever for, when she wanted him so badly? "No, I don't believe I will."

He reached down and adjusted himself in his trousers. "Come, Patience."

Her breath quickening with excitement, she paused only a moment before crossing to him.

"Closer."

She had stopped only a pace or two before him. Taking a step forward, and then another, she stopped again when she stood in the vee of his open legs. Feeling bold, she gazed down at him. The gold in his hair glinted in the firelight.

"Take off your dressing gown and put your arms at your sides," he ordered.

Oh God. Though her clitoris throbbed with excitement, her daring immediately slipped a notch. Why was that simple directive so difficult? After last night, it should be easy. Yet, it wasn't. And he offered no kind word to set her at ease.

Forcing her arms to move, she slowly let the cream-colored velvet slip off her shoulders. It landed with a soft *thwump* at her feet. Patience clenched her jaw as she pressed her reluctant hands down her sides and against her thighs.

She could see the rise and fall of her own chest as she looked down at Matthew. His nostrils flared as his eyes moved over her. Beneath his intense scrutiny, her nipples hardened and her cunt quivered.

He swept his fingers over his tongue and, leaning forward, slipped them between her legs. Patience gasped and shuddered as he rubbed her vigorously. She could feel the warm wetness of her own body as he reached between her folds and touched the opening of her quim. Then he moved his hand forward again, his slick fingers plying her quickly swelling bud.

Patience sucked in her breath and moaned. She'd been yearning for this all day—yearning for *him* all day. She reached for his broad shoulders, gripping them for support. His fingers moved in tighter and tighter circles. Her blood rushed. He looked up at her and she shivered with desire at the dark ferocity in his eyes. Faster and faster he stroked her. She tensed and her thighs trembled. *At last. At last!* His eyes narrowed. Her hips jerked. *A moment more!*

And then he snatched his hand away.

Patience gasped and choked back a cry. She didn't even realize she'd moved her hands between her legs until he grabbed them and held them against her sides. She looked down at him through suddenly blurry eyes as her desperate clitoris throbbed with excruciating tenacity.

Why did she feel no ire? Her body was clamoring for fulfillment, yet she felt only ardor as she looked at him—he, who was preventing her pleasure.

No, not preventing her pleasure—preventing the culmination of her pleasure.

His gaze softened as he got to his feet. Vetiver floated in the air. Patience leaned close, and his hands moved again to hers, holding them against her. Undeterred, she pressed her hips against the hard ridge of his erection as she lifted her trembling mouth to his. He would give her release—surely he would.

Clasping her wrists, he wrapped his arms around her and held her hands captive against the small of her back as he kissed her gently. Patience leaned into him. His soft kisses only fanned her fire. If only he would kiss her more deeply. Gasping, she continued to rub against the thick strength of his cock.

He lifted his mouth just above hers. "There," he breathed. "Now, the next time I tell you to send your maid away—the next time I tell you to do anything—I shall expect your immediate obedience."

Yes, of course. Patience sighed as he brushed his lips lightly against hers.

"Yes, Matthew," he prompted her, as he released her hands. "Say, *yes Matthew*."

Patience reached her arms around his neck and lifted onto her toes. "Yes, Matthew," she said against his lips.

His arms crushed her against him and his tongue thrust deeply into her open mouth. Patience arched against him and her own embrace tightened. She felt his hand slip over her bottom and squeeze her firmly. Then his hips tilted toward her and he ground his prick against her as he swept his tongue over her teeth. Moaning with desire, she lifted against him—almost climbing his body as she curved one of her legs around his hip.

She felt him tremble and then she felt his warm hand on the under-curve of her thigh. But just when she thought he might finally be beyond restraint, his hand fell away and, pulling back, he set her firmly apart from him.

His eyes were dark with passion, but as she stared at him she watched the rest of his features shift into calm, composed lines. His breathing slowed, and when he released a deep breath even the heat of his gaze had lessened. Another moment and he regarded her with a serene control.

"Come along now," he said casually. "It's time to dress for dinner."

She looked at him in wordless disbelief. But he just stepped near and, placing his hand against the small of her back, pushed her toward her dressing table.

With every step she took, her clitoris pulsed. It tortured her and yet . . . the sensation was sweet. She glanced at Matthew. His expression looked even more relaxed, and she marveled at his control.

Once at her dressing table, Matthew stroked his hand over her bottom before turning her to face him. Looking directly into his eyes she could see that a fire still smoldered there, it was just contained. His voice was low but firm. "Now, be good and keep your hands at your sides. For if you don't, I shall have to punish you again."

Patience's heartbeat quickened. She thought of touching herself just to see what he would do—but she was already aching so much between her legs that she thought better of it. Besides, she was curious what her obedience would get her. "Yes, Matthew."

He nodded his approval.

She watched him cross to her bed where all her garments were already laid out. As he looked over her things, she admired his formidable erection. It tented his trousers, but he seemed content to disregard it. Did it torment him as much as her swollen clitoris tormented her? She swallowed as she remembered the feel of the smooth head in her mouth. How she longed to touch it and taste it again.

Patience let her eye wander over him as he picked up her silk stockings and garters. Her chest tightened and her womb grew heavy as she studied his profile. He was so handsome—his features beautiful in tenderness, and fierce in lust. And, always, there was the dark intensity of his regard, as if he were trying to perceive her every thought and desire.

Tossing her garters and one of her stockings over his shoulder, he gathered up the other stocking with his fingers as he returned to her. "Sit," he said gently as he knelt before her.

Patience briefly paused. She was accustomed to doing most everything for herself. Even her maid she only utilized for tightening her laces and straightening the room.

But she couldn't resist him. So, perching on her dressing table stool, she lifted her foot. With an ease that suggested practice, he slid her stocking up her leg, smoothing it with his hands afterward.

Patience frowned as he gathered up the second one. How many times had he knelt at a woman's feet assisting her to dress? Had he done so with Rosalind?

A tiny rivulet of jealousy trickled down her back. What did it matter? It shouldn't matter.

Yet it did.

"Matthew?"

"Yes?" He slipped her stocking over her toes.

"How many . . . ? I mean how often have you . . . ?" She didn't know how to put it.

He raised his eyes to hers and they were soft.

Patience felt herself blushing. "Well, I mean how many ladies have you—"

"It doesn't matter," he interrupted her gently. "Anyone before you was simply an overture to you—a necessary preparation for the magnificence that is you." His beautiful eyes held her. "Never question that I value you above all others, Patience." He patted her calf. "Now stand."

Patience stared down at him for a moment before she slowly stood on her trembling legs. He had a way of saying the most astounding things when she least expected them. Her stomach fluttered. She usually didn't appreciate compliments, but this was different. Such words, so easily spoken, made her feel something soft and indescribable. Pride and—perhaps, happiness?

She slipped one hand through his thick hair as he tied her garters. His eyes closed for a moment as she traced the curve of his ear, then he turned his mouth into her palm and kissed it before rising.

He pressed her arms gently back against her sides. Lord, but she wanted to touch him—everywhere. Standing before her, his eyes moved over her features and then dropped to her breasts. Patience drew in her breath and her nipples tightened. Without thinking, she drew back her shoulders and lifted her chest. In the next moment, she realized what she'd done, and she flushed with embarrassment. But despite her discomfort, she craved his touch so much that she held her lifted posture.

Matthew's eyes darkened and a small smile turned his mouth. "Ah, that's lovely. That is just the response I want from you, Patience." He brushed the backs of his fingers over her stiff nipples and she gasped as he pinched them firmly. "You may always demonstrate your desires to me in such a way, and if it pleases me, I shall accommodate you."

Patience bit her lip as he rolled her nipples between his fingers. It felt so good that she drew her shoulders back farther, begging more. In the next moment she sucked in her breath as he landed three light slaps upon her right nipple and three more upon the left. A hot sensation that was equal parts pleasure and pain washed through her and made her cunt water. But then he turned away, and she expelled her breath in a disappointed gasp.

Matthew spoke as he crossed to her bed. "Just as you reacted a moment ago, so will you be taught to react at all times and for any pleasure I require." He held up her pantalets. "And no more of these. Your quim and your bottom are to be accessible to me at all times." He tossed the garment aside and picked up her chemise and corset. "You will learn to live in a state of sensual readiness that is only for me." He held her with his powerful gaze as he returned to her and set her things on the stool. "This takes training and tending. But have no fear, for I am completely devoted to your education."

Why did this notion thrill her and comfort her? "But why must I learn this?"

His eyes moved slowly over her features. "Because it will please me." He fingered one of her long curls. "But, equally as important, because it will please you. It's essential to your happiness and fulfillment, Patience. There is a strong part of you that longs to submit and obey. A part of you that wishes everything weren't so easy—so attainable by your own will. A part of you that craves a shoulder stronger than your own to lean upon."

Patience's throat tightened and tears suddenly stung her eyes. "Yes," she whispered.

He held her with a soft and steady stare. "Oh, Patience, you crave a kind of rapture that most people will never understand, let alone achieve—a kind of rapture that can only be accomplished by complete submission of the self to one who is completely dedicated to your fulfillment." He touched her cheek and his gaze flickered over her features. "And your greatest fulfillment comes through struggle. You respect nothing that's effortless. So you see, it is not only I who adore the sweat of your submission, it is you as well." His eyes darkened. "And I *shall* make you sweat—sweat, writhe, and weep, and beg me on bended knee for release or respite. And as I pleasure you and punish you, it shall be my greatest joy, for I shall know that it is yours as well."

Patience trembled as her tears escaped her eyes. Tears of . . . joy? She swiped them away but then her thoughts tumbled upon each other as Matthew reached between her legs and stroked her budding clitoris. Her hips tilted, and in three strokes she was undulating against him.

"You see," he breathed by her temple, "one of the ways you will learn is through stimulation—regular and rigorous stimulation."

She gasped and her eyelids shuttered closed at the pulsing intensity his touch aroused.

But after just a brief moment, he stopped and kissed the moist corner near her eye. "Unconsummated stimulation."

Patience let out her breath on a rush, but then drew it in again as he gave her distended nipples a firm pinch and then a light slap. A shudder wracked her body. Her legs shook, and it felt as if all her blood were rushing to her breasts and to the beating heart between her legs. And all the while, he watched her.

His mouth turned in a soft smile as he picked up her chemise and slipped it over her head. "It will seem unrelenting at first—but so it must be if you are to attain more than superficial surrender."

Patience shivered as the batiste fabric brushed her swollen nipples. His words fascinated and delighted her. She strove for perfection in all things. This would be no different.

He tied the bow beneath her breasts. "I expect exceptional submission from you. Therefore, the more accomplished you become, the more I shall demand of you."

Yes, more!

"So it is best you become accustomed to a strong hand from the start."

Patience moaned and grit her teeth as he brushed his fingers firmly over her thinly veiled nipples. Her chest jutted out and then he was squeezing them, depressing and pulling the thick, agitated nubs as he spoke. "Ah, Patience, your sensual distress is beautiful to behold. It pleases me well and makes me eager for all the delightful trials and rewards that shall be yours."

Her skin tingled and her mind raced. How much more acute could her pleasure be? Let him try her and reward her now. She couldn't wait!

Patience gasped as he pinched hard upon her thickened flesh before finally releasing her. She glanced down at her distended nipples. Her breasts felt heavy and full and her cunt ached as if every vessel there were engorged. She hovered at some lush pinnacle of sensation. It was like balancing on a precipice—both terrible and wonderful at the same time.

Matthew picked up her corset. "Lift your arms, my beauty."

Patience did as he asked, and enjoyed a rush of pleasure at his endearment.

Wrapping her corset around her waist, he set to securing the hooks and eyes down the front panel. As he did, she couldn't help staring at his erection, which now tented his trousers to an extreme degree. Just looking at it made her mouth water and her quim weep. If only she could feel its meaty thickness against her tongue. She quivered as her clitoris throbbed at the thought.

"Go to the bedpost," he ordered gently.

Patience went, luxuriating in the pulsing pleasure that came with each step. She could feel the slick moisture that wet her thighs. Setting her legs a little apart, she gripped the bedpost and felt Matthew's hands taking up her laces. In a few strong pulls, her stays were hugging her torso with a comfortable snugness.

When he stepped close, she felt the warmth of his body and the nudge of his erection behind her. "Good?" he murmured by her ear. His breath sent a shiver over her skin.

"Yes."

He stroked her bottom through her chemise and then took a moment to massage it firmly. Leaning her cheek against the bedpost, Patience arched her back at the wonderful feel of his firm grip.

But, again, he quickly stopped and moved to fetch her corset cover.

Patience sighed luxuriantly. Her bottom tingled, her breasts felt hot and full, her cunt ached, and her clitoris maintained a steady pulse.

"Come, my beauty," Matthew said low.

Patience moved to him and put her arms through the delicately embroidered garment. Before closing it completely, he bent close and pressed a kiss to the corner of her mouth as he slid his fingers inside the top of her corset. Patience moaned and kissed him back as he nibbled her lip and pinched her swollen nipples.

She thrust her hips against his prick. It felt as hard as steel, but, yet again, he quickly withdrew. Patience shivered. As he closed her corset cover, her eyes kept dropping to his magnificent erection. She longed to touch it, at least. But though he surely noticed where her eye wandered, he did not acknowledge it in any way.

Instead, he ushered her back to her dressing table. "Sit," he murmured.

Patience obeyed, squirming a little as her swollen sex was pressed deliciously by the seat cushion. She felt some surprise as Matthew picked up her brush and began taming her wild curls with firm strokes. Seemingly intent on his task, she took the opportunity to study, through the mirror, the soft curves and hard angles of his face.

His brow was smooth. His nose would have been completely straight but for a small chisel-like dip in the bridge that, somehow, served to make it more perfect. His wide, sensual mouth made her want to kiss him, and his chin, firm and square, hinted at his dominance. And then there were those expressive, long-lashed eyes that seemed to look inside her.

"God must have modeled you after an angel." She didn't realize she'd spoken the words aloud until his lashes lifted and she was staring into the reflection of his dark orbs.

Something flickered in his expression. "I assure you, I'm no angel."

She thought of her dream. "Perhaps you are to me."

He picked up her hair combs and looked at them for a moment before sweeping back her hair from each side of her face and pushing them in. He met her gaze in the mirror. "Your aunt says you're an angel." His hands rested on her shoulders and his long fingers traced her collarbone. "And I'm inclined to believe her."

As she admired the sight of his sun-darkened hands against her pale skin, Patience smiled softly at the thought of Aunt Matty lauding her. "Well, you mustn't believe everything my aunt says. She's rather prone to exaggeration."

Matthew stared at her for a long moment, his own mouth turning up slowly at the corners. Then he stepped even closer to her, his hips against her shoulder blades as he slid his hands over the curves of her breasts. "You mean you aren't really the best croquet player in the world?"

Patience pressed back against him and shivered as his long fingers squeezed her breasts. "Well, that may actually be true," she breathed.

Matthew leaned over her and kissed the curve of her ear. His moist mouth and warm breath lifted gooseflesh on her skin. Patience sighed as his hands swept lower, pressing between her thighs. She immediately let her legs fall open, and her body jolted as he rubbed her through her chemise. She groaned and, leaning back against him, her hips tilted up as strong prurient pulses erupted from her enflamed flesh.

"God, your clitoris is so swollen," he whispered. "Look at it, Patience, look at how full it is."

Panting, Patience looked down. Matthew had pressed the thin batiste of her chemise against her and, through it, she could see her clitoris, plump and round. He pressed his finger gently against it and Patience jerked—first back and then forward.

"So pretty, Patience," he whispered against her ear. His other hand slipped into the top of her corset. "That's how I like to see it—full and ready to burst."

Patience gasped and moved her hips in tiny thrusts as he kept pressing it and stroking it gently. Then, shuddering, she choked back a groan as he pinched her nipple firmly between his fingers. He pressed and rolled the thickened nub harder and harder while he tenderly fondled the heart of her cunt.

Her mind reeled as the piercing sensation in her breast shot straight to her aching quim. They were connected—the feeling in one communicating to the other in a rapid pass of blood.

"This state—this heightened state of voluptuous readiness—is what you will learn to keep simmering at all times, Patience." Matthew's whispered voice spoke directly into her ear, overwhelming any other thought. "I shall help you, and soon you shall move through your days, doing all the things that normally fill your time—only you will do them with a swollen sex and a ready mind."

Yes! God, yes! An unstoppable trembling began in Patience's body as the pressure he exerted upon her nipple became acute. She had no idea when she'd drawn her legs up, but now she pulled them back farther as she raised her eyes to her mirror. She sucked in her breath at the image of Matthew wrapped around her like some dark, beautiful demon. As she watched, his tongue slipped from his mouth and touched the outer whorls of her ear. Suddenly, she envisioned great golden wings fluttering at his back—not a demon, an angel. *Her* angel. And then her eyelids dropped as she listened to his whispered words.

"Tonight, as you dine, your breasts will throb and your sex will ache. And while you smile and exchange pleasantries with others, you will be aware of your body's hunger. It will please you because you will know it is your proper state. It will please you because you know it pleases me. Isn't that so?"

"Yes, Matthew," Patience breathed.

He pressed his lips into her neck, and then he pulled slowly away from her, supporting her upper arms so that she didn't tip off her stool. She shuddered and gripped the edge of her dressing table as he went to collect her crinoline and gown.

As he returned, she noted a small wet stain on his trousers. It darkened the part of the pearl gray fabric that was tight over the head of his erection. Moisture filled her mouth at the sight. Surely he would allow her to taste him again.

"Come," he said firmly.

Patience forced herself to rise. Her legs felt tingly, and she almost moaned at the full, inflated sensation she felt between her thighs as she crossed to him.

He quickly dropped her layered crinoline over her head and secured the waist. Her gown followed and, just as efficiently, he worked the intricate closure. Her slippers came next and then her jewelry—a parure of dainty cut-steel beads. He regarded the pieces briefly before helping her to don them. Then he dropped a soft kiss upon her lips. "I'll see you at dinner."

Patience's eyes widened as he stepped away. She glanced at his powerful erection. "But—but what about you?"

Matthew paused. "What about me?"

"Well"—Patience dropped her eyes to his wet trousers and licked her lips—"shouldn't I assist you with that?"

Matthew crossed his arms over his chest. "No. If I allow you to fellate me, you'll come and that would be counterproductive to my purpose."

Patience shook her head. "I won't, I promise." She felt desperate for the taste of him. Once was not enough to fulfill the desire of a lifetime.

His eyes seemed to darken. "This is not a negotiation, Patience. When I say no, the answer is no."

Patience bit her lip. How could he be so controlled, when he was in such obvious need? Wet and throbbing, she felt like a disciple of Priapus.

Stepping close, he stroked her cheek. "You are a goddess. My Persephone," he murmured. "Your beauty is unmatched, and the sensual fire in your eyes makes you magnificent. If only you could see yourself through my eyes . . ." He shook his head, then frowned. "Your admirers will be clamoring after you tonight. Though you will be needy, allow none of them to touch you. You belong to me."

Patience felt a swell of pride at his possessiveness. Of course she wouldn't allow anyone else to touch her. No man but he would ever touch her again.

But she didn't say that.

She just said, "Yes, Matthew."

Chapter Eight

Nobles

They all hold swords, being expert in war . . .

Song of Solomon 3:8

"I'm so glad that you are recovered from your headache, Miss Dare. I was mightily disappointed to miss my dance with you last eve. Indeed, I do believe at least half the gentlemen at the ball were quite put out with you."

Patience lifted her emerald silk skirts as she descended the stairs with Lord Farnsby. Guests were slowly moving down to the main floor for dinner. But she barely noted them as each step she took sent luscious reverberations through her engorged sex. "I'm sorry to have disappointed you, my lord."

Patience searched discreetly for Matthew's broad shoulders and gold-tipped hair. She wanted to see him—to look into his eyes and feel the touch of his dark, possessive gaze.

"Well, you're forgiven, of course." Farnsby pushed back his thinning hair. "Ah, there's Asher. Did I tell you, Miss Dare, that Asher and I are cousins?"

"No, my lord, you didn't."

Patience saw Lord Asher talking with another gentleman at the foot of the stairs. But where was Matthew? Her breasts felt heavy. Would he attend dinner? Her nipples tightened and tingled. What of the musicale afterward? Would he come to hear her play?

"I say, Asher!" Farnsby called over the din of the milling crowd. "Look who I've had the good fortune to run into—Miss Dare."

Farnsby's raised voice seemed to get the attention of every man in the immediate vicinity. Eyes turned toward her and remained on her. Indeed, it felt as if the entire crowd of males took a collective step toward her all at once. She paused but then raised her chin. Where was Matthew? With him, she felt protected.

Taller, leaner, and more handsome than his cousin, Asher smiled up at her and extended his hand as she approached. "Miss Dare, you have made this evening bright. Though I hardly know how it is possible, you look even more beautiful this evening than you did last night." He hovered a bit over her hand before turning to his companion. "I believe you were introduced to Lord Fitz Roy at the ball."

Patience smiled at the man who also seemed to be observing her intently. Though most all the gentlemen she had met the night before had blurred in her memory, she remembered Lord Fitz Roy for his black hair and extraordinarily pale blue eyes. "Good evening, my lord."

"Good evening, Miss Dare," the man drawled. "I can't tell you what a relief it is to see you. Are you aware that you are one of only a handful of ladies here this evening who can claim some understanding of style and subtlety?" Fitz Roy raised his brow at a passing group of giggling young women before turning back to Patience. "What horrid plague has clouded the minds of ladies, that they adorn a single gown with enough lace and trimmings to easily ornament a dozen? I ask you"—he gestured to the crowd at large—"have you ever seen so many gewgaws, bow-ties, and gimcracks?"

The man had a beautiful voice, but he spoke in a bored monotone that made Patience smile. She nodded as she glanced around. "It does appear to be rather a strong night for gewgaws, bow-ties, and gimcracks." She turned back to him. "Personally, I don't mind a bow-tie or two. It's the gewgaws and gimcracks that I cannot abide."

The smallest of grins turned the man's mouth.

"Good God, Miss Dare, you've actually got a show of teeth from our supercilious Fitz Roy." Lord Asher turned to his cousin. "Surely, this is an incident worth recording in your Journal of Extraordinary Events."

Farnsby nodded. "I shall make a note of it."

"Well, while you're at it," Lord Fitz Roy drawled, "be sure you document the fact that the Lady Humphreys has actually adorned her shapeless personage in fewer than seven hundred fifty-two flounces today. Heavens, I barely recognized the lady in such a simple gown."

Smiling, Patience glanced over her shoulder as three women passed behind her. The large lady in the middle wore a gown with at least a dozen lace flounces from waist to floor, and more upon her sleeves. Patience turned back to her companions and lowered her voice. "I think seven hundred fifty-two may be a slight exaggeration, my lord."

"Only this eve, Miss Dare. Only this eve."

Just as Patience began to smile, she heard the unmistakable voice of one of the gossips from the previous night.

"Doesn't Hawkmore know that his presence is an embarrassment? No one knows what to say to him. You'd think he'd stay away for his brother's sake, at least."

When Farnsby began to speak, Patience stayed him with a hand upon his arm.

"I couldn't agree more," came the reply. "What do you say to a man whose illegitimacy is announced in the papers—and in such a scandalous manner? And what of his mother? Nobly born, but with both feet in the gutter. Why, if *my* mother were proven as low and horrid a woman as she, I'd never show my face in public again."

Patience felt herself growing hot with anger as her companions shared uncomfortable glances. How dare these women speak of Matthew or his circumstances with such derision!

"Well, she's our host's mother as well," said a third voice.

"Yes, but she clearly favored her illegitimate son. What must it have been like for the young earl, tolerating that all those years? And then to almost lose the love of his life, all to protect a bastard brother. It's unconscionable, I tell you."

Patience's hands clenched in her skirts. Fitz Roy took a step forward but she stayed him with a shake of her head.

"Yes. And just what does one say to a gardener's son who walks about in our midst as if he were our equal?"

"You say, 'Pardon me, but can you tell me how to rid my roses of mildew?' "

More tittering. "Oh, Mildred! You're shameless."

Patience had heard enough. In a fury, she whirled around the column that separated her from the nasty gossips. "Yes, Mildred, you are shameless. Shameless and cruel."

She glared at the three ladies, who drew back in surprise at the sight of her. They were none other than the Lady Humphreys and her two companions. The two smaller women looked aghast. Lady Humphreys, who must be Mildred, looked haughty. It was the haughtiness that made Patience's blood boil. Employing all her restraint, she kept her voice low. "How dare you? Tell me, are you Christian women?"

"Of course," Lady Humphreys snapped.

"Then have you forgotten the words of our Lord?" When they looked at her blankly she took a step closer. "Very well, though I am only a common vicar's daughter, I shall remind you. 'But I say unto you, that every idle word that men shall speak; they shall give account thereof in the day of judgment. For by thy words thou shalt be justified, and by thy words thou shalt be condemned.'" Patience took a deep breath. "You demean no one but yourselves with your malicious gossip. I pity you, and I shall pray for the redemption of your souls." She started to turn away, only to turn back. "And so that you will not be tempted to engage in any more wrongful speculation, I will tell you that the earl loves his brother, and my sister loves him, too. Matthew Hawkmore is welcome in this house whenever he chooses to grace it with his presence."

Though she had tried to keep her voice low, Patience realized that her tone had drawn the attention of those in the immediate vicinity. *Fine. Let them hear.* "And as to how to speak to him—you speak to him as ever you would have. For he is the same man as ever he was."

While the other ladies stood in stunned silence, the Lady Humphreys stepped forward with a glare, her skirts pushing against Patience's. "Do you know whom you are addressing, Miss Dare?" She was a woman of formidable size, who was no doubt accustomed to intimidating people just with her presence.

But Patience was taller than both her sisters, and she stared straight into the eyes of the older woman. Refusing to step back, she lifted her chin and raised her brows. "Though, clearly, you already knew my name—I have only just learned yours, Lady Humphreys."

The Lady Humphreys's beady eyes narrowed. "I am the *Marchioness* of Humphreys, and I will be addressed with the respect my title merits. And the only reason I know who you are, *miss*, is because of your conspicuous appearance. And I do *not* mean that as a compliment." She glared at Farnsby and Asher and the small crowd of other gentlemen who had paused behind Patience, but she seemed to excuse Fitz Roy. She lifted her strong chin. "Any woman who is so constantly surrounded by men cannot be a woman of any quality or dignity. I pity you, Miss Dare. And I pity you your low brother-in-law, Mr. Who-ever-he-is."

Patience trembled with her fury. "Pity me? Rather pity yourself. Any woman who is so constantly surrounded by her own malignant pride cannot be a woman of any kindness or decency. And if *you* are what exemplifies good breeding, then Mr. *Hawkmore* ought to count his blessings that he is not a member of your illustrious society." Patience leaned forward. "He is good and honest, and I would thank *you* not to speak his name unless you can do so with the respect *his* character merits."

The Lady Humphreys's face turned dark red. "Respect? Shall respect a man who just last eve attacked Lord Danforth over the gaming table—out of malice and jealousy?"

Patience stiffened and felt her own hands fisting. Had Mathew been in a fight? "While violence is obviously regrettable, if my brother-in-law struck Lord Danforth, then Lord Danforth must have provoked him to do so. And as for jealousy, what posible reason could my brother-in-law have to be jealous of Lord Danforth? Rather, the other way around I should think, for Mr. Hawkmore has many enviable attributes."

Fitz Roy's bored drawl sounded from beside her. "Actully, Lady Humphreys, it was Lord Danforth who attacked Mr. Hawkmore."

Patience lifted her chin. "There, you see."

The Lady Humphreys cast a quick glance at Fitz Roy but therwise ignored him. Her lip curled as she regarded Patience. Perhaps you are not aware, Miss Dare, that Lord Danforth just became engaged to Lady Rosalind Benchley, your brother-inlaw's former fiancée."

A small but decidedly unpleasant tremor moved down Paence's spine.

"And you declare that he has no reason for jealousy? Really, Miss Dare, I think you are being a bit naïve. If there is one thing everyone knows, it's how completely in love Mr. Hawkmore was, and likely still is, with Lady Rosalind. Lady Rosalind, who, I might add, is a woman of elegant beauty and impeccable breeding."

Patience tamped down the surprisingly painful feeling that the marchioness's words evoked, and pulled herself up. "If there's one thing everyone knows, my lady, it's that gossips are most always wrong. Therefore, I can hardly take anything you say seriously. Besides, since Lord Danforth was the one who accosted Mr. Hawkmore, then clearly any malice or jealousy must lie in the heart of Lord Danforth."

"You are certainly passionate in your defense of your brother-in-law, Miss Dare." Lady Humphreys raised her thick brows and gave Patience the once-over. "I can only wonder at why that might be?"

"Mr. Hawkmore is a respected member of my family—and that, my *lady*, is reason enough." Patience took one step closer to the Lady Humphreys and lowered her voice. "Do not slander him again."

The marchioness narrowed her eyes. "Wait till people hear how you have spoken to me. I hope you have no aspirations of marrying a title, Miss Dare. For you have most certainly ruined any hope of that this evening."

Patience didn't back up. "I have no aspirations to marriage at all, so your threats are meaningless."

The Lady Humphreys narrowed her eyes. "Yes, well, you may be unmarriageable, Miss Dare. But you've also just stolen your sister's chances for admittance into the best drawing rooms."

Patience's anger flared. How dare this woman punish Passion. "*My* sister won't care one whit about that."

"So you hope."

"So I know."

The Lady Humphreys drew in her breath with a hiss. "I do not bid you good evening." And with that she turned and stomped off, her friends hurrying after her.

Patience drew short breaths and tried to still the trembling that had suddenly started in her legs. Her wonderful mood was gone.

She turned back to her companions and the circle of gentlemen who had stayed by to listen. They were all staring at her with a kind of awe.

No comfort there. Where was Matthew?

Lord Fitz Roy stepped forward, breaking the silence. "By God," he said in his bored drawl, "that was exceptionally well done, Miss Dare." Her crowd of onlookers, including Farnsby and Asher, nodded and a few *Hear, Hear*s were raised to her.

Patience managed a small smile, and tried to ignore the unsettled feeling in her stomach. Her throat felt tight. What was the matter with her?

Where was Matthew?

She glanced back at Fitz Roy and found his pale gaze upon her. He regarded her for a moment before turning to address the group in his bored drawl. "I do believe that this is, perhaps, as great a day as when David slew Goliath." He raised his brows as he turned back to her and offered her his arm. "Perhaps greater." Patience tucked her hand into the bend of his elbow as everyone laughed. "Now, if you'll excuse us my lords, gentlemen, I'm going to escort our heroine for a brief, resuscitative walk." And with that, he led her away.

Patience breathed a sigh of relief. Sometimes she felt like she couldn't breathe when so many were clustered around her. And for a horrid moment, as she'd turned and faced the mute circle of amazed gentlemen, she'd thought she might cry. She glanced at Fitz Roy. "Thank you, my lord. Had you not taken my part, those gentlemen might not have either."

Fitz Roy looked at her and raised one black brow. "My dear Miss Dare, your victory this evening was entirely your own. The Lady Humphreys is one of the most feared members of our—what did you call it?—our 'illustrious society.' "

Patience frowned. "I apologize, my lord. I didn't mean you."

Fitz Roy shrugged. "It's quite all right. We're a worthless lot, really. Far too much time and money on our hands, and an unfortunate disinclination to do anything substantive with either. So"—he paused by the doors to the grand salon and looked over the milling guests—"we're more starch than substance, I'm afraid. Stiff, and full of little more than air, we shy away from the weight of true morality for fear it will crush us." He turned back to her. "Which is why your brilliant and passionate defense of Mr. Hawkmore was so enthralling. It isn't often that we see such exceptional displays of decency, and loyalty."

Patience frowned. If her defense had been so brilliant, why did she feel defeated? Matthew wasn't in the salon either. She met Fitz Roy's pale gaze. He was being so kind to her, but . . . "Forgive me, my lord. I'm afraid I seem to have lost my good humor."

Fitz Roy nodded and then regarded her a moment longer. "Miss Dare, the fight between Mr. Hawkmore and Lord Danforth had nothing to do with Lady Rosalind—nothing whatsoever."

Patience stiffened as, yet again, her eyes welled. She lifted her chin. "No, of course it didn't." She blinked and swallowed down her tears. "But thank you, my lord."

He bowed his head. "You're welcome, Miss Dare."

Flushing at her own discomfiture, Patience nodded. "Please excuse me. I find I am in need of a moment."

"A moment, if you please."

Matthew turned from his search for Patience and followed his brother. Mark led him across the foyer to the library and closed the tall doors behind them.

"What is it?" Matthew asked. He could see by his brother's tense face that it was something significant.

"Benchley is here. He demands to speak with you."

Matthew stiffened as his hands tightened into fists. A cold fury burned away all vestiges of the good humor he had cultivated with Patience. He spoke through his clenched jaw. "How rude of him to arrive at the dinner hour."

Mark nodded. "Do you want me to throw him out?"

"No." Matthew shook his head. "Where is he?"

"I had him escorted to your office."

"Good. Rear of the house. That way, if I murder him, no one is likely to hear," he snarled, as he wrenched open the library door.

Striding down the broad corridor to his office, Matthew took long, deep breaths. He needed to remain calm—calm and controlled, no matter what.

Without pausing, he jerked open the office door. Benchley

stood in the middle of the room, but Matthew managed to ignore him as he slammed the door and walked behind his desk. Only then did he meet the older man's glaring blue eyes.

Matthew gritted his teeth and his heart pounded as he prepared for battle. "What do you want?"

Benchley strode forward, his coat swinging back from his bulky frame. "I came for my mine, Hawkmore. Danforth informed me this afternoon that you cheated him out of it. I demand that you return it to me, at once."

Matthew leaned his fists on the desk. "Call me a cheat again, and I'll sue you for slander." A muscle in his arm twitched. "As for the mine, Danforth's name was on the deed to Gwenellyn, not yours."

"You know damned well that means nothing. Danforth can't tie his own cravat, let alone run one of my mines. Now give it back to me!"

"And why the hell should I do that?" He was barely able to bite out the words.

Benchley stepped closer and pointed his finger accusingly. "Because you bloody owe me."

Heat flooded Matthew's head as he leaned forward and planted his hands on the desktop. "I owe you?" he repeated slowly. His arms trembled with the effort it took not to hurl himself at Benchley. "I don't owe you anything but the bottom of my boot."

The earl's face grew florid. "You bastard! You sullied my daughter and me with your lies and your low attempt to pass yourself off as a man of pure and noble blood. You embroiled us in your hideous scandal and then you embarrassed and shamed us with your attempt to see Rosalind, even after I told you myself that she didn't ever want to see you again!" He slammed the flat of his hand on the desk. "And thanks to our association with you, upon which we embarked in good faith, we have been tainted to such a degree that now the only husband I can get for my daughter—*my* daughter who can trace her pure, perfect line back to the Conqueror—is a penniless gambler! And *that* is why you owe me."

Matthew heard the papers crinkling on his desk as his fingers curled into fists. His whole body was stiff with suppressed rage. "I never lied to you because I never knew," he snarled, baring his teeth. "But despite that fact, you cast me off—adding derision and insults to your public denouncing of me. You sullied *me* with your lies about my paternity until, I am sure, doors closed to me based on that alone. And as if it weren't enough for you to run me into the ground personally and socially, you have the unmitigated gall and villainy to try to ruin me financially as well!" He ground his knuckles into the top of the desk. "So, thanks to my association with *you*, upon which *I* embarked in good faith, I have suffered losses tenfold what they would have been without you!" Matthew picked up a long, silver letter opener, and with the full swing of his arm, stabbed it into the desktop. "I owe you? I owe you nothing!" he roared.

Benchley's hand clenched over a large marble paperweight. His breathing came hard and fast. "Why shouldn't you suffer financially, you son of a bitch? I am! Danforth is practically penniless, yet he is the best I can get for Rosalind now. His earldom is the only thing he shall bring to this marriage, but small consolation is the title of countess when I shall have to fund my daughter's life entirely while keeping her gambling husband out of fucking debt!"

Matthew drew back. Just let Benchley make one move with that paperweight. "Forgive me if I do not weep for you," Matthew sneered. "Had you stood by me, you and Rosalind would have had the benefit of all my money. You chose your path, now you deal with what lies in it."

Benchley began to shake. "I swear, you will rue the day you lied to me."

"I never lied to you!" Matthew bellowed.

"You did! You knew!" Benchley's fingers whitened around the block of marble. "What man can look upon a bastard child—the incarnation of his wife's betrayal—without making that bastard suffer the knowledge of his own low birth?" He shook his graying head. "No. With *your* slut of a mother at the root of things—the way she always favored you. No man could tolerate that. So don't tell me you never knew."

Matthew's fury escalated at the mention of his mother. A muscle pulled in his shoulder. He hated that he was her son, and he hated Benchley for reminding him that he was. He clenched his jaw. "Get out."

"Give me back my mine!"

"Go to hell!"

Benchley's eyes narrowed to slits. "By God, I shall ruin you."

Matthew leaned forward, his blood racing. "The only ruination to come will be your own."

"Have you forgotten?" Benchley pulled back, his mouth twisting into a sneer. "You're not the son of an earl anymore. And the last I heard, no one will do business with you. Ruin me? You don't have the resources."

Matthew's heart beat with a deadly determination. "I am going to bury you."

Benchley lifted his heavy chin. "Do you think I quiver at the paltry threats of a worthless bastard? They mean nothing. *You* mean nothing!" He strode to the door and yanked it open before looking back over his shoulder. "You're finished, Hawkmore. Do you hear me? Finished!" The door slammed behind him.

A heavy silence filled the room.

"Good then," Matthew growled. "War, it is."

Chapter Nine
The Musicale

. . . yea, he is altogether lovely. This is my beloved . . .

Song of Solomon 5:16

Patience drew her bow across the strings of her cello with calm concentration. She played Vivaldi's "Largo" from the *Winter* concerto. Though the piece was meant for violin, she liked the deep, resonant sound of it on the cello.

As she played, she saw the music in her head—each note and cue appeared before her, one leading to the next. She executed each one perfectly, and each completed measure was a triumph. Perfectly and precisely, she moved through the piece until reaching the end. And as she played the last notes, she felt victorious.

Lifting her head to the applause of the audience, Patience smiled at the rows of seated guests that filled the large music room. There were always two factions amongst the people who watched her play. There were those who really admired music and appreciated her skill. And then there were those who came only to gawk because she played an "indelicate" instrument that required the parting of her legs. She could see in the face of each guest who fell into which group. Many of the ladies, including the odious Lady Humphreys and her followers, looked at her with barely repressed censure. Many of the gentlemen, including Lord Fenton and others she had danced with the night before, looked at her with barely repressed lechery.

How she loathed the sly glances that passed between these so-called lords and ladies. Ignoring any disdain or venery, she nodded appreciatively to those who showed genuine enjoyment. She smiled at Mark, Passion, and Aunt Matty, who all sat together in the front row of seats. Her smile widened as she saw Lords Farnsby and Asher standing at the back of the room, clapping enthusiastically alongside Lord Fitz Roy, who nodded and lifted his gloved hands for three short claps.

Then, at last, she found Matthew. Her heart skipped a beat. Where had he been all evening? He stood alone, leaning against the jamb of the open music room doors. Her blood rushed and her clitoris pulsed in recognition of his presence. He was so amazingly handsome, and he wore his flawless evening attire as if he'd been born in it. But, as always, it was his dark stare that made her breath quicken and her body tremble.

He looked at her with an admiring pride and, suddenly, what anyone else thought was unimportant. The disdain of certain ladies, the salaciousness of certain lords meant nothing. Matthew was the only one who mattered—he who tied her to his bed at night, and brought her tea in the morning.

In the quiet after the waning applause, Aunt Matty's loud voice echoed across the room. "Oh look, it's Mr. Hawkmore. Why don't you ask him to join you, my dear? I do so enjoy duets."

Patience blanched and looked at her aunt, who had turned around in her chair and was gesturing to Matthew. Patience shot a beseeching glance at Passion, but her sister sent her a what-can-I-do look as Mark chuckled silently. Murmurs rose, and people glanced alternately at her aunt and over their shoulders at Matthew.

Patience felt her blood rushing to her cheeks as she saw the snickering and disparaging glances that passed amongst many of the guests, including, of course, Lady Humphreys and her circle. Patience lifted her chin. Her aunt might be a bit unsophisticated, but she had a heart of pure gold.

Matthew had taken a step into the room and was regarding her carefully. Patience tensed. She didn't want to play with him. The last time she'd played with a man who meant something to her, it hadn't gone well. And while she may not love Matthew, she definitely—

She definitely what?

Matthew's low voice carried across the chamber. "I thank you for your enthusiasm, Mistress Dare, but I wouldn't dream of intruding upon your niece's performance."

Patience caught Lady Humphreys raising her haughty eyebrows at her companions, and the fullness of the situation became clear to her. This was not the moment for absurd insecurities. This was the moment to demonstrate her allegiance, both to her aunt and to Matthew.

She looked at him, and, though her heart beat nervously, she lifted her voice so that all might hear. "Please, Mr. Hawkmore. I am to play the prelude from Bach's Cello Suite Number One as my encore." She glanced at his cello leaning in its stand. "Your fine instrument is here, and I would be honored for you to join me."

Matthew kept his eyes unwaveringly on her and, for a moment, she thought he might refuse. But then he stepped forward. "Very well, Miss Dare." He spoke as he removed his gloves and walked down the aisle between the seats. "For you, I am most pleased."

Patience's stomach fluttered, and she heard whispers emanating from the audience. They quieted as Matthew took a chair beside her and accepted his instrument, a beautiful Domenico Montagnana, from the footman. The gold strands in his hair looked bright against the dark ones, and the faintest note of vetiver moved in the air. He positioned his cello between his legs and then slid his long fingers almost sensually up the fingerboard to the peg box.

He looked at her and his eyes were soft. "Suite Number One, you said?"

Patience felt tense and flushed, but not with arousal. "Yes."

She waited as he made some slight adjustments to the tuning pegs. Then he lifted his beautiful eyes to her and nodded.

Patience drew a deep breath. She hated that he looked so calm while she felt so ridiculously nervous. Positioning her fingers, she set her bow. *Just see the music . . .*

She brought forth the first notes of the suite on her own, and then Matthew joined her and the music filled the room.

As she played beneath his unbending gaze, her stomach slowly tightened. The piece had never sounded more beautiful, but not because of she.

It was him.

He was better than she.

But how was he better?

She frowned as she listened. Bach's prelude was one of her favorite pieces, and she was playing it perfectly. She glanced at him and her frown deepened. He played with a seeming ease and fluidity. And, as they moved into the piece, he added subtle yet provocative variations that fit exactly into each measure she played.

Yet, for all his skill, he did not try to outplay her, or even lead the melody. He kept to the low notes and moved in flawless accompaniment with her. And the whole while, he kept his soft gaze upon her—watching her, and watching her play.

Patience found herself meeting his expressive eyes again and again. They seemed full of both her and the music. How did he watch her so intently and play so wonderfully at the same time?

Her shoulders tensed as she almost missed a note. The shock of that made her keep her eye pinned to her bow. But her ear still searched the music for what made him better. Hard as she tried, she couldn't lay her finger on it. So as the final notes of the suite floated into silence, rather than her usual satisfaction, she felt perplexed and a bit peeved.

Lifting her eyes to Matthew, she saw a slow smile turn his beautiful mouth, and then enthusiastic applause filled the room. As footmen stepped forward to take their instruments, Matthew stood and offered her his hand. Patience paused only a moment before slipping her fingers in his.

Rising, her heart quickened as Matthew bent to place a kiss on her fingers. His lips felt firm and warm and, again, she smelled the deep scent of vetiver.

Lord. Despite her contrary emotions, all she could think of was that she wanted so much more from him than just a kiss. But then he was presenting her to the audience, and she blushed uncomfortably as he stepped back so that she might have the guests' gratitude for herself.

She didn't deserve it. Turning back to him, she dropped into a low curtsy. What was it about his playing that made him better than her?

She raised her eyes and found that he was looking down at her. One dark eyebrow tilted, and then he held out his hand and lifted her to her feet.

As the applause died, he discreetly stroked her palm before

releasing her. Her skin tingled at his touch and her blood rushed, but she had no time to enjoy the lovely sensations, for Aunt Matty was hurrying forward.

Her aunt grinned broadly. "That was wonderful, my dear. Just wonderful. Isn't she wonderful, Mr. Hawkmore?"

Patience blushed as Matthew looked at her. "She is beyond wonderful, Mistress Dare."

Aunt Matty's grin deepened and a knowing gleam lit her gray eyes. "Oh . . . yes, isn't she though. And my goodness, don't you both play wonderfully together. Of course, I knew you would. And I'm so rarely wrong about these things." She raised her silvered brows at Matthew. "What a happy coincidence that you and my beautiful niece should play the same instrument, Mr. Hawkmore. I find that ladies and gentlemen who share one thing in common, often share many things in common. And you know what they say about ladies and gentlemen that share so many things in common."

Matthew regarded Aunt Matty with an expression that bespoke great interest. "No, what do they say?"

Aunt Matty shrugged and flipped open her fan. "Well, I don't know what they say exactly. But I can tell you that many married people share less in common with each other than you and my beauteous niece."

Patience looked to her sister for help, but Passion and Mark had been waylaid by a sophisticated-looking couple who didn't seem likely to move off soon. So, slipping her arm through her aunt's, she gave her a warning squeeze. "I do believe that is quite enough, Aunt Matty."

Aunt Matty batted Patience's hand with her fan and then pointed it at her. "Rotten peaches. That is all I have to say to you, young lady." And with that, she turned back to Matthew, who seemed able to regard her with complete seriousness. "You mustn't mind her, Mr. Hawkmore. She really is a good-natured girl." She lowered her voice and leaned closer to him. "It's just that she doesn't always know what's in her best interest."

Patience bristled. "I beg your pardon, but I always know exactly what's in my best interest."

Aunt Matty looked at her sympathetically but then sent Matthew a small, conspiratorial shake of her head.

"Oh, really!" Patience exclaimed.

Matthew's lips twitched at the corners. "Perhaps we should continue this conversation later, Mistress Dare. It seems to be distressing your niece."

Aunt Matty nodded. "You're right, Mr. Hawkmore. Better to discuss her future out of her presence—especially when she is so contrary to its proper course." Aunt Matty sent Patience a brief glare before turning back to Matthew and patting his arm. "We shall continue this little chat at another time, Mr. Hawkmore. But don't worry"—she winked—"I am for you, sir."

Matthew bowed and clasped Aunt Matty's hand. "My thanks, Mistress Dare."

Patience shook her head as Aunt Matty smiled adoringly at Matthew.

"You know," her aunt said with a sigh, "I must insist that you address me as Aunt Matty, Mr. Hawkmore. After all, we are already related through marriage, thanks to the good sense of your brother, who could have no finer woman in the world than my eldest niece. For though she is common born, Passion has a nobility and grace of spirit which is unmatched—except by her sisters, of course, who are equally blessed"—Aunt Matty glanced at Patience and managed to smile and glower at her at the same time before turning back to Matthew—"even if they don't always show it."

Matthew smiled. "Very well, Aunt Matty. If you insist upon such familiarity, then I must insist upon the same. Please, call me Matt."

Aunt Matty actually batted her lashes as she fanned herself idly. "Dear Matt. I could tell this morning on the ride from the station that you and I were going to get on swimmingly. I don't care what anyone says, *I* like you."

Patience tensed and glanced at Matthew, but if he took offence to her aunt's backhanded compliment, he didn't show it. "Thank you, Aunt Matty. I like you, too."

Aunt Matty blushed like a girl. "Dear Matt."

Patience cocked her brow at her aunt as a brief silence ensued.

Aunt Matty sighed and then started slightly as she met Patience's pointed stare. "Oh." Her adoring look faded. "Well, if you'll excuse me, I'm going to go fetch some refreshment." She raised her brows. "A cup of hot punch, perhaps, as it seems to have gotten a bit chilly in here." No sooner had she started off, than she turned back. "Don't let her intimidate you, Matt, dear. She has an extremely annoying way of doing that to men."

As Patience's eyes widened at her aunt's audacity, Matt glanced at her and the corner of his mouth curled. "Don't worry, *that* I won't allow."

Patience met the dominant look in his eye, and her heart skipped a beat as her aunt nodded approvingly and finally moved off.

A brief silence settled between them as the buzz of multiple conversations floated around them. With his back to the room, Matthew held her in his steady gaze.

Patience released a breath and smiled. "You really should disabuse her of the notion that you are interested in marriage. She will hound you unmercifully if you don't."

Matthew regarded her for a moment, his eyes moving over her features. "Do you know, it makes me hard just to look at you?"

Patience's nipples tightened with a sharp, tingly sensation.

Slipping his hands into his pockets, he massaged himself discreetly. "Here's what you're going to do," he said, quietly. "After the next performance, I want you to excuse yourself for the evening. The hunt is tomorrow, so no one will think it odd if you retire early. Go to your room directly, remove all your clothing, and await me. Do you understand?"

"Yes," Patience breathed.

"Is your cunt wet?"

She shivered. "Yes."

His eyes were so dark. "Good." He glanced quickly over her shoulder. "Now smile. Here come Farnsby and Asher."

Patience drew a deep breath and smiled as the two lords hurried over. Farnsby was juggling two glasses of champagne and a plate of cheese with sugared grapes. Asher came quickly behind him, trying not to slosh champagne over the tops of the etched glasses he carried.

With his breathing coming quickly, Farnsby extended one of the glasses to Patience. "There you are, Miss Dare, a little refreshment after your marvelous performance."

Patience took his offering. "Why thank you, my lord."

As Asher handed a glass to Matthew, Farnsby nodded victoriously at his cousin. "I reached her first—carrying two glasses and a plate." He shook his head. "And I didn't drop a single grape." His brows lifted at Asher as if to say, *and what's the matter with you?* "You may pay me my five pounds later."

Ignoring Farnsby, Asher lifted his glass. "A toast to the lovely Miss Dare. You play magnificently."

Patience smiled. "Thank you, my lord, but it is Mr. Hawkmore who plays magnificently."

"Right, and to her accompanist as well. Fine job, Hawkmore."

Matthew raised his brows. "My thanks, Asher."

Once they had lowered their glasses, Asher smiled broadly. "Did you know, Miss Dare, that I play the violin?"

"Do you, my lord?"

"I do indeed. Perhaps *we* might play a duet together sometime."

"Good Lord!" Farnsby exclaimed before Patience could respond. "You're bloody awful, Asher, and you know it." He jerked his vest down and leaned closer to Patience and Matthew. "Saws upon the poor instrument as if he were a woodcutter hacking at a tree. The man has no finesse, no subtlety." He grinned and slapped the peeved-looking Asher on the back. "No, I advise you to avoid any offer to play with him as you might avoid the plague."

Patience could barely contain her smile and Matthew coughed into his glass. "I can't believe that such a dire warning is necessary," she replied.

Asher shook off Farnsby's hand from his shoulder. "I'm not as bad as all that, Miss Dare."

Oblivious to his cousin's discomfort, Farnsby guffawed. "It's true. He's worse!" The stout man broke into a wheezing laughter. "He's dreadful!" More laughter. "Positively, run-for-the-hills horrid!"

Patience choked back a giggle and Matthew coughed again, this time over his shoulder. Farnsby was almost bent over with mirth.

Just when she thought she wasn't going to be able to stand it, Asher cracked a smile and then a chuckle. "Well, I may not be very good, but I'm better at the violin than you are at tennis." His smile widened as he pointed at Farnsby, who was still laughing. "Ah, it's true! Abysmal—say it! You're absolutely abysmal."

Patience laughed, and as she noticed Matthew chuckling at her side, her chest tightened at the incredible handsomeness of his face filled with humor. She realized then that she'd never seen him laugh.

"Oh, all right," Farnsby wheezed after they'd all calmed. "It's true. I am an abysmal tennis player. But at least my tennis doesn't offend the ears."

"Well"—Asher drank from his champagne—"perhaps I shall hire a new music master."

"Say, that reminds me," Farnsby interjected. "Won't you be off to London soon, Miss Dare? To study with that Italian chap?"

In a matter of a moment, Matthew's face became cold as stone. He slowly turned his glacial gaze upon her. "What's this?"

Chapter Ten

Decisions

Thou hast ravished my heart, my sister, my spouse; thou hast ravished my heart with one of thine eyes . . .

Song of Solomon 4:9

Matthew stood rigid. "What Italian chap?"

Patience looked at him. "I've been invited to study with Fernando Cavalli." She blinked. "In approximately two weeks time, I'm leaving for London."

No! Matthew gripped Patience's elbow. "My lords, if you will excuse us. I require a moment with Miss Dare."

Without waiting for Farnsby or Asher to reply, Matthew turned Patience down the hall and guided her straight to the library. His heart was beating uncomfortably fast as he pulled her into the large room. Releasing her, he closed the doors and turned the lock. Leaning against the polished wood, he drew a deep breath and watched her walk toward one of the hearths.

The oil lamps were turned low but the two fireplaces in the room burned high. Their flickering flames illuminated the gold-leafed spines on the books so that the walls seemed to sparkle with gold flecks. But their brilliance was as nothing to Patience's hair, which looked like molten lava in the dim light. And when she turned to face him, the fire lit her with such a radiant glow that it made his heart ache to look at her.

He would not let her go.

"What's this about London and Cavalli?" he asked.

Patience regarded him from her spot by the fire. "While on his way to Belton House to visit the Brownlows, Mr. Cavalli heard me play at church. As he was so complimentary of my skill, Father invited him to dine with us and, that evening, he invited me to study with him in London. Father considered the idea, obtained several references, and then finally agreed to allow me to go." She clasped her hands before her. "I shall be the first woman to ever study with him, which is a great honor as he is considered one of the best cello masters in Europe."

"I know perfectly well who he is. I trained with him myself for almost eight years." Matthew pushed away from the door. "He's a lecher. Did you know that?" he asked as he closed the distance between them.

"He's married," Patience replied.

"Yes, he's a married lecher."

"He's seventy-three years old."

"He's a seventy-three-year-old married lecher."

One red gold brow arched as she pinned him with her green gaze. "Are you implying that the only reason he invited me to study with him is so that he might have an opportunity to throw up my skirts?"

He stared at her and caught a trace of gardenia. "I'm not *implying* anything, and this has nothing to do with your worthiness to be his student. I'm *telling* you that Fernando Cavalli has had his aging, but still vigorous prick up every female in his household. And then, of course, there are the women in the households into which he is invited."

Patience nodded, her expression bland. "Very well, thank you for informing me."

"You're welcome," he said tightly. "And when, exactly, were you thinking of informing me of your plans?"

Her chin lifted. "Well, if you must know, upon the few occasions that you and I have been together, I've been a bit distracted by other thoughts."

Matthew stared into her amazing eyes. *Then distract her every day, every moment. Woo her to distraction.* "I don't want you to go."

Patience gazed at him and something flickered in her eyes, but she quickly blinked it away. "Why not?"

Because you belong to me.

Because you're the only thing in my life that is wonderful and unsullied by scandal.

Because I need you—because I . . .

He stepped closer to her. “Because you and I have embarked upon something extraordinary—something that cannot be interrupted or stopped.” Did her eyes darken? He took another step and felt the press of her skirts against his legs. “I know you feel it, too, Patience.”

Her lips parted and the pulse in her throat fluttered, making her cut beads twinkle. “Yes.”

“What’s between us has just begun.” He drew the backs of his fingers across her soft cheek. “I have so much more to show you, and to teach you.” He let his hand drop. “But I cannot if you are in London.”

Her intelligent eyes never left his. “You could come to London. I’ll be at Aunt Matty’s. Your brother used to scale the trellis to lie with my sister.”

Matthew shook his head.

Patience frowned. “Why not?”

“Because what I am teaching you takes time. I require you more often than for just a few hours at night.” He lifted his hand and rested it on her breast. “I need you near and accessible at all times.”

Patience’s breathing quickened and her brow creased. “For how long?”

Forever.

“For now,” he said softly. He could feel her heartbeat.

“And what of my music?” Her voice was low. “Apparently, I did not adequately express to you how important it is to me.”

He hooked his fingers inside the top of her bodice. Her nipple was hard and stiff, and she drew in a breath as he squeezed it gently between his fingers. “So your music comes before everything, even your own fulfillment?”

Patience’s frown deepened. “Physical pleasure is only one aspect of fulfillment. My cello fulfills other parts of me.” She pulled away from him. “I’ll never give it up.”

Matthew watched as her expression turned guarded. Why was she so defensive? “I’m not asking you to give it up.”

She took another step back. “Well, it certainly sounds that way to me.”

Rather than step close to her again, Matthew leaned his shoulder against the mantel. “I’m asking you to give up a teacher, Patience, not your instrument.”

"And do you think teachers like Cavalli come along every day, Matthew? I'm a woman. The opportunities that you take for granted are minor miracles to me."

"And what of us, Patience? Do you think pairings like ours come along every day?"

She didn't reply, but she didn't look away either.

"You know they don't. What *we* have together is a minor miracle." He let his gaze move over her slowly. His pulse quickened as he watched her breasts rise and fall with her breath, and his cock moved as he imagined her moist thighs. He raised his eyes back to hers. "And I'm acutely aware of your womanhood. What we have begun magnifies and illuminates your womanhood." He felt his blood flowing steadily into his cock as her lips parted and a glimmer of soft desire lit her eyes. "Soon, Patience, you will understand that what we have begun is so much more than mere physical pleasure. Is the exploration of this wonder not equal, at least, to the pursuit of your music?"

He could almost see her mind flowing from thought to thought. Her beautiful brow creased as she moistened her lips. "Perhaps it is. But I will not sacrifice my cello."

Matthew studied her for a moment. "Then let me teach you."

Her eyes widened, and even in the rosy glow of the fire he could see her pale. "No."

He frowned as the shuttered look returned to her eyes. "Why not? I trained under Cavalli for years. There is nothing he knows that I cannot teach you. In fact, I can teach you more."

"I said, no." She turned away from him, only to turn back. "I told you from the beginning—my cello comes first."

Matthew's frown deepened and a spark of anger ignited in him. He crossed his arms over his chest. "Why? Why do you put your music before all—before marriage, before children, even before yourself? Why must everything be sacrificed upon the altar of your musical pursuit?"

Patience shifted, and he saw her hands tremble as she pressed them against her skirts. "You play, you should understand."

"No." He shook his head. "Actually, I don't. I adore my instrument. Indeed, my playing was the one thing that my fath—" he paused at his slip—"that George Hawkmore admired me for." He met her troubled gaze. "But right now I would toss my cello into the fire rather than give up what is between us."

His declaration didn't surprise him. It was true. He would do anything to keep her. Why didn't she feel the same, damn it? "Why, Patience? Why does your bloody instrument rule your life? Do you aspire to the stage?" His voice was growing harder, but he couldn't help it. "Is it fame you want? Will you be traveling the world—you and your cello—moving from place to place in a perpetual performance?"

"No!" Patience's hands closed into fists. "Why must people always assume that fame and fortune are the reasons for my dedication?"

"Tell me, then! What are your reasons? Why is your cello so goddamned important?" he yelled.

"Because it's all mine!" she yelled back. "And as long as I love it enough, it will never, ever leave me!"

What?

Matthew's anger melted away, only to be replaced by a fierce protectiveness.

Patience sucked in her breath and then squeezed her eyes shut. When she finally opened them again, her expression was one of forced calm. "My cello is important because it challenges me, and it never disappoints me." Her voice was tight but quiet, and her eyes glistened. "And despite the fact that it is but wood and string, it comforts and satisfies me."

Crossing to her, he stared into her exquisite face. Her lower lip was trembling, but she didn't allow a single tear to fall.

His heart constricted.

I'll never leave you.

Resting his hands on her slim waist, he bent and pressed his lips softly to hers. Her mouth was tender and her breath sweet. Once again and twice more, he kissed her before pulling back. A wet streak glistened on her cheek, and he could feel her shaking. This was about more than some bastard music master. He brushed his thumb across the remnant of her tear. "At least consider my request."

Patience held him in her green gaze for a long silent moment. "Yes, Matthew."

He nodded and drew her into his embrace.

But as he pressed her head to his chest, he knew that he wouldn't take the chance.

He would do whatever it took to keep her.

Whatever it took . . .

Patience took off her dressing gown and stood before the fire. The bright flames warmed her naked body, helping her to resist covering up. Several times already, she had put her dressing gown back on; for it felt strange to walk about with nothing on. She was determined, however.

Matthew's demand had been clear. Undress and wait for him.

But what of his request?

And what of *her* words, words that had snuck up on her so stealthily. Turning to face the fire, she stared into the flames. Were they true? Was her dedication to her instrument based on some desperate, pathetic need? The thought was repugnant.

Other than the fulfillment of her physical passions, which Matthew was now tending to, she'd felt she had everything she needed in life. She was not some weak woman who bemoaned her lot or pined for love. She was strong and her days were full.

Pacing before the fire, she twisted one of her long curls around her finger. Yes, she'd experienced a broken heart, but she'd repaired it beautifully. She felt no scars, no tortured need. Indeed, there was very little she needed. That had been one of her discoveries during her quest for love—that she didn't really *need* anyone. She could take care of herself. And since love evaded her, why marry?

So, she had turned fully to her instrument, which she did love.

Besides—she continued pacing—everyone should have some passion, some pursuit. And why pursue anything if one were not going to work toward perfection? Of course, the pursuit of perfection required focus and discipline, which romantic love invariably robbed a person of.

Releasing her twisted curl, she nodded. Yes, all her decisions seemed perfectly sound.

Turning from the fire, she frowned and bit her lip. Then why did she feel that something was amiss? Why had she felt such sorrow at the moment her surprising words had escaped her? She had no reason to feel sorry for herself.

Her frown deepened. She wished she could take the words back.

With a frustrated sigh, she rubbed her hands on her thighs and glanced at the clock. Almost eleven. Where was Matthew? Her nipples tightened and her stomach fluttered as she poured a brandy from the decanter he had left.

His request that she give up her opportunity with Cavalli had both pleased and distressed her. She couldn't deny that she was glad he didn't want her to go. But she couldn't possibly give up the prospect. Cellists from all over Europe vied for the chance to study with Cavalli. She and Matthew could continue their relationship later.

But when later?

Her muscles tensed as she thought of the alternative he had offered—to teach her himself. Shivering, she took a sip from the brandy. She couldn't possibly allow that. Studying with Cavalli was one thing. She felt nothing for him but a detached admiration for his expertise as a cello master. Matthew, on the other hand, inspired her passions and made her feel . . . things . . .

. . . things that might infect her playing were she to allow him too close.

And yet, she couldn't help thinking of how he'd played—easily, fluidly. She frowned. Better than she.

What if he could make her better?

What if he ruins you?

She shuddered.

No. He may touch her body, but he may *not* touch her music. Besides, what if he weren't really recovered from the loss of Rosalind? Her stomach tightened. Taking another sip from the brandy, she began pacing again. It was a thought that had been plaguing her off and on since her encounter with the horrid Lady Humphreys.

What if Matthew still ached for Rosalind? Rosalind who was "a woman of elegant beauty and impeccable breeding." Rosalind, who, "everyone knows," Matthew had been "completely in love" with.

Was he thinking of Rosalind when he was with her? Was he

comparing her to Rosalind? Just how intimate had he been with Rosalind?

God . . . Patience halted her pacing. She had to stop this nonsense. She had no claim upon Matthew, therefore no right to jealousy. And why was she allowing some vile woman's words to infect her? Matthew had conveyed his desire—his desire for *her*. *Never question that I value you above all others, Patience.* That's what he had said. And she believed him.

She would not allow the vile Lady Humphreys's words to supersede Matthew's. Matthew had done nothing to deserve her distrust. So he hadn't told her of the fight with Lord Danforth—so what? He was trying to survive the scandal with nobility and honor, and, clearly, many people were against him. He didn't need her faithlessness as well. " 'A prophet is not without honor, save in his own country, and in his own house,' " Patience quoted the words quietly as a rebuke to herself.

Taking a last sip from the brandy, she placed the snifter on the hearth to warm. As she bent, she felt the weight of her breasts. They swayed and tingled with the gentle pull of gravity.

She straightened slowly. She had never noticed the pleasant weightiness of her own breasts before.

But now the feeling made her think of other, more delicious sensations—like the sharp slap of Matthew's fingers upon her nipples, the firm press of Matthew's hand against her quim, and the swollen shaft of Matthew's cock in her mouth.

Slowly, she walked to the long cheval mirror by the window. She knew her body well. But tonight, she saw it with fresh eyes. Tonight, she saw a body whose secret cravings had been revealed to her—a body that suddenly knew itself.

She saw long limbs that yearned for restraint. She saw pale skin that blushed for firm pinches and strong words. Her nipples, thick and rosy, showed no sign of the sharp slaps they had endured the night before. But as she gently touched the dark bruise at her inner thigh, she almost wished they did. Maybe then, she might still feel some remnant of that splendid sensation. Oh, to feel that hot heaviness again would be heaven.

Her clitoris, tender with want, throbbed in eager agreement. She pressed her fingers to her pulsing, needy flesh. She could bring her own release now. But she had no desire to do so. She let her hand fall away.

She wanted Matthew.

With a sigh, Patience moved back to the hearth. Though her clitoris was aching, a comfortable calm suffused her. It was similar to the feeling she'd had the night before, when she'd lain alone, tied to his bed. Only tonight it was stronger and deeper. Tonight, she had some understanding, some experience. Tonight, she knew her proper place.

She dropped to her knees before the fire.

Her sex felt bloated.

Where was Matthew?

Matthew leaned back in his desk chair and read the letter he'd just composed.

Dear Maestro,

You have often asked if there were not some way you might repay me for the financial assistance that I have given you over the years. I find, at last, that there is.

You recently agreed to take into your tutelage my sister-in-law, Miss Patience Dare. However, I am unwilling to be parted from her at this time. So I must ask that you forward her a letter detailing your change of heart in the matter of her musical training.

I would have this letter be as gentle as possible, so I would like you to inform her that, after conferring with your wife, you have realized that teaching a beautiful young woman would not be in the best interests of your marriage, and that, regretfully, you must rescind your offer to instruct her.

Thank you, Maestro. I have enclosed herein a cheque in the amount of five hundred pounds, which should more than offset the loss of Miss Dare as a student, and should line your wallet nicely. I shall expect for Miss Dare to receive your letter forthwith.

Regards,
M. M. Hawkmore

Matthew stared at the letter a moment more. It was wrong. He shouldn't send it. But neither could he tolerate the thought of Patience leaving him. Fitz Roy had been right when he'd called Rosalind's missive an act of desperation. So was this.

Shoving his conscience out of the way, he quickly folded the letter and the cheque into an envelope and addressed the front to Maestro Fernando Cavalli. Tomorrow, he would give it to Mickey Wilkes to deliver. Then the reformed thief, con artist, and knave could return to Benchley Manor—but only after he delivered a message to Rosalind.

Placing the letter to Cavalli in his top desk drawer, his eye landed upon the note from his former fiancée. Pointing at it, almost like an arrow, was the corner of another letter protruding from the stack of mail he'd dropped there that morning. On that protruding corner was a bit of large, curling script that he recognized immediately.

A bitter feeling moved through him as he pulled his mother's letter from the stack. Since the scandal, he'd received only three letters from her. They had gone from cajoling, to indifferent, to angry. And each one had been entirely taken up with her—*her* reasons, *her* woes, *her* needs—her, her, her. She'd barely spared two lines at the end of each letter in reference to how he might be faring. Once she'd even put it in the postscript. What more could she possibly have to say to him? And why should he care?

He loathed her. He turned over the letter as boyhood memories of her fawning attention flashed through his mind. She had seemed to favor him so much, but the truth was that, despite the lavish shows she had made over him, her attentions had actually been shallow and inconsistent.

He remembered all too well how she would disappear for days, weeks, or even months, whenever she acquired a new lover. And then she would reappear bearing expensive gifts for him that often bore no relation to his childhood interests. And how often had she seemed to overindulge him in front of others, especially before Mark and her husband, while treating him with only mild affection when they were alone? There had been times when he'd hated her, even then. But, though he had periodically spent his rage upon her, he'd let everything happen.

He'd let it happen because she had told him, over and over and always, that she loved him.

And she was his mother . . .

. . . so he'd believed her.

He stared into the flames flickering in the fireplace then, rising, he crossed to the hearth and tossed the letter in the fire. He watched it curl into ash. That passage of his life was over.

As the last bit of his mother's letter burned to dust, he returned to his desk. His ledger still lay open. He stared down at the balance. In three months, the figure had been reduced by almost two thirds. Though his outside investments continued to earn, the huge payments he'd made to keep GWR afloat had far surpassed his monthly income. But he hadn't built Grand West Railway by being conservative. As dangerous as it might be, now was not the time to tighten his purse strings. Perception was even more important than reality. To win his war with Benchley, he needed to inspire confidence. He needed to give the impression that his pockets were bottomless. He needed to spend.

And he needed to move forward with his life. As he closed his ledger and put it in the drawer, the letter to Cavalli stared up at him. He drew a deep breath. He wasn't going to stand by, ever again, and let life just happen to him. He would collar it and drive it down the path of his choosing.

And Patience was no exception. He wouldn't—couldn't—allow her to wander from him. She was his hope and his desire.

His eye shifted to Rosalind's note. So different from *her*. He picked up the pink paper and flipped it open.

Matt, Darling, I know you must hate me . . .

Yes.

. . . so perhaps it will please you to hear that I am suffering.

Yes.

But I want you to know that I think of you every day as Father parades suitor after suitor before me, none as handsome or as "bold" as you.

But all just as blind.

Darling, if you regret our parting as much as I . . .

I thank God every day for our parting.

. . . then send me word.

On a cold day in hell.

Just because we cannot marry, does not mean we cannot be together. Yours, R

He stared at that last line. If the truth of his parentage had never been revealed, he would have married her. Then, one day, she may very well have sent a note, bearing the same line, to some other man. Maybe even to one of the footmen or underbutlers of his own household. On that day, he would have become a cuckold, just like the man he had always called "Father." Perhaps, like the late earl, he would even have raised a child not of his seed. And just like that, his life would have come full circle.

God, why hadn't he seen before just how much like his mother Rosalind was? His gut clenched. The thought was vile.

Shoving the note back in his desk drawer, he slammed it shut and began to pace. He wanted nothing to do with his former fiancée. Yet, his financial and social survival depended upon taking Benchley down. He must use every advantage at his disposal—even Rosalind. He would contact her. Then he would see how she could be of use to him.

He stopped pacing and rubbed his aching brow. He wished it were all over. He wished he could jump forward in time, and find Benchley defeated and himself restored to his former stature.

But he couldn't. He had to play it all out. He had to have patience.

Patience.

She would never betray him.

Matthew felt his shoulders slowly relax. Patience had the Dare family decency and goodness. It enshrouded her like a cloak and was plain for all to see. He thought of her perfect chin lifting proudly when Aunt Matty's loud invitation for him to play had raised brows and caused murmurs. He remembered her fiery retort to Fenton and her proud demeanor when she had walked with him through the ballroom at the masque. She was loyal and true. She was honest and strong.

He stared across the room into the flickering flames of the fire.

She was going to be his wife.

His heart thumped and then beat fast.

Had he just decided, or had he known all along?

He suspected the latter. They were meant for each other. God had made her to fit his hand, and God had made him to take her in hand. And since he had no intention of sharing her, or ever letting her go, then marriage was only logical.

Besides, that morning he'd been reminded of how much he wanted a family. He wanted to father children who would never need question their paternity, with a woman who would never give them cause.

Patience was that woman—whether she knew it or not.

Chapter Eleven
Second Submission

A garden enclosed is my sister, my spouse; a spring shut up, a fountain sealed.
Song of Solomon 4:12

Matthew stood still and quiet by the hearth as he watched Patience come to him. The lamplight in her room and the dim light from the fire gilded her beautiful nudity with a golden glow. The long muscles in her thighs lifted as she walked. The curls between her legs glinted, and her smooth stomach and dainty navel drew his eye to the curve of her waist, and then to her amazing perfect breasts—breasts crowned with thick, edible nipples that made his mouth water and his hands twitch.

His cock filled and lifted as she took her last steps and came to a stop before him. He stared into the stunning beauty of her face and brushed his fingers against her soft cheek. "Thank you for defending me to Lady Humphreys."

A frown puckered her brow. "Who told you?"

"Fitz Roy—just as I was on my way here." He clenched his jaw against his anger and embarrassment, and kept his eyes on Patience. "On the one hand, I *hate* that my circumstances require defending. But on the other"—he smoothed his hand over her hair—"the thought of you taking my side so openly makes me feel strong and invincible."

She rested her hand on his chest. "It does?"

"Yes."

"Good, because I would do it again." She laid her other hand against the tensing muscle in his jaw. "And I wasn't defending you against your circumstances, Matthew, for there is nothing there to defend. I was defending you against an evil woman's malice, for which you bear no responsibility."

Matthew stared into her clear, earnest gaze and his heart ached at her goodness, her honor, and her nobility. How would he ever deserve her—he who was shunned and on the brink of ruin—he who wrote desperate letters to music masters? He who was impure.

"You offer me comfort," he murmured, "when it is I who should be comforting you."

Patience's head tilted. "For what, Matthew?"

He threaded his hands in her hair. "My fight with Danforth had nothing to do with Rosalind." He frowned as her lashes lowered, hiding her eyes. Damn it, he should have realized how his duel with Danforth would look to some—the ladies especially. He gripped her thick curls. Her eyelids lifted. "Patience, I don't care who Rosalind marries—Danforth or the fucking King of Siam—I don't care. *You* are the only woman who matters to me. The only one." He searched her eyes. "Do you believe me?"

Her green gaze was unwavering. "Yes, Matthew. I believe you."

He let out his breath and snatched a kiss from her soft mouth. "There's one more thing," he said against her lips. "I'm sorry I didn't join you for dinner. Fitz Roy tells me that Montrose took the seat I left empty at your side." Montrose, who was popular, rich, and legitimate. Montrose, who would never need defending.

"Yes"—Patience slid her hands over his shoulders—"and his company was a poor substitute for yours." She paused. "I missed you, Matthew—your presence."

Her sweet words and the press of her body quashed the bitterness that had reared up in him. "I'm sorry," he said again. "I would rather have been with you, than where I was."

"You didn't give it back to him, did you?"

Matthew tensed and drew back. "What?"

"The mine. Lord Montrose said he was certain you would give it over to Lord Benchley. But Lords Rivers and Fitz Roy told me you won that mine in a fair game, so why should you."

Matthew looked into her beautiful and intelligent face. She would be privy to the same gossip as everyone else. He needed to be sure it was all favorable.

Patience suddenly looked uncertain. "You didn't give it back, did you? You shouldn't have to, Matthew."

God, she made him feel good—and protective. He drew his finger along her jaw. "No, I didn't." *And I won't give you back, either.*

A small smile turned her lips. "Good. Fair is fair."

Matthew's gut tightened as he swooped down to cover her mouth with his. As he kissed her, he thought of the pained declaration he had forced from her in the library. Whatever had happened to hurt her, he would discover it. He would tear down every barrier she had built, until her heart lay as naked to his view as her body was now.

Breaking the kiss, he stared into her glittering green eyes—eyes so full of urgent expectation. He would keep her and protect her, and shield her from the world's hurts. He would take care of her and give her the strong hand she craved. Then she would truly be his.

He stroked his thumb across her full lower lip.

And in return . . .

He lowered his head, and her eyes closed.

. . . she just might give me . . .

. . . something.

He stopped just short of her mouth.

Something important.

Her soft exhalation felt warm and shaky against his lips. It took all his will not to kiss her. Rather, he spoke low, his mouth barely touching hers. "Earlier, I assisted you to dress for dinner. Now you will assist me to undress." He brushed his lips against the corner of her mouth, and then along her cheek. Closing his eyes, he breathed in the smell of her—gardenia mellowed by the tender scent of her skin. He stroked his lips against her ear and felt her shiver. "And throughout your ministrations to me, you will touch me and demonstrate to me, sweetly and submissively, the extent of your desire for my attentions." Matthew drew back slowly and stared into Patience's upturned face. Her lips were parted and her cheeks flushed. His cock throbbed as her beautiful eyes flickered open. "Won't you?"

A slow blink and a small shudder preceded her answer. "Yes, Matthew."

With a groan, he swept his arms around her and, lifting her to him, he thrust his tongue possessively into her mouth. The sound of her soft moan reverberated in his ears as he tasted her and ground his cock against her pelvis. With one arm tight around her slim waist, he stroked his other hand over the curve of her hip, squeezing her buttock as he pressed her harder against him.

God, she felt both soft and firm, and he wanted to fuck her so badly. He wanted to kiss her and hold her while he pushed into her tight cunt. He wanted to break the barrier to her womb, bathe his cock in her virgin blood, and then plant his seed deeply inside her. Moaning, he tightened his grip on her firm buttock as he thrust hard against her. She shook and her fingers threaded through his hair.

But he needed to be patient—patient, yet demanding.

Patience undulated in Matthew's demanding embrace. His kisses stole her breath and the hard press of his thick, engorged penis made her cunt drip with desire. His hand squeezed her bottom, his fingers biting into her flesh. It hurt and felt good at the same time. His grip eased and then tightened again. Moaning into his mouth, she curled her fingers in his thick hair.

Yet, suddenly, she felt his arms relaxing and the pressure of his kiss easing. She gasped and tried to hold him as he pulled his mouth from hers. But he was stronger than she. Gripping her upper arms, he supported her as he held her away from him.

Patience shuddered as she gazed into his dark eyes. They were full of fire, yet his demeanor seemed completely controlled.

"That was lovely," he said gently. His brow lifted. "But you have not yet earned your pleasure."

Patience stared at him. His words both rankled and excited her. He had to know she was yearning for release. She had been obedient. Why must he make her wait? Her pulse raced and her clitoris throbbed. And why must her body thrill at the very denial that tormented her?

Her gaze dropped to his lapels. For some inexplicable reason, she found his command for her assistance to undress more difficult to comply with than his command for her sexual submission. She was perfectly willing to take his penis in her mouth, but she didn't want to take his jacket. She frowned. It made no sense. Especially when such relatively easy obedience would likely get her the orgasm she longed for.

"Tell me what you're thinking, Patience."

Matthew's low voice made her shiver. She met his dark eyes. "I don't know why, but I find your demand for assistance—difficult."

"You will find punishment far more difficult," he said calmly.

His words, resolute and remorseless, sent a spark flaring along Patience's nerves and rushing to the swollen flesh between her legs. It enflamed her and burned away her resistance, replacing it with capitulation. How did he do that? How did he inspire such surrender just with his words and his tone?

Stepping around him, moisture smeared her thighs. She reached over his shoulders and carefully helped him out of his jacket. She brushed the fine fabric with her hand as she laid it on the chair.

"No." Matthew nodded across the room. "Take it to your dressing table."

Patience bristled but then forced down the feeling. For goodness' sake, what was so difficult about that? Crossing to her dressing table, she could feel his eyes pinned to her back, magnifying her nakedness. She felt like hurrying, yet she was forced to walk slowly, for every step she took stimulated her aching sex.

Carefully, she laid his jacket over the stool. His eyes never left her as she returned to him. The aching between her legs grew worse. Did her walk seem unnatural? Did she appear graceless? Blushing fiercely beneath his steady regard, Patience finally stopped before him. Staring at his cravat, she frowned as her emotions veered in a different direction. She hated the idea that she might appear ungainly. She hated the fact that she felt embarrassment over her own nakedness. And she hated the fact that she was finding it difficult to do simple tasks. She was supposed to be striving for perfection.

"Patience."

She looked up at the warning tone in his voice.

His brow was creased by a frown. "I'm waiting."

Patience dared a frustrated sigh. She never minded lending aid when it was needed. But this was not a case of need. "Why must you demand something of me that you can so easily do for yourself?"

The expression in his eyes shifted, and his frown eased a bit. "Because it pleases me."

"Yes, but why?" She shook her head. "I never ask for help—unless I can't possibly avoid it."

"Really?" He stared at her intently for a long moment. "Why not?"

Her frown deepened. "Why not?" It seemed a pointless question. "Why would I?"

Matthew's frown twitched, and Patience shifted uncomfortably as he stared at her. "Tell me, Patience," he said low. "Did you enjoy your breakfast this morning?"

She flushed with a deepening discomfort, and with embarrassment, too. She'd forgotten to thank him. "Everything was quite delicious." She nodded. "Thank you."

Matthew shook his head. "I didn't ask you if it was delicious. I asked you if you enjoyed it. Did it please you?"

Patience's discomfort escalated. "Well, if it was delicious, I must have enjoyed it, mustn't I?" She lifted her shoulder to ease the tension there and glanced at the floor for a moment before returning her gaze to his. "It's just that normally I practice in the morning and . . ."

His brows lifted. "Oh, you don't eat breakfast?"

Patience frowned. "Well, of course I eat breakfast." She could hear the frustration in her voice. Looking away from Matthew's casually inquiring gaze, she drew a deep breath, and when she looked back at him she managed a small smile. "It's just that you needn't have gone to all the trouble."

"Trouble? What trouble is that, Patience?" His eyes dropped to her mouth. "Don't you see? You're no trouble to me." He lifted his gaze back to hers. "And even if you were, I would go to the ends of the earth to be troubled by you."

Patience drew in a breath, and she must have done it too quickly or too deeply because she felt a sharp pain in her chest. It made her eyes sting. Looking away, she exhaled and blinked back her tears. Drawing shallow breaths, she tried to relieve the ache in her chest, but it wouldn't ease. She lifted her gaze back to Matthew's. Did it help to look at him?

Or did it make it worse?

"Am I a trouble to you, Patience?" His eyes were soft as down.

Tears welled again. "No." She lowered her eyes and stroked

her hand down his waistcoat. "Of course not." Lifting her hands to his cravat, she slipped the loop. As she slowly untied the long piece of silk, she felt a tear slip down her cheek. She ignored it, for she had no idea why she was crying.

Matthew watched her as ardently as ever. She could feel his gaze. He seemed to appreciate her displays of emotion, even if she did not. She glanced up at him.

"God, but you're beautiful," he whispered. He lowered his head and nuzzled her hair.

Pulling free his cravat, Patience let her moist eyes close as he pressed his lips to her brow.

"Being tended to by you is lovely," he said between kisses. "I like to see you naked before me. I like to see your hands touching me." He pulled back to look at her and she saw that desire had infused the softness she'd seen just moments before. "Give me the cravat."

Would he tie her again? Lord, it would be so much easier—so much easier than having to do all these things—these difficult, intimate things. She draped it across his palm.

"Hold up your hair."

Her hair? She did as he asked. But then he reached through her arm and put the cravat around her neck. She stood completely still as he tied and knotted the soft fabric around her neck—snug but not too tight.

He lifted his brow. "Better?"

She looked down at the cravat falling between her breasts One long end brushed her thigh. As with her bonds the previous evening, the sight of it, and the comfortable snugness around her neck, worked some sort of calming magic upon her.

She looked up at him with a small frown. "Yes. I don't know why; but, yes, it is better."

His lips curled slightly. "There are many levels of submission Patience." His voice was gentle yet firm. "The first is passive This is what you experienced last night. Tied, you submit while give to you and take from you. This is relatively easy because you must do nothing but react and respond."

Yes. It was so much easier.

He moistened his lips. "The next level, however, is active. In this case, I do *not* tie you, and I require you to do things that please me—things that may or may not involve sex. As you have discovered, this can be more difficult. But"—he stroked his thumb across her lower lip—"only at first—only until you recognize that your misplaced pride is a hindrance to your happiness and fulfillment. Once you learn to take pride in your submission and obedience, all will be well. For now"—he touched the silk at her neck—"think of this collar as a stepping stone. You aren't tied, but it serves to remind you of your place, and the fact that I can bind you at any time I choose."

Patience listened intently. She found everything he said fascinating and stimulating. "You said 'many' levels."

Something flickered in his eyes. Lust? Excitement? "The next level entails surrendering to your punishments." His gaze probed hers. "You will do this because you will discover that punishment is good for you. Punishment keeps you soft, secure, and obedient. But punishment also strengthens you—just as tempering strengthens steel." He stroked his hand over her hair. "You will learn to love your punishments as dearly as you love your pleasures."

Patience remembered how, the night before, he had stopped stroking her when she had given him unsatisfactory answers. Her clitoris pulsed. "Have I not already experienced punishments?"

"Punishments come small and large. What you've experienced is a mere slap on the hand, my sweet." He adjusted his erection in his trousers. "Once you've suffered a proper punishment, you'll know it."

Patience's heart pounded in her breast and her quim let down a rush of moisture. What were these punishments?

"Enough conversation." Matthew held out his hand and his eyes darkened. "Put your leash in my hand. And know, as you do so, that you are subject to both my wishes and my whims."

Patience lifted the trailing piece of fabric, and then looked at Matthew's open hand. A chill raced down her back. Then she laid the silk across his palm.

"Good." He pulled her to him and pressed a soft kiss to her lips. "Now, my brandy, if you please."

Patience almost forgot that she had left it on the hearth. As she began to bend her knees, Matthew pulled on the silk. She glanced at him. His expression had a hard intensity. "Bend at the waist. And don't turn from where you now stand."

Patience felt her face flushing. She looked down at the snifter and wished she hadn't put it there. Before she could consider further, she quickly bent. Her leash fell free and, as fast as she reached the glass, Matthew was behind her, his hands caressing and squeezing her bottom. As she began to straighten, he pressed her back down. Then, with his foot, he slid her petite footstool before her. "Stay."

Patience bit her lip and reluctantly placed her palms atop the low little stool. Matthew's long fingers kneaded her flesh, squeezing it hard and grabbing it. It felt so good, but her position made her face flame with embarrassment. Still, he rubbed her and smoothed his hands over her bottom, following the outer and inner curves.

Sucking in her breath, she tried again to straighten.

Again, Matthew's hand moved to her back. "I said, stay." His voice sounded tight. Then he squeezed her bottom again, drawing a moan from her at the strength of his grip. "Does it feel good, Patience?"

"Yes," she gasped.

"But you feel embarrassed." He released her, only to grip her again. "Vulnerable."

"Yes!"

"You've no need to feel embarrassment, for I find every part of you beautiful. And there is no indignity in pleasing me, ever." His grip eased, and, closing her eyes, Patience tried to relax. "Your vulnerability, however, is something you must learn to embrace." His hands swept over the curves of her hips and her lower back. "Vulnerability will both soften and strengthen you. Not to mention"—he bent over her and kissed the curve of her back—"that it is amazingly beautiful to behold." His hands slid over her shoulder blades as he pressed another kiss along her vertebrae. "And those who can be vulnerable, despite their fears, are oh so rare." He pulled back, his hands sliding firmly along her sides. "Now, don't move."

Patience's eyes flew open and widened as Matthew crouched behind her. Despite his words, she felt like her face was on fire.

"Oh, Patience," he said thickly. "My sweet, Patience." His hands gripped her bottom again, pushing up to better expose her quim. "You're so swollen and wet."

Groaning, Patience lifted her head for a moment. Her whole sex felt like it was ballooning.

"God, I've never seen such a beautifully needy cunt. It makes my prick hurt just to look at it."

His hands left her, and looking back down, she saw him tip his knees to the floor and undo his lower trouser buttons. Then he pulled out his magnificent cock and scrotum. The thick trunk was hard, while the knob, dark and red, wept steadily. His cods looked tight and full.

Patience lifted her head and swallowed the saliva that had filled her mouth. She cried out as Matthew squeezed her bottom with one hand and jerked himself vigorously with the other. But just as quickly, he released himself and gripped her other buttock tightly. Then Patience leapt in her skin as she felt the broad stroke of his tongue near the inside of her thighs. Breathless, she trembled as he licked the moisture from her legs, then nibbled and sucked her skin. The warmth of his mouth sent her embarrassment fleeing in the face of her desire.

Softening her elbows, she bent lower. Keeping her legs straight, she pushed out her hips. Her hair brushed the ground, the muscles behind her thighs stretched, and her breasts felt heavy. As he laved her other thigh, his hips lifted toward her and his prick swayed ponderously. She couldn't resist it. Sucking in her breath, she reached between her legs and curled her hand around him.

Matthew moaned and then, as if in reward, laid his tongue in broad, wet strokes right on her aching and swollen folds. Patience groaned and shuddered, then pushed against him as she squeezed and stroked his truncheonlike cock. It felt so heavy in her hand, and she adored the cords of veins that fed its magnificence. God, what might it be like to be penetrated by such an organ?

Her cunt clenched and watered. Her heart was pounding and she felt almost frantic for release. Matthew's hands briefly eased on her buttocks, only to move and grip her hard again as he thrust his tongue between her nether lips, lapping up the wetness she couldn't stop. And all the while, her clitoris, hidden and untouched, throbbed ever more painfully.

Panting, and almost crying, Patience pushed against him, trying to reveal more of herself. His tongue thrust deeply and she could feel the rough press of his chin, but it wasn't enough. Her hips bucked, and her tears began to fall again. Suddenly she felt full of want—desperate want, old want, new want, want she'd never known she had. And her hidden, inaccessible clitoris represented all of them.

She struggled and writhed, and tried to jerk against him, but then he ran his tongue over the curve of her buttock. Groaning her anguish, she was stroking him frantically when he suddenly bit firmly into the flesh of her bottom. Patience sucked in her breath and let it out on a whimper as the sharp little pain shot straight to the aching heart of her sex, making it throb violently—making it respond though it could not be touched. Gasping, she thought the sensation would take her to release, but, instead, it hung her suspended on the brink as Matthew opened his mouth and sucked hard on the flesh of her buttock.

Patience shuddered, and tears of desperation continued to fall as Matthew suddenly pulled away. Getting quickly to his feet, he gripped her bottom a final time then kicked the footstool closer to the fire. "Stand on it," he ordered, brusquely.

She almost forgot about the brandy, but then she picked it up as she straightened. Her legs trembled with the strain of having been stretched and her bottom tingled with a delicious soreness. She could feel it, almost as if it were swollen and large. She looked at Matthew through her wet lashes as she handed him the brandy. His eyes were dark fire. As she stepped carefully onto the footstool, he quickly placed the brandy toward one end of the mantel.

No sooner had she stepped up than his hands were under her arms. "Jump," he commanded.

Jump? She could barely stand. All her energy was held prisoner between her legs. She shook her head. "I can't."

"Do it," he growled.

Patience felt more tears fall. She couldn't stop them, even as her heart beat with anticipation. Gathering her strength, she jumped, and at the same moment, Matthew lifted her.

Her bottom landed atop the wide marble mantel with a soft *thwap*. Matthew supported her for a moment then released her. Her legs dangled, but the fire had burned so low that she felt no excessive heat, and the mantel was deep enough that she was in no danger of falling. Brushing away her tears, she shook as she stared down at him.

He paced a little, stroking his cock with short, quick strokes. "Spread your legs and rest your heels on the edge of the mantel," he ordered.

Patience wanted to reveal herself, yet she suddenly didn't know if she could. But she must, mustn't she? Trembling uncontrollably, she obeyed.

Matthew's nostrils flared as he stared at her. "Bring your bottom closer to the edge and lean back against the wall."

God! Patience carefully positioned herself. Again, a hot blush heated her face. Her legs were open, her hips tipped up, and her cunt fully exposed—and she was sitting on the mantel, like a piece of art positioned for his view.

Matthew moistened his lips as he stared hard at her sex. "Christ, that's fucking beautiful," he said thickly, more to himself than to her. Finally, he raised his dark, intense gaze to hers and Patience felt her blush darken. "You will learn to be completely comfortable in your nakedness, Patience." He pulled firmly on his cods and stroked himself steadily as he spoke to her. "Many women can only bear their own nudity during the throes of their passion. You, however, will relearn what it is to be Eve. Eve, who was created to pleasure and serve her husband in all things. Eve, who was created to *be* pleasured and protected by her husband in all ways."

Her husband?

"Your nakedness is perfection," Matthew continued. "Clothing is only for covering what is mine from the world. But when we are alone together, you will learn to take pride in your nudity." Releasing his incredible phallus, he bent a stern frown upon her. "And unlike earlier, you will soon go happily about the fulfillment of my will, knowing that you do so just as God intended you—with a naked body and an obedient heart."

Yes!—just as God made Eve. Patience moaned and tilted her hips wantonly as Matthew moved away. The aching between her legs was so acute that she couldn't stop moving. She slowly rocked and gyrated her hips in an attempt to ease the excruciating want that he had been driving in her for hours. It was torturous, and her tears flowed at the intensity of her feelings, both physical and emotional. For as much as her body pined for release, her heart thrilled at her surrender.

And surrender she had—wonderful, willing, feminine surrender. She felt the sweetness of her vulnerability. She felt the comfortable snugness of her collar, and despite her sensual distress, touching herself was out of the question.

He must do it. Only him.

She followed Matthew with her eyes as he moved across the room, unbuttoning his waistcoat. He walked with an easy, yet dominant grace. Her heart skipped as she watched him. He was the lord of her pleasures, and she would have her release only when, and if, he allowed it. She must show him the extent of her longing. Perhaps then . . .

Seemingly engrossed in his own thoughts, he did not look at her as he shrugged out of his waistcoat. He laid it with his jacket and then paused before her dressing table to remove the diamond studs from his shirt. The longer pieces of his hair had fallen forward, framing his brow and temples with the wavy strands. She drew in her breath as he took off his shirt, the muscles in his chest and arms flexing. He removed his shoes and socks then his hands went to his trousers. Bending, he swept them down and laid them atop the rest of his clothes.

Patience couldn't take her eyes off him. He was so beautifully built—and so clearly comfortable in his own skin, which was golden in the dim light of the room.

Though he acted as if he'd dismissed her, his beautiful erection proved he hadn't. It lifted solid and proud before him, and when he walked back toward her, it barely moved it was so thick and hard.

As he approached, Patience tilted her hips and thrust up her quim in a silent offering and plea. She moaned at his nearness, but he didn't touch her.

Picking up his brandy, he stood back before her, sipping it as he stared at her bloated and dripping sex. "I've never seen a virgin in heat before." He moistened his lips. "Your clitoris is so full, like a ripe raspberry ready to be eaten."

Patience writhed and undulated, and gasping breaths escaped her as she demonstrated what her swollen flesh already indicated—desperate, frantic desire.

"That's good, my beauty." Matthew's features were hard with lust. "Show me. Show me how right now the only thing that matters is what's between your legs. Put away the world, and show me Eve."

He stroked his cock enthusiastically, and Patience felt her tears begin to fall again as her hips jerked and lifted. "Please, Matthew."

He raised lust-blackened eyes to hers. "What was that?"

She blinked back her tears and briefly lifted her hips entirely off the mantel. "Please, Matthew!"

His strokes quickened. "Please, what?"

She shook and bit down on her lower lip. He had said he would make her beg. "Please—help me!"

Matthew stared up at her from beneath lowered brows. "Why should I?"

"Because you're the only one who can!"

He took a step toward her, and his eyes were like fire. "Tell me that you need me, Patience."

Patience stiffened and squeezed her eyes shut. Did she surrender to desire or to need? It couldn't be need. She didn't need anyone. But then—she opened her eyes and stared into Matthew's—why did that feel like a lie now? Her chest hurt.

"Tell me," he urged.

"Yes," she breathed.

Stepping close, Matthew slid his brandy onto the mantel. He stood right before her exposed sex but his eyes held hers. "Yes, what?" he murmured.

Patience's eyes filled with hot, stinging tears, and all at once, she felt as if she might shatter into a thousand pieces. Was she so brittle? "Yes." Her voice was a choked whisper. "I need you."

His eyes closed for a moment then opened. "It's all right," he said. Reaching up, he swept the tip of his finger over one of her tears. "I need you, too." Then he spread his arms wide across the mantel and lowered his head.

Patience held her breath but then she cried out as Matthew's tongue pressed directly upon her overfilled bud. She jumped and jerked at the hot, piercing sensation. It was too much! She tried to escape. But when she scooted back, he gripped her bottom and pulled her right back to the edge of the mantel.

Patience writhed and gasped as he relentlessly laved her distended flesh. Then just when she thought she couldn't stand another moment, the excruciating edge suddenly exploded inward, suffusing her womb and then her heart with a deep and primal lust.

A long, low moan escaped her and then she thrust her cunt forward, pushing hard against Matthew's mouth. His tongue pressed against her pulsing bud, but now it wasn't enough. Thrusting her hand into his thick hair, she held him to her as she rubbed the whole of her wet woman's parts against his nose, mouth, and chin, marking him with her scent and claiming him for her own. Her heart pounded and her blood roared in her veins. Her eyes squeezed shut. She was all pleasure—all lust—a being reduced and concentrated into her most primitive and sensual self.

Yet, there was no end. Only a need for more.

Thrusting her other hand into Matthew's hair, she lifted her hips off the mantel and rutted against him in a wild frenzy. Panting and grunting, she moved faster and faster. Matthew's saliva dripped over her straining sex. His rough chin scored her swollen vulva. His fingers bit fiercely into the flesh of her bottom. Her hips thrust. Her knees pressed downward and her muscles stretched. And then everything inside her broke from the strain, and on a long, pealing cry, she shattered—parts and pieces of the woman she'd always been flying away from her. But she didn't care. For as her body and heart convulsed in the throes of her agonizing bliss, and as her orgasm poured out of her in an ecstatic rush, she realized that if she didn't need those parts for this, then she didn't need them at all.

She didn't need them because tonight she was Eve—freed from the burden of thought and inhibition, yet filled with the joyous wonder of her simple and sensual purpose.

Matthew shuddered beneath the burden of his own lust. His heart thundered and his cock felt like steel. Patience's fierce and wild surrender was too delicious. The taste of her, the smell of her, the sounds that were wrenched from her, spurred a strong and primal carnality in him.

Swallowing the last of her passionate release, he pulled back.

His cods churned at the sight of her. One heavy, corkscrewed curl hung forward over her brow, while the rest of her luscious red mane fell in untamed disarray around her pale shoulders. Her cheeks were tear-streaked and her lips moist. Her legs hung loose and open. And just beneath that rebellious curl, her eyes, half closed, were lit with a sated yet sensual fire. Matthew's blood surged. She was a vision of feminine submission. But he wasn't finished with her.

Growling low, he grabbed her leash and pulled her forward. She gasped as she fell over his shoulder, and Matthew's lust boiled as he carried her long, naked body across the room.

With one heave, he tossed her onto the bed. While the surprised cry was still passing her lips, he leapt upon her, pinning her beautiful body with his. Patience's eyes widened and a soft protest escaped her, but Matthew ignored it. Grabbing her wrists, he ground his cock against her soft thighs while he pressed hot, open-mouthed kisses to her gardenia-scented neck.

The feel of Patience's body struggling against his roused something dark and dangerous in him. Sweat broke on his brow as he fought the sudden urge to take her against her will. And acknowledging the desire only made it worse.

Biting back a snarl, he pulled up and pinned her arms over her head. "Be still!" he barked.

Patience quieted immediately and stared up at him, her green eyes shining and her breast heaving.

She was so goddamned beautiful, and he wanted to get inside her so badly. But he'd made a promise. He clenched his jaw. "Be still and cross your ankles," he said sharply.

Patience stared up at him. He could see her pulse throbbing fast in her throat and then he felt her legs move. Holding her wrists with one hand, he reached down and pushed his aching prick between her moist thighs. As the length of his cock pressed firmly against her hot, wet folds, he moaned.

Patience shivered beneath him and her lips parted on a soft gasp. Releasing her wrists and bracing his elbows on either side of her head, Matthew shifted higher, increasing the pressure his erection exerted on her swollen sex.

"Oh, Matthew." Patience bit her lip and her eyes closed.

Jesus, a slight withdrawal, a few guided thrusts, and he could claim her. He threaded his fingers in her soft, thick curls. But that wasn't how he wanted it. Her lashes fluttered. "You know I could take you right now." His voice came tight and tense as he thrust between her thighs, rubbing his heavy length hard against her. "I could shove my cock in your tight little cunt and have done with your virginity in a thrice." Patience sucked in her breath and her eyes flickered open as her hips tilted up. Matthew tightened his fingers in her hair. "But when the moment arrives, that isn't how I'm going to do it." He pumped slowly against her. "I'm going to do it gradually and carefully, because so magnificent a gift cannot be rushed."

Patience stared at him with rapt attention, and he could feel her thighs tensing. His cock throbbed a warning but, gritting his teeth, he held himself in check.

"I'm going to penetrate you slowly, Patience, so that I can enjoy every splendid moment of stretching and filling you. It won't be over in an instant. I'm going to draw it out, so that you never forget it, and so that you see how much it means to me."

Patience stared up at him and her hips jerked. Lust and submission sparkled in her eyes, but there was something else there, too—something poignant and tender.

Matthew's heart pounded and he gasped at the sudden rush of hot moisture that bathed Patience's thighs. God, he couldn't hold back any longer. She felt too fucking good. "Get used to the feel of me," he murmured thickly. "Soon you'll be bearing my weight often."

And as Patience moaned and curved her arms around him, Matthew let his passions go. Swooping down, he caught her mouth in a hard kiss, thrusting his tongue into her as he pumped his cock between her legs.

Patience panted and gasped, but he refused to release her from his kiss. Her arms tightened around him and her hips began to rut. His blood rushed and a hum started in his ears. With each strong surge beneath him, Patience enflamed him all the more. He could feel the soft wetness of her swollen vulva as he drove against her, but his body and his mind shouted for more—for supremacy and domination—for penetration.

He tore his mouth from hers just as she submitted to orgasm Her body shuddered and then her soft cry stole the last of his control. "Shit!" Jerking back onto one knee, Matthew gripped Patience's hips and flipped her onto her stomach. Pressing his cock against the firm globes of her bottom, he held it there with his thumbs as he thrust in a frenzy of ravenous and possessive desire. His heart pounded and his ears rang. Soon—soon he would have all of her! Soon she would be his, body and soul! And as he stared at the master's mark he'd left on her bottom, and watched his cock slide against her high, round cheeks, the power of his intent overcame him at last.

Throwing back his head, Matthew shouted his release as his sperm came roaring up from his cods and exploded from his prick in a hot and exultant burst. Grunting his dominance and pleasure, he let his head fall forward as he continued to spew his possession over Patience's curving back.

Patience shivered beneath the wet heat of Matthew's ejaculation. Closing her eyes and letting her hips relax, she lay quiet and unmoving. Her clitoris still pulsed dimly in the aftermath of her second orgasm and she felt as if her whole body were humming at some low, inaudible level. The silk coverlet felt soft against her cheek. She could hear Matthew's shuddered breathing and feel the press of his legs on either side of hers. She sighed as he smoothed his hands over her hips. She was completely content. So content, in fact, that she realized she couldn't remember ever having felt more so.

She frowned. How could that be true? She lived a very contented life.

Didn't she?

"What's the matter, Patience?"

She opened her eyes at the sound of Matthew's gentle voice. She could feel him moving, and, glancing back, she saw him rise and fetch his shirt. "I don't know," she murmured. "I just . . . Everything feels different."

Returning to her, Matthew used his shirt to wipe his cum from her back. Then he lay down beside her and, bracing his head in one hand, pulled her close against him with the other. His lashes flickered. "Everything feels different, you say?"

"Yes."

He stroked his fingers over her cheek. "Everything feels different, Patience, because *you* are different. And every day you shall be a little more different."

She frowned—not because she disagreed, but because she knew he spoke the truth. Her heart thumped, hard and heavy. "But what am I becoming?"

Matthew regarded her for what seemed like a very long moment. Then he blinked. "Your true self, Patience. You're becoming your true self."

She stared up at him, her chest so tight that she didn't seem able to draw a deep breath. If she was becoming her "true self," then who was she now? And who had she been?

Matthew laid his hand over her pounding heart. "You mustn't worry," he said, calming her immediately with his soft touch and voice. "It may feel strange at the moment, but the more different you become, the more you shall recognize yourself."

Patience held his stare and covered his hand with hers. "And what of you, Matthew? What are you becoming?"

His gaze grew so tender that his beautiful eyes looked like velvet. "Enraptured." He slowly lowered his mouth to hers. "I'm becoming enraptured."

Chapter Twelve

Sleeping Beauty

I sleep but my heart waketh . . .

Song of Solomon 5:2

Matthew woke slowly from a deep and comfortable sleep. Before even opening his eyes, he became aware of the warm body beside his and the faint smell of gardenias.

Patience. My sweet Patience.

Tightening his arm around her slim waist and forcing his eyelids to lift, he stared into the face of his sleeping beauty. Though it was still dark, he could see her well enough in the dim glow of the oil lamp he'd left burning on the bedside table. Lying on her back, her head was turned toward him, her cheek resting on her bright curls. Her lashes fluttered like delicate fans, and he wondered what she might be dreaming of. One of her red gold brows lifted and dropped, and then a soft sigh passed her full lips.

Matthew's chest filled with a deep contentment. This was what he wanted—to wake up beside her forever.

He drew a long breath and released it slowly. He wanted to dance a thousand dances with her. He wanted to play alongside her at a hundred musicales. He wanted to stand at her side as her acknowledged mate. And most of all, he wanted to protect and care for her, so that she never had to fear that he would ever leave her.

He lifted one of her thick curls to his nose. He needed to know what had happened with the damned music master. Had she loved him?

He hated the thought and pushed it from his mind.

It didn't matter. Whoever he was, he was gone. What mattered was that she'd made decisions about her life based on whatever he'd done to her—wrong decisions.

Even her playing was wrong. Though technically perfect, it was devoid of emotion, which was surprising considering how vehemently she claimed to love her instrument and her music. It didn't make sense. The bloody music master was surely responsible for that, too.

He looked at the pale expanse of her soft skin revealed above the sheet, and then returned his gaze to her flickering lashes. She *was* Sleeping Beauty. And while he didn't yet have the answers to the riddle of her captivity, he would. For he was bent on waking her and claiming her.

Excitement simmered in his gut. Battling down her defenses would be a great pleasure. He would be both her conqueror and her emancipator.

Carefully, Matthew rose onto his elbow. His blood coursed as he gazed down at her. "I will have you, Patience," he whispered low. "I *will* have you."

Her angel whispered into her ear, yet all she could hear were hushed bits of words. The low rush of sound caused by the movement of his wings cut his message into indecipherable fragments. But it didn't seem to matter because his embrace and the threads of his voice conveyed his message—you're safe and I'll never leave you.

"I know," Patience breathed.

She wrapped her arms around him and pressed her cheek to his shoulder. How long had it been since she had felt so sheltered? She didn't know. But once, long ago, she had lain in an embrace that reminded her of this one—warm, protective, and perfect.

She sighed as she felt the press of a kiss upon her brow, and she wanted to weep because even the kiss reminded her of one long forgotten.

But then, the strong arms of her angel began to pull slowly away. She clung to him and tried to keep him by her. "No, don't go . . ." she pleaded.

More broken whispers. But still he drew away. She felt a lingering touch, and then, just like that long ago embrace, he was gone. And just like long ago, all her comfort and happiness went with him.

The heavens disappeared from around her. She stood, alone, upon a barren hill. A breath of wind blew and she felt cold.

But there were no arms to warm her.

So she wrapped her arms tightly around herself.

Matthew wrapped the collar of his coat more securely around his neck as he looked up at the dawn sky. His breath, and that of the big bay beside him, steamed in the cold air. Fortunately, Hawkmore House and Gillyhurst, the Filbert residence, were set relatively close, with their lands stretching in opposite directions. Still, it had been over an hour's long ride to Lord Filbert's estate. Matthew checked his watch. A little after six. It had been three o'clock in the morning when he'd forced himself from Patience's sweet embrace.

His heart tightened. She'd asked him not to go, but he had decided it was better to leave her then, than to have to leave her later. He had plans for her later. Besides, if he could inconvenience Rosalind, all the better.

Rosalind. He shoved his hands in his coat pockets. He'd better get something useful out of her, for he would rather have never seen her again. Even still, he was tempted to change his mind and leave.

Behind him, a couple of ravens cawed. Turning, Matthew found them perched on the old mill wheel that hung, still and decaying, alongside the crumbling wall. A river had once fed the sad stone building, but Lord Filbert had diverted it long ago. Meadow grass now brushed the lower slats, forever touching and pushing, but forever ineffectual at bringing the mill back to life.

Matthew stared at the moldering wheel.

Patience was his river. Her very presence brought him to life—her strength, her loyalty, her goodness, and her guarded heart. She moved him and fueled him with the desire to succeed. That's why he couldn't leave this meeting. He was going to make Patience his wife, and he needed to give her everything he could—wealth, status, and security. Not poverty, contempt, and worry.

He drew back his shoulders. She would never regret choosing

him. He would give her a brilliant life. And no one, least of all Archibald Benchley, would prevent him.

In the quiet, Matthew heard the muffled canter of horses' hooves approaching. The ravens took flight with loud caws and squawks. He turned as the horses rounded the bend—Mickey Wilkes at the front and Rosalind following.

Pulling his hands from his pockets, Matthew crossed his arms over his chest and waited. It was strange. Before he received her recent note, Rosalind had receded so far from his mind that he'd hardly thought of her. Rather, it was her father who had become his fiercest enemy. But as she rode toward him, a smile on her face, he realized how much he really did hate her. Not because she'd left him—he was glad of that. But because of *how* she'd left him. Because of how she'd vilified him after leaving him. And because of how she was trying to come simpering back to him.

Mickey and she drew up. The boy dismounted and then moved to assist her when it was clear Matthew wasn't going to. Rosalind didn't say anything, but she kept her smile as she accepted Mickey's assistance and handed the lad her reins.

Regarding Matthew coyly, she closed the remaining distance between them. Her dark hair was tied back loosely at her neck and loose strands fell around her cheeks, which were reddened from the cold. Her dark eyes held a flirtatious satisfaction, and her smile deepened as she stopped before him.

He'd once found her beautiful, but now all he saw was a selfish, shallow fraud. He wished he were back in bed with Patience. He shouldn't have left her for this.

Rosalind stayed silent as Mickey collected Matthew's horse and then moved off. Matthew let his arms fall to his sides as he remembered the last time he'd seen her. It had been in her London home. She'd turned her back on him, before quietly disappearing behind a closed door. Her father had raged at him—and then had him thrown out. Yet, this morn, there was no sorrow or remorse in her expression for that day. In fact, she was looking at him as if he owed her something.

"I knew you would come to me," she said.

Matthew gritted his teeth. "Really." He entertained himself with thoughts of slapping the cocky smile right off her face. "How did you know?"

She took a step closer to him. "Because you loved me, Matt. And love doesn't disappear in four months." She looked up at him through her lashes. "Which means you still love me."

It was all he could do not to blurt out the truth—that she was right, love didn't disappear in four months. Which proved that he'd never loved her at all. He clenched his hands into fists. It only made him angrier that he'd thought he had—that even when he'd known better, he'd clung to the illusion that he loved her—and the illusion that she loved him.

He looked into her brown eyes and spoke around his hatred. "What of you, Rosalind? Do you still love me?"

She pressed her hand to her breast. "Yes, my dearest."

Liar. Goddamned liar.

"Look." She opened the neck of her cloak. "Look what I'm wearing."

Matthew stared at the sapphire necklace while ignoring the bit of bosom she artfully revealed when she opened her cloak. He'd given her the necklace as an engagement gift. He wanted to rip it off her neck. Rosalind was wearing sapphires—sapphires he'd bought for her—while Patience wore cut beads.

"Is that supposed to prove something?" He couldn't keep his lip from curling. "Because I'm afraid it doesn't. You already failed the ultimate test of love, Rosalind." He could still remember the horrified look on her face when he'd told her he was a bastard. "And then you sealed the break in writing."

"You know Father made me write that letter. I didn't want to do it."

"Yet, you *did* do it."

A pained frown twisted Rosalind's brow. "You're not being fair. I've been in such shock, Matt." Her frown deepened. "Your news was devastating, and I was very hurt by it. What woman wouldn't be?"

Patience.

"And, yes, I admit I was angry with you." She shook her head. "But can you really blame me? Mine is an old and pure line, which has had its dignity besmirched by this scandal." Her lower lip trembled. "Yet, despite the sad truth of your parentage, and despite the awful consequences that have been forced upon me as a result—still, I am here. I am here, Matt."

Christ, he hated her more with every word she spoke. "I repeat, is that supposed to prove something? Am I to feel grateful that you have deigned to dignify me with your presence?"

Tears welled in her eyes.

"Oh, stop it," he snapped.

Her expression looked truly repentant. She clasped his hand between hers and then clutched it to her breast. "Dearest, I know I hurt you. But I regret it. Really I do." She leaned close, her eyes brimming. "No one loves me like you, Matt. No one treats me like you did. How could I have known that what we had was so special, when I'd never experienced any love but yours? Oh, Matt"—she released his hand and pressed herself against him—"please, I miss you so much."

Matthew stood unmoving. She didn't miss *him*. She missed how he made *her* feel. She'd thought he would be easily replaceable, and now she felt fucking sorry for herself.

He forced himself not to hurl her away from him.

She looked up, her dark eyes glistening with a sudden sensuality. "Kiss me, Matt. Kiss me like you used to—with all your strength and passion. Just kiss me and everything will be fine."

"No." *Never.* His kisses were only for Patience now.

She stared at him for a long moment before lowering her eyes. "It's all right. I know you're angry with me. But I also know you still love me." She paused and looked up at him through her lashes. "And I know you're furious over my engagement to Danforth. I heard about the fight, dearest." The smallest of smiles turned her lips. "And while I admit that the thought of you fighting over me is thrilling, you must never, ever be jealous of him. Promise me you won't be."

Matthew wasn't sure if he wanted to laugh or spit in her face. He did neither. "Very well, I promise."

Her small smile faded only to be replaced with a resentful frown. "Danforth is such a dimwit. But soon I shall be a countess in my own right, and I'll do what I want."

He stared at her for a moment and couldn't resist forcing her to show her true colors. "Or, we could go to Gretna Green right now."

A flash of shock and then dismay showed in her eyes.

Matthew held back a sardonic smile.

"But . . ." She looked down, and when she looked back up at him her expression was full of regret. "I wish we could, Matt—I truly do. But Father is completely against you. He would disown me. I wouldn't get a penny." She touched his cheek. "And who knows what *your* future holds."

"Yes, who knows?" *Patience.*

"But if I marry Danforth, as loathsome as it will be, I will get his title. And I'll keep my money." Rosalind gave him a small hopeful smile. "Dearest, I could even find a way to help you if you ever needed it. You know, financially." Her smile deepened. "Wouldn't *that* get Father's goat. Of course, I could never let him know."

"Of course not." *Because you're a lying cheat.*

"But the important thing is that we will be together, dearest—secret lovers forever." She pulled him close. "Oh, Matt, it will be so wonderful and exciting. And Father and Danforth will never know."

"No, never." *Because it'll be a cold day in hell before I ever become your lover.*

She pulled back and covered a giggle with her hand. "Father is so angry that Danforth lost that mine to you. You should hear him. He's still raging about it."

At last. "Is he?"

"Yes. Do you know, he practically threw Danforth across the room when he found out? He called him an imbecile, and accused him of 'ruining everything.' "

Matthew tensed. "Really?"

Rosalind's expression shifted to one of concern. "Oh, I'm sorry, dearest." She pulled him close. "I shouldn't be speaking about this." She gripped his arms and brushed her cheek against his chest. "But I want you to know that if Father does succeed in taking over GWR, that I don't care. No matter what, I want to be with you always. And I want . . ."

Matthew stood frozen as Rosalind's voice faded.

Taking over GWR? Benchley wanted to take over GWR? Benchley wanted to fucking take over Grand West Railway?

Matthew's body stiffened with rage. Yes, of course he did, the goddamned son of a bitch! Benchley need only starve GWR and wait. After all, barring any brilliant escape, it would have just been a matter of time before Matthew could no longer sustain the railway's losses. Stockholders would have dumped their shares, and he, a bankrupt, would have been forced from the board. Then Benchley, and likely the other large mine owners as well, would have swept in to save the day. And in one fell swoop, Matthew would have been thoroughly ruined, whilst Benchley would have acquired GWR for a fraction of its value.

Matthew felt as if his blood were boiling. Benchley was to have been his father-in-law for Christ's sake. Yet the man was not only plotting Matthew's ruin, but, simultaneously, his own ascension—upon Matthew's back and in pursuit of Matthew's throne!

Matthew clenched his jaw in an attempt to contain his wrath. Benchley's villainy, it seemed, had no bounds. What else was the man capable of? Matthew curled his fingers into fists. He couldn't afford to find out. He must destroy Benchley completely. He had a future to protect—a future with Patience.

"Matt, dearest, are you listening to me?"

Matthew stared down at Rosalind, and his anger was almost as much for her as for her father. "I have to go soon."

Rosalind's expression turned to one of surprise. "But I only just arrived. I thought—well, I thought we might spend some time together."

Matthew turned her toward the mill path. "Another time, perhaps. I can't stay today . . ."

Why hadn't he stayed with her?

Patience stretched her arms across the bare sheets where Matthew had lain. For the second night in a row, she'd fallen asleep with him at her side yet awakened alone. She didn't like finding him gone. For some reason, it made her sad.

She wanted to wake and see his strong angel-face beside her. She wanted to be able to reach for him and feel the comforting warmth of his presence. She wanted . . .

Her chest suddenly felt tight, like she might cry. Lord in Heaven, she'd cried more in the past two days than she'd cried in years.

Annoyed by her emotions, she jerked away from the empty

spot beside her and turned onto her other side. Right before her, on her bedside table, was one of her small note cards propped against a candlestick. Her heart quickened as she picked up the note.

My Sleeping Beauty ~

I kissed you, but you did not wake. I find this strange for I know I am your prince. Later, I shall kiss you again . . .

I'm thinking of you, always,

M

P.S. I've left breakfast for you. Be obedient and eat it.

A smile turned Patience's lips as she read the last line, and then she read the note all over again—and again. Such a brief little note, yet it banished her ill humor completely.

Sitting up, she saw the breakfast tray by the hearth. A silver dome hid the contents. Considering her ungratefulness for the previous day's breakfast, she was surprised that he had brought her another. But she also felt exceedingly happy that he had. Happy and—and, well—happy.

Hurriedly scooting out of bed, she crossed to the hearth and peeked beneath the dome. A poached egg, toast, and tiny sausages were prettily arranged beside a baked apple. The plate was still very warm. He could not have left it long ago.

She inhaled the smell of cinnamon. Would he have stayed and breakfasted with her if she'd awakened to his kiss? That would have been nice.

Replacing the lid, she crossed to her dressing table. As she opened the small drawer on the left, she read the note one more time, pausing on the words "for I know I am your prince."

Her heart fluttered.

Her prince?

Was he?

Clearly, he thought so.

Yet she'd been certain there was no prince for her. She'd been certain she would reign over her life alone—certain that she needed no one.

She brushed her thumb across the cleanly penned letters as a small frown turned her brow. Only, last night, she had admitted she needed him. And he had confessed a need for her. Her frown deepened. But what did they need each other for? Pleasure and physical fulfillment? Clearly, there was that.

But there was more. She felt it at the deepest moments of her submission—a profound peace and comfort. And happiness—sweet and undiluted.

She felt it at other times, too—as when they'd danced together, and when she'd seen him leaning against the doorway at the musicale. And when he said things. Those startling, wonderful things she would never forget. And now, when he wasn't even with her—but was thinking of her.

She slipped the note in her drawer along with the folded slip of paper that had graced her breakfast tray the day before. Lifting her gaze, she looked at the reflection of her torso in the dressing table mirror. Bringing one hand to her breast, she smoothed her other hand along the curve of her waist. Were they destined for each other—for a life together? Her hands trembled and her heart beat fast at the thought. Was that the inevitable something she had sensed from the first moment she'd seen him?

That would mean all her certainties were wrong. How could that be? How could that be when she'd been so sure, so decided?

Turning slowly, she let her gaze wander down the curve of her waist to her bottom. Her eyes widened and, looking over her shoulder, she turned more. Pale little bruises dotted the skin of her buttocks, and a larger, darker love-bite sat on the curve of her left cheek. Her clitoris pulsed and a sigh passed her lips. The sight pleased and excited her. Like the fading love-bite on her thigh, it was a small view of her submission—tangible proof of something sweet, yet secret—tangible proof of Matthew's strong touch upon her.

She smoothed her hands over her bottom, gently pressing the pale bruises. She barely felt them, and wondered at why that was disappointing. As she continued to stare at the small marks, she realized that the sight of them made her feel proud and protected. But while she could recognize her feelings, she could not explain them.

She sighed as a small frown turned her brow. Was this the woman she was becoming? One with strange, inexplicable emotions that made no sense?

She turned and stared at her cello case. How could she trust such odd emotions? Was she being blinded by the intense experience of her submission?

She frowned. Or was it, rather, that her eyes were being opened?

Lately, everything seemed to be working in opposites. Submission was power. Vulnerability was strength. Bonds were freeing. There was pleasure in punishment.

Her frown deepened as she stared hard at her cello case.

And old truths felt like lies.

How he hated telling lies.

Matthew leaned back in his desk chair and shoved his fingers through his hair. Rosalind merited the fullest expression of his honest loathing and disgust. But, instead, he had participated in a revolting exchange that, in the end, had left him feeling unclean.

Even though Rosalind had provided him with valuable information—information that had increased his determination to destroy Archibald Benchley—he still could not get rid of the feeling that he had somehow tainted himself.

He frowned. When he'd returned and found Patience still sleeping, he had thought to wake his Sleeping Beauty with a kiss. Only she had not awakened. It stuck him now that it was as if his kiss were not pure enough—as if he were not worthy to be her prince, strong and true.

His frown deepened. It was a silly thought. A fanciful thought.

But he couldn't shake it.

A knock on the door interrupted Matthew's thoughts. He called for admittance, and Mickey Wilkes sauntered in.

Matthew indicated the chair across from his desk. "I'm sorry to have awakened you so early this morning."

Mickey sat. "Tha's a'right, Mr. 'Awkmore. I's a'ways up fer a early mornin' ride."

"Pinter's riding lessons have served you well. No one would know that you only recently learned."

"Thank ye." Mickey smiled. "I really enjoy th' ridin', I do. And me mum were so surprised when I rode right up t' 'er 'ouse las' month. She were out milkin' our cow, Molly. An' she thought I were some fancy trav'ler stoppin' fer a cup." Mickey winked. "Didn't e'en recon'ize 'er own son, she didn't."

Matthew nodded as he jotted a brief note on a piece of his stationery. "A few lessons in etiquette, and you could pass for quite the young gentleman."

"Really, Mr. 'Awkmore?"

Matthew raised his eyes to Mickey. "Yes, really. Get me what I need and I'll see that you get those lessons."

Mickey smiled. "I will, Mr. 'Awkmore. I will indeed." He leaned forward. "So, did ye get wha' ye wanted, this mornin'? Are ye goin' back wit' th' lady?"

"Hell, no." Matthew frowned as he shoved the note in an envelope. "Rosalind Benchley is merely a means of getting information—a necessary evil in my war with her father. I'd rather never see her again. Which is why you need to hurry up and get me something I can use."

Mickey grinned. "I mus' say, I's 'appy to 'ear you ain't goin' back to th' lady what lef' ya."

"Are you?"

Mickey shrugged. "Well, yeah. I jus' cain't respec' a man 'oo goes grovelin'. 'Sides, yer rich an' yer a'right t' look at. Ye'll find yerse'f a new lady in no time."

Matthew lifted his brows as he put his seal on the envelope. "Rich" was relative. "I've actually already found the one who shall be mine."

"Yeah?" Mickey leaned forward. "Good fer you, Mr. 'Awkmore. Wha's she like? Pret'y?" He raised his brows. "Fair or dark?"

"None of your business." Matthew opened his desk drawer and took out the letter to Cavalli. "All you need to know is that the lady's name is Miss Patience Dare. Since I plan for her to be in my company often, I'm certain you shall meet her at some point. When that happens, say nothing of the Benchleys." He tapped the letter on the desktop. "For I'm of the strong opinion that she would not approve."

Mickey nodded. "I got it, Mr. 'Awkmore. Me lips are sealed. Mum's th' word. Devils couldn't drag i' out o' me."

"Very good." Matthew slid the note to his jeweler and the letter to Cavalli across his desk. The moment his fingers left the latter, he almost grabbed it back. But then he envisioned Patience, asleep beside him, as she'd been that morning. His heart thumped. He couldn't let her go. She would wake to his kiss. And she would be his.

He looked back at Mickey as he was picking up the two missives. "You will take the next train to London. Before you do anything else, deliver the letter to Maestro Cavalli at the address written on the front. Then, take the note to Smithfield and Sons Jewelers. You may get directions for both at the train station. Once you've finished those errands, return to Benchley Hall and get me what I need. I have it from Rosalind that they have no plans to be there anytime soon, so it's the perfect opportunity for you to do some deep digging. In the meantime, I have business to attend to; so I will keep you informed of my whereabouts by messenger. Now"—he pulled out his cash box—"let's discuss how we'll handle the finances of this venture. Bribes may be necessary."

"They might be." Mickey grinned. "Tho' I's very persuasive, 'specially wit' th' ladies."

Matthew watched his letter to Cavalli disappear, along with the note to his jeweler, into Mickey Wilkes's breast pocket. He, too, could be persuasive.

He would persuade Patience that he *was* her prince—for now and forever.

Chapter Thirteen

The Hunt and the Capture

. . . behold, he cometh leaping upon the mountains, skipping upon the hills.

Song of Solomon 2:8

"The sky is far too dark today, my dear. I think it very ill advised of you to attend the hunt. Why don't you stay at home with us?"

Patience turned from the window where she had been looking at the clouds overhead. She crossed to Aunt Matty and Passion, who were sitting comfortably before the family drawing room fire eating their breakfasts. Patience poured her aunt a fresh cup of tea. "I'll be fine, Aunt Matty. What's a little water, after all?"

"My dear, if it were just water I would have no worries. But it is sure to storm. What if you catch a cold? What if your horse becomes skittish and throws you? Oh"—Aunt Matty's eyes widened—"what if you're struck by lightning? Passion, tell her what happened to my good friend, Mrs. Nobhew."

Passion smiled at their aunt. "But, Aunt Matty, I don't know what happened to Mrs. Nobhew. I don't even know who Mrs. Nobhew is."

Aunt Matty looked worriedly at Passion but then patted her hand. "Dearest, I'm afraid your delicate condition has started to affect your memory, for I am quite certain that I told you all about my good friend, Mrs. Nobhew."

Passion nodded. "I'm sure you're right. Forgive me."

"Always, my dear. And, of course, I shan't say a word to Mrs. Nobhew about your completely forgetting her harrowing story." Aunt Matty sipped her tea. "And if I do say a word, I shall be certain to explain the reason for your forgetfulness, which is, after all, completely understandable."

Patience shook her head and exchanged an exasperated glance with her sister. At this rate, it would be noon before they discovered what had happened to Mrs. Nobhew. "Well for goodness' sake, Aunt Matty, tell us what happened."

Aunt Matty frowned up at her. "Really, Patience, you would do well to exercise the attribute for which you were named. Heavens, let me catch my breath a moment, will you?"

Patience crossed her arms over her chest while her aunt made a show of clearing her throat. Passion hid her smile behind a spoonful of baked apple.

"Gracious, look at the time," Patience said casually. "I suppose I should be going."

"So," Aunt Matty immediately continued, "as I was saying about Mrs. Nobhew. Just last month she accompanied her son and his family for a picnic in the park. They were having a splendid time until a sudden storm came up. Well, in their haste to leave, no one considered the dangerous ramifications of packing the silverware beneath Mrs. Nobhew's seat."

"Good Lord." Patience raised her brows at her sister, unsure whether their aunt's story was going to go down a serious or an amusing path.

"Good Lord, indeed," Aunt Matty said dramatically. "Imagine their shock and dismay when a ferocious bolt of lightning came down right behind my good friend, Mrs. Nobhew, electrifying the picnic utensils to such a degree that, right before the horrified eyes of her entire family, every hair on Mrs. Nobhew's head sprang into curl!" Her eyes widened. "Including, even, her eyebrows!"

Patience and Passion both looked at her for a brief moment before breaking into laughter.

Aunt Matty frowned at them sternly. "This is no laughing matter, girls. It's positively dreadful. You should see her—tufts of wiry curls sticking out in every possible direction. She can't do a thing with them. And the last time she invited me to tea, my eye was constantly drawn to her eyebrows, which, no matter how I tried to tell myself otherwise, looked like two fuzzy caterpillars creeping across her brow. It was terribly distracting."

Choking with laughter, Patience held her aching side and leaned over the back of a chair as her sister covered her face with her hands, her shoulders shaking with silent hilarity.

Aunt Matty sipped her tea whilst waiting for them to contain themselves, which they did fairly quickly despite a couple of relapses.

Aunt Matty raised her own silvered brows. "If you two are quite finished, I shall return to my point."

"Which is?" Patience asked, trying to keep from laughing.

"Which is that lightning can have a frightful effect upon the hair, and possible contact with it should be avoided at all costs."

Patience swallowed her laughter. "But Aunt Matty, my hair is already curly."

"Exactly. So it stands to reason that lightning would have the opposite effect upon you, causing your magnificent curls to fall completely straight and limp. Now wouldn't *that* be a disaster?" She sipped her tea. "I tell you, Patience, you simply *must* stay at home."

Just as Patience was preparing her rebuttal, Passion spoke. "Perhaps Aunt Matty is right, darling." Her sister paused. "Of course, Matt will be quite disappointed. I believe he was hoping to ride with you." Passion shrugged. "But I think Aunt Matty has a good point. The safety of your curls is far more important."

Aunt Matty put down her teacup with a clatter and cleared her throat. "Gracious, Passion, you really mustn't coddle her so." She turned to Patience. "I tell you, my dear, you simply must attend the hunt. What do you mean even thinking of not going?" She sniffed. "What's a little water, after all?"

Patience frowned. She appreciated her sister's assistance, but she was also annoyed by her aunt's blind determination to push Matthew and her together. "But what about the lightning?"

Aunt Matty looked at her as if she'd lost her mind. "I hardly think you'll be packing picnic utensils in your saddle, hence you have nothing whatsoever to worry about, my dear. Go, and have a wonderful time."

Patience rested her hands on her waist. "Matthew and I are not going to get married, Aunt Matty."

"You're not? Well then who are you marrying?"

"I'm not marrying anyone—not Matthew, not anyone! You must put the notion from your mind immediately."

Aunt Matty shook her head. "I'm sorry, but I simply can't put notions from my mind so quickly. You'll have to wait."

"I'm serious, Aunt Matty."

"Well, so am I!" Aunt Matty pushed aside her tea and frowned. "I do not understand you, Patience. Why do you persist in eschewing the very roles for which God created you? Do you think you know better than He what will make you happy? Do you think your woman's heart and your woman's womb are irrelevant?"

Patience stood stiffly before her aunt. "You cannot deny that some women are ill suited for marriage and motherhood."

"I don't deny it. But whatever do those unfortunate creatures have to do with you? You will make an excellent mother. Look at the children at the church school. They admire and respect you because you are both firm and fair. And as for marriage—well, I told you just yesterday that you, my dear, are a peach." Aunt Matty paused and then raised her brows. "A peach is soft, sweet, and juicy. A peach is meant for eating. And because it is so soft, sweet, and juicy, it is a great tragedy when a peach is *not* eaten. For it is only by being eaten that it can truly fulfill its purpose—which is to be loved and adored for how soft, sweet, and juicy it is."

Patience stared at her aunt and her chest felt a little tight. Despite her strict demeanor with the children at the church school, she did care deeply for them. However, most of the time, she didn't feel very soft, sweet, or juicy. She glanced at her sister and found that Passion was regarding her intently. She turned back to her aunt. "But what if you're wrong? What if I'm not a peach, Aunt Matty?"

"Humph, believe me, you are. And Matthew Hawkmore is desperate to pluck you from the branch. I hear wedding bells whenever he draws near."

Marriage to Matthew? Patience's heart skipped then raced nervously. He may want her to stay with him for a time, but he'd specifically said that he wasn't interested in her hand. She shook her head. "Matthew Hawkmore is no more interested in marriage than I am."

"Oh, of course he is. Heavens, Patience, for such a bright girl, you can be so very obtuse."

Patience frowned and looked to her sister. "Will you say something, please?"

"All right." Passion met her gaze. "I, too, believe you're a peach."

Patience's brows lifted with surprise. "What?"

"There," Aunt Matty said superciliously.

Passion leaned forward. "As for Matt"—her gentle eyes looked so certain—"he's a good and decent man—a man who, I believe, longs to be yours."

Mine?

Passion smiled softly. "I see how he looks at you, darling—with such tender intensity. Last night at the musicale, everyone saw."

Patience stood tense. Was everything turning topsy-turvy? She had a plan for her life—one that did not include peaches and marriage. Yet her aunt and her sister seemed to see things differently. And most unsettling of all, she seemed to be seeing things differently, too.

Why?

Because you *are different. And every day you shall become a little more different. But you mustn't worry, for the more different you become the more you shall recognize yourself.*

Patience frowned. She'd believed it last night, and it only seemed truer and truer. How could Matthew, who knew her so little, be so right? And how could she, who knew herself so well, be so wrong?

Her frown deepened. She hated being wrong. There was something very uncomfortable and inconvenient about it. She lifted her chin as she looked at her sister. "Thank you for mentioning the musicale." She turned to Aunt Matty. "I am reminded that we shall soon be leaving for London and Cavalli. I hope you will be ready when the time comes."

Aunt Matty rolled her eyes and shook her head. "Oh, Patience. What's more important? Another music lesson or your eternal happiness?" She lifted one silver brow. "Cavalli or Matthew?"

Matthew.

Patience clenched her hands into fists. "This is ridiculous. Matthew isn't interested in marriage. He told me so himself." She picked up her gloves from the table. "Now, I must go. Or I shall surely miss the hunt."

Patience hurried to leave, but before she could close the door, she heard Aunt Matty's voice.

"Rotten peaches. I shall never forgive myself if she becomes rotten peaches."

Frowning, Patience shut the door a bit harder than was necessary and then strode down the hall. Matthew didn't want to marry. He'd said so. But then—she pulled on her gloves as she walked—he'd also written in his note that he was her prince.

What did that mean?

She turned the corner that led away from the family quarters. Likely nothing. It was just a whimsical note, meant to be fun and frivolous. It had no special meaning, no import. It was just a note—

Her thoughts careened to a halt as her brisk entrance into the third-floor foyer brought her face-to-face with the Lady Humphreys and her constant companions.

The marchioness raised her brows haughtily and gave Patience a head-to-toe once-over. She turned to one of her friends. "Do you remember, Amelia, the stunning habit that Lady Rosalind wore to this hunt last year?" Her friend nodded mutely. "If memory serves," the marchioness continued, "it was a rich olive color, embellished with gold braid and gold buttons. So much more subdued and tasteful than the *common* colors"—she looked pointedly at Patience—"like blue."

Patience gripped her sapphire velvet skirts. She was in no mood to spar with the Lady Humphreys. "If memory serves, my lady, you were adorned in blue just last eve. So if you are concerned about looking common, perhaps you should see to your own wardrobe. Excuse me."

With that, Patience brushed past the ladies and quickly descended the stairs. She frowned. Her response had lacked brilliance, but it was the best she could do under the circumstances. Pausing halfway down the stairs, she let her eye flicker over the scene below. In their red hunting jackets, the gentlemen were bright dots and clusters in the loitering crowd. But she didn't see Matthew's broad shoulders and gold-tipped hair—no dark, penetrating eyes. Why was he never there when she wanted him? Her frown deepened. Why must she want him at all?

Hurrying down the rest of the stairs, she turned in the opposite direction of the milling crowd and moved toward the rear of the house. She felt cross, tense, and off-kilter. Her boot heels briskly tapping the floor, she passed several rooms. She didn't even know where she was going, she just wanted . . .

"Patience."

She froze, and her heart raced. His voice had come from the room she'd just passed. Her ill humor urged her to keep walking, but she couldn't do it. Turning slowly, she found Matthew standing just inside the doorway, his beautiful eyes fixed upon her. Dressed in a red jacket, fawn breeches, and black riding boots, he was too handsome for words.

Her body quivered and her breath grew short as she stared into his sweet and tender gaze. The gaze that made her feel like running into his embrace and never leaving. The gaze that made her want to hope.

She tensed. Hope was dangerous. Hope was not to be indulged. Better just to enjoy what was than to hope for what would never be.

Patience's thoughts were interrupted as a tall boy appeared at Matthew's side.

"Christ in 'eaven," the boy gasped, his eyes widening as he stared at her.

Matthew raised his brows as he stepped forward and drew Patience into the room. "Miss Dare, please allow me to present Mr. Mickey Wilkes."

The boy swept off his cap, revealing straight black hair that fell forward around his face. "Lady," he said reverently.

Patience tried to shake off her mood. The lad had a boyish handsomeness and intelligent eyes. She mustered a small smile. "I'm not a 'lady,' Mr. Wilkes, I'm just a 'miss.' "

Mickey Wilkes crumpled his hat in his hand as he shook his head. "Fergive me fer disagreein', Miss Dare, but you—you could ne'er be *'jus'* anythin'. I mean, you"—he looked her up and down before returning his gaze to hers with a shake of his head—"you—yer *everythin'*."

Patience gave him another small smile. "Thank you, Mr. Wilkes."

He smiled. "Thank *you,* Miss Dare."

Matthew shook his head. "All right then, off with you, Lancelot. You've got dragons to slay."

Mickey frowned. "Oo's Lanc'lot?"

"A valiant knight," Patience offered.

"Who poached on another man's woman," Matthew added, giving the boy a glare. "Now get about your business."

Patience's blood warmed. Was she Matthew's woman? How could she be, when she would soon be leaving him?

Don't leave him.

The boy's frown deepened as he flipped his hat back on his head. "Yeah, a'right." His brow cleared as he turned to Patience. "Fergive me fer takin' me leavc so sudden like, Miss Dare. I look fo'ward to 'aving me day brigh'ened again soon by yer beau'eous face." He smiled and, though there probably weren't more than three years between them, he suddenly looked very young. "Good'ay, Miss Dare."

Patience nodded. "Thank you, again, Mr. Wilkes. And good day."

As the lad walked off, Patience returned her gaze to Matthew.

His dark eyes moved over her in an intense perusal. "Close the door," he ordered quietly.

Patience's heart leapt with excitement, but in the very next moment her petulance flared. She stood there, unmoving, as her peevishness fought with her desire. Then, annoyed with her own indecisiveness, she squared her shoulders and turned to close the door.

When she turned back, Matthew was walking to his desk. Sitting against the facing edge, he crossed his long legs at the ankles and folded his arms over his chest. Though the room was dim due to the grayness of the day, she could see that, as always, his dark gaze moved slowly over her. The tips of her fingers tingled.

"You're beautiful," he said softly. "Pluto could never have resisted a Persephone such as you." He paused. "Come here."

Patience shivered at the sound of his voice, and she took a step forward before she was able to stop herself. But then she stood, stiff with the effort to remain rooted. She didn't have to obey. "You come to me," she said stiffly.

Matthew's handsome mouth turned up a little at the corners, and he shook his head. "Really, Patience. That's a rather small stand to make, isn't it?"

She frowned and suddenly felt a little foolish, which only served to vex her more. "Nonetheless, it is my stand."

"Do you often stand against your own wishes—and such simple ones?"

Patience clenched her jaw and hated that he spoke the truth.

When she didn't answer, his brows lifted. "I know you want to come to me. Look at you, all tense and rigid with the effort not to. It does not please me to see you like this, Patience."

God, she began to fear that she had embarked upon a losing battle. "Then put an end to my tension and come to me."

He braced the heels of his palms against the edge of the desk. "You know I won't do that."

"Why not?" Her voice sounded so tight. "As you said, it's only a small stand. Surely you can indulge such an insignificant request?"

"No." He held her with his steady gaze. "And don't try to manipulate me by equating smallness with insignificance. You're testing me—over something small and petty—but the test itself is not insignificant."

Patience bristled at the words *small* and *petty*.

"You think that if I come to you, you will have won some battle. You think you'll feel better about the emotions that are rising up in you. Perhaps it will even prove that the last two nights were all wrong."

Yes! Patience swallowed the lump in her throat.

"But the truth is that the battle you're fighting isn't with me, it's with your pride and your old, mistaken notions. I am not your enemy. I am the ally of your true self. But if I give in to your 'insignificant request,' I will have deserted you. You'll feel a fleeting victory, only to be followed by monumental disappointment."

God, was that true? She stared into his dark, unflinching gaze.

"Don't worry," he murmured. "I won't fail you."

Patience drew a choked breath as relief, and the realization of what that relief meant, flooded her at the same moment. God in Heaven, what was happening to her?

"Now"—he planted his feet apart and laid his hands atop his muscular thighs—"save this disobedience for something that truly taxes you and come to me."

She paused as the last of her resistance made a weak stand.

He slowly held his hand out, palm up.

Patience's heart pounded in her breast. *Just go to him. You want to.*

In only a moment, her hand was in his and he'd drawn her between his long legs. She stared into his dark, heavily lashed eyes. This was better. It felt so good to be near him.

"What are you thinking now?" he asked.

"I'm thinking of how much nicer it is to be near you, than far from you."

His expression softened. "Kiss me, Patience."

Patience felt her whole body ease as she slipped one hand behind Matthew's nape and curved the other along his jaw. Tilting her head, she pressed her parted lips eagerly against his mouth. Though he remained still and didn't kiss her back, she knew he would soon relent. Again and again she touched her mouth to his, tasting him and nibbling the fullness of his lower lip. She saw his eyes close, and he sighed softly as his head tipped back. Her desire flaring, Patience pressed supple, open-mouthed kisses along his chin and jaw. The smell of his vetiver-scented skin intoxicated her.

Finally, with a low moan, he brought his mouth to hers, capturing her in a deep, possessive kiss. His tongue thrust and his arms pulled her tightly against him. Patience's blood rushed to her core and filled the needy little heart that pulsed between her legs.

She curled her fingers in the short hair at his nape and leaned into him as he stroked his tongue over hers. His hand pressed against the layers of her skirts in an attempt to draw her hips closer. This—this urgent embrace—was what she had longed for upon waking.

She gasped into his mouth as she felt his hand upon her breast. Her nipples tightened behind her stays and tingled against the press of her garments.

"Touch me," Matthew said against her lips. "Touch me and feel how much I want you."

Reaching between them, Patience pressed her hand against the thick column of his erection. He moaned against the corner of her mouth, and her clitoris pulsed as a sudden rush of moisture wet her thighs. God, she loved the feel of him. He was so hard and so big around that she wondered at how she was able to take so much of his thickness into her mouth. Curling her fingers around him firmly, she grew wetter as he thrust repeatedly against her grasping hand.

Her breathing quickened, and, yet again, she found herself wondering what it would be like to feel him pushing between her legs. Her cunt clenched and throbbed.

His arm tightened around her and his voice came by her ear. "Does the feel of my cock make you wet and hungry?"

"Yes," Patience gasped. She cupped her fingers around his swollen cods and arched against him.

Matthew groaned and pressed harder against her as he squeezed her breast. "Does the feel of it make you long for release?"

"Yes. Yes!" Patience squirmed as her clitoris began to pulse in earnest.

Matthew continued to thrust against her hand. His breath tickled her as he bit tenderly, yet firmly, upon her earlobe. "Do you want me to give you release now?"

Her body trembled with desire. "Yes."

"Are you desperate for it now?"

"Yes!"

Patience bit back a cry as Matthew suddenly whirled her around and bent her back on the desk. He was between her legs and, despite the many layers of her skirts, she could feel the press of his body against her most tender need. Her hips tilted and she gripped the lapels of his jacket. *Yes!*

Bent over her, his handsome features were tight. "But I say no."

It took a moment for his words to register in Patience's mind. She froze. "What?"

His dark eyes regarded her intently. "I said no. I'm afraid you must be punished for your disobedient little outburst."

Patience's eyes widened in disbelief. "You don't mean it."

"Of course I mean it. Did you think there would be no repercussions?" Matthew raised his brows as he drew back from her. "My sweet Patience, your disobedience will always be punished. I was lenient with you last night, but it is time you begin to learn your lessons."

Patience bolted to a seated position as hot anger roared

through her. She could see his erection, thick and strong. Her clitoris pounded. "I demand satisfaction," she said fiercely.

Matthew straightened his jacket. "You will demand nothing. For if you do, you will get nothing."

Patience felt her cheeks burning with fury and resentment. "Very well," she snapped as she grabbed at her skirts. "I shall satisfy myself."

Matthew leveled his dark gaze on her. "Lay one finger between those lovely legs, and I will put you over my knee and give you the spanking of your life."

Patience drew back in shock, even as her clitoris palpitated. She narrowed her eyes. "You wouldn't dare."

"Oh, I most certainly would."

Patience held his dark stare, but she couldn't detect the slightest note of jest or insincerity. She pushed herself off the desk and put her hands on her waist. "You'd really do it, wouldn't you?"

"Not only *would* I do it, I *will* do it."

Patience stood completely vexed and speechless as the distant cry of the horn called the guests to the hunt.

Matthew ran his hands through his hair and brushed a speck of lint from his sleeve. "We should be going. Do you need a moment to compose yourself?"

"Do I—?" Shaking her head, Patience cut herself off and stomped past Matthew. Yanking open the door, she threw it open and then slammed it behind her.

There. She lifted her chin and strode down the corridor. *All composed.*

With his topper under his arm, Matthew lifted his chin and straightened his cravat as he descended the stairs to the main floor. He smiled as he thought of Patience—her sweet resistance, her brief capitulation, and her ill-humored exit. Poor thing, she really was in need of some serious punishment. His blood rushed. Today, he would accommodate her. Today, he would have time with her. His heart felt full. Today, they would have time *together*.

Stepping out onto the front portico, Matthew found the wild chaos that always preceded a hunt. People and horses were everywhere. Half the guests were mounted, half not, while the stable boys rushed to supply appropriate mounts for those who had not brought their own. The horses pranced and whinnied in their excitement, while the hounds spoke loudly to the proud Master of the Foxhounds. The whipper stood by and the terrier man barked sharp orders to the sprightly fox terriers, which he kept on a short lead. Hunt servants, already mounted, milled about at the rear of the throng. Required to aid the less experienced riders by opening gates and offering ways around hedges, they were also to help riders stay on course. Nonetheless, despite the hunt servants' best efforts, many guests would get lost. It was a circumstance that suited his plans perfectly. He spotted Patience in the throng and let a small smile turn his lips. She was mounted on the very mare he had instructed Jimmy to saddle for her. He pulled on his gloves. It was going to be a *very* good day.

Setting his topper on his head, Matthew trotted down the wide steps of the portico and headed for the front of the crowd. As he passed amongst the guests, he was well aware of the ebb and flow of murmurs that followed him. He ignored them. Earlier, as he'd passed the library, he'd seen several important personages, including Lord Wollby, scanning the newspaper. They could not have missed the business page headline: *Grand West Railway Wins The Bet And Beats The Odds*. The article had credited him personally with the acquisition of Gwenellyn, and gone on to speculate that if GWR could successfully mine its own coal and reduce rail costs in the process, more rail companies were sure to follow in GWR's footsteps. *Certainly*, the article had observed, *this would change the face and power structure of these two monumental industries*.

It was a bloody marvelous article. One that would surely cause a shift in the tenor of the gossip surrounding him—if it hadn't already.

Matthew tipped his hat as he passed the Countess of Mayfield and her daughter. The ladies smiled and so did he. If he could pull this off, it would revolutionize the rail business. Matthew cocked his brow. And all because the Earl of Benchley had chosen to be a son of a bitch.

Matthew found his brother with the other experienced riders who would lead the chase—Lords Brammley, Hillsborough, and Sefton were only a few.

Mark smiled. "I'd hoped you'd come. Jimmy's got Dante saddled for you. Mount up and join us."

"Thank you." Matthew stroked the neck of his brother's stallion. "But Farnsby asked me to join Asher and him."

"Bloody hell, don't tell me you accepted?" Roark Fitz Roy drew up alongside Mark. "Most excellent Farnsby and Asher, but if you ride with them, you'll be relegated to the rear."

Matthew looked at Fitz Roy. "Yes, but *they* asked me. Apparently they're not afraid I'll stop to trim the hedges as we ride."

Fitz Roy paused and glanced at Mark, who was grinning. Apparently, the man wasn't sure if he should laugh or not. And Matthew wasn't sure either. Had he actually made a joke at his own expense?

He felt a slow smile turning his mouth.

Fitz Roy chuckled, but then he shrugged. "Would've asked you m'self, but ever since you became such a bloody recluse, no one knows what to do with you."

Matthew sent Fitz Roy a mock scowl as the man moved off.

Mark leaned over his saddle. "By the way, I heard about what happened last night between Patience and the Lady Humphreys. This morning, I told 'the Humph' to leave. I also gave Fenton the heave-ho." Mark frowned. "Did you know he was the author of that petition for your removal from White's?"

Matthew nodded. "Yes, but the man's uniformly regarded as an inconsequential ass, so it won't serve me to engage him."

"Are you saying I shouldn't have asked him to leave?"

"No, tossing him out on his 'inconsequential ass' is actually quite perfect—and I love the irony."

Mark chuckled. "I've missed you."

Matthew glanced into his brother's blue eyes and smiled. "It *is* good to be getting back in the saddle."

Mark grinned. "Speaking of saddles, why don't you have Farnsby and Asher join us at the front."

Matthew shook his head. "I don't want to be responsible for their deaths. Besides, I intend to get lost today."

Mark frowned. "You intend to get lost?"

"Yes, along with a certain young woman."

Mark's frown deepened. "Damn it, Matt," he said quietly. "I can't permit this. As long as Patience is here, she is under my guardianship."

Matthew almost smiled at the notion of his brother as the guardian of a woman's virtue. Love and marriage really had changed things. "I didn't have to tell you my plans."

"But you did."

Matthew met his brother's stern gaze. "You can't keep me from her, Mark—any more than I could keep you from Passion. The only person who will ever keep me from Patience is Patience herself."

At that moment, Jimmy walked up with Dante. Matthew quickly mounted the big gray as Mark sat back in his saddle. His brother stared at him, and Matthew could see that he was mulling over his options. But unless Mark was going to lock him up and send Patience home, there was little he could do. "Where do you plan on taking her?"

"Gwyn Hall."

"Christ, why so bloody far?"

"I don't want any interruptions."

Mark looked up at the cloudy sky. "If this storm gets fierce, you'll be stuck."

"That's exactly what I'm hoping." Matthew winked. "Cover for us, will you?"

Mark glowered from beneath the brim of his topper. "Why don't you just marry her, and then I won't have to cover for you," he growled.

"Actually, I've decided to do just that." Turning Dante around, Matthew glanced back into his brother's widening eyes and allowed a small grin. "Say nothing. The lady is prickly on the subject."

As Matthew rode off, Mark's laughter rang out behind him. It made his smile deepen. He hadn't intended to tell his brother his plans, but now he was glad he had. Besides making his courtship of Patience a lot easier, telling things to Mark always made them seem more real.

Matthew headed back in the direction of where he'd last seen Patience. He spotted her easily and, pulling up, studied her from a distance. Her lovely posture and her bright hair, even tucked into a snood, made her stand out in the crowd. She sat her sidesaddle gracefully and the veil of her short-brimmed topper fluttered against her cheek in the breeze. He frowned as he noted Montrose and two other men engaging her in conversation. She couldn't be anywhere without an entourage of male admirers. He hated that. She should be at his side, and the whole world should know that she was his.

Soon . . .

"I say, Hawkmore, there you are! You see, Asher, I told you he would come."

Farnsby and Asher drew up in front of him, blocking his view of Patience.

Matthew nodded. "Gentlemen."

"Asher was convinced you would give us the brush-off. But I bet him ten pounds you wouldn't. And here you are." Farnsby glanced at Asher. "You may pay me later."

Asher shifted uncomfortably in his saddle.

"That's all right, Asher." Matthew patted Dante's muscular shoulder. "I might have bet against me, too. I haven't been very social lately."

Asher smiled just as Mark's voice rang out over the assemblage. Matthew listened to his brother welcome his guests to the hunt and lay out the general direction of the course. Then the stirrup cup was served.

As everyone drank heartily, Matthew glanced in Patience's direction. His heart beat a little faster when he saw that she was looking at him. Oh, what a day he had in store for her.

He nodded and touched the brim of his hat. A blush darkened her cheeks but she didn't look away. Indeed, her green gaze almost seemed to challenge him. But in the next moment, she was blocked from his view as the call for the hunt was sounded, and everyone began to move out. Falling in at the rear with Farnsby and Asher, he located Patience ahead of him and then settled into his saddle to await the chase.

It seemed to Matthew that the hounds took an interminably long time to catch the scent of the fox. During which, Farnsby and Asher engaged him in idle and seemingly endless conversation. At another time, he would have enjoyed their company more, for they were actually decent and amusing fellows. But he was anxious for the hunt, and kept his eye on the straight back and bright hair of his personal prey.

When the horn finally sounded, his heart leapt and his blood rushed. *Finally!* With a touch of his heels, he urged Dante forward. He yearned to ride full-out as he watched the lead group of riders quickly break from the rest. But today he needed to be patient.

In only moments, they were gone, leaving scattered groups of riders to follow in their wake. His lovely prey rode straight and strong, in a group toward the middle. Keeping to an easy canter, Matthew stayed with Farnsby and Asher, who did their best to keep up with him. He indulged them for some time as he watched the distance between Patience and him grow wider. But when she finally disappeared into a stretch of woodland, he made his decision to break from them.

A tall hedge loomed in the distance. His companions would have to go around. He called over his shoulder to them. "I've got to give Dante his head. I'll see you later."

Farnsby and Asher raised their hands in farewell, and Matthew was off. Beneath the darkening sky, he bent low over Dante's neck and urged the horse to a gallop. The gray bolted, and Matthew felt his heart quicken as the big horse found his stride. The hedge grew ever closer and ever taller. Dante's hooves churned the earth with a drumming power that echoed Matthew's heart. Thunder rolled in the distance. Faster and faster Dante galloped. The hedge grew closer, until it seemed a great wall before them.

Matthew sucked in his breath, and then they leapt. Suddenly, everything was silent as they flew through the air, hooves and heart stretched and straining. Then, almost as soon as it had begun, their flight ended as the ground rose up to meet them. And once again, hooves and heart pounded together.

Hedge after hedge, gate after gate, Matthew closed in on his prey. His blood rushed as he broke through some woodland and caught sight of her topping the ridge before him. Like the hounds that bayed in the distance, he let out a whoop of victory.

Patience could hear the horn in the distance. Plunging down a steep hill into a dense grove of oak and birch trees, she followed its call. Those with whom she rode appeared and disappeared between the trees. The ladies were fleeting shadows, the gentlemen bright flashes of color. But less experienced than they, she was forced to slow considerably as she made her way through the thick wood. It wasn't long before she wondered if she'd somehow gotten turned around.

Wind moved the crowded canopy of foliage above her. The leaves and branches rustled and whispered, but then they quieted and a heavy silence followed. Despite the muffled thump of her mare's hooves on the leafy ground, she was distinctly aware of the quiet. It crept through the still vegetation, and hovered in the static air.

Patience urged her horse forward, looking for a break in the darkening wood. It was then that she heard it—the sound of thunder. It rolled upon her from behind, and seemed to grow louder and louder.

A chill scurried down her spine as she set her heels to her mare's sides. The trees began to thin and she increased her pace. But the thunder became a drum in her ears. It echoed the swift pounding of her horse's hooves. And the faster she rode, the faster it seemed to follow. She gasped thanks to God as she saw a break in the trees. Veering to the right, she took her mare over a broad stump and leapt into the wide expanse of an empty meadow.

Relief flooded her, but in two strides she cried out in fright as a huge horse and rider hit the ground alongside her. Gasping with fear and spurring her steed, she looked briefly into dark, predatory eyes.

Matthew!

Her heart pounded, but though her fear turned to a dangerous excitement, she did not slow. Rather, she gave her mount its head and urged her to greater speed. The surging body of the beast beneath her became an extension of herself. The cold wind whipped Patience's face, but the thunder of hooves was too loud to be her horse alone. Chancing a glance over her shoulder, she gasped to see Matthew only a half a length behind her. His expression was fierce and deadly serious, and, God, his huge gray didn't even seem to be straining.

With a small cry, Patience set her heels to her mare's sides yet again, but the lovely beast was at her limit. Thunder rolled overhead and thunder rolled behind her. Both seemed to be overtaking her. Suddenly she saw the gray's giant head beside her, his black mane flying. She veered away, but he followed. Her blood pounded in her ears as she tried to evade him. But he was as unshakable as his rider, whom she could feel at her side. She tensed. Turning, she stared directly into Matthew's fiery eyes.

A clap of thunder crashed as he snatched her from her horse.

Chapter Fourteen

THIRD SUBMISSION

Thy lips, O my spouse, drop as the honeycomb: honey and milk are under thy tongue . . .

SONG OF SOLOMON 4:11

Patience gasped as Matthew pulled her firmly against him. Flushed from the excitement of the chase, she was suddenly overcome by a deep and primitive exhilaration at being captured. Matthew's arm was strong around her waist and his chest hard against her back. She could hear his breathing, quick and shallow, and she could feel his power. It enveloped her like a warm cloak.

This was where she belonged—with him.

He said nothing, but turning his horse about, he cantered back to the tree line. Remembering her lovely mare, Patience glanced over her shoulder. Surprisingly, the soft-eyed beauty was following right behind them.

Matthew's voice came by her ear. "Beatrice is Dante's stall mate. She follows wherever he leads."

Patience shivered at the feel of Matthew's breath. Lightning flashed behind the clouds and thunder rolled overhead. The sky was growing darker. They reentered the wood and waited for Beatrice to draw up beside them. Once she had, Matthew tethered her reins to the back of his saddle.

"The storm may frighten her," he said, turning back to Patience and gathering her tightly against him. "She'll feel more secure tied to her mate."

"Yes," Patience breathed as she leaned into the warmth of Matthew's body.

And then they were riding quickly through the dense trees—faster than she had ridden through before. But he did not follow the path she had taken. Instead, they were traveling deeper into the forest. A thrill tingled just under her skin. Where was he taking her?

She pressed herself more snugly into the shelter of his arms as a sharp wind began to buffet the wood. Thunder rumbled and lightning cracked, but still they rode on. At last, the rain began to fall. Cold and heavy, it permeated the dense canopy above them.

Slowing only slightly, Matthew bent his head near hers. Just as Patience began to wonder if they would ever reach their destination, she glimpsed a light through the trees. A moment later, they broke from the wood. Beneath a circle of open sky sat a rambling Tudor house. With its mellowed brick exterior and light glimmering from a couple of the lower windows, it looked warm and inviting.

Riding around the side of the house and across a wide courtyard, Matthew brought them straight into an open stable. It was dim but dry.

Matthew's hold on her loosened as he leapt down. But then he reached for her. His hands circled her waist, and he pulled her against him as he lowered her to the ground. She could feel his tension.

"Stay," he ordered.

She drew in her breath. Her clitoris pulsed. But other than removing her hat and placing it atop a barrel, she didn't move.

Turning, Matthew led his horse and her mare into the shadows and lit a lamp. The soft light illuminated him. He hung the lamp from a hook affixed to a center beam between two stalls, which were now occupied by the horses.

As Patience watched, he removed his hat and riding jacket before tending first to her horse and then to his. He didn't even look in her direction as he removed the saddles and tack from the mare and the big gray. There must have been fresh water and food in the trough, for the beasts dipped their heads in repeatedly. Outside, the rain continued to pour down.

Though she was wet, Patience stood completely still. But as she watched Matthew throw a blanket over the mare's back, an inescapable inclination to disobey began to overcome her. It bubbled up beneath the heat of a rising excitement, and her bruised pride from earlier lifted its head and said, *Yes, do it.*

Tense, she waited for him to finish. He blanketed the big gray and murmured some words to the beasts. Then he grabbed the lamp and latched the stall doors before finally turning to her.

Patience met his dark gaze across the distance. Her heart quickened. Then she took one large step backward.

Matthew's brows lowered. "I said, stay."

She shivered at the ominous sound of his voice, but her blood was rushing in her veins. She took another large step back.

In the light of the lamp at his side, she could see his penis bulging beneath his tight riding breeches. Her mouth watered.

His frown grew fierce as he hung the lamp on a hook outside the stall and then slowly removed his gloves. "Take one more step and I shall make you sorry for it."

She stared at him. Her quim moistened. There was nowhere to go. Wherever she went, he would catch her. But she'd already begun, and something—something more than just her pride—wouldn't let her submit so easily. So she turned and fled into the rain.

Her blood raced as she lifted her skirts and flew across the broad courtyard to a leafy lane that bordered the house. Cold droplets pelted her, but she barely felt them as she made her wild dash. God, it was farther than she'd thought. She glanced back. Lightning flashed, and she gasped as she saw Matthew running at her at full speed.

Her heart leapt and she tried to run even faster, but her wet skirts were heavy and cumbersome. She turned the bend toward the front of the house. She could see the broad, shallow steps of the entry. *Almost there!* She looked back again and shrieked at finding Matthew just behind her. Then his arms clamped around her waist and he hauled her back against his body.

Beneath the noise of the storm his breathing was ragged by her ear, and a hot thrill coursed through her veins at being captured yet again. But then he was dragging her, not to the house, but across the wide drive to the circular front garden. A waist-high wall of brick enclosed it, and Patience gasped when he forcefully bent her over the top.

Lord, he was really going to do it!

Exhilaration washed through her, followed by a shock of mortification as he threw her skirts over her back and proceeded to tear her pantalets to shreds. The low wall pressed against her abdomen, and she felt the cold and wet on her bottom and legs. Her face grew hot even as her clitoris began to throb. She thought of trying to bolt once more, but then Matthew's arm clamped around her waist, and with the rain pouring over her bared bottom she felt the first sharp and stinging swat of his hand.

She sucked in her breath and her body jolted, but Matthew immediately spanked her again, and then again and again. Flashes of heat burst across her flesh. Each quick strike landed in a different spot, igniting a new fire. A prickling warmth spread rapidly across the entirety of her bottom. Her cunt pulsed. The rain fell and thunder rolled above them. Patience found herself pushing against Matthew's body—leaning into his strength even as he laid on more stinging spanks. Her tears welled. Not because of pain, but because of promise. Every spank seemed full of it. Powerful and seductive in its beauty, it called to her and drew her ever closer to its source. Matthew—

Patience yelped and her tears overflowed as Matthew's hand came down much harder. The sudden pain of the heavy-handed blow suffused her body and overwhelmed her thoughts. She tensed for more, but no more came.

As Matthew pulled her up and spun her away from the wall, she felt a flicker of disappointment. But when she looked into his beautiful face, rain dripping from the strong planes and angles, she shuddered at the dark passion etched across his features—the dark promise.

He wasn't done with her.

Without a word, he grabbed the lapels of her velvet jacket and ripped it open. Buttons flew and Patience gasped as he pulled it roughly from her arms and tossed it on the wall. Her blouse and corset cover followed, each one torn from her more swiftly than she had imagined possible and then thrown with her jacket.

The trees encircling them swayed with gusts of wind. Patience shivered, but Matthew didn't pause. He and the elements were one—powerful and primal. His mouth was set in a tight line, and his nostrils flared as he yanked at her laces and then unhooked her corset. He tossed it with her other garments and Patience shuddered at the realization that she would soon be naked.

A soft cry escaped her as he sundered her chemise down the

front and pulled it to her waist. Rain fell on her bare breasts, and her thick, hardened nipples. Matthew paid them no mind as he whirled her around and yanked at the fastenings of her skirts and crinoline. Patience tensed as she felt them loosen, and her fingers gripped reflexively at the drenched layers of fabric as they began to fall. But Matthew snatched them down, and then tore at the remnants of her chemise and pantalets.

Gooseflesh lifted across her skin. She could feel Matthew's strength and relentless intent as he moved around her, rending the last of her garments. And then she stood in naught but her stockings and riding boots. Cold rain fell upon her naked body. Patience looked down at herself. There was nothing between her skin and God's tears. The drops poured over her, cleansing her of inhibition and filling her with an ancient and pure need to possess and be possessed.

She blinked against the rain as she raised her gaze to Matthew. He stood before her, his wet hair framing his face and his handsome features carved into merciless and predatory lines. His clothes were plastered to his body and his magnificent cock bulged thick and tumescent beneath his breeches. The last shreds of her chemise were still hanging from his fists, but he threw them down and then began to walk slowly around her.

She followed him with her gaze, her body frozen with a tense anticipation. Her breasts heaved and her thighs quivered. Between her legs, she felt a fierce heat. Was this how Persephone had felt? In the moment of her capture, had she stared into the fiery eyes of Pluto and known that her life would never be the same? And in that breathless moment, had she rejoiced?

Matthew moved behind her. A startled gasp broke from her as he grabbed her and lifted her from her pile of skirts.

His voice was a low growl by her ear as he dragged her back to the wall. "You belong to me. You are mine and only mine. And I will brook *no more* of your petty disobedience."

Patience swallowed a cry as, once again, Matthew forced her over. Her pile of clothes protected her from direct contact with the hard brick, but she was acutely aware of the weight of her dangling breasts and the wash of the rain upon her naked body.

Matthew's arm clamped around her waist. She felt the press of his hip against hers. Then his hand landed and a hot explosion of pain burst across her bottom. Patience jerked up and bit back a cry as tears sprang to her eyes. Matthew pushed her back down and brought another heavy-handed spank down upon her. Patience groaned and her cunt clenched. Matthew's hand lingered on her buttock, caressingly, then lifted. Another hard spank came and another. Patience's tears overflowed as the strong blows continued—each one another shocking eruption that reverberated through her and into her. And while Matthew laid them on hard and heavy, claps of thunder boomed in accompaniment to the wet, smacking sound of his hand and the cries she could no longer contain.

She wept and writhed against him—against the force of his will and the force of his hand, neither of which could be stopped or diffused. His arm was a circle of iron around her, and his hand rained down fire. She struggled to escape. But she knew she wouldn't. She knew she mustn't. And as Matthew ground his prick against her hip and landed a barrage of blows on her burning bottom, she suddenly felt as if she were cracking—as if, spank by heavy spank, Matthew were causing an irreparable fissure to inch through her. She wept and wept. Yet, even as she longed for each spank to be the last, she hoped for another. What would happen if she broke entirely?

Patience cried out loudly as Matthew's hand came down stronger than ever. His cock pushed against her hip. She wailed as another fierce blow landed. But then he was stroking and squeezing her heated flesh. She moaned around her tears. Her bottom felt hot and huge, yet she trembled with a desire unlike any she'd ever felt—a desire for Matthew.

A desire that stretched both backward and forward in time.

A desire that reached into forever.

Her chest tightened and fresh tears sprang to her eyes. There was no going back. He was the one she'd always wanted. Before she'd even known him, he was the one. The moment she'd seen him, he was the one. He would always be the one.

God, how would she ever do without him?

Her tears fell, indistinguishable from the rain that ran down the slopes and into the crevices of her bent body. And Matthew's touch was as unrelenting as the water. Patience sucked in her breath as his fingers slipped between her legs, and then she groaned and twisted as she felt the hot, slick wetness that was sluicing from her cunt.

Matthew shuddered against her, and then he pulled her up. She fell into his arms, and when she lifted her eyes to his, her body quaked at the passionate gaze he bent upon her. For there was, in that gaze, absolute certainty—absolute possession.

Stepping away, he picked up her skirts and swept her things from the wall. Then he returned to her and, bending, tossed her over his shoulder. Patience's breath left her in a rush, and exhilaration coursed through her as he headed toward the house. His arm was tight around the backs of her knees, his shoulder strong beneath her hips—and still, the storm raged.

From her strange upside-down angle, Patience watched Matthew's long legs as he strode across the drive and mounted the wide steps. Her heart pounded as he threw open the door and carried her over the threshold. Then, just as quickly, the door slammed shut. In the sudden quiet, her panting breaths sounded loud. A red and gold rug whirled below her and then receded as Matthew crossed the wide foyer and moved down a hall with long, purposeful strides.

Patience listened to the striking of his boots on the wide planks of the hardwood floor and the sound tantalized her, for each step he took brought her closer to some new fulfillment—or punishment.

Her nipples tightened.

Perhaps fulfillment and punishment were one and the same.

They entered a well-lit room, and Matthew dropped her sodden clothes over a wooden chair before crossing to the fireplace. Patience expected to be put down, but instead, he landed a sharp spank on her left buttock. She gasped and then sucked in her breath when another fell on her right buttock. Biting her lip, she curled her fingers in his shirt, for though the spanks weren't nearly as hard as the last ones, her bottom was sore and tender.

She felt his lips brush against her hip, and then he was setting her down before the low burning fire. Her legs shook and she swallowed as she met his stern gaze.

"There is a bootjack beside the hearth." His voice was low and velvety. "Take off your boots and stockings. And be quick about it."

Moisture spilled onto Patience's thighs and her heart beat wildly. Immediately, she went to the jack and used it to remove her riding boots. As she rushed back before the fire, she glanced briefly around the room. They were in a large library, made cozy by the illumination of oil lamps and comfortable-looking furniture. But she had no time to admire it. She could feel the heat in her bottom as she moved, so she returned her gaze to her task and, as quickly as she could, began to unknot her garters.

While she worked to untie them, her attention kept being drawn to Matthew. He undid his cravat. Then he opened the top of his shirt and, slowly and deliberately, rolled up his sleeves—as though he had much work to do. His cock looked huge and hard beneath his wet breeches. And, all the while, he held her in his dark gaze, which somehow managed to be both soft and stern at the same time.

Patience shook as she dropped her garters and then rolled down her stockings. Though she knew it was impossible—though she didn't even want to run—she couldn't help glancing toward the door.

"Don't even think of it."

Her nipples immediately hardened at his quietly ominous tone. She met his gaze as she straightened. She craved something in that tone—perhaps the strong and uncompromising quality of it. For even as it threatened, it made her feel safe. It said that what she did mattered—that *she* mattered, and that he wouldn't let her go. Letting her stockings drop, she stood before him, naked and shivering with tension.

Matthew pulled free his loosened cravat. "Take down your hair."

Patience watched the black silk dangle from his hand. God, was he going to tie her? Did she want that or not?

She jumped as he suddenly whirled her around and bent her over. Then she was gasping and writhing as he held her against him and swatted her bottom with strong, lifting spanks that came from below rather than above. Her gasps turned to cries, as each one seemed a little harder than the one before. Also, she felt the power of his hand more against her drying skin than she had in the rain. Heat rapidly spread across the tender underside of her bottom. But despite this new torment, her cunt felt heavy and her clitoris ached. Her tears came easily now, and she wept with mortification as she felt her desire running down her legs.

Matthew whirled her back around and spoke each word slowly. "Take down your hair."

With her bottom throbbing and her chest heaving, Patience quickly pulled the pins from her snood and laid them on the mantel with shaking hands. As she reached to remove more, she swiped at her tears.

"No," Matthew said, low. "Leave them."

Patience drew her brows together in puzzlement.

"Your tears—leave them. I want you to feel them on your face. You hide a part of yourself when you brush them away, and I won't have that." He tipped up her chin with his finger. "For how can I touch you where you need to be touched, if you hide from me?" His eyes delved into hers. "Now. Take—down—your—hair."

Patience trembled as she stared into Matthew's gaze. Was there no part of her he would not insist upon seeing? He was looking at parts and places of her that even she had never seen. What would he find? Her heart tightened and more tears welled.

Now was not the time for such questions. She lifted her hands back to her pins and, as she removed the last ones, her eyes dropped to Matthew's beautiful and formidable erection. As trembling and tense as she was, she adored the shape and thickness of his engorged organ—adored the way it rose up before him, a proud symbol of his masculine power.

Removing her snood, she let her damp curls fall down her back. There was nothing more for her to take off; and when she returned her gaze to Matthew's, she suddenly felt her nakedness. Impulsively, she wrapped her arms around herself.

Matthew frowned. "Put your hands at your sides, and keep them there until I tell you otherwise."

Oh God! Squeezing her eyes shut, she forced her hands against her thighs.

"Look at me," he said sternly.

Patience's eyes flew open, and she felt them well yet again. But she felt no sadness or regret, only a fierce desperation.

"Your nakedness is for my pleasure," he said more gently. "You will not cover it. Indeed, you will open yourself for my view whenever I command it. And as you do, you will look at me with the grateful knowledge that all I command of you is for my pleasure—and therefore, for yours."

Patience's clitoris ached with its fullness.

"Even if what I command is your punishment, you will endure it for my pleasure. And you will look at me and pay me the tribute of your emotions, no matter how difficult. Is that clear?"

I cannot oblige you at this time. She could utter the words whenever she wanted . . .

His frown deepened. "I said, is that clear?"

She bit her lip as one of her tears spilled over. "Yes, Matthew."

His gaze seemed to follow the path of her tear. "Good." He bent close, and thunder rolled outside as he pressed an open-mouthed kiss to the wet trail on her cheek. She trembled with want as he pulled away. His dark, long-lashed eyes were hard and full of the fire's reflection. "Now, lift your hair."

Patience did so immediately, and as Matthew reached around her she breathed the smell of him—rainwater and vetiver. He looked down at her as he drew the silk slowly across the back of her neck. His eyes seemed to look inside her and he paused. "Above all, Patience, remember that you ran from the barn because you trust me. You ran because you yearn for a strong hand, and you trust that I know how to wield mine. Isn't that so?"

Still holding her hair, she stared into his firelit eyes and her tears overflowed. It was true. "Yes," she admitted softly. *But why?* She lowered her gaze. Why did she crave what most would find intolerable?

Her tears fell as the rain fell without. She could feel each one rolling down her cheeks and dropping upon her breasts. But she could not dry them or conceal them. She could not run away so that they could not be seen. And she could not pretend they didn't exist.

For he wouldn't let her.

She lifted her wet face to Matthew.

"There," he said softly. His gaze moved over her face like caress. "There's my beauty."

Patience's blood surged, and suddenly her heart felt overfull.

Matthew stroked his fingers gently along her jaw. "Your tears make me hot and hard, and I will never tire of them. But, of course, they are not a reprieve."

Shaking with emotions and needs she couldn't explain, Patience waited as Matthew tied the silk snugly around her neck. Lightning snapped. Her breathing quickened. The leash offered some comfort, but not as it had the night before. Everything was heightened now—everything was more than she thought she could bear. Yet, at the same time, it wasn't enough.

Gripping her leash just below the knot, Matthew drew her close and brushed his lips tenderly over hers. Keeping her hands at her sides, Patience pressed up against him and tried to seduce a deeper kiss from him, but he pulled back just enough to keep her reaching for more. She lifted onto her toes, but still he drew back, giving her only the lightest of kisses.

"Set your feet apart," he said against her lips.

Patience expelled a frustrated gasp, but she complied. Her clitoris throbbed as Matthew stepped to her side and stroked his hand over her breast and down her belly. Then he reached between her parted thighs, and she gasped as he stroked her wet folds.

"Ah, my disobedient beauty," he said near her ear. "See how wet you are—and with such little punishment. Why, I've barely begun to give you what you deserve."

Barely begun?! Patience trembled as she felt him parting her. Then she moaned as he slipped two fingers just inside her quim, and gently massaged the slick interior.

"Did you think I would let your insolent departure from my study this morning go unpunished?" He rubbed a little faster and a little deeper. Patience shivered and her hips began to tilt, forward and back. But then she cried out and her body jolted as Matthew's other hand landed a sharp swat upon her bottom.

"And what of your reckless attempt to escape me upon Beatrice?" Another stinging spank heated her other buttock. But, still, he was rubbing her wet opening.

Patience swayed and her legs bent and straightened as she tried to ease her need. Her bottom felt hot and sore, but somehow the discomfort amplified her desire. She was wild for release, but Matthew wasn't touching her clitoris, and he wasn't deep enough inside her. She groaned and wagged her hips wantonly.

As if in answer, he slipped another finger inside her, even as he laid a spank on the underside of her enflamed bottom. Patience yelped and her quim tightened. "There," he murmured by her ear. "Do you see how the pain and the pleasure are connected?"

Patience panted through her tears as she tried to thrust her clasping cunt more deeply over his fingers. She couldn't speak, could only pant and jerk her hips.

"Do you see how little there is," he insisted, "one between the other?"

Another quick, lifting slap stung her tender buttock.

"Yes," she cried. "Yes!"

Patience ground fiercely against Matthew's fingers. She could feel the barrier of her virginity. Her hips tilted and her tears fell. And just as she felt her climax cresting, he pulled his hand away and stepped before her.

Patience cried, and her hips undulated uncontrollably. She wept with a frustrated desire that was, somehow, both mortifying and exciting. Her cheeks felt hot beneath her tears. Her bottom felt sore and tingly. And her cunt felt wet and heavy.

Matthew watched her, his eyes shining with both lust and admiration. Then before she could think what he might do next, she gasped as he delivered a light slap to each of her nipples. The stinging sensation shot, like an arrow, directly into her throbbing clitoris. Shuddering, Patience drew back her shoulders as he gave her another and then another. And the more he gave her, the more her nipples throbbed and darkened, and the more her cun watered. Her knees weakened and her head fell back as she thrus her hot and swollen nipples forward. They felt enormous, bu each light slap only made her crave another. Her hips gyrated an her clitoris strained and stretched. Her tears fell and her thigh shook, but she couldn't reach her orgasm!

It evaded her, leaving her suspended upon some relentles peak. She groaned and stretched, but then the spanks stoppe coming and everything was still. Only it wasn't, for her whol body was alive and humming with a heightened sensual aware ness. Dizzy and desperate for release, she straightened her hea and met Matthew's fiery gaze.

"Sometimes the worst part of punishment is not the pain, Pa tience. It's the need"—he stepped close to her—"the rampar desire that cannot be assuaged." Pressing his hands over hers, he slowly rubbed his erection against her pelvis. "For your orgasm is no longer your own. It belongs to me as much as it belongs to you." Patience ground against him, wild for the feel of his firm flesh. "And you will not have it until I say you will have it." Then he stepped away from her.

Patience dropped her head with a sob. Her body was pulsing, and her thick nipples were dark and incredibly distended. They tingled with a hot, electric sensation that both tortured and tantalized her, for it echoed the feeling of her punished bottom. Moisture trickled down her thigh, and her clitoris ached. It was marvelous and unfathomable.

"This is how I like to see you—hot, flushed, and soundly spanked. Punishment becomes you, Patience."

It took all her energy to lift her head. Matthew reclined on the couch facing her, his long legs open and his erection bulging. Her mouth watered and her quim tightened as she stared at it.

"You can't know how beautiful you look." His hands moved to his breeches and he undid them. "All pliant from punishment." He unveiled his thick cock and then, reaching in, lifted out his swollen cods. "All wet with tears and need."

Patience swallowed and her heart skipped a beat. His prick was dark red and the head looked purplish and inflated. He demonstrated such masterful control, but he was clearly as desperate for release as she.

"Come," he said firmly, indicating the floor between his legs.

She practically flew to him, but when she settled on her heels and wiggled in an attempt to ease her pulsing clitoris, Matthew sat forward quickly and grabbed her by her upper arms. "No." He shook his head. "Knees wide apart."

As Patience complied, he pinched her tender nipples firmly. She gasped and immediately drew back her shoulders.

"Good," he murmured. Then, scooping up her breast, he sucked her dark and thickened nipple into his mouth, while he teased and rolled the other between his fingers.

Patience shuddered as he laved and compressed her titillated flesh. She lifted and arched against him. He released her breast, only to scoop the other to his mouth. His fingers brushed the inside of her thigh. She groaned and, pressing her hands against her thighs, tilted her hips in an attempt to coerce his caress. If only he would touch the pulsing heart between her legs. If only . . .

He released her and drew slowly back.

"Oh, God . . ." She met his hard, dark gaze. "Please!"

Matthew's jaw clenched as he leaned against the couch-back. Gripping the thick trunk of his cock, he pushed it toward her. "Show me some appreciation, and I'll think about it."

Patience dove forward, her clitoris throbbing, but then he stayed her. She looked up at him, her desperation growing.

He gazed back at her from beneath lowered lids. "Keep your hands on your thighs. And if you come without my leave, you'll regret it."

Patience nodded, then took him into her mouth with a hungry urgency. Moisture washed from her cunt at the taste and feel of his thick flesh filling her mouth. She sucked the salty fluid that flowed from him in a steady stream, and swept her tongue across his satiny glans.

The feel and taste of him made her wild with lust. She felt a heady power as she sank more deeply over him, pressing her tongue firmly against the thick underside of his prick. With long, slow passes she moved up and down, milking rivulets of pre-cum from his enflamed member.

Matthew groaned and slid his hands into her hair as his hips tilted, pushing more of his meaty thickness into her mouth. Patience opened for him and took what he gave her. Then his fingers tightened in her hair and he began to thrust, steadily and deeply. Patience moaned when he ground the head of his cock against the back of her throat. Her clitoris throbbed dangerously. She heard Matthew draw in his breath, and then she held hers as he sent several hard, fast thrusts against the tight turn of her throat. He withdrew in time for her to take a gasping breath and then he pulled her down again. But this time he did not thrust. He simply pushed his meaty thickness slowly and deeply into her until she was completely filled. Then he held her to him as he rocked his hips in small, tight motions that gently yet inexorably forced more and more of his heavy organ down her throat.

Patience's back arched up. Her clitoris swelled and her hips jerked. Her release rushed toward her.

Only, before it could wash over her, Matthew pulled her back

Light-headed, she drew a ragged breath in preparation for him to pull her down again. But he didn't. He got up and was dragging her to her feet.

"No!" she cried. She was so close! Jerking her wrist from his grip, she threw herself into his arms and rubbed herself desperately against him. She could feel his strong phallus—his warm body. "Please, not again, Matthew!"

Grabbing her, he spun her around to face the fire. He held her against him and kicked her legs apart as he thrust his cock against the small of her back. "Yes, again!" he rasped near her ear. "And again and again, if it pleases me, Patience."

Then he stepped to her side and the spanks came hard and fast. She struggled and strained. But then he was behind her again, thrusting against her hot skin. "There is no pleasure for you, but through me, Patience." She moaned as he gripped her nipples, depressing them ever more tightly between his fingers. "So, think of nothing but satisfying me, and know that everything you suffer for my pleasure works to bring you that much closer to your own fulfillment. Submit," he breathed.

He released her swollen nipples, and Patience let out her breath on a gasp. She felt a desperate desire to submit. The word itself seemed synonymous with relief and freedom. "I want to submit." She spoke around her tears. "I do. But my body is aching—and my pride . . ."

Matthew slid a feathery touch down her arms. "I want your body to ache. I want you to feel all the sensation it is capable of. And I want you to experience each punishment and each pleasure with the awareness that it is I who am giving it to you." He squeezed her sore bottom. "*I* am the one, Patience. I am the *only* one who can bring you this beautiful, blissful ache." His grip tightened on her aching flesh, causing her to gasp. "For it is blissful, isn't it?"

"Yes." Even as she longed for release, his strict refusal to bow to her comforted some deep part of her soul. And the pain, there was something unfathomably satisfying in that as well.

"I think you love it." He kissed the curve of her ear. "And you will grow to love it even more and more, until you can't do without it." She gasped as his grip released then tightened yet again. "But that's all right, for I will be with you—always."

Patience's tears slipped down her cheeks.

Was it true?

God, let it be true.

Matthew's lips touched her ear. "As for your pride"—Patience's hips tilted back as, from behind, he stroked his fingers over the wet and swollen folds of her cunt—"soon you shall discover a new pride—a pride in your feminine submission." Her skin tingled as he kissed her shoulder. "You shall feel pride when you please me. You shall feel pride when you endure your punishments gracefully. You shall feel pride when I reward you with orgasm. And you shall feel pride when you recognize that your submission makes you stronger, not weaker." His hands slipped slowly from her. "And when all this comes to pass, you will know a new truth."

Patience trembled as Matthew came to stand in front of her. His ponderous prick rose florid and dark from its impossibly broad base, and the head bobbed as it dripped clear fluid. It was beautiful. Lifting her wet eyes to Matthew's, she found his dark orbs were lit with an unreadable glow.

"You're so wet," he said, softly. "And I'm so hard. I could fuck you beautifully."

Patience's cunt tightened and a choked groan broke from her. God, but she wanted it—she wanted him! Her legs began to shake. *Yes* trembled upon her lips.

But she bit them to hold the word in. If she gave that part of herself, she would have no defense. Tears of distress welled as she looked into Matthew's angel eyes. No defense at all . . .

"Very well," he breathed. "Go stand in front of the chair by the fire, set your legs apart and place your forearms on the armrests."

Patience's pulse quickened. Was he going to punish her for refusing him? Her clitoris pulsed painfully as she moved to the heavy-looking wingback chair and did as he asked.

"That's lovely, Patience. You have such long legs, and your bottom is blushing beautifully."

Patience jumped as she felt his hands brush gently over her heated flesh. But he didn't spank her. Rather, he slid his hands to her hips. "One day, soon, I'll take you just like this. I'll spank your pert little bottom until it's hot and red, and then"—she held her breath as she felt the head of his cock touching her wet folds—"and then I'll push my prick into your sweet, tight cunt and I'll fuck you, fast and hard. And I won't stop. Even when my cock is dripping with your cum, I won't stop. Even when you beg me because you can't come anymore, I won't stop." His hands tightened on her hips. "Still, I'll fuck you and fuck you until there's nothing left in you but Eve—pure, undiluted Eve, who knows nothing but the perfect purpose of her creation. And then I will fill your womb, as it was meant to be filled—and only then, will all be as it should be."

Patience shuddered as her resistance flowed out of her. But when she pushed back, he wasn't there. He'd moved. Crouching a bit behind her, his hands were slipping between her legs and reaching forward to brace around her pelvic bones.

"Don't worry," he said. "I won't drop you."

Drop her? Patience cried out as he quickly lifted her by her hips. Her head went down and her feet flew into the air. She grabbed at him, her cheek against his thigh, but he had a firm grip upon her, and, lifting her by her hips, he settled the tops of her thighs over his shoulders.

Upside down, Patience gasped. She was right in front of Matthew's wet prick, and she could feel his breath between her legs. His arm was tight around her waist while his other hand squeezed her sore and flaming bottom. Patience moaned, and then Matthew's tongue was stroking her wet folds. She shuddered as his hips thrust toward her in a silent demand. She answered it immediately and took his thick cock into her mouth.

He groaned against her cunt and his hot breath touched her as he kissed and tongued her swollen sex. Patience moaned as she pushed down farther on his thrusting organ. Her blood rushed and her toes curled in the air. She was both pleasuring and being pleasured, but she couldn't distinguish the two. They seemed to be the same, and she couldn't tell which drove her desire more.

She tilted her hips as he drove his tongue into her cunt and his prick into her mouth. Her head spun as he thrust faster and faster. Her hair swayed and her body strained. She felt her pleasure cresting.

But then he was lifting her away from him. She heard herself wailing "Noooooo!" as she slid down his body to the floor.

Weak and trembling with need, she got to her hands and knees. She swayed. Then she cried out as the spanks came again, sharp and pitiless on her burning bottom. Hot, stinging tears fell, but the more Matthew spanked her the more strongly her clitoris throbbed, until her bottom and her sex pulsed with an equal demand.

Grabbing her leash, Matthew pulled her up so that she was on her knees. Dazed with desire, she managed to look into his dark, plundering eyes. He was Pluto. He was her prince and her angel. He was Adam—and she was his Eve. As a shudder wracked her body, she groaned, low and long, in a desperate and wordless plea for release.

Matthew cupped her cheek, and his voice was like gravel. "Yes. Now you may." And then he pulled her to the right with the leash. "Use my leg."

Patience fairly leapt upon him. Sitting on her heels, she straddled his foot with her splayed knees. She hugged his thigh and thrust her hips. She gasped and panted, and ground her bulging clitoris against the smooth leather of his boot. Faster and faster she humped against him, beating the tortured little nub of flesh that held her release.

Matthew's hand clenched in her hair, and she pressed her cheek to his thigh. "That's it, Patience. Do it. Do it!"

Sucking in her breath, she hammered against him. Every muscle drew tight. Her cunt pulled and her womb lifted. And then she squeezed her eyes shut, and with a long and throaty cry, her clitoris ruptured, filling the entirety of her body with the hot and succulent nectar of submission.

Crying and convulsing with the sweetness of it, she ground against him until her rapture was spent. Then, too weak to stay upright, she slipped to the floor and onto her back. Through her tears, she looked up at Matthew as he moved to stand between her legs. The rug was rough on her sore bottom but she didn't care, for he was staring down at her and furiously stroking his enflamed phallus. "To whom do you belong?" he demanded.

Patience's heart thumped, as if too much blood had rushed into it. "To you."

And with her knees splayed open and her tears falling, she watched him as he jerked a hot, wet splash of cum onto her palpitating clitoris and cunt.

She gasped and winced, but her knees drew back, revealing more of her virgin quim.

"Yes," he groaned. And grunting hard, he milked thick ropes of cum over her swollen sex, abdomen and breasts.

Her clitoris pulsing beneath the hot blanket of his ejaculate, Patience shuddered and wept silent tears at the complete peace that filled her.

Matthew stared down at her, his breath coming fast. A dark glow still simmered in his eyes. "That's my beauty."

His endearment made her moan softly. She had no words.

Stepping beside her head, he crouched then tipped onto his knees. Sliding his hand into her hair, he lifted her and pushed his half-hard penis into her mouth. "Suck it," he ordered softly.

Her nipples tightening and tingling at this new command, Patience obeyed. She sucked him hungrily, pulling and stroking his softened member deeply into her mouth. But when he reached between her legs and began rubbing her aching clitoris, her hips jerked back and she moaned her distress around his hardening flesh. It was too much—she couldn't bear it. But he kept on, and she groaned as he pushed his semen-drenched fingers inside her. And as he withdrew and pushed in again and again, he plied her wounded clitoris continually with his thumb.

Her mouth full, she mewled and squirmed as she tried to convey her distress. But staring down at her, he only pressed his prick deeper and rubbed her harder. She sobbed and sucked as he worked her, forcing her exhausted nub to fill and stretch. And all the while, he regarded her with an expression that was both tender and uncompromising.

She wanted to close her legs. Her muscles shook to do so. But she didn't. She forced them wider. For this was for his pleasure and she must endure whatever pleased him, gracefully and gratefully. Her heart pounded and her blood rushed as she gave herself up. And the moment she did, her distress faded and her desire reared.

Her hips lifted and her clitoris fattened. This was bliss. And this was who she was—this woman—with Matthew's cock in her mouth and Matthew's fingers in her cunt.

And as she wept hot tears of surrender, and drew ravenously upon his thrusting penis, she came. And as she came, he praised her and filled her mouth with a faint, watery ejaculate.

Chapter Fifteen
HE LOVES HER

O thou whom my soul loveth . . .

SONG OF SOLOMON 8:7

Shaking, Matthew rested on his heels. He stared down at the beautiful vision of Patience. Her eyes were closed, her lips parted, and a blushing glow tinted her high cheekbones. He'd worked her hard. But it had all been to her benefit, for he had seen the totality of her surrender in her eyes, observed it in her straining body, and felt it in the enthusiasm with which she gave of her wet, succulent mouth.

But he wanted more than her mouth.

Leaning forward, he stroked her bright curls back from her forehead. Her lashes fluttered, then she lifted her vivid eyes to him. Still sparkling with unshed tears, they were full of peaceful and submissive adoration.

His chest filled with a deep and primeval pride. *Soon.* Soon she would be incapable of refusing him anything. He would take her virginity, and he would take her hand. And most importantly, he would take her heart.

Yes, her heart was what he wanted most of all.

Reaching down, he clasped her hand. Drawing it to his lips, he kissed the soft, fragrant skin over her pulse. Her fingers gently cupped the side of his face. He looked at her—at the tenderness in her eyes, the softness of her expression—and something sharp and almost painful pierced his chest.

He stared down at her for a long while, carving the image of her into his mind. Then he pressed another kiss into her palm before drawing her hand from his face and laying it on her chest. "Stay," he murmured.

She didn't move as he got to his feet. Crossing to the hearth, he slipped his prick into his breeches then buttoned up. He used the jack to remove his riding boots, then he pulled off his socks and removed his shirt. Though Patience was still and quiet, he could feel her gaze as he drew a wooden chair before the hearth. He threw more wood upon the fire. Her eyes followed him as he collected her clothes, then draped them over the chair to dry.

Turning back to her, he crouched by her side and untied her leash. Then he scooped her up. As he stood, the smell of gardenias and sex wafted from her. She felt so soft and supple. The feel of her arms around him and her eyes upon him made his gut quiver and his heart beat a little faster.

He carried her into the foyer and up the wide stairs of Gwyn Hall. The storm was still battering the house. He thanked God for it. The longer it poured down, the longer he could keep her with him. The tall clock at the landing read twelve fifteen.

He carried her to the small bathing room and was gratified to see that, thanks to a brazier of coals, the copper tub was still steaming. He would have to put an extra pound note or two in the underbutler's pocket. The man had seen to all of Matthew's requests, and in short order.

He stood beside the tub. "Touch the water and tell me if it's too hot."

Patience extended one long leg and dipped her toes in the water. "It's perfect."

Matthew let her legs down, and then he watched her as she lowered herself into the tub. Though she drew in her breath as her bottom entered the water, her green eyes, normally so knowing and assessing, glowed with a calm docility. Once she was seated, she leaned against the high back of the tub with a long sigh. But she never shut her eyes to his regard.

His heart skipped as he moved to a small table that held a snifter and a decanter of brandy. Splashing some of the amber liquid into the glass, he handed it to Patience. As she sipped, he admired how her breasts floated in the water, her thick nipples just breaking the surface. His mouth watered and a prickling sensation moved through his cods. She had such beautiful breasts—breasts tipped with buds that flowered into magnificence with a spanking.

He met her steady gaze. "Your nipples crave punishment."

Her chest lifted slightly at his words. "Yes."

His blood quickened as he thought of her reddened bottom. "Your whole body craves punishment."

Her moist lips parted. "Yes."

His cock throbbed. "That's very good."

Patience handed him back the glass. "It pleases you?"

"Immeasurably."

Tossing down the remaining brandy, he moved to the stool that had been placed at the head of the tub. Breathing the sweet smell of her hair, he reached around her for the soap and lathered it.

"Matthew?"

"Yes."

"Have you always been like this?"

His prick stirred as he laid his hands upon her chest and began washing her. "Yes."

She took another sip from the brandy. "But how did you know?"

"I didn't at first. It took time for me to begin to make sense of the feelings and urges I had." He pressed his fingers against the muscles of her neck and shoulders, drawing sighs from her. "But it all became much clearer to me the day I ripped the belt that was meant for me from my governess's hand, pushed her over my school desk, and belted her bare bottom."

Patience twisted around, her eyes wide. "Did you really?"

He almost smiled as he saw her nipples tighten. "Yes, I did. And if she hadn't run off shrieking, I might have fucked her, because the whole thing made me incredibly hard."

Patience's eyes darkened, even as her lovely mouth turned down in the corners. "I think I feel jealous."

Matthew's cock throbbed. "Of what? The fact that I belted her, or that I would have fucked her? Neither of which I've done to you."

She lowered her lovely eyes and seemed to be considering for a moment. "I'm not certain." She looked at him, a quizzical frown creasing her brow. "Both, I think."

He couldn't resist a small smile. Her honesty was too lovely. "Don't bother with jealousy. She couldn't hold a candle to you." He reached out and brushed the backs of his fingers against her protuberant nipple. "As for the belt, it has its uses. But I require no implements to punish you properly." He gave her distended bud a quick, hard pinch. Patience gasped and then shivered. He stared into her beautiful gaze. "And as for the fucking—well, that's one control I agreed to let you keep, didn't I?"

"Yes." Her green eyes looked dark and almost contrite. "You wanted to fuck me today."

Yes, damn it! "It would have been nice."

"I'm sorry."

Not half as sorry as I am. Standing up, Matthew clasped her hand and pulled her to her feet. "I suppose I'll survive. I've always preferred fellatio to fucking anyway." *Until you.*

Patience's brows lifted. "You have? Why?"

"I don't know." He soaped his hands. "Trained early, I suppose." Bending, he lathered her long, shapely legs.

"What do you mean, 'trained early'?"

As he straightened, he noted that the master's mark on her thigh was fading. The sight of it reminded him of the one on her bottom, which reminded him, yet again, of how incredibly beautiful her taut and reddened buttocks had looked as he'd spanked them. A dim throbbing started in his prick.

He stared into her curious gaze as he rubbed the soap all over her breasts, belly, and hips. "I always wake hungry. When I was a boy, the cook knew to have a tray sent to me early every morning. The same kitchen maid brought it every day. But the day came that she found me with my prick sticking straight out from beneath my nightshirt. Open your legs."

Patience set her legs apart, and he ran his soapy hands over her soft folds.

"So," he continued, "she quickly explained that she could help the situation. And that day, as I stood there with my biscuit in my hand, she fellated me nicely." Matthew slipped his fingers over Patience's clitoris and found it a little enlarged. Ignoring her indrawn breath, he lowered his gaze and gently scrubbed his soapy fingers through the red curls over her mount. How beautiful those bright curls were against her pale skin. How beautiful the moist, virgin quim just beneath. Christ, he could feel his cock beginning to swell. What had he been saying? *Ah, yes.* "Most every day thereafter," he continued, "she would milk me while I breakfasted."

"And who performs this daily service for you now?" she asked, her voice tight.

Matthew looked at her and found an angry, resentful frown twisting her brow. His heart pulsed strongly and a wave of something washed through him—something powerful yet tender. "No one does." He stepped closer to her and stroked his hand along the soft outer curve of her breast. "Why? Do you want the job?" he asked gently. Her frown slowly faded, and she drew in a breath as he slid his other arm around her waist. He stared into her green gaze. "Because if you do, it's yours. Of course"—he brushed his lips across her brow—"we ought to discuss what other services I will require of you, and what services I shall render in return." He kissed her soft temple and felt her arms slip around him. His heart skipped a beat. "And then"—he kissed the delicate corner of her eye—"there should be some kind of formal"—her hand smoothed over his nape—"and binding"—he kissed her cheek—"agreement." Her mouth opened beneath his, and he thrust his tongue possessively. His head spun as he tasted her and plundered her. God, she was so warm and sweet, and her lips clung to his so passionately. Would that a vicar still attended the tiny chapel behind the garden. He would drag her there now.

Yes, now!

Patience moaned as he broke their kiss. He stepped back. He felt his knee begin to flex. But then he froze, for even as he was regarding her, a slow and bewildered frown was turning her brow. Jesus Christ, what was he doing? As her frown deepened and her head tilted, he straightened the infinitesimal bend of his knee. In the pursuit of Patience, *im*patience was his enemy.

He drew a slow breath then raised his brows. "Naturally, any such agreement would necessitate your canceling certain travel plans. For though I have always considered myself satisfactorily endowed, I can assure you that my cock, on its most randy of days, is incapable of reaching London from here."

Patience's frown eased and a small smile briefly turned her lips. Then she shivered and her nipples stuck out like hard little fingers as Matthew made a show of adjusting himself in his trousers.

"Are you cold?" he asked casually.

"Yes—no." Patience shook her head. "I mean, I don't know."

Matthew held back a smile and, stepping forward, soaped his hands again. "Let's see, where was I?"

"The maid," Patience said.

He met her gaze. "I meant, where was I on your body?"

Patience's lashes fluttered. "Oh."

"Turn around."

Patience obeyed, and Matthew's cock throbbed strongly as he stared at her reddened bottom. It was bright and beautiful, and, though it showed no signs of serious punishment, it was blushing vividly both on top and beneath. The contrast against the rest of her pale skin was dramatic and alluring. "Ah, Patience, don't you look lovely."

She glanced over her shoulder at him, and he could see that a flush was pinking her cheekbones as well. Eagerly, he smoothed his soapy hands over her bottom. He could feel the heat radiating from her, but it only made him long to throw her over his knee and spank her more. His voice caught a little in his suddenly dry throat. "I think, my beauty, that you will find it all too easy to earn punishment." Patience sighed as he laid a string of kisses along her soft shoulder. "No doubt, this will spoil you terribly," he breathed. "But how can I resist such temptation? Especially when it serves you so well." Her back arched and she moaned softly as he grabbed her bottom and pressed his fingers into her firm flesh, squeezing and massaging it.

Christ, though he'd come twice and was exhausted from lack of sleep, his cock was at half-stand. He needed to stop, or he would find himself having another go at her. He smoothed his hands up her back and then down her arms. "Turn," he murmured.

Patience faced him, and he could see in her eyes that his words had stoked her desire. He slid his soapy fingers over hers, and took a moment to admire the long, fine bones of her hands. They were lovely hands, cellist's hands.

"Are you going to finish telling me about the maid?"

Matthew raised his eyes to hers and sighed at her persistence. "There isn't much else to tell. Later, I found out that she was fellating Mark before supper. We thought we were quite the young masters until we discovered that she had a daily schedule of fucks and sucks that included the chef, the underbutler, the second footman, and the steward." He shrugged. "Anyway, I was only twelve when these morning pleasures began, so I suppose that explains my preference for sucking over fucking. Although, if I'm being exact, I actually prefer irrumatio to fellatio." He rinsed his hands in the water. "You may sit."

A curious frown turned Patience's brow as she sat back down and idly scooped water over her soapy shoulders. "What's irrumatio?"

Matthew regarded her for a moment as his cock throbbed. He may be exhausted, but he really couldn't resist giving her a brief education. Unbuttoning his trousers, he removed them along with his undergarment. Half hard, his penis swayed and felt heavy. He met Patience's avid gaze. "Come."

She swallowed then immediately came to lean against the side of the tub. Her tongue flicked out over her lips as she faced his bobbing prick. His blood raced. "Go ahead."

Without pause, she gripped the edge of the tub and took him into her moist mouth. He drew in his breath as he watched her full lips slip repeatedly over his shaft and glans. His legs tensed, but he didn't move. Her soft tongue stroked around the rim of his knob, and then pressed firmly against the swelling underside of his shaft. Turning her big green eyes up to him, she began to slide her lips back and forth on his growing member. As usual, one of her heavy red curls fell over her brow, bouncing as her head bobbed on his ever-thickening cock.

Matthew bit back a moan at thc beautiful deference with which she pleasured him. But his muscles had begun to quiver and his hands were twitching. He pulled back from her and touched his finger to her pouty lower lip. "*That* is fellatio. Now"—he set his legs farther apart—"let's begin again, shall we?"

Patience leaned forward eagerly, but, this time, he curled his fingers in her hair and held her immobile while he pushed into her warm mouth. He groaned and withdrew slightly before pushing back in more deeply. Then, with a shudder, he began to pump into her in long, slow strokes until he could feel the wall of her throat.

Sucking in his breath he paused there, and looking into Patience's lust-filled eyes, he held her captive as he withdrew and thrust and withdrew and thrust, each time feeling the pressure against his eager glans as he pushed farther down the tight corridor of her throat. He grunted at the delicious depths to which she took him—swallowing his meaty thickness so deeply that his balls churned and boiled at the feeling. God, he could come again. And he could feel by her saliva-filled mouth that she wanted it. But she, and he, would have to wait. This was, after all, only a vocabulary lesson. Tightening his hands in her hair, he allowed himself a final volley of deep thrusts before pulling out.

Patience sucked in a ragged breath. He tipped up her face. She was flushed and her long lashes fluttered over her glistening eyes. "And *that* is irrumatio," he said, his voice rough. He traced the curve of her red gold eyebrow. "Two words, referring to the same act, but separated by the very significant distinction of who moves." He traced the full curves of her wide mouth. "Few people even know what irrumatio is. They lump every beautiful and subtle variation of *coitus per os* under the term *fellatio*. I, however, am a connoisseur. And you, as a French artist par excellence, should also know the proper terms of that which you perform so magnificently."

As he drew back, Patience smiled up at him. "Do I? Perform it magnificently?"

Matthew's heart quickened at the brilliance of her smile. It was genuine and . . . happy. He found his own mouth turning up as he drew the stool to the side of the tub and sat down. "You, my eauty, are masterful." He touched her lower lip. "Your mouth s wide and your throat is deep. But more importantly, you truly njoy it. And *that* is what makes you extraordinary." He handed er a small washcloth. "For your face, my lady."

Patience took it, and her smile widened. "I do enjoy it. And I uess all that practice really made perfect."

"What?" Matthew tensed, and in an instant, searing jealousy looded him. "You told me you'd never done it before."

Patience nodded. "That's right. But I've fellated more cucumers than you can imagine."

Matthew's brows shot up. "Cucumbers?" His body relaxed, nd he felt laughter rising.

"Yes." Patience soaped the cloth. "And I'll have you know I ecame very expert at not scoring the skin."

She looked so adorable and proud of herself. Matthew felt a arm flutter in his gut and he laughed out loud. "Well, that's very good, miss." He spoke around his laughter. "You must show me this trick of yours some day. In fact, I'm very anxious to see it."

"Yes." Patience raised her brows saucily. "I'm sure you are."

Matthew laughed as she lifted the washcloth and scrubbed her face. But his laughter faded as, once again, that gentle, yet inescapable, wave of something wondrous welled up within him. He gazed at her with her lovely red curls falling all around her shoulders and down her back. The wet end of one long tendril was affixed to her breast, right above her delectable nipple. It made his heart ache to look at her.

God, I want you, Patience.

She splashed water on her beautiful face.

I want to be with you every moment of every day and night. I want to know every inch of you, body and spirit.

He put a towel into her searching hand.

I want to give you babies. I want to grow old with you. And I want to take my last breath in your arms.

She patted her cheeks dry and then raised her sweet, smiling face to him.

I love you, Patience.

He stared into her grass green eyes. His heart felt like it was going to burst in his chest. Could he breathe?

Patience's smile slowly faded. "What?"

I love you.

Bloody goddamned hell—I love you.

Matthew drew a shuddering breath.

And I want you to love me.

Patience stared at him, and her eyes looked like polished glass. "What is it, Matthew?" She spoke in a whisper.

Lowering his eyes, he leaned down to her and brushed his lips softly against hers. "Nothing," he whispered.

Then he stepped into the tub and, sinking into the warm water, gathered her into his arms. "Nothing at all."

Chapter Sixteen
Long Lost Dreams

. . . my heart waketh . . .

Song of Solomon 5:2

"There," her angel whispered in her ear, "see how your heart bleeds."

Patience stared into his dark dove's eyes for she couldn't bring herself to look at her own heart.

Her angel cupped his hand against her cheek. "Look at it, or I shall punish you," he said softly.

"But I'm afraid," Patience whispered.

"Don't be. I am with you."

Slowly, Patience lowered her gaze. Blood, dark and red, poured from a deep wound on her breast. But then she realized that there wasn't just one wound. There were many, and as she watched, they all began to bleed. Choking on a panicked gasp, she clutched her arms across her chest as she looked up at her angel. "Am I dying?"

"In a way." His great wings beat the Heavens. "But I can bring you back, Patience. I can heal you."

"How?"

"Just open your arms. Take me to your breast, and I shall do what is needed." His dovelike eyes were full of hope and yearning. "But know that if you take me, it must be forever. There is no in-between for us. There is only all—or nothing." He held her in his unwavering regard. "Tell me, Patience, which will you give me?"

She paused. Then thunder crashed, scattering her weightless dream world into pieces. With a choked cry, she grabbed for her angel.

Patience's eyes flew open as her arms tightened—not around a dream, but around flesh and form.

Matthew!

Her heart constricted as she stared down at him asleep upon her breast. *Finally.* Finally, she did not wake alone. All thoughts of her panicked dream faded. He was with her. And the reality of him was stronger than any dream, for she could feel the weight and warmth of him. She could feel the touch of his breath and the softness of his hair upon her skin.

Her heart welled with an old pain and a new happiness.

He was with her . . .

She glanced around the comfortable bedroom. It was a large chamber built into an odd little tower at the rear of the house. Matthew said it was the only part of the old Tudor manse that rose above the forest around it, and that, on a clear day, you could see Hawkmore House from the bay of mullioned windows. A fire crackled in the wide hearth and two overstuffed chairs sat cozily before it. She and Matthew were snuggled into a high four-poster bed covered with old velvet quilts and, above them, dark beams crisscrossed to support the canted roof. The storm sounded loud, as there was no attic above.

She sighed. It was a heavenly room.

A small bedside clock chimed twice. She'd napped for a little over an hour, but she had no desire to rise.

She drew her arms more tightly around Matthew and, breathing in the smell of him, pressed a lingering kiss to his forehead. With his cheek pressed to her chest, his arm snug around her waist, and his leg tossed over both of hers, he captured her even whilst he slept. A tear of happiness slipped into her hair. It was the most comforting confinement she'd ever felt.

What would it be like—?

She closed her eyes against more tears. She shouldn't think of it. But, God, she couldn't help it. What would it be like to feel this warm contentment—this sweet serenity—all the time?

Opening her eyes, she studied the curves and angles of Matthew's face. What would it be like to give herself to him? To belong to him—forever?

At the moment, nothing seemed as important, or meaningful. At the moment, her carefully constructed plan for her life seemed ill conceived and contrived—Cavalli, an obstruction, not an opportunity. With Matthew pressed to her breast, dreams of an entirely different life filled her head—dreams of husband and home, dreams of children and laughter. She gazed at him and gently smoothed his thick, gold-tipped hair back from his brow. Dreams of pleasure and punishment.

But unlike ever before, her dreams now had form and substance. She stroked her fingers across Matthew's cheek. Now, her dreams came with the eyes of a dove, the face of an angel, and the strong hand of a pagan god.

"What are you doing to me, Matthew?" she whispered softly. His dark lashes twitched. "Are you really my prince?"

He lay still and quiet as the question echoed in her mind. Could it be true? Her heart yearned to believe it, but did she dare? She bit her lip to keep it from trembling. What would happen if she did?

What would happen if he proposed to her right now?

Matthew stood quietly in the doorway to the large kitchen. He had donned fresh trousers and a shirt, and was holding a dressing gown that he had slipped from Patience's closet that morning. But looking at her now, he dropped it on the upholstered bench that sat just outside the entry to the kitchen.

Dressed in her corset and petticoats, Patience was preparing a tea tray on the large table in the middle of the room. She wore an apron around her slim waist and one red curl, having escaped her loosely upswept hair, bobbed before her eye as she settled things into place.

He loved her. Why had he bothered resisting it? He'd loved her from the first, deeply and desperately. He'd known because the feeling was unlike any he'd ever experienced before. It was exhilaration, hope, happiness, and desire all bound tightly together with a ribbon of bliss. Only one thing could possibly lift him higher—her love in return.

He watched her for a moment longer and smiled as a tiny frown turned her brow. God, did she know—could she possibly know—how beautiful she was?

"I have only one question," he said gently, drawing her immediate attention. "*What* is that heavenly aroma?"

Patience smiled and pushed back her curl. "Lemon cream scones."

Matthew stared at her and his heart wavered. There was something new in her eyes. A tender susceptibility, perhaps. *Yes.* It was tentative and fragile, like the glimmer of light that halos a barely opened door. But it was there. He swallowed. "Scones?"

"You said that you always wake hungry." She smoothed her hands on the front of her apron. "And you were sleeping so deeply . . ." Her fingers clenched the fabric and then let it go. "Besides"—she shrugged—"it's about teatime and you've brought me breakfast twice. It was the least I could do."

Oh, no you don't—no platitudes. "Was it?" Matthew slipped his hands in his pockets and tilted his head. "So you made scones in order to pay me back for the breakfasts I've brought you?"

Patience looked at him for a moment, and then a small frown turned her brow. "No," she said softly. "That's not why."

Matthew stood very still. "Then why?"

She looked down for a long moment and a curl fell against her temple. When she finally raised her eyes back to his, Matthew's heart wrenched. Behind a glistening veil of unshed tears, her gaze seemed fraught with both hope and dread.

Matthew tensed with anticipation and the desire to take her in his arms, but he forced himself to remain still. If he moved, he might chase away the words that she seemed on the brink of speaking. His gut tightened. The patter of the rain and the snap of the kitchen fire filled the silence.

Patience released a long, tremulous breath.

Matthew held his.

"It's just that you've—" Her voice shook and her lips trembled. "You've made me so happy, you see. And—and, I'm not certain, but I think that I haven't been happy in a very long time." Her tears spilled over, and she quickly swiped them away. "So, I—I wanted to do something for you. Something that would please you." She swallowed and her chest heaved with a quick breath. "I made the scones because I wanted to make you happy." Her voice trailed off and she stood stiffly, her fingers clenched in the fabric of her apron.

Matthew felt like his heart was going to burst. He wanted to rush to her and hold her against him. He wanted to discover all the reasons for her unhappiness, and then he wanted to banish that unhappiness forever. He wanted to pledge his love to her and give her everything—heart, home, family, and fortune.

But he had to proceed with a delicate seesaw of push and release, push and release. For Patience was like a wounded bird. Although he'd coaxed her to eat from his hand, if he tried to grab her too soon, she would surely claw and peck to fly away.

So he crossed to her slowly. He took her hands gently, and drawing her fingers to his lips, he kissed them reverently. Then, holding her hand to his heart, he looked into her moist gaze. "You make me intensely happy. Thank you."

Patience's lashes fluttered and then her lovely mouth turned up in the corners. "You're welcome."

Patience felt Matthew's heart flutter beneath her hand. Then he smiled at her with such a happy, carefree light in his dark eyes that it made her own smile deepen.

They stood there for a moment, and it suddenly occurred to Patience that they were grinning at each other like a couple of—well, like a couple of love-struck children. With a shake of her head, she pulled her hand away. But as she crossed to the oven, her smile remained. Removing the scones, she returned to place them on a rack on the table.

Matthew's eyes widened. "God, those look absolutely marvelous." Moistening his lips, he took a seat on one of the benches and rubbed his hands together enthusiastically. "I'm famished."

Patience couldn't suppress her pleasure, and laughed lightly as she sat across from him. Her bottom was a little sore, but while she was grateful for the padding that seven layers of petticoats offered, she had already discovered that she rather liked the achy, tender feeling. As she moved, bent, and sat, it was a constant reminder of what had occurred between them—a constant reminder that, even if only for now, she belonged to Matthew. "I'm glad you're hungry." She reached for the tea tray. "The scones need to cool just a little, though."

"Very well. But I'll have you know that when it comes to food—and you—I hate waiting." He leaned his chin in his hand with a smile, but as he watched her pour the tea a tiny frown marred his brow.

Patience paused. "What's wrong? You don't care for any tea?"

"No, I'm quite eager for tea." His frown deepened. "I'm just wondering what you're doing sitting way over there?"

"Oh." Patience glanced at the wide expanse of table that separated them. "Well, it's customary to sit across when one is conversing, isn't it?"

"My sweet Patience, nothing between us is customary. How can I possibly ogle and fondle you from such a great distance? I can barely see you across this vast wasteland of a table, and I most certainly can't touch you."

Patience grinned. "No wonder you and Aunt Matty get on so well. You're as prone to exaggeration as she is."

"Yes, now stop stalling and come sit beside me immediately."

Patience started to move but the feel of her sore bottom made her pause. Had her submission to punishment gained her any leniency? Surely it had. Her heart beat faster as she met Matthew's gaze. "You could come over here."

Matthew's eyes seemed to darken slightly but his expression remained mild. "Ah, my sweet Patience. I see you need reassurance."

Did she? What exactly did she need to be reassured of—that he would yield, or that he would *not* yield?

A small smile turned Matthew's mouth. "I love your challenges, Patience. They give me something to rise to. They give me a special purpose."

Patience tilted her head. "What purpose?"

"To bring you to your proper place—which, at this moment, is beside me. To help you grow in your obedience. To reassure you and comfort you." He stood up and his cock was a hard, thick bulge in his trousers. "To make you happy, my beauty."

Patience's heart thumped and the tiny heart between her legs answered with an echo. "Is that your purpose, Matthew? To make me happy?"

"But of course." Matthew regarded her as he began to roll up his sleeve. "Your happiness is one of my foremost desires. Now, come to me immediately and bend over the table."

Patience's eyes widened and her cunt throbbed. "You mean to punish me? Again? Just for a question?"

Matthew raised his brows as he turned up his other sleeve. "Oh, come now, Patience. Stop acting so surprised. I told you this morning that I would not tolerate this sort of petty disobedience." He rested his hands on his lean hips, and her attention was drawn again to his prominent erection. "Or is it that you thought I would spare your sore bottom?"

She snapped her eyes back to his. *Yes!* That was exactly what she'd thought.

He shook his head with a small smile. "If you think submitting to punishment is a pass to disobedience, you are *sorely* mistaken." He lifted one brow. "No pun intended."

Patience tried to slow her racing pulse as she rested her chin in her hand. "Hmm." She knew she was being cheeky. "And if I refuse to obey?"

Matthew regarded her for a moment, and then his smile lifted slowly on one side. "I wouldn't, were I you."

Patience felt the tingle of her nipples hardening. She was surely escalating the situation, but she felt no inclination to stop. She shrugged. "Why not? I can always speak 'the words' if I want."

Matthew crossed his arms over his chest with a sigh. "You can, but that would be a mistake. The words of refusal are not really meant to be spoken, Patience. They exist to comfort you. They are the escape that always *can* be taken, but never *is* taken."

It was true. Several times she'd thought of saying "the words," but she hadn't. It was enough that she knew she could. But what if she actually did voice them? She tilted her head. "So if I spoke 'the words,' you would not heed them?"

"Of course I would. But it's a moot point, for if I serve you well enough, you never will speak 'the words.' " Matthew leaned his hands on the table. "Remember, Patience, it isn't submission if you only do it when you want to. It isn't submission if you only do it when it's easy. And it most certainly isn't submission if you start avoiding it with the speaking of a simple sentence." He held her with his dark gaze. "Is it?"

Her clitoris pulsed as she stared into the depths of his beautiful eyes. "No."

He was quiet for a moment and then his voice came, soft as velvet. "You will submit to me when it pleases you and when it doesn't. You will submit to me when it is easy and when it is difficult. You will submit to me through pleasure and through pain. And you will most definitely submit to me despite the existence of certain words to the contrary." He straightened slowly. "Come."

Patience regarded him only a moment longer before she found herself getting to her feet and walking slowly around the table. Her heart beat fast and she felt a little uneasy for her sore bottom. Yet, the closer she got to Matthew, the wetter she felt between her legs. How strange it was to feel both dread and desire at the same time.

She paused beside him and felt herself blushing as she met his determined gaze.

"Lean forward," he said quietly, "forearms on the table."

Patience did as he said. The position was quite comfortable, but the moment she felt her petticoats flipping up, she tensed as both her anxiety and her excitement escalated.

"Ah, Patience"—Matthew smoothed his warm hand over her bared curves—"your beautiful bottom is still rosy. However, you can well afford this little reminder."

Patience bit back a surprised yelp as his hand came down fast and firm on her sore flesh. Despite all he'd said, she had really expected to feel a gentler reprimand. But such was not the case, and in no time she was gasping and writhing as Matthew heated the entirety of her aching posterior with short, sharp spanks.

The moment he stopped, she dropped fully onto the table. With her cheek pressed to the smooth wood, she drew shallow, panting breaths that quickly slowed and deepened. Her bottom was hot, sore, and throbbing. The sensation pulsed through her body with a strange and sensual deliciousness that massaged her from the inside out. She felt completely relaxed and completely at peace. But most fascinating of all, she felt a deep and intensely satisfying sense that she was Matthew's—that she belonged to him and that he would take care of her.

A flood of relief and overwhelming gratitude washed through her. Her eyes stung with fresh tears.

God . . .

For how long had she felt neglected? How long?

Matthew pulled her up, and she immediately wrapped her

arms around him. She breathed in his skin, and pressed soft, urgent kisses against the warm column of his throat and the smooth line of his jaw.

He held her with his whole self. His body braced her, his arms encircled her, his fingers pressed her tenderly, and his head bent over her. She was enveloped in his protective embrace, and she felt entirely safe—entirely happy.

She nestled her face against the curve of his neck. Would that such feelings could last forever. "Thank you, Matthew."

His arms tightened around her and his mouth turned to hers. "You're welcome," he whispered against her lips. Then he kissed her with a slow gentleness that made her feel weak.

Chapter Seventeen

Questions, Answers, and Explanations

. . . let me see thy countenance, let me hear thy voice; for sweet is thy voice, and thy countenance is comely.

Song of Solomon 2:14

"Patience, I have never had scones as delicious as these."

Sitting gingerly beside him, on what he was sure must be a nicely aching bottom, Patience grinned. "I'm glad you like them."

Truly, the spanking he'd given her hadn't been a very hard one at all. But she was just beginning, so everything seemed more than it was.

She leaned her pretty chin in her hand. "Would you care for another?"

"Yes. But how many have I had?"

"Three."

Matthew raised his brows. "Only three? Then I'd better have one more."

Patience's smile deepened as he picked up another scone and took a big bite. Not only were they delicious, but *she* had made them—for him.

Since he was sitting astride the bench, he stared into her smiling eyes as he swallowed the fluffy mouthful. *She* had made them. The more he thought about it, the more it pleased him. "You know, this is the first time in my life that I have ever eaten food that was not prepared by a kitchen staff or purchased from a merchant."

She looked him up and down. "Spoiled."

Matthew looked at the sugar-glazed scone and then back at Patience. *I love you.* "No—not spoiled." Leaning forward, he kissed her soft lips. "Not until now."

Patience's mouth curled back into a smile as he withdrew to finish his scone. It was such a sweet and endearing smile—one he hadn't seen before. His heart beat a little faster. *Ah, Patience, your walls are crumbling.*

"If you keep smiling at me like that," he said, "I will soon be robbed of all my wit, and you will have naught in me but a dumb and drooling mute who trails incessantly at your heels in hopes of the smallest favor."

Patience laughed. "Somehow, I doubt that." She leaned close and would have kissed his cheek, but he turned to catch it on his mouth instead. Her lips were soft and warm. She lingered a moment before withdrawing with a sigh and a smile. "In fact, if anyone is in danger of such a fate, it is I."

"Are you?" Matthew swallowed the last of his tea. "Excellent."

Patience laughed lightly. "Oh, you'd like me witless, would you?"

"No. Witless would be boring. But I wouldn't discourage you from trailing incessantly at my heels. Of course"—he traced his finger along her collarbone—"you couldn't do that from London, could you?"

Patience grinned and shook her head. "Were I constantly in your presence, you would become bored with me."

Matthew felt a surge of hope. She hadn't voiced a flat refusal. "Patience, I would happily spend my every waking moment with you."

Her smile faded but her eyes were soft. "Never having spent your every waking moment with me, how can you know that?"

Because I love you. Because we are meant to be together—forever. "I just know. But why don't we put it to the test?" Matthew gently fingered the thick curl that had fallen forward from her upswept hair. "Agree to stay with me, and I'll prove my point."

Patience regarded him for a long, silent moment. Her beautiful gaze was tender.

Matthew's heart quickened. Slowly, he closed the small gap between them. "Say yes, Patience," he murmured against her lips. When she didn't speak, he took her mouth in what he intended to be a brief kiss. But her lips were so soft, and the smell of her filled his head.

Say yes, my love—say it . . .

For a moment, he struggled to keep the kiss from becoming demanding. But then his arms swept around her, and he held her tightly as he plunged his tongue into her sweet mouth. His head spun as Patience moaned, and he could feel her embrace, close and clasping. With a gasp, he broke the kiss and pressed his forehead to hers as he tried to calm his racing pulse.

Patience's breath came in short, shallow pants. "Oh, Matthew"—her hand curved against his cheek—"you're not playing fair."

Clasping her hand, he laid a kiss in her palm. "I know." He pressed her hand over his heart as he drew back. "But there is nothing I won't do to keep you, Patience." By now, Cavalli had likely received his letter. A shiver of doubt scurried up his back, but he shoved it away. "There is *nothing* I won't do."

Her mouth turned up in a soft smile. "Wouldn't you rather have my answer without coercion?"

Yes. "Oh, I don't know. I rather like coercing you."

Patience's smile deepened. "And I rather like being coerced by you." Her smile softened as she regarded him. "But in this case . . ."

"Yes." He stared into her bright green eyes. "The answer is yes." He studied her a moment longer before releasing her hand and expelling what he knew was a petulant-sounding sigh. "But I hate waiting."

Patience grinned. "Why, you only just asked me yesterday." Wrapping her arms around his waist, she tucked her head beneath his chin. "You've barely waited at all."

Matthew's heart lifted at her spontaneous embrace. He pulled her as close as he could, so that even her legs were resting over his thigh. "Well, it feels like forever," he murmured.

Patience pressed a gentle kiss to the underside of his jaw, but she said nothing. In the silence, the kitchen fire snapped and the rain pattered against the windows. Content, Matthew held her. He breathed the scent of her hair and stroked his hands over the curves of her back and waist. He could feel the occasional flicker of her lashes against his neck.

"Matthew?"

"Yes?"

There was another brief pause, and then, "How many women have you taught what you are teaching me?"

Matthew pressed a kiss to her brow. "None, Patience. You are my first, my one and my only."

Patience drew back, her expression incredulous. "How can that be? You must have done this before. You know everything about it."

Matthew paused. It had been inevitable that she would ask the question. He met her gaze. "There are houses, Patience, that specialize in the fulfillment of specific desires. When I came of age, it didn't take me long to find a place where I might explore my particular interests."

"These 'houses' are houses of prostitution?"

"Yes."

A small frown turned Patience's brow. "So I'm *not* your first. I'm just the first you're not paying for." The words were spoken calmly, but he heard sadness in them.

"No." Matthew tipped up her chin and stared into her deep green eyes. "You *are* my first—my *one* and my *only*," he repeated. "There is a universe of difference, Patience, between what we are building together, and what I paid for at Mr. Stone's. There, the young women are trained to submit to any customer. Therefore, their submission rarely reaches beyond the physical. They need their regular discipline and fulfillment, and though they have their favorites, generally it matters not who metes it out—or in what way it is meted out—so long as Mr. Stone's rules are not broken. The submissive gets what she wants, the customer gets what he wants, and the evening is over. It's all very superficial—and so it must be."

He stroked his hand down the soft curve of her cheek. "But what you and I have is altogether deeper. What I do for you is only for you. You are my only study, and my only desire. My devotion to you is total. And the surrender I want for you is total. So that whether I am with you, or miles away from you, you will be mine—in all things and in all ways guided, and made happy, by your submission to me." Her beautiful eyes never left his. *God, I love you. And I am only going to love you more and more.* "I shall master none but you, Patience." He pressed his lips to the corner of her mouth. "And you will belong to no one but me—ever."

Patience released her breath on a soft sigh. Her parted lips and the small, almost pained frown that turned her brow sent a strong pulse to his prick. She wanted what he offered. Capitulation was close. He could feel it.

Patience. He must have patience.

He forced his face into casual lines. "So you see, just as you observed the practice of fellatio by your maid and butler, I observed the training and submission of many a young woman. Just as you practiced upon your garden cucumbers, I practiced upon some of those ladies." Matthew smoothed the frown from her brow with his finger. "But just as you had never actually fellated a man, I had never chosen a woman to teach and to train as my own."

Patience regarded him for a long, quiet moment. "Could you have, though?" She tilted her head. "I mean, if you'd wanted to, could you have purchased such an opportunity from this Mr. Stone?"

Matthew paused. Apparently, she needed answers from him. "Yes," he admitted. "Not because that was on the menu, because it wasn't. But because Mr. Stone has a philosophical and biblically based belief in feminine submission, and he knew I was dedicated to gaining a deeper understanding of it."

Patience raised her brows. "A brothel owner with biblically based beliefs?"

Matthew smiled and refrained from commenting on their own break with biblical law. "Yes."

Her expression settled back into thoughtfulness. "So if Mr. Stone offered you the opportunity, why didn't you take it?"

Matthew stared into her intense green gaze. "I was waiting for you."

Her lashes flickered. "You didn't know me."

"No." A stillness floated in the air between them. "But I knew the dream of you. And the moment I saw you, I knew you were the one—the one I'd been waiting for."

"Waiting, Matthew?" Her voice was soft. "You weren't waiting; you were engaged." A small, disbelieving smile turned her mouth. "Do you mean to tell me that you never shared your desires with Rosalind?" She lowered her eyes and began straightening her apron across her lap. "Really, Matthew, everyone knows how completely in love with her you were."

Matthew frowned. "No one knows anything of the kind." He lifted her chin and was surprised to find her eyes shiny. His heart tightened. He looked directly into her eyes. "I *never* loved Rosalind." *I love you.* "What she and I had was just a façade."

Patience smiled shakily and a flush pinked her cheeks. "I shouldn't have brought her up. You told me Rosalind is in the past, and I believe you."

Matthew's frown deepened as the image of Rosalind pressing herself against him that morning replayed in his mind. He shouldn't have allowed her to touch him.

Patience's smile faded. "I'm sorry, Matthew. Please don't frown so. My doubts stem from . . . from my own uncertainties. You've done nothing to deserve them. In fact, you've given me so much—and offered me even more." There was such gentle regret in her eyes. "Forgive me."

Matthew's heart lurched. Pulling her to him, he masked his own regret with a kiss that was born of love and desire. If he gave her enough, if he showed her with his heart and with his body what he felt, then nothing else would matter. Nothing.

Breathlessly breaking the kiss, he cupped her exquisite face in his hands. "I've never hidden the way I am, Patience—for I'm not ashamed of my proclivities or beliefs. But I'm telling you that Rosalind and I were not even a shadow of what you and I are. All the months I knew her do not compare to the days I have spent with you." He held her gaze, willing her to see the truth in his eyes. "You, Patience—you're the dream I thought I would never find. So how, in a thousand seasons of eternity, could Rosalind ever compare to you?"

. . . a thousand seasons of eternity . . .

. . . the dream he thought he would never find.

As his hands slipped from her face, Patience let his words soak beneath her skin and into her soul. She didn't question them. She didn't minimize them or dismiss them. She accepted them and believed them—and let them make her happy—incredibly, marvelously happy.

She smiled into Matthew's gaze, even as she silently vowed to never again bring up Rosalind. His dark eyes delved so deeply into hers. God, how was it possible that they were even more beautiful than ever? "Thank you, Matthew." Leaning forward, she pressed a quick but urgent kiss to his lips. "And thank you for answering my questions honestly. I like knowing the truth, even if it does involve a house of prostitution. It never occurred to me that such places might specialize in particular desires."

Matthew's serious expression eased and the corners of his mouth lifted. "Really? The subject never came up over the dinner table in your home?"

Patience's smile deepened. "No."

"Imagine that." Matthew grinned and leaned his cheek on his fist. "Mr. Stone's is only one house of many that caters to similar desires."

"One of many? I didn't know that it was so common." Patience felt herself blushing as she shifted on her sore bottom. "I thought, perhaps, that I—that we—were strange."

"Oh, Patience"—Matthew's smile gentled and he stroked his hand across her cheek—"I assure you, we are not. Desire comes in infinite variety. Besides, what is strange about the feminine desire to submit, and the masculine desire to dominate? Are these not the roles we most often see acted out in nature? Are these not at the most basic of levels, the natural tendencies of the sexes?"

"Yes." Patience lifted her brows. "But then I've known plenty of men who could have used a sound thrashing. And Mrs. Hawkings, the poulterer's wife, clouts her husband all the way to market and home again."

Matthew chuckled. "There are always exceptions, aren't there? But do exceptions belie general truth? Do exceptions belie us?"

"Well, no. But I can't help feeling that *we* are the exception."

"Perhaps we are, in that few actually understand and live this life to its fullest—and more's the pity. But does that mean we shouldn't?"

Patience wasn't certain she actually understood what living "this life to its fullest" meant either, both in the context of submission and in the context of their relationship. But she did know how she felt right now—awakened, fulfilled, happy, and cared-for. What would it be like to feel this way all the time? And what depths of feeling would she discover if she stayed with Matthew?

"I'll tell you something, Patience." Matthew's voice drew her attention back to him. "I think this life—one shared between a man and a woman in true and deep accordance with their natural predispositions—must be very close to the life God meant for us."

Patience lifted a brow. "Are you bringing God into this conversation in order to sway me?"

Matthew grinned, but then he said, "Not at all. I think there's merit in the notion." He traced his finger idly along her collarbone. "Did God not create Eve in answer to Adam's needs and desires?"

Patience shivered at his touch. "Perhaps. But some scholars believe they were created together."

Matthew stroked his hand down her arm to her wrist. "Whether they were created individually or together"—lifting her hand, he held it against his own larger one—"did God not create Eve more delicately, more softly, because she was not meant to resist Adam, but rather to submit to him?" He brushed his nose against the skin over her pulse. His eyes closed briefly, then he turned his dark gaze back upon her. Patience felt her heart quickening. "In fact," he continued, "did He not create her so that in order to be filled with the seed of life, she must submit to Adam's penetration?" Patience drew in her breath as he pulled her hand down and pressed it to his thick erection. "Men carry the staff of their dominance between their legs, Patience." He held his hand over hers and thrust against her palm. "What greater proof could there be that feminine submission is God's will?"

Patience curled her fingers around him and her clitoris throbbed as he continued to thrust gently against her hand.

His expression remained relaxed. "What say you? What says my vicar's daughter?"

Patience tried to concentrate. "I'm thinking."

"You're beautiful when you're thinking. In fact, you're beautiful all the time."

Patience grinned and shook her head. "And you're distracting me."

"Sorry." Matthew released her and, leaning his chin in his hand, waited.

"All right." Patience gathered her thoughts as she squared her shoulders and drew a deep breath. "I can't say I disagree with the points you've made. However, it's hardly fair to hold women to God's will whilst men walk around ignoring His will entirely. If woman is meant obey her husband, then it must be acknowledged that man is meant to protect and provide for his wife. And if he is to wield authority, and expect obedience to that authority, then he must bear the responsibility that comes with it. He must be trustworthy, and self-disciplined. He must use good judgment and always have the best interests of his wife in mind. And if his authority is never to be questioned, then he must be a man whose goodness and strength of character are unquestionable."

Patience nodded decisively as she warmed to her subject. "Yes, like any king, lord, or leader of men, a man who would be a husband must be held to a very high standard. He must do the work for which he is suited—work that will provide a life of safety and security. What's more, he must cherish his wife and strive to make her happy, just as she so strives for him. He must care for her and show her affection. And, if God wills it, he should give her children, for children are our earthly immortality."

Patience frowned. "Which brings me to the point that if the staff of a man's dominance rests between his legs, then he'd best be sure that it is pressed only to his wife, for *she*, and only she, is the one who is bound to it through her holy vows. She, and only she, is the one who kneels before it in submission. And she, and only she, is the one who is entitled to its pleasure."

Sitting back, Patience expelled the last of her breath in a short burst and waited for Matthew's rebuttal.

A slow smile lit his face, and it suddenly seemed that his dark dove's eyes were deeper and gentler than ever. "I agree completely."

Patience felt her brows shoot up. "You do?"

"Of course." Matthew stood up and crossed to the wide entrance of the kitchen. He turned and leaned against the doorframe. "There's only one thing you left out."

"There is?" Patience quickly reviewed her points in her mind. "What?"

"Love. You failed to mention love."

Patience felt as if everything stilled. "Did I?"

"Yes."

"Well, there must be love—mustn't there?"

"Yes." His dark gaze touched her like an embrace. "There must be love."

Patience suddenly felt flushed, her chest too full for breath. What was happening?

Matthew's expression shifted. He raised his brows. "For example, if a man were to say to his wife"—he looked at her expectantly—"*come*."

Patience stood and crossed to him, feeling her sore bottom the whole way.

Matthew nodded approvingly. "Then she will do so, without question, because she knows that whatever the reason for his bidding, even if it be to punish her, it comes out of his love for her."

Patience felt wet between her legs. She shivered and her nipples tightened.

"Of course," Matthew murmured, "much of the time she will find that answering his summons leads to something quite pleasant." He reached around the doorframe and produced her dressing gown.

Patience raised her brows in surprise as he held it open for her.

"I packed a full set of your undergarments and a fresh gown as well."

Patience smiled as she turned and slipped her arms into the sleeves of her gown. "You thought of everything, didn't you?"

"That's what I do, Patience." He settled the gown over her shoulders. "I think of everything you need."

She sighed as he pressed a kiss against the back of her neck, and her legs trembled a little as she turned to face him.

His eyes searched hers. "I hope you don't mind that I went into your wardrobe."

Did she? Three days ago, she might have. But nothing was as it had been three days ago. She shook her head. "No, I don't mind at all."

"Good," he murmured as he began closing the tiny buttons of her dressing gown. She watched his long, deft fingers as they quickly accomplished the task. His attentions were growing on her. She liked when he dressed her—and undressed her.

She looked up at his face. His eyes were lowered, but his hair had fallen forward on his temples and his beautiful mouth was soft and relaxed. With her eye, she traced the curve of his brow to his cheekbone, and then the plane of his cheek to the sweep of his strong jaw. Lord, he was so intensely handsome—and so wise and tender.

As he lifted the collar of her dressing gown more snugly around her neck, Matthew raised his dark eyes to hers. "I like when you look at me. It makes me feel warm."

Patience's stomach fluttered. "Isn't that funny? When I look at you, I feel warm, too."

He smiled. "Then it serves both of us, and you should do it more."

Patience smiled, and, somewhere in the house, a clock chimed.

"Four o'clock," Matthew said softly. "We ought to go, but the storm is still raging." He stroked her cheek with his finger. "I don't think it's safe."

Patience shook her head. "Neither do I." Leaving was the last thing she wanted to do. She sighed. "But we'll surely be missed if we don't return."

"Mark knows where we are. If we're asked after, I'm sure he'll think of something to say."

"I'm glad he knows where we are." That meant Passion would know, too. "But I don't like him having to lie for us."

Matthew smiled. "He won't lie. He'll say something ambiguous." He traced his finger along her lower lip. "I have an idea. Why don't we stay the night and return early—before anyone rises?"

Could they? Patience smiled, and happiness coursed through her. She couldn't resist the idea. She couldn't resist *him*. "I think that's an excellent plan."

Matthew's smile deepened. "Good, then."

There they were, smiling again.

Patience let her gaze flicker down the wide corridor that led to the front of the manse. Earlier, she had paused to admire the landscapes and hunt scenes that decorated the paneled walls. She looked back at Matthew. "I like this house."

"Do you?"

"Yes, it feels strong and sound. Yet it's also warm and comfortable."

He nodded as he ran his hand gently over the worn wood molding of the doorframe. "I like it, too."

"I'm not surprised, it suits you."

"Do you think so?" He cocked his brow at her. "It's old, drafty, and gerrymandered."

"That's what gives it character."

"It's too secluded and hidden away."

"Then only those worthy of it will find it."

He began to smile. "It's worn and ragged in places."

"Aren't we all?"

Matthew laughed, and Patience smiled at the happy sound for his happiness fed her own.

Taking her hand, he led her slowly down the corridor. "It's called Gwyn Hall, and it was built in 1530 by the Earl of Marsham for his young bride. They were married in the tiny chapel behind the garden."

"How romantic."

Matthew smiled at her. "Yes, it is." Drawing her arm through his, he led her into the long dining room. "The house came into Hawkmore hands after the Restoration. Charles II granted the house and its land, which bordered the western edge of the Hawkmore estate, to the fourth Earl of Langley as a gift."

Patience admired the beautiful linen-fold paneling of the room.

"The fourth earl ignored the place," Matthew continued, "but the fifth earl used it as a hunting lodge. It was he who had over a hundred trees planted around the house. He thought it looked more rustic that way. The sixth earl kept the place up but rarely used it, and my fa—" Matthew cut himself off. "George Hawkmore gave the house its modern improvements."

Patience felt him stiffen. She smiled and pulled his arm close. "Well, thank goodness for George Hawkmore, because I particularly enjoyed that deep copper tub. And the kitchen is a wonder."

Matthew looked down at her, and she watched the tension melt from his face.

"As I was looking for the kitchen," she continued, "I noticed that there's a study off the library with a number of model trains on the shelves. Are those your trains?"

"They are. Before I bought Angel's Manor I used to spend

quite a lot of time here. I believe my practice instrument is there as well. Would you like to play?"

"No, thank you." She felt absolutely *no* inclination to play. "But I'd like to see the trains. Will you show me?"

He clasped her hand and pulled her with him.

The spacious room was chilly as no fire burned in the hearth. And even though a large bay window and two tall side windows let light in through diamond-shaped mullions, the fury of the storm and the hour made that light dim and watery. As Matthew lit some lamps, Patience crossed to the shelves behind the desk. Interspersed throughout the books were models of engines, carriages, and depots. There were so many, and they all sported the gold initials of GWR—Grand West Railway wasn't a company, it was an empire.

Patience remembered the gossip of Lady Humphreys and her companions. They had said people didn't want to do business with Matthew anymore—that he would find himself in the poorhouse. She shook her head as she scanned the many models. Ridiculous! GWR was huge—even the Swittley sisters knew of Matthew's wealth. He'd taken ten thousand pounds to the gaming table for heaven's sake. And now he owned a coal mine as well!

Besides—she picked up the heavy model of a shiny black engine—what possible effect could a scandal over illegitimacy have on a rail company the size and stature of GWR? Especially when that illegitimacy had no real or practical consequence upon anything.

Matthew joined her. "That's the model for our first engine."

"It looks different from the engine of the train that brought me from Lincolnshire," Patience said, returning it carefully to the shelf.

"Yes." Matthew pointed out another black engine that was far bigger and heavier looking. "This is the beast that brought you here. It's called the Black Dragon—so named for its strength and speed." He raised his brows. "And its insatiable appetite for coal."

"Well, fortunately you own a coal mine. By the way, I read the article in the paper this morning. It's credits you with 'changing the face of two monumental industries.'" She smiled. "That's very exciting, Matthew. Congratulations on your success."

"Thank you." Matthew's dark eyes studied her for a moment. "You know, when I went to play cards, I had no idea that Danforth was carrying the deed to a coal mine in his pocket. I could have come away with nothing."

"When I attended the ball, I had no idea you were carrying the deed to my desires in *your* pocket. God often sends blessings when we least expect them, Matthew."

Pulling her into his arms, he kissed her deeply and thoroughly. Patience moaned and pressed more tightly against him as his hands squeezed her sore bottom.

Breaking the kiss, he spoke against her lips. "Are you sure you want to continue discussing trains?" He held her to him as he rubbed slowly against her. "Because I do believe I have something in my pocket for you right now." He smiled. "Something I think you should see."

Patience laughed as she pulled back. "I believe that I'm already acquainted with what's in your pocket, sir."

"Ah, but not nearly well enough, miss."

Patience shook her head with a smile. "Are you going to tell me anything more about your business or not?"

Matthew sighed. "What do you want to know?"

"Well, what about this new coal mine? You know, despite the laws, conditions in mines and mining villages are typically horrible. Do you have plans to visit?"

Matthew regarded her thoughtfully for a moment. "You really are a vicar's daughter, aren't you?"

Patience grinned and felt herself blushing again. "Well, it may not always seem like it, but yes."

His arms came around her. "I'm aware conditions for miners are typically poor." He pressed kisses to her brow and temple. "And, yes, I plan to visit."

She sighed and leaned into him. "What if it's terrible?"

He nuzzled her ear. "Then I'll fix it."

Patience smiled into his neck and held him tighter. "You're the best of men, Matthew." She shivered. "The best of men."

Chapter Eighteen

A Promise and a Decision

Thou that dwellest in the gardens, the companions hearken to thy voice . . .
Song of Solomon 8:13

"So tell me, Matt, dearest. How are things progressing?" Aunt Matty sat in a chair beside Matthew on the large terrace overlooking the garden. The storm of the day before was gone and, as the autumn party and hunt was over, most of the guests had left that morning after breakfast. The house was peaceful. "Can we expect an announcement soon?"

Yes. Matthew tipped his head toward her. "Well, you know Patience, Aunt Matty."

Narrowing her eyes and pursing her lips, the woman drew a breath in loudly through her nose. "I most certainly do."

Matthew held back his smile and shook his head. "There's just no rushing her."

"Oh!" The word came out as a frustrated exhalation. "That girl—I could just . . ." Aunt Matty clenched her hands as she looked across the rose garden at Patience.

She was walking the gravel paths with Passion, and the late morning sun made her hair look like fire.

Aunt Matty's hand clamped down on his arm. "You've got to take her in hand, Matt."

Matthew met the older woman's gaze. "Really? You think so?"

"I do." Aunt Matty said definitively. "For her own good, someone's got to do it. The girl has rebelled against God and common sense for too long. It's time to put an end to it."

"What do you recommend I do?"

Mathilda Dare raised her silver brows. "You mean besides put her over your knee, which is what she *really* needs?"

Matthew regarded the woman with a new respect. For all her eccentricity, she understood certain things perfectly.

She shook her head. "If only her father had done so long ago, I'm sure we would not be having this conversation. Of course"—the peeved look washed from her face—"I'm so glad we *are* having this conversation, because I know I wouldn't have liked anyone else she'd married so much as I like you." She patted his arm.

"Thank you, Aunt Matty."

She smiled. "You're welcome, Matt dear. Now"—the peeved look returned—"what to do with her?" She tapped her fingers on his arm. She sighed and tapped some more. "You see, this is the problem I've always faced. I can never come up with a workable plan because nothing works on her. She sees through everything. She resists everything. She's positively incorrigible."

Matthew nodded in what he hoped was an empathetic fashion. "It seems we're just going to have to be patient with our Patience."

Aunt Matty lifted her eyes heavenward. "God knows I have been exercising patience with Patience for years. So many years, that I'm entirely out of patience. I've spent it all, Matt." She snapped her fingers and made a *ptht* sound. "I don't know where patience is kept, but if you could look there, you would see that mine is entirely gone. It's tragic really, how she's used up all my patience—and it being such a virtue." Not looking at all tragic, she glanced across the garden but then looked quickly back at him. "I mean, how will I ever acquire more? I don't even know if it's possible. Do you?"

Thoroughly entertained, Matthew nodded. "I believe I've heard of some kind of secret reservoir of patience. Just when you think you have none, it bubbles up from somewhere."

"Really?"

"Yes. I think you'll be all right."

"Well, thank goodness. But let's not tell Patience. After all, it's because of her that I am currently bereft of a very important virtue. I think she should be made to suffer over my present state."

She pressed her hand to her breast as if something hurt. "I mean really, Matt, you have no idea what it feels like to be positively parched for patience."

Ha! That morning he'd awakened with such a fierce desire to fuck his sleeping beauty that he'd had to leave the bed or risk taking her. Then, as he'd given her a light morning spanking, his desire had flared all over again. The spanking wasn't a punishment, but rather a means of beginning her day in her proper state—soft, sensual, and submissive. In time, such spankings would grow firmer. But for now, the light one had served her very well. His cock throbbed at the memory—both of her pink bottom and her wet cunt. God, if he didn't get to fuck her soon, he was going to move past parched and into pained.

Aunt Matty's brows came together in a worried frown. "You're my last hope, Matt dearest. Tell me you won't give up. Tell me you'll be strong and steadfast in your pursuit of my stubborn niece. Tell me that, whatever it takes, she *will* be bound to you in marriage—before Christmas would be nice."

Matthew smiled then looked across the garden at Patience. She and Passion had stopped walking and Patience had her hand on her sister's belly. *Soon, Patience—soon I shall fuck your pretty cunt and you will be as full-bellied as your sister.* Matthew's cock pulsed. "I won't give up, Aunt Matty. I will be strong and steadfast. And I will do whatever it takes to bring your beautiful niece down the aisle."

"Oh, Matt! Dear Matt!" Aunt Matty gripped his arm. "Uh, ah—before Christmas?"

Matthew looked at her.

"Well, it's just that Christmas is such a family time, and it's only three months away. It would be nice . . ." Her eyes were moist and her smile quivered. "Forgive me. It's only that I love her so. And I have been afraid"—her eyes sparkled with tears—"I have been afraid she would be left alone."

Matthew felt a surge of tenderness for the woman as he gave her his handkerchief. "I won't abandon her, Aunt Matty. I promise."

"Thank you, Matt." She dabbed her tears. "Spinsterhood has many things to recommend it, but it's not for her. Much as she tries to be an apple, there's simply no denying she's a peach."

Matthew tried to deduce her meaning, for he was beginning to think she made more sense than anyone gave her credit for. Perhaps she was referring to the fact that apples were hard and peaches were soft? Uncertain, he just nodded.

She looked across the garden at her two nieces. "Look at them together. You know, Matt, before their mother died those two were inseparable—laughing and giggling all the time and everywhere. You couldn't find one and not find the other. They were so close."

"*Were* so close? It seems they still are."

"Oh, yes—in many ways. But not like they were as children."

Matthew leaned closer. "Why?"

Aunt Matty sighed. "Because everything changed when their mother died. Penelope, God rest her soul, was an extraordinary woman. Everyone was affected by her passing."

"Of course," Matthew replied. "But why should their mother's death have driven anything between them? When my father . . . When George Hawkmore died, Mark and I grew even closer. We needed each other more."

"Yes, well, there were only the two of you. And forgive me, dear Matt, but I don't think you or your brother had the pressing and practical concerns of running a home that is not populated by a large staff." Aunt Matty looked around. "How many are the staff here at Hawkmore House?"

"Including groundskeepers and stable-hands, about seventy-five," Matthew admitted.

She raised her silver brows at him. "The staff at the vicarage are six—butler, cook, upstairs maid, downstairs maid, gardener, and driver. They all do more than their titles suggest, and, even so, the girls must assist with things—not to mention their responsibilities at the church school and to the community."

"Forgive me, Aunt Matty, for being so obtuse."

She smiled and squeezed his hand. "You're not obtuse, Matt dearest. In fact, I think you're acute, which is one of the reasons that you and Patience are so well suited. She cannot abide fools, that girl." Aunt Matty raised her chin. "And, come to think of it, neither can I. She and I are cut from the same cloth in that regard. I disdain foolishness of any sort. Fools will never fool me." She nodded and, narrowing her eyes, scanned the garden. "I'm foolproof." She turned back to him and lifted one eyebrow. "I'm in-fool-able."

Matthew swept his fingers across his lips to erase his smile. "Oh, I can see that."

She smiled beatifically. "Well then, you see, you're not obtuse at all. You're incisive and sharp." She poked the air with her finger. "Like an arrow. Like an arrow shot from the bow of Robin Hood, that's what you are." She nodded knowingly. "You always hit your target. You can knock the peach right out of the tree."

Matthew jumped on the segue she offered. "Speaking of peaches, weren't you going to explain what happened with Patience and her sisters? I'm gathering from what you said that they didn't have as much time for each other after their mother's death."

"Yes, that's exactly right." Aunt Matty's expression turned inward. "Without ever needing to be asked, Passion stepped quietly into Penelope's shoes. Bless her heart, she tried her best to fill the void created by her mother's passing. This included caring for Prim who, at five, was too young to be without a mother." Aunt Matty shook her head and smiled softly. "How that child used to cling to Passion's apron strings. Passion couldn't do anything, or go anywhere without Primrose trailing behind her."

"And Patience?"

"Patience and her mother had a special bond. I can't say exactly what it was, but Penelope always seemed to know and understand Patience in ways that no one else could." A small frown turned Aunt Matty's brow. "Poor thing. When Penelope passed, she was ten. Such a tender age for a girl—no longer a baby, and not yet a young lady—old enough to never forget her mother, and young enough to still need her." She shook her head. "And as mature as Passion was at twelve, she couldn't really manage herself, a home, and the mothering of *two* girls. So Patience had to take care of herself. And help her older sister, too."

Matthew frowned as he imagined a ten-year-old Patience standing alone while Passion tended to Primrose. No child should feel alone. For all his troubled upbringing, that was one thing he'd not suffered. Mark had always been there for him. Mark was still there for him. "What of their father? What part did he play in this? Surely he could see that one of his daughters was more alone than the others."

"More alone?" Aunt Matty tilted her head as she seemed to consider the question. "No. You see, this is just how it was, Matt. It all happened quietly and without incident. Passion never complained or cried over her lost childhood. And Patience never complained or cried. I mean, how could she when she saw her older sister working so hard."

Matthew suddenly remembered Patience's words from the night he'd spent in her room: *I never ask for help—unless I can't possibly avoid it.* He thought of her discomfort over the first breakfast he had left for her, and her obvious reticence over allowing him to dress her the night of the musicale. And then he remembered her poignant admission about her cello: . . . *as long as I love it enough, it will never, ever leave me*!

Matthew stared across the garden at Patience.

Oh, my love. I begin to see the whys and wherefores of you. It's no wonder you hid your heart away.

Aunt Matty had followed his gaze. "You mustn't think there was any strife between them, Matt. There wasn't. Three more loving and loyal sisters you will not find. And, you know, in many ways Passion and Patience were uniquely predisposed to the roles they took on. Passion, the nurturing mother, and Patience, the strong-minded independent. It isn't surprising that things happened the way they did."

Matthew fixed his gaze on Patience. She may be strong-minded and independent, but she'd suffered—badly. And he was beginning to think no one knew it.

Not even Patience.

Aunt Matty smiled softly. "They are both versions of their parents, Matt. Passion is so like her mother, both in appearance and temperament. There were tiny moments when, with Prim in her arms, it almost felt as if Penelope were still with us. Almost . . ." She sighed. "And Patience—though she got those curls from her mother, their fiery color came from her father. She is so like him—strong and stoic, but with a heart as deep as the ocean. Being so deep, I sometimes find it untouchable, but I know it's here. If I were only a better swimmer . . ." Her voice faded to thoughtfulness.

Matthew looked at her. "I think you're a better swimmer than you think."

Aunt Matty beamed at him. “Really? Do you know what I think, Matt dearest?”

“What do you think, Aunt Matty?”

“I think you’re the best swimmer I’ve ever met. I think you’re so accomplished that you could be one of those amazing South Sea pearl divers that I recently read of.” She nodded and her gray eyes sparkled with a determined excitement. “Dive deep, Matthew. Dive deep, find the pearl, and bring it to the surface. For if you really mean to marry Patience, you’ll have to have it.”

He stared across the garden at Patience. She looked toward him, almost as if he’d called her. Then she smiled and lifted her hand in a wave. She did it with such immediacy. She hadn’t paused to think.

Matthew smiled and his heart lifted as he waved back. “I’ll have the pearl, Aunt Matty. I’ll have it before Christmas.”

“Look at Aunt Matty.” Patience watched her aunt chatting excitedly with Matthew. “She’s like a child at Christmas when she’s with Matthew.”

Passion smiled. “And he really likes her.”

“Oh, I know. They’re birds of a feather, those two.” Patience shook her head. “Though what they have in common, I couldn’t tell you.”

Passion looked at her with raised brows.

Patience raised her brows in return. “What?”

“*You* are what they have in common, darling.” Passion slipped her arm through Patience’s, and they continued walking. “Aunt Matty wants Matthew to marry you. Matthew wants to marry you.” Patience snapped her eyes to her sister, but Passion just smiled. “That makes them allies in the battle against your formidable castle of spinsterhood.”

Patience’s heart beat a little faster. “But Matthew told me he wasn’t interested in marriage.”

A puzzled frown turned Passion’s brow. “When did he say that?”

“The night of the masque.”

“Then he masked his heart that night, rather than his face.” Passion stopped walking and turned to face her. “Darling, I know

I'm right. I see how he looks at you. From the very first, I've seen how he looks at you." She tilted her head and her warm hazel eyes looked so certain. "I know what that look means because it's the same way that Mark looks at me. And speaking of my handsome husband, guess who else once disavowed any desire for marriage?"

"Your handsome husband?"

Passion smiled and nodded. "And I, too, had said that I wouldn't marry again. Yet, here I am—and with child, which I had also believed was impossible." Passion clasped Patience's hands. "Upon occasion, we misunderstand ourselves, or we lose faith. Whichever the case, we say things we think are true, only to find they are not." One of Passion's auburn brows lifted. "Perhaps, even you are capable of being wrong?"

"You know how I hate being wrong," Patience murmured.

"I know."

Patience stared into her sister's soft gaze. "But in this case, I think I might be happy to be wrong."

Passion's eyes widened. "Really?"

Patience felt a nervous giddiness welling up at the prospect of making the decision that had been growing more and more irresistible. "Oh, Passion, do you think it would be terribly foolish of me to give up Cavalli?" Releasing her sister's hands, she pressed her fingers against her temples. "I can't believe I'm even asking you the question. But Matthew asked me not to go. And, right now, I—I don't really want to go."

"Then don't go."

"But how can I *not* go?" She dropped her hands. "Who turns down Fernando Cavalli?"

Passion shrugged. "I guess you do."

"How can I do that? Am I mad? I mean, really, have I lost my mind?"

Passion tilted her head, and her gaze was tender and searching. "I don't know. Have you?"

Patience shook her head slowly. "I don't know. Part of me thinks I must have."

"And what does the other part of you think?"

Patience closed her eyes, and the memory of the spanking Matthew had given her that morning filled her mind and immediately eased her tension. He'd spanked her not because she'd disobeyed, but because it *pleased him*, and because *she needed it*. As it was turning out with everything that pleased him, somehow it pleased her, too. And maybe she had needed it, for even though it had hurt, it had made her wet; and afterward she'd felt soft, sensual, and happy.

Patience opened her eyes. Her nipples were hard, and her clitoris felt achy. She took a slow, deep breath before meeting her sister's unwavering gaze. "The other part of me thinks that staying with Matthew is all that matters. That staying with Matthew is all that has ever mattered"—she swallowed—"or ever will matter."

Passion nodded slowly. "Then stay, Patience. Stay."

Patience trembled at her sister's unknowing echo of Matthew. "Stay?" Slowly, she turned her head to look at him. She wasn't surprised to find his dark gaze riveted upon her. Even over the distance she could feel his powerful intent. God, how desperately she wanted him. "Stay," she repeated more to herself than to Passion. "Put away *for now*, and live in the possibility of *forever*?"

"Yes."

Patience turned back to her sister. "Even though there are no promises between us?"

"I think his promise is in his eyes."

Yes. "He has such beautiful eyes, doesn't he? And he says things, Passion. Such wonderful things."

"Then have faith in him."

"I want to. It's just that 'forever' has so often eluded me. Whenever I think I have it, I find I'm wrong. And, this time, I—" Patience blinked back sudden tears. "Well, it's just that in these few days, I feel changed—or perhaps, as Matthew says, I'm just returning to myself. I'm not entirely certain. But what I am certain of is that I won't survive being wrong again—not now. Not now that I feel so alive."

Passion looked toward Matthew. Aunt Matty had returned to the house so he stood alone, staring across the garden at them. Passion regarded him thoughtfully for a moment then she looked back at Patience. Pressing a kiss to Patience's cheek, she smiled softly. "Stay."

It took only a moment for the lovely word to inspire her response.

Yes!

Patience smiled and threw her arms around her sister. Her heart bloomed with happiness and sudden confidence. “I shall stay. I shall stay, and I shall have faith in forever.”

Patience heard Passion’s laughter and it made her laugh. She squeezed her sister tighter. “I love you. And I’ve missed you.”

Passion pulled back with a puzzled grin. “Missed me?”

“Yes. I’ve missed the part of you that used to be mine.” Patience stared into her sister’s hazel eyes—the eyes that were so like their mother’s. “And I’ve missed the part of me that used to be yours.”

Passion’s head tilted.

Patience’s smile deepened. “I love you,” she said again. Then, kissing her sister on the cheek, she turned and ran to Matthew.

Matthew watched Patience run toward him. A magnificent smile on her face, her bright red curls bounced and her petticoats frothed like sea foam beneath her raised blue green skirts. His heart pounded with love and anticipation. She looked so exuberant, so full of happiness. What was she coming to tell him?

Just as she turned toward the path that would lead her to the terrace steps, she drew up short. A footman appeared and handed her a letter. Matthew tensed as he watched her smile fade. Who was it from?

The Royal Post was so famous for its speed that people often used it more like a messenger service, sending notes back and forth across town in the same day. If Mickey Wilkes had done his job, then it was entirely possible that a letter from Cavalli was now being delivered into Patience’s hand.

Gripping the stone rail, Matthew moved toward her. She was staring at the front of the unopened envelope. Dread surged in him as he slowly descended the stairs. She turned over the envelope and opened it. He paused, and his gut tightened when she drew out and unfolded a single sheet of paper. As she read it, he forced himself to continue down the steps, watching her for any sign of distress.

Though her face was slightly lowered, her expression didn’t seem to change.

Matthew stepped off the last stair and moved toward her. "What is it, Patience?"

She looked up at him, her expression a little bewildered, but then she smiled. "It's from Maestro Cavalli. He's rescinded his offer to take me as a student. It seems his wife has become concerned about the 'intimate nature' of the teacher and student association." Patience shrugged. "She doesn't want her husband teaching a woman."

Matthew stared at her, his breath shallow. "You're not upset?"

Patience paused and seemed to mentally search herself. When her gaze returned to him, she smiled. "No. I'm not."

What? A tentative relief flickered beneath Matthew's skin.

She stepped closer to him, and he breathed the scent of gardenias. "Do you know why?" she asked.

"No." Despite her smile, he held his breath. "Why?"

"Because I'd already decided to stay."

He let out his breath in a rush. "You had?"

She tilted her head and the corners of her mouth curled oh so sweetly. "Yes, I was coming to tell you just now."

With a joyful shout, Matthew swept her into his arms. She laughed as he whirled her around. The sound of her laughter, the smell of her skin, and the feel of her body all made him giddy. She was his! She was his and he would never let her go. Never . . .

Slowing to a stop, he threaded one hand into her hair as he held her tightly. "I'm so happy you're staying," he whispered against her temple. *Because I love you.* "Because I—I need you."

Her arms tightened around him. "I need you, too."

Yes! She needed him. Which was why she must never discover that he was the source of the letter. Why the hell had he sent it? He should have trusted in himself—he should have trusted in her.

But it was too late—and what did it matter? She was staying. All on her own, she was staying.

Matthew pulled back to look at her. "I want you to come to Angel's Manor—you and Aunt Matty."

Patience's smile widened. "You do? When?"

"As soon as possible. I have some business I need to atten

to, first in London then at the mine. After that, I can meet you there."

"Oh, Matthew, I'd love to see your home." She laughed. "Aunt Matty will be ecstatic. I just need to write to my father for his permission."

"Write your letter, then. For though I have much to do, I want you with me."

Holding her tight, Matthew pressed his lips against her brow then closed his eyes and breathed the smell of her hair. "I'm glad the letter didn't hurt you."

She drew back to look at him. "Before you, it would have. But not now." She cupped her hand against his cheek. "Now it's just confirmation—a beautiful and unexpected confirmation from God that my decision to stay is the right one." She lifted onto her toes and touched her soft mouth to his. "How could I possibly be upset by that?"

Chapter Nineteen
Diamonds and Sisters

. . . the keepers of the walls took away my veil from me.

Song of Solomon 5:7

Matthew surveyed the parure of diamond jewelry. It was an exceptionally fine collection that included combs, a necklace, earrings, two bracelets, a belt buckle, and a ring. Each piece was set in gold and the diamonds sparkled against the black velvet of the box.

He remembered Patience wearing her cut steel. She deserved real jewelry—jewelry that matched her in beauty and quality. Now if only she would agree to marry him, he could adorn her properly.

Snapping the box closed, Matthew realized the jeweler's apprentice was still standing before his desk. He'd already thanked him and given him his tip. "Thank you," he said again. "They are lovely. I accept them."

The young apprentice looked nervous. "My master was sure you'd be pleased, Mr. Hawkmore. The only thing is—and he heartily regrets this inconvenience—but he insisted—he insisted that I must give you this." He whipped a piece of paper from his pocket and extended it with a shaky hand.

Frowning, Matthew took the paper and unfolded it.

It was the bill!

Heat suddenly radiated up from his collar. Never, in all his years of patronage, had he ever been billed upon delivery. Never!

Furious, he raised his eyes to the jeweler's apprentice. "My credit is impeccable. I have never failed to pay for that which I have ordered."

"Yes, Mr. Hawkmore! That's true. *I* know it's true." The young man was red-faced with embarrassment. "But my master felt that—well, that this time—because of the number of pieces in this—this particular collection—that this time—just this once, mind you—that he must—well, that he simply must secure—must secure payment. Just—just this once. Under the circumstances." The young man's trembling voice trailed off.

"What circumstances?" Matthew ground out.

The apprentice paled. "I—I, uh . . ." He swept his hand across his brow. "Mr. Hawkmore, you know Lord Benchley is also my master's patron. Well, Lord Benchley, he's—he's insinuating things."

Matthew's hands clenched into fists. "What things?"

"That—that he might not do any more business with Smithfield and Sons. And that no one else of any quality will either so long as my master is"—the apprentice swallowed convulsively—"is servicing you."

Matthew suddenly had a visceral understanding of why Roman emperors often killed messengers. He wanted to heave the box in the apprentice's face.

But where else might he expect this treatment? Archibald Benchley patronized many of the same artisans and merchants that he did. Matthew's humiliation and rage grew as he imagined Benchley infecting them all. Today his credit was denied. Tomorrow he could be refused service altogether.

He looked at the black velvet box.

If he sent it back, Patience would have nothing.

Shaking with fury, he pulled out his ledger and, with a stiff hand, wrote a cheque for the full amount of the bill. His jaw clenched as he stood and held out the note, which the apprentice suddenly seemed reluctant to take.

But he did take it, pulling his hand back quickly once it was between his fingers. "Thank you, Mr. Hawkmore."

"I don't want your thanks," Matthew snapped. "Tell your master he needn't worry about losing his customers of quality, for that is the last cheque he will ever see from me."

The man bowed as he backed across the room. "Very well, Mr. Hawkmore. I'm sorry, Mr. Hawkmore." Then he turned and scurried out the door.

Matthew gripped the edge of his desk as he stared down at the black velvet box. He forced his hands to open it.

He let his eye wander over the sparkling jewels.

It was an exquisite parure. But now it gave him no pleasure.

It gave him no pleasure because it was, without doubt, the most costly thing he'd ever purchased.

Not because of the exorbitant sum he'd paid for it.

But because of the deep measure of pride it had cost him.

He closed the lid.

Only for Patience.

"Oh, Patience, when are you leaving? Have you written to Father? What does Aunt Matty say?"

Patience smiled across the table at her sister. "Yes, I've written to Father. Assuming he approves, we leave in ten days. And Aunt Matty is beside herself with excitement."

Passion grinned. "I'll bet she is. I wish I could watch the unrelenting matrimonial assault she is sure to wage upon the two of you. I'm certain it will be vastly entertaining."

"Oh, she's already acting as if it's a fait accompli. The moment I told her I wasn't going to Cavalli and that we were going to Matthew's home instead, she raised her eyes heavenward and thanked God for answering her prayers and 'making me see reason.' Then she began planning the wedding."

Passion laughed as she picked up her teacup. "Did you tell her Cavalli had cancelled your instruction?"

"I did. She said it proved that the very forces of the universe were moving to insure that I marry Matthew." Patience cocked her brow. "Which, she said, was exceedingly fortunate, as I 'cannot always be counted upon to know what is for my own good.' She did, however, praise me for finally accepting that I'm a peach."

Passion smiled softly and sipped her tea before returning the cup to its saucer. "You seem reconciled to her ambitions for you."

"Aunt Matty may have whatever ambitions she likes." Patience looked down and adjusted her napkin in her lap. Matthew had said he wasn't interested in marriage. Yet everything he did, and everything he'd said since then, seemed to negate that declaration. Even Passion believed he had intentions toward her. Patience tried to contain the happy exuberance that seemed to be welling up in her continually. *One step at a time.* With a sigh and the remains of a smile, she shrugged as she looked at her sister. "Her ambitions will not decide our lives."

"True." Passion leaned her chin in her hand. "Though I sometimes wonder if she doesn't have some singular power that brings about marriage for whomever she sets her sights upon. She was trying to marry off Father when he met Mother. She was trying to marry off me when I met Mark. She introduced her neighbor's daughter to her now husband, and the summer before last, I believe she worked her matrimonial magic upon the twin nieces of the Swittley sisters." Passion raised her brows. "Perhaps you *should* start planning the wedding."

Patience smiled as she shook her head. "I think, despite Aunt Matty's seeming powers, that Matthew must be the force that moves me. I will make no plans until he gives me reason."

Passion regarded her gently. "You really trust him, don't you?"

"Yes." The answer had come immediately and unequivocally. "I trusted him from the very first."

Passion tilted her head. "How unusual. Typically, your trust is hard won."

"I know." Patience stared at the steam rising from her teacup. "I think it's because of the way he has always looked at me—as if he saw all the hidden parts of me." Patience looked at her sister. "Parts of me even I dared not look at."

Passion reached across the small tea table and clasped Patience's hand. "Like the pain of Henri?"

"I don't know." Patience looked back down at her tea and curled her fingers against Passion's palm. "Perhaps the pain of you."

Silence drew out. Finally, Patience lifted her eyes.

A deep frown cut between her sister's brows and her expression was completely confounded. "What? What pain have I caused you?"

At the question, a flood of hurt welled up in Patience. Her eyes stung. "What pain? You left me. You left me, and we were never the same."

Passion stared and her lip trembled. "Patience, what are you talking about?"

Patience felt tears slip down her cheeks, but she didn't care. "I'm talking about how we used to be. How we used to be so close. How we used to do everything together. Don't you remember?" Patience clasped her other hand around her sister's. "Oh, Passion, don't you remember?"

The pulse throbbed in Passion's throat and her eyes looked shiny.

Patience could feel her own heart, aching with every beat. "You must remember—how we used to pick each other's clothes and brush each other's hair. How we used to ride down the banister together every morning, and race up the stairs every night. How we used to walk in step and speak in rhyme." She shivered, and her tears continued to fall as she was overrun with memories. "Don't you remember how we used to make daisy chains together and leave them around the neck of Mr. Higgin's cow? How we used to swim together at the lake, just the two of us, and pretend we were mermaids, trapped there by an evil witch?"

Tears slipped from her sister's eyes.

Patience shook her head. "Don't you remember how we used to tell each other everything, and keep from each other nothing? How we used to share our secrets and our dreams—and our pains and our fears? Oh, Passion"—Patience clasped her sister's hand to her cheek—"don't you remember how we used to love each other?"

In a moment, Passion was there, her arms tight around Patience's shoulders. "Of course I remember, my darling. I remember everything."

Patience pressed her cheek against her sister's side. Something had happened. Something had opened inside her, and she suddenly felt the painful depth and fullness of how much she had missed Passion over the years. And rather than minimize the feelings, or hide them away, she let them out. "You left me," she wept. "You didn't have time for me anymore. Always, Prim was between us. You picked her clothes and brushed her hair, and there was no more time for me—for us." Patience turned her face into her sister's side and clung to her. "There were moments I felt I hated Prim for taking you away from me. But how could

I hate her when I love her so much? And she was so young, and needed you."

"Oh, my darling." Passion bent around her and smoothed her hair.

But the loving touch only made Patience cry more. "Sometimes I hated you, too. Sometimes I was so angry with you." She squeezed her eyes against the sting of her tears and her emotions. "But then I hated myself for having such feelings, and for being so selfish."

Dropping to her knees, Passion clasped Patience's hands. Her face was tear-streaked. "My darling—my sweet Patience, I'm so sorry."

Patience's heart twisted at the anguish in her sister's eyes. "No, you mustn't say you're sorry. You're an angel—a saint—you always have been. It's just me. I—I couldn't bear the weight of my own feelings. And I didn't know what to do with them, so I—I just buried them." Patience cupped her hand against her sister's wet cheek. "And I did everything I could not to be a burden to you. I took care of myself, so you wouldn't have to. I stayed out of the way so that you could give Prim what she needed. And I thought I was strong and perfect and whole. But now . . ." Fresh tears welled, and she couldn't go on.

Leaning forward, Passion pulled her into her arms. "Oh, my Patience—my sister." Her voice was choked. "You know, we were such little girls when mother died. I was but twelve and you were but ten. There were so many times that I wanted to be only with you. So many times that I yearned for you, and for the joy and freedom we had shared together. But I didn't voice my feelings because I feared they would only magnify what we no longer had. So I just—I bowed my head and did what I thought I had to." She pulled back, her hands cupped around Patience's head. "But when I did that, I lost sight of you, didn't I?"

Patience shook her head.

Passion's frown deepened. "Yes. Yes, I did. And when I finally looked up again, it was too late. You didn't seem to need me. But I didn't see my part in that." Her tears fell freely. "Can you forgive me, Patience? Can you?"

Patience couldn't stand the grief in her sister's face. She loved her with the love of their childhood. "There's nothing to forgive. Nothing. There are only feelings to share and hearts to mend."

Passion pulled her close again. "I love you," she murmured.

Tears still welling, Patience slid onto the floor with her sister and curled into her embrace.

Passion rocked her gently. "I love you. I love you so much."

The words soaked beneath Patience's skin; and they touched her in the deep, completely comforting way that they had when they were children. "I love you, too."

Another tear slipped down her cheek. But though there was some sorrow in it, there was also relief—and even a peculiar happiness.

Chapter Twenty

Revelations

My vineyard, which is mine, is before me . . .

Song of Solomon 8:12

Matthew frowned across the huge, opulent desk that presided over Benchley's former office at Gwenellyn. "Tell me."

Mickey Wilkes shoved his black hair from his brow and sat back in his chair. He looked reluctant and, more worrisome, he was quiet.

Matthew's frown deepened. "Miss Dare is arriving at Angel's Manor today. I had planned on being there to greet her. But when the messenger informed me you were coming here with some news, I waited. So, surely you can tell me why I'm sitting here with you, rather than enjoying the incomparable company of Miss Dare."

"I'm sorry 'bout ya no' bein' there fer Miss Dare. But I kin get 'ere faster than I kin t' Angel's Manor. An I knows ya be in a 'urry fer somethin' 'gainst the Benchleys."

"Out with it, then."

"I don't think yer gonna like it."

"Let me be the judge of that."

"Cain't prove it neither. 'Ave to get the proof."

Matthew leaned forward and calmly laid his hands flat atop the desk. "If your next sentence does not begin to convey to me what you have discovered, I'm going to reach across this desk and throttle you to within an inch of your life. Is that clear?"

"Yeah." Mickey nodded but seemed otherwise unaffected by Matthew's threat. "Look, Mr. 'Awkmore, ya paid me t' find Benchley dirt, an I's got it. Only, maybe, it's more dirt 'n ya want."

Christ. What could be so bad? Whatever was bad for the Benchleys should be good for him. "I'm waiting."

Mickey sighed. "Yeah, a'right, 'ere it is. I been makin' it a point o' chummin' it up wit' Mrs. Biddlewick, an t'other night I finally got 'er to join me in a bot'le. After I got a few cups down 'er, I made like I was real bo'rd and asked 'er if nothin' int'restin ever 'appened round there. She 'llowed as it did. Naw, says I. This place be dull as dust, says I. Then she starts tellin' me alls 'bout what 'appened 'tween you and the Benchleys. An meanwhiles, I'm pourin' more gin in 'er cup t'make sure 'er tongue stays nice an loose. An she gabbed on an on 'bout you an them an the scandal, an I'm thinkin' I'm gettin' nothin'—till she says somethin' 'bout ain't it funny how some people git chased by the same skel'tons their 'ole lives."

Tension trickled down Matthew's back.

"So I asks 'er wha' she means. She says nothin'. I says, tha's right, you don't know nothin'. She 'llows 'ow she knows ever'thin'." Mickey leaned forward. "An then she leans real close, burpin' and breathin' 'er gin on me, and says, Mr. 'Awkmore ain't the only one what was born on the wrong side o' the sheets." Mickey held Matthew's stare. "Says she, they perten's to be pure, an cry shame on 'Awkmore, but Benchley blood be bastard as well."

Pain.

Shock.

Disbelief.

Pain!

Matthew's breath left him in a ragged gasp as all the emotions from when he discovered the truth of his own birth washed over him yet again. His eyes stung, and he sucked in air. Breath filled his lungs, even as reason and fierce realization filled his heart. *Bastard Benchley blood.*

Paper crumpled as his hands closed into fists.

The Benchleys claimed one of the purest lines in England. They were more English than the Royal Family, and every one of them noble born. It was their selling point, their point of pride. Even when Archibald Benchley's business acumen had added wealth to their family status, it was the banner of their bloodline that waved above all else.

Lies?

Deceit and treachery?

Matthew's blood boiled with rage.

Hypocrisy. Bloody fucking hypocrisy!

Villainy!

Matthew lifted his gaze back to Mickey. "Go on."

Mickey shrank back in his chair. "I tol' ya ya wouldn't like it."

"Go—on," Matthew ground out from between clenched teeth.

"By now, Biddlewick were real drunk an a'most droppin' off. But I kep' at 'er. She tol' me 'ow 'is Lordship were violent when 'e found out. 'Ow 'er Ladyship wouldn't ne'er tell 'oo 'er lover was, an 'ow she died soon after." Mickey shoved his hair out of his eyes. "I ask'd Biddlewick if that were why Benchley'd changed o'er the 'ole 'ouse'old. She 'llowed it were. An ya know wha's amusin'?" He raised his brows. "Turns out Benchley kep' the one person what knew the mos'. Turns out, in fact, that 'er Ladyship's lover be none other than Biddlewick's cousin. 'Parently, 'e were the Benchley coachman. But when 'er Ladyship go' with child, they decided 'e should leave. 'Is Lordship found the 'ole thing out when 'e caught 'is wife writin' to the bloke. Only there were no name on the let'er—only me darlin'."

A letter. Always there was a letter. "But you have a name."

"That I do, Mr. 'Awkmore. The man be Roger MacQuarrie."

"And you know where he can be found."

"Bryntoogle. Lit'le village in the north o' Scotland."

"Go there." Matthew forced the words through his clamped jaw. "Go there. Find the man, and get me some proof of this."

"Yes, sir, Mr. 'Awkmore." Mickey got to his feet.

"Mr. Wilkes."

Mickey looked at Matthew. "Yes, sir?"

"Does she know?"

"That were the las' thin' I ask'd Biddlewick 'fore she went dead drunk. Does the Lady Ros'lind know?" Mickey shook his head. "She don't."

No, she couldn't. Her conceit was too genuine. But Benchley—he knew. The son of a bitch was vilifying Matthew for being both a bastard and a liar when he'd been shielding the bastard in his own house for years.

Goddamn it, he didn't blame Benchley for protecting Rosalind from the truth. However, the malice and viciousness he'd leveled against Matthew for that same truth, the defamation of his character, the attempted ruination of his finances, and theft of his company—for all that, Archibald Benchley must pay. *The goddamned lying villain!*

Reaching into his desk, Matthew withdrew several bills and tossed them across the desk to Mickey. "Go. Go and get proof."

The boy swept up the money and put it in his pocket. "Yes, sir." With a nod, he flipped his cap onto his head and left.

Matthew sat, unmoving, for a long moment. Then he exploded from his chair and, with an enraged shout, heaved a desk lamp across the room.

In the heavy silence after the crash, he stood stiff with fury. Fury at Benchley, and fury at the forces of circumstance.

For despite his hatred of Rosalind, he didn't know if he could do to her what had been done to him.

It wasn't him.

Angel's Manor was a monumental neo-Gothic edifice—complete with decorative crenellation, ornamental ironwork, and a courtyard. But unlike a real medieval castle, there wasn't a broken stone, a clinging vine, or a hint of character in sight. The gray stone walls and slate roof were smooth and perfect in their newness. Tidily trimmed hedges were the only things growing along the walls. Innumerable windows of expensive plate glass stared out over the courtyard, and a multitude of tall chimneys and turrets jutted from the seemingly endless roofline.

It wasn't a house, it was a statement.

No, it was more than a statement. It was an exclamation—an exclamation of wealth, status, and modernity.

Patience frowned.

But it wasn't Matthew.

At least, not the Matthew she knew.

Where was Matthew?

"Wherever is dear Matt?" Aunt Matty asked loudly.

The footman who was assisting them bowed. "The Master has been delayed, ladies. He bids you welcome, but sends his regrets. He is expected tomorrow."

Disappointment coursed through Patience's veins.

"Oh," Aunt Matty pouted, "we had so hoped that Mr. Hawkmore would be here to meet us. I don't know how we shall do without him for another day."

Patience sighed. For once, she felt in complete accord with her aunt.

"Oh, well. I suppose we shall just have to be patient. If only I had any patience left . . ." Aunt Matty shrugged then shielded her eyes from the sun as she gazed up at the house. "Well, my dear, one thing's certain. Once married to Matthew, you shall never want for room."

Mortified, Patience glanced at the footman who was assisting them, but he demonstrated no reaction to her aunt's words. Patience leaned close and spoke softly. "Aunt Matty, you *must* stop being so presumptuous."

Aunt Matty raised her brows imperiously. "I am *not* presuming. I am merely stating a fact," she said in her regular volume.

Patience leveled a warning glare at her aunt before turning to Lord Fitz Roy, who was assisting Lord Rivers to their side of the carriage. In Matthew's absence, the two lords had accompanied them to Angel's Manor and had proven excellent escorts and traveling companions. Farnsby and Asher rounded out their party. They were exiting the carriage behind.

"Well, here we are at last, ladies." Lord Rivers stepped forward and offered Aunt Matty his frail arm. "And before tea—just as you had hoped, Mistress Dare."

Though he was taller than she, Aunt Matty looked far more capable of supporting him than he did her. But she smiled and laid her hand gently on his arm. "Yes, my lord," she agreed as they moved toward the house. "And how fortunate, for it so happens that I am terribly prone to swooning when forced to do without tea."

Fitz Roy lifted one brow as he gave Patience his arm. "Is she really?"

Patience looked into his pale eyes. "So far as I know, my lord, my aunt has never swooned in her life."

Fitz Roy's mouth lifted at the corners as they turned to wait for Farnsby and Asher. The cousins were engaged in their usual banter.

"I told you it wouldn't rain today," Farnsby was saying. "I'll collect my five pounds later. You know, if you don't win a bet soon, I shall have to record your losing streak in my Journal of Extraordinary Events."

Asher rolled his eyes as they approached. "Why don't you record the fact that you cracked your knuckles no less than two dozen times between the station and here? That, surely, must be some sort of record—and a supremely annoying one, at that. I warn you, do it one more time and I shall rap them soundly."

Farnsby held his hand up before Asher and, drawing his finger down with his thumb, cracked it.

A scuffle ensued as Asher grabbed for his portly cousin and, despite Farnsby's laughing resistance, managed to rap the back of his hand several times. Farnsby retaliated by delivering several pokes into Asher's sides. The two were still pushing and prodding each other as they drew up to Patience and Fitz Roy.

Fitz Roy looked down his nose at them. "Infants." Then he turned and drew her up the wide walk to the house.

The cousins followed. "I say, Asher, Fitz Roy just called us infants. What are we going to do about it?"

"*I'm* not going to do anything. He was referring to you, no me."

"No, I most definitely heard an *s* at the end of the word." Shor pause. "Would you care to bet on it?"

Patience's smile deepened, but as she stepped over the thresh old of Angel's Manor, the house stole her attention. The entry hal was huge, and the voices of their party, especially Aunt Matty's echoed off the stone floor and up the heavy stair to the vaulte ceiling. There, large iron light fixtures were suspended, and be neath each lamp, a spearlike shard pointed downward. Thoug they were meant to enhance the shape and line of the chandelier Patience's first thought was of being impaled should one fall.

Pushing the gory image aside, she chided herself for her a titude. Whatever was the matter with her? This was Matthew home—and, really, it was decorated perfectly. A giant tapestr depicting a joust hung on one wall. Landscapes filled the othe Splendid furniture and objets d'art drew the eye around the e pansive space, and tall plate-glass windows let sunlight stream i from the rear of the house. Yes, Angel's Manor was impressiv and magnificent.

What was there not to like about it?

Besides Matthew's absence.

Before leaving Hawkmore House, he'd told her he intended to be home in time for her arrival. Clearly, important business had kept him at Gwenellyn.

She missed him.

Fitz Roy introduced Mr. Simms, the butler. Then they were all led upstairs, Aunt Matty waxing lyrical on the virtues of tea the whole way.

"I've ordered that tea be served in the main parlor in half an hour," Fitz Roy said as they all paused on the landing.

"My lord, you are a saint," Aunt Matty said.

"Really?" Fitz Roy raised his brows. "Had I known sainthood came so easily, I would have aspired to it long ago."

Patience smiled as the gentlemen set off toward a different wing of the house. She and her aunt followed the footmen to their rooms, which were just across the wide hall from each other.

"Remember, my dear, tea in half an hour," Aunt Matty said before disappearing into her chamber.

Patience nodded as she crossed to her room. Like the entry below, it was huge—and beautiful. Decorated in shades of mauve, violet, and taupe, it had exceedingly high ceilings and a row of large windows. A young maid bobbed a curtsy and introduced herself as Annie while the four footmen carrying Patience's trunks placed them in an adjoining dressing room.

"May I unpack yer things, miss?" the maid asked.

Patience watched another footman carry in her cello case and valise. He placed both in the sitting area that was arranged by the windows. "Yes, Annie. Thank you."

While the girl went to work in the dressing room, Patience moved to her instrument. Matthew had told her to bring it with her so that he could begin tutoring her.

She stared at the case. Why had she been so obedient?

She ought to have left it behind. It didn't belong with her for now.

She turned away from it.

But Matthew did.

Would he come home tomorrow?

She'd endured ten days without his attentions, but now she

was becoming peevish. She needed a spanking—and an orgasm. But more than either of those, she just needed him. She needed to smell him and touch him.

She sighed forlornly as she looked around the giant room.

God, but she missed him.

God, but he missed her.

Matthew hurried down the stairs after having rushed through washing, shaving, and dressing for dinner.

He hadn't seen Patience in ten days, but it felt like forever. He'd missed her smile and her intelligent, assessing eyes. He'd missed the smell of her gardenia-scented skin. He'd missed her voice, her company, and her conversation. He'd missed her passionate kisses, her soft body and sweet submission. But perhaps most of all, he'd missed the warmth of her presence—her simple proximity—the delicious awareness that she was near him, rather than far from him.

In fact, he'd felt her the moment he'd entered Angel's Manor. He felt her now. She hung in the air, calling to him.

She dimmed his bitter anger over Benchley's treachery, hypocrisy, and malice. She balanced darkness with light—rage with joy. She made him feel clean and renewed. She was his Persephone—his love.

As he neared the dining room, he forced himself to slow. He heard low, male voices, and then he heard Aunt Matty.

"You know, my lord, it's very dangerous for a man to do without marriage."

"Is it, Mistress Dare?" It was Lord Rivers' gentle voice.

"Why, yes. All sorts of maladies may be attributed to marital deficiency. Boils, hangnails, the plague."

"Oh really, Aunt Matty—the plague." There it was—the tender and slightly annoyed voice of his love.

"Yes, the plague." Matthew could almost see Aunt Matty glaring at Patience. "Which is why certain young women, more especially those with exceptional beauty . . . ahem . . . have an obligation to marry."

"Whatever does beauty have to do with preventing the plague?" His love again, sounding slightly more annoyed.

"Really, Patience. Have you ever seen a beautiful plague victim?"

"I haven't seen a plague victim at all."

"Well neither have I, because here in England, thank the Lord, we support the healthy institution of marriage. But, I assure you, they don't call it the plague for nothing. I'm certain the disease comes with all sorts of plague-ish type bumps, lumps, and spots."

"Aunt Matty, the plague has nothing whatsoever to do with a marital deficiency. It is understood that plague comes from filth and rats."

"Exactly. And as everyone knows—forgive me, my lords—men are naturally messy creatures. Whereas women are naturally tidy. So when a man marries a woman, he brings into his home one who will see to it that it is kept neat, and clean. And there you have it, prevention of the plague." Short, silent pause. "I mean it's so simple, really."

Long, silent pause.

Smiling, Matthew turned into the room. "Good evening, ladies—my lords."

He slowed, and the greetings of his guests jumbled together as he drank up the vision of his love. Her red curls were pulled back but for one thick tendril that lay against the gentle rise of her breast. Her lips moved in a breathy exclamation of his name. A flush touched her cheeks. And as he held her gaze, her eyes—her beautiful, intelligent eyes—glistened with a tender and urgent yearning.

"Patience."

He stepped forward, his heart pounding. Had he said her name aloud? Taking her hand, he inhaled gardenias as he bent and pressed his lips to the soft kid of her glove. Still holding her hand, he met her moist gaze. "Miss Dare, whenever I have the misfortune to be out of your presence, I never seem able to envision you as beautiful as you truly are."

Patience's lips parted and her fine nostrils flared.

Matthew's cock throbbed as he imagined kissing her and . . .

"I say, Asher," Farnsby said quietly, but still loud enough for all to hear, "that's a bloody good line, isn't it? We'll have to remember that one."

Matthew smiled into Patience's shining eyes, and then she coughed a giggle that turned into a laugh, which made everyone else laugh. Even Fitz Roy smiled.

With a gentle squeeze, and a passionate glance, Matthew released her hand. He saw it tremble before she tucked it into her lap.

"You'd best write it down," Asher said to his cousin. "Otherwise you're sure to say it all wrong."

"Good idea," Farnsby replied, and actually pulled a small notebook and pencil from his breast pocket.

Making his way to Aunt Matty's side of the table, Matthew bent over her hand. "Mistress Dare, you are looking particularly lovely this evening."

"Thank you, my dear. But how dare you be so formal." She clasped his hand in hers. "I am, after all, your—your"—she looked to Patience—"what? Aunt-in-law?" She frowned. "Is there such a thing as an aunt-in-law, Patience?"

Matthew expected Patience to refute her aunt. But, instead, she just smiled. "I don't know, Aunt Matty. But if there isn't such a thing, there surely should be." Patience lifted one beautiful brow. "Perhaps you've just invented the term."

"Have I?" Aunt Matty released Matthew's hand and positively beamed. "Well, who would have thought that *I* would invent a term? I mean, now that I've done it, I can see how easily it comes to me. Why, I could likely invent a hundred terms."

"Or a thousand," Fitz Roy said wryly.

Aunt Matty nodded. "Or a thousand."

Matthew smiled and took his seat at the head of the table. Fitz Roy, Aunt Matty, and Farnsby sat to his right, Lord Rivers, Patience, and Asher to his left. As Aunt Matty went on about her new term, and as a footman ladled soup into his bowl, Matthew stared at Patience. His beauty was wearing a peach-colored gown that was arranged in small pleats around her shoulders and across her décolleté. Tortoise shell combs were nestled in her red curls, and a cameo hung from a brown satin ribbon around her neck.

She looked like autumn.

Chapter Twenty-One

He Makes Her Look

Set me as a seal upon thine heart . . .

Song of Solomon 8:6

Matthew looked at Patience. Sitting relaxed in her lawn chair she watched Farnsby and Asher's tennis game. She wore a wide-brimmed black straw hat and a ciel blue gown. A bib of pleated white organdy filled the square neck and was tied with a black ribbon at her throat. White organdy cuffs turned back at her wrists. Her long curls were pulled back from her face, but left to cascade from beneath her hat. The sunlight filled them with red and gold glints.

Matthew sighed. In the week since his arrival at Angel's Manor, his nights had been blissful. Spending them almost entirely with her, he was able, for a few hours, to forget his troubles. Unfortunately, there were no secret passages in Angel's Manor, so he was forced to come to her room late and depart early. But he would tolerate anything to be with her—anything, even just to sleep at her side.

His days were less peaceful. He worked to strengthen the position of GWR whilst organizing a production, loading, and shipment schedule for Gwenellyn—which was proving logistically challenging. Further, no matter how he'd shifted the figures, he'd been unable to avoid giving GWR another infusion of his own money. He couldn't do it again—not a sum that large. And word was circulating that Benchley was preparing to contest his ownership of the mine.

Where the hell was Mickey? He needed the proof Mickey was looking for. Once he had it, he would make Benchley entirely and eternally irrelevant. For he was in a fight to the death.

He looked at Patience.

And he had too much reason to live.

He watched her sip her lemonade, and let the vision of her soothe his tension. They had a music lesson scheduled for that afternoon. He'd given her three in the past week, but she was proving a difficult student. She was very resistant, and continued to claim that she didn't even want to play—which was a curious sentiment for someone who had formerly played every day. It didn't make sense. Nothing about her playing had ever made sense, which was why he had to get to the bottom of it. Besides, he didn't want her to go without instruction, as he was the reason she'd given up Cavalli.

And then there was her virginity. His desire to claim it was becoming almost impossible to control. When would she give him her whole self? He turned back to the tennis match.

"So, are you really going to attend Lady Millford's ball?" Fitz Roy asked, not taking his eyes from the game.

"Yes," Matthew answered, following the ball.

Fitz Roy turned to him. "The Benchleys will be there."

Matthew nodded as he continued to watch. "Of course, they always are."

"You know, Lady Millford's reasons for inviting you are entirely selfish. By having you and the Benchleys at her circus, she ensures that everyone who's anyone will be in attendance—just so they can be present for the drama that is sure to unfold. Everyone who knows I'm staying with you has written to me about it, asking if it's true you're really going. They can barely contain themselves."

Matthew turned to Fitz Roy. "I am entirely aware of Lady Millford's motivations. The woman will do anything, including ask *me* into her home, to ensure she has the most talked-of event of the season."

"So why give her what she wants?"

"Because if I don't go, it will be presumed that Benchley's presence is the reason." Matthew frowned. "He will walk around with his chin in the air, and everyone will start talking about how I was too ashamed or too afraid to appear. Anyone who has any belief in me will begin to doubt. Those who are uncertain will fall into Benchley's camp. And those who already malign me will look righteous. No." His frown deepened. "I'll be damned if I'm going to turn tail and hide whilst Benchley holds court at Lady Millford's."

Fitz Roy rested his chin lazily on his fist. "Shame you two can't just whip your cocks out and lay them on the table for everyone to measure. Then we could put this whole thing to rest."

Matthew was forced to smile. "I'd win."

The corners of Fitz Roy's mouth twitched. "I'm sure."

They both turned back to the tennis match, in which Asher seemed to be completely eclipsing his cousin.

After a moment Fitz Roy asked, "Will you bring Miss Dare and her aunt as your guests?"

Matthew glanced over at them. "Of course." He wanted everyone to see Patience on his arm. He wanted everyone to know she was with him.

Fitz Roy nodded as he turned back to the game. "I heard Miss Dare asking you about visiting Gwenellyn the other day."

"Yes."

"I never heard a lady make such a vehement argument for visiting a coal mine." He still watched the game. "In fact, I've never heard a lady make *any* argument for visiting a coal mine."

"Yes, well"—Matthew looked at her—"Patience isn't just *any* lady." She made him feel proud. Rosalind had never been to one of her father's mines, yet Patience was insisting upon going.

"So I take it we're all paying a visit?"

Matthew turned back to Fitz Roy. "I have to return to Gwenellyn for about a week. I thought I'd invite you all up for the day. We'll go on a tour of the place, take dinner together, and then you can escort Miss Dare and her aunt back home the following morning."

"Very well."

They both turned back to the game.

"Thank you, Fitz Roy."

"You're welcome, Hawkmore."

"You're a dear," Aunt Matty said as she accepted Patience's help with her coat. "But hadn't you better get to your lesson? You don't want to be late."

Patience took her time arranging her aunt's collar. "Are you sure you don't want me to go to town with you and the gentlemen?"

Aunt Matty drew back, looking shocked. "Absolutely not! My dear, it's vitally important that you spend time with Matthew engaged in mutually satisfying activities. This is the sort of thing that brings a couple closer together."

Patience sighed. She and Matthew engaged in more mutually satisfying activities than Aunt Matty could ever imagine. But the music lessons were not nearly as satisfying as everything else they did together. "You know, I really do need some new blue ribbons for my velvet bonnet."

"I'll get the ribbons for you, dear," Aunt Matty said, pushing her toward the door.

"Royal blue," Patience added.

"Yes, dear." Aunt Matty opened her bedroom door and waited.

Frowning, Patience strolled out. She looked back at her aunt. "Satin. They must be satin, and not too thin."

Aunt Matty nodded. "Yes, dear. Now off you go." She made a shooing motion.

Reluctantly, Patience turned and meandered down the quiet hallway. She looked back once more, but her aunt was gone. Clasping her hands behind her, she continued toward the upstairs parlor. It wasn't that she didn't appreciate Matthew's efforts to teach her—she just didn't understand his methods. At her first lesson, he'd spent the whole time trying to reposition her. She hadn't played a note. At her second lesson, he'd attempted to get her to play without thinking. *Impossible.* And at her third lesson, he'd asked her to play off tempo. *Equally impossible.*

She paused at a window to watch Aunt Matty leave. Fitz Roy led the way to the carriage. Lord Rivers walked beside her aunt, and Farnsby and Asher brought up the rear. One by one, they boarded, and the conveyance left. It bobbed and swayed as it picked up speed then finally disappeared around a curve in the long drive.

Apart from the servants, she and Matthew had Angel's Manor to themselves. Perhaps she could gently coerce him into a more exciting exchange than a musical one. She smiled to herself and her heart beat a little faster as she hurried the rest of the way to the parlor.

She found Matthew standing by a window, his arms crossed over his chest. "You're late."

Patience nodded. "I was seeing Aunt Matty off."

She immediately noticed that Matthew's Montagnana and another chair had been placed beside her chair and instrument.

Crossing to her seat, he laid his hands on the back. "Come."

Patience obeyed immediately, but instead of sitting down, she stood close to Matthew. He smelled so good. Sliding her hand over the semifirm bulge in his trousers, she lifted her gaze to his and smiled. "It's such a beautiful day, Matthew. And we're alone."

His dark eyes delved into hers but their intensity didn't seem to shift or soften. "Yes, we are. Take off your clothes."

Patience's eyes widened. That had been a little too easy. A shiver of excitement tightened her nipples as she raised her hands to the row of tiny buttons on her bodice.

Stepping away, Matthew took off his jacket and set it over the back of his chair. His broad shoulders and narrow waist were even more apparent clad only in shirt and waistcoat. She watched him as he moved to the hearth and put on more coals. Thank goodness; for though the day was unseasonably sunny, there was a definite nip in the air.

"Thank you, Matthew."

"To keep you warm," he said, turning from the hearth, his impenetrable gaze moving over her.

Shrugging out of her bodice and corset cover, Patience laid them on another chair before reaching back to loosen her skirt and crinoline. Her clitoris pulsed as Matthew watched her step out of her skirts. Per his rule, she wore no pantalets; and he had cut several of her chemises to midthigh. This was so that he need only pull her into a private corner, or claim a brief but private moment to avail himself of her body. Just that morning, he'd brought her to the brink of orgasm three times—and all whilst his staff and guests had been in fairly close proximity. And the day before, he'd given her a firm spanking during their walk through the wooded portion of the rear garden.

Patience laid her skirts with her other things.

His gaze moved slowly over her stocking-clad legs as he crossed the room. Turning, he closed the double doors. "The upstairs staff is belowstairs this afternoon," he said, removing his cuff links as he returned.

They were? A small tremor of tense anticipation moved through her. No wonder everything had seemed so quiet. And no wonder he'd been so quick to have her undress. He'd had other plans for her all along.

Reaching behind her, she pulled the laces of her corset then unhooked the front. As she peeled it away and put it aside, Matthew began rolling up his sleeves. Patience's sensual tension grew, for that simple act, which revealed his handsome forearms, was portentous.

Crossing her arms, she grasped her shortened chemise and, pulling it over her head, added it to the pile of her clothes. She watched Matthew watching her. His eyes seemed to darken as he stared at her in naught but her black high-buttons, black silk stockings, and blue garters. His erection was full and prominent.

When she bent to untie her garter, he said, "No. Stay."

Patience stood straight and let her hands fall to her sides. Her cunt tightened. She was gaining greater comfort with her nudity, but it felt different to be wearing her shoes and stockings. It felt different to be standing before him in the full light of day. And he was regarding her differently.

He was deep in thought. Below his obvious arousal and his powerful gaze, he was weighing and considering . . . something. She looked at him intently and when his eyes returned to hers, she saw . . .

What?

Her heart beat a little faster when he moved, but it was only to step toward the chair that was beside her cello. "Sit."

Patience frowned as she looked first at the chair and then at him. What did he mean to do? She moved slowly to the chair and sat. Then she watched Matthew as he came around to sit beside her.

"Now, take up your cello," he said, placing his own instrument between his trousered legs.

Astonished, Patience stared at him. "You're still giving me a lesson? But I thought . . ."

Matthew looked at her. "You thought what?"

Patience raised her brows then, expelling an exasperated huff, she shook her head. "I can't play in the nude, Matthew."

His gaze gentled. "But you must." He brushed the backs of his fingers softly against her arm. "For I desire it."

His touch elicited a tingly shiver that lifted the gooseflesh on her skin and stiffened her nipples.

"Trust me, Patience."

His eyes were so deep.

With a disgruntled sigh, she parted her legs and swung her instrument before her. "I do trust you."

"Good." His eyes moved slowly over her as he spread his knees wide. His Montagnana fell close against him. The fingerboard rested against his shoulder. "Now," he said in a low voice, "I want you to bring your cello close, like I have mine. Then I want you to touch it. I want you to touch it as if it were your lover. Like this."

Placing his hands on either side of his instrument, he stroked slowly along the curving body—down the shoulder, into the waist, and back up. Then he went down again, his fingers tracing the delicate edges and purfling before slipping to the f-holes. His fingers rubbed the upper holes, swept along the elegant curves, and then pressed just inside the lower holes. Top to bottom and bottom to top, then back again.

Patience's mouth went dry. She knew the feel of those long fingers pressing her clitoris, sliding along her folds and pushing into her cunt.

She lifted her gaze to Matthew's face and found him looking at her, his dark eyes full of fire. Holding her in his stare, he moved his hands down and, flattening them against the lower belly, pulled his cello even closer. His legs opened wider, and then his hips began to rock.

Patience's blood rushed to her womb as she watched him thrust sensually against the back of his instrument. His eyes closed and he turned his face toward the fingerboard. His cheek pressed to it. His lips parted. His fingers stroked up the strings.

And then he stilled.

His eyes opened and captured hers. "Show me that, Patience."

Patience stared at him, enthralled and enflamed—sorrowful and desolate. "I can't."

"Why?"

Tears welled in her eyes. "I just can't."

Matthew frowned as he set his cello in its stand. When he turned back he rested his elbows on his knees and clasped his hands. His head fell forward. A heavy silence filled the room.

"Did you love him, Patience?" He lifted his head, and there was tension in every line of his face. "Did you love this music master who filled your head with lies?"

"No." The answer had come quickly and unequivocally. Patience stared into Matthew's beautiful, bottomless eyes. How could she have ever thought she loved Henri Goutard? "I once thought I loved him." She shook her head. "But I never did."

"Then why do you cling to his lies?"

Because they aren't lies.

A tear slipped down her cheek.

Perhaps if he read Henri's letter he would understand. "In my cello case, there's a bit of loose lining at the bottom. Inside is a letter. You may read it."

"A letter?" He frowned as he retrieved it. Then, sitting back down, he unfolded the single sheet.

Patience braced her hands on the shoulders of her cello as she watched his eyes move across the page. She silently recited the words she knew so well.

Patience,

I caught you watching me yesterday, and I realized immediately why your performance of late has been so unpleasant. Though you tried to hide it, I saw love in your eyes. I was repulsed. Your love for me has infected your music. Your playing has become soft and insipid, and I can no longer endure listening to it.

I told you when you became my student that the pursuit of art and the pursuit of love are antithetical. I thought you understood this. Yet, look what you've done. You've ruined a fine talent, and you've stolen almost a year of my life, during which I might have taught someone more worthy.

I ought to have known better than to have placed my confidence in a fifteen-year-old girl. I made the mistake of believing that you were above the emotional responses so common to females. Clearly, I was wrong—you are all the same.

Since you have proven yourself incapable of perfection, and therefore greatness, you would do well to quit playing altogether and marry one of those eager-faced young men who are always running after you. Yes, give your love to one of them, and take your joys from the more simple pursuits allotted to your sex—marriage and breeding.

Henri Goutard

Matthew dropped his hand and looked at her, his eyes dark with anger. "This is shit."

Is it?

Another tear fell.

His lip curled. "Why have you kept this?"

Why? "As a reminder."

"Of what? That you had a cold son of a bitch for a teacher? Because that's the only truth that I can take from this letter."

"Is it?"

"Listen to me, Patience. The pursuit of art and the pursuit of love are eternally bound. One who denies love will never be a great artist. One who rejects love will never be a great person. One who repudiates love, repudiates God. And as for marriage and the creation of children, I know of no greater pursuits."

Patience trembled, both at his words and the fact that *he* was saying them. "Is that what you believe, Matthew?"

"That's what I know, Patience." He leaned close. "The question is, why don't you know it?"

Patience lowered her gaze. "I want to know it. It's just that . . ." She shook her head.

"What?" Matthew lifted her chin, forcing her to look at him. "Patience, if it wasn't love this Goutard saw in your eyes, what was it?"

"I don't know. Pain, perhaps. And the ridiculous hope that he might soothe it." She shrugged and smiled, which was strange because her tears fell at the same time.

Matthew's frown deepened. "What pain?"

"I don't know, Matthew. Just pain. I mean, sometimes there's just pain, isn't there?" Closing her eyes, she sighed and rested her head against her arm for a moment. Then she returned her gaze to him. "I was fifteen and impressionable. He gave me attention—but not the superficial sort that other men did. In fact, he only really looked at me when I played. And when I did play, he barely looked at anything else. So I played and played. And I came to confuse his attention for caring." Patience paused. "I was foolish."

"You were young and—alone?"

"Alone." Patience repeated the word. She'd felt alone for a very long time. She thought of her last conversation with Passion. At the time of Henri, Passion had just begun to be courted by her first husband, Thomas Reddington. It was then that Patience had realized that her sister would soon be leaving—leaving to make a life of her own. It was then that she, herself, had begun to look outside her family. A part of her had longed to be courted, too. So after the painful failure of Henri, and after many sleepless nights, she'd decided to search for love—a real love—all her own.

She looked at Matthew.

He looked at her.

"Know what I know, Patience." He held up the letter. "And renounce this man's lies."

Patience stared at the paper. She wanted to.

Matthew got up and walked to the hearth. He lifted the letter and then dropped it in the fire.

Patience watched it burn. The center blackened, then the ends curled and flamed. In only a short time, it was ash and dust. Tears slipped down her cheeks, but she wasn't sure why because she felt nothing but a vague satisfaction at its destruction.

Matthew came back and sat before her. "It's gone."

"Yes." Patience nodded. "Thank you."

"You're welcome."

The fire crackled in the silence.

Matthew's gentle gaze moved over her. "So, here we are again. You, me, and your cello."

Patience looked at her instrument and then down at herself. She'd almost forgotten she was naked.

"I am with you, Patience. The past is gone, but I am with you."

She stared into Matthew's beautiful, dovelike eyes.

"I will always be with you," he said softly.

Always? Was there really such a place as always? Patience's tears spilled over. "You shouldn't make such promises," she whispered.

"You shouldn't question what I know," Matthew returned. "Now, touch your instrument, Patience."

No. Her tears kept falling. She shook her head. "Why can't you just leave it alone, Matthew?"

His frown deepened. "Because I can't. I can't leave it alone any more than I can leave you alone." His head tilted. "*Alone* isn't good for you, Patience. You've had too much of *alone*."

Patience's tears fell. Her heart was hurting so badly. "Stop it," she gasped.

"I won't stop it." His eyes bore into hers. "Touch it."

"I can't." She choked on the words. Her body trembled uncontrollably.

"You can." His voice was hard. "Touch it, Patience."

"I can't!" she cried, her heart cracking. "I can't!"

"Can't or won't?"

"I won't!" she shouted at him, heaving her cello away from her.

He grabbed her wrist. "Why, Patience?" His eyes held the fire of the heavens. "Why?"

She tried to pull away.

"The truth, Patience." His hand was a vise. "Look at the truth! Just because you refuse to look at it, doesn't mean it isn't there."

With a choked sob, she twisted her wrist frantically.

"Look at it, Patience! Look at it, or I will make you!"

"I won't!" she screamed.

And then he pulled her down and she was falling—falling over his lap. She fought and flailed, but he was too strong. His arm cinched around her waist, pinning her. Then his hand came down upon her bottom like a crack of thunder. She cried out and her body stiffened as the pain shot through her, fiercer than any she'd felt before. Another strike fell and another, each one as strong as the one that preceded it. Yet the pain grew exponentially, and she couldn't escape it. She cried and jerked against Matthew's body, but he kept on—spanking her and spanking her. And as she wept and writhed, it seemed that the pain he laid on from without reached inside her, touching and releasing a pain from within. A pain that was old, deep, and bleeding. A pain that was too terrible to look at.

She wailed and squeezed her eyes shut, but there was nowhere for her to go, and nowhere for her to hide. For the pain was spreading and Matthew kept on, his unrelenting hand landing upon her flesh over and over, and again and again, breaking down the last of her barriers—the last of her resistance.

And then it happened.

The final door over her heart split and broke, and there was nothing but a swirling eddy of pain before her—and Matthew beneath her, holding and supporting her. Sobbing, she collapsed over his lap. His arm loosened from around her waist. His hands stroked up her back. His lips touched her spine.

Blinded by her tears and deafened by her cries, Patience let her legs slide to the floor. But she held on to Matthew, for he was her rock in the storm of her emotions. Grasping his thigh, she curled into the vee of his legs and wept into his lap. He bent around her, protecting her with his body and his touch, from the full fury of her pain.

Then his voice came softly by her ear and his words reached past her cries. "Tell me, Patience. Tell me, what ails your heart?" His hand smoothed back her hair. "Why won't you touch the instrument you profess to love?"

My instrument. Anger and loathing whirled from the storm of Patience's pain and floated before her, clear and distinct.

She lifted her head and, looking over the top of Matthew's thigh, glared at her cello through her tears. It lay facedown, where she'd thrown it. And the more she stared at it, the angrier she grew.

"Why can't you touch it like a lover, Patience?" Matthew asked low.

"Because *you're* my lover," she cried, her voice thick with tears. "Not that thing!" She spat the word, and her anger ignited into something bigger.

Matthew bent closer to her. "You don't love it at all, do you, Patience?"

"No!" A violent fire flared in her.

"Do you hate it? Is that why you won't touch it, or let it touch you?"

"Yes, I hate it!" Patience's fingers curled into the fabric of Matthew's trouser leg. "I hate it!" She sprang to her feet, and leaping to her cello grabbed it by the fingerboard. With a cry of rage, she swung it over her head and dashed it to the floor. It groaned as its ribs cracked. Over and over she swung it, venting the wrath and resentment of years upon the instrument of her emptiness. Slivers of wood and loose strings flew everywhere. And as she expelled gasping cries, she threw down the fingerboard and stomped upon the splintered remains, grinding the heel of her boot into the scroll and pegs. She stomped and kicked, and cried and whirled, slowing only as the fire inside her began to burn itself out. And when the last spark died, she stood there, her breast heaving, the remnants of her cello all around her.

She didn't move as the realization of what she'd done sunk in.

Oh, God . . .

Had she really done it?

She looked at the broken shards and twisted strings. Shocked, she began to tremble. She looked at Matthew. He stood near his chair, unmoving, his features drawn into tense lines, his dark eyes fixed upon her.

Oh, God . . .

Her tears welled and spilled over. "Look what I've done." She dropped to her knees as fear whirled out of the storm. "Now I have no place to hide. Where will I go if you leave me?" Shaking, he bent and gathered some of the broken pieces of her cello to er.

But it was useless.

Sitting back on her heels, she covered her face with her hands nd cried.

"Patience." Matthew drew her hands from her face. He was itting right before her, one leg folded beneath him and the other ent against his chest. The gold in his hair gleamed in the sunght. "I will never leave you. You and I are forever."

His words made her eyes sting even more. Her tears fell. What if there is no earthly forever, Matthew? What if forever only exists in heaven and fairy tales?" She drew a shuddering breath. "What if *our* forever, isn't really forever?"

Matthew's dark eyes caressed her. "Love is eternal, Patience."

Her heart quaked, and sorrow loomed. "I know," she mewled. "But so is loss. And, for me, the two are never far apart." She touched one of the splinters of her cello. "That's why I need an empty place—an eye in the storm."

"No. You *don't* need it. That's why you broke it."

She looked at him through her tears.

"You can't live in the eye of a storm, Patience. There's nothing there. It's calm and empty, but it's not life. Life is in the whirlwind." His gaze was so earnest. "Love and happiness are in the whirlwind."

"And sorrow."

"Yes, sorrow, too." He cupped her face in his hand. "And tears." His thumb brushed her wet cheek. "But there's no sorrow that can't be borne, Patience, so long as we're not alone."

Alone.

The word and all that it meant—pain, sorrow, fear, anger resentment, and, finally, emptiness—reverberated through he memories. It echoed backward in time to the defining momen that had been its beginning, and from which every other loneli ness had been born—her mother's death.

The moment appeared in her mind like an image viewe through a stereoscope, three-dimensional and real. She looke at it for the first time in twelve years. Pain ricocheted throug her. Grasping Matthew's hand, she pressed her face into it as high mewling sound came from somewhere deep inside her. Hi arm came around her. He pulled her into his lap, and his lip touched her brow. And then as her memory began to move, sh pressed against him and told him everything in gasping whispe and choked sobs.

"The night my mother died we were all there—Father, Pa sion, Prim, and I. We'd been there all day, for she'd been grow ing weaker over the hours and we knew she'd soon be goin She was so pale and fragile, and we didn't know if we wou hear her speak again. But then, at about nine o'clock, she opene her eyes. She smiled at us, and then she looked at me. And wi what seemed like a monumental effort, she said, 'Play for me, pigeon.' So I ran. I ran to get my cello. I ran so fast because I was afraid she might die while I was getting it. But when I returned, her eyes were still open and she was just as when I'd left. So I sat and I played Handel's *Sarabande*. It was her favorite. And I played and played, and I kept looking at her to see if it pleased her, but her eyes never moved or blinked. I played till the end. And it wasn't until then that I realized—when my father closed her eyelids—that I hadn't run fast enough." She turned her face into Matthew's neck. "My father collapsed over my mother. Prim turned into Passion's arms, and started calling, 'Mummy! Mummy!' And I didn't know what to do, or who to go to, because there were no arms left—no embrace for me. There was nothing for me. So I just stood there." She looked up at Matthew through tears of anguish and remorse. "If only I'd had my cello there already. A few notes, or a couple of bars—that would have been enough to escort her to heaven. She wanted that. She asked me for that."

Sobbing into Matthew's neck, Patience surrendered to the pain.

All she could feel was pain. All she could see, touch, and taste were tears. All she could hear were sobs.

But she let herself feel all of it.

And she didn't hide.

How long she cried before she began to calm, she didn't know.

Matthew whispered into her ear, yet all she could hear were hushed bits of words. The low rush of an angel's wings cut his message into indecipherable fragments. But it didn't matter because his embrace and the threads of his voice conveyed a message—you're safe and I'll never leave you.

"I know," Patience breathed.

She wrapped her arms around him and pressed her cheek to his shoulder. It had been so long since she'd felt sheltered. Only her mother's embrace had been like this one—warm, protective, and perfect.

She heaved a sigh as she felt the press of a kiss upon her brow, and she wanted to weep again because even this kiss reminded her of her mother's kisses.

But it was Matthew's arms around her. He pulled her closer, and she clung to him.

More broken whispers. But still he held her. She felt his lingering touch, and it filled her with comfort and peace.

Heaven was around her. She wasn't alone. A breath of wind blew, and she felt warm.

For there were arms embracing her—strong, beautiful arms that would never leave her.

Matthew's arms.

Chapter Twenty-Two
She Loves Him

I have found him whom my soul loveth: I held him, and would not let him go . . .

Song of Solomon 3:4

Matthew pressed his lips to Patience's brow and stroked her curls back from her cheek. He didn't know how many times he'd already done so, but it didn't matter. He'd kiss her brow and smooth her hair for a thousand years if it comforted her—if it made her understand that his embrace, his heart, and his soul were all eternally hers.

He tightened his arms around her protectively. She rested, still and quiet now. But her collapse, her painful confession, and the tortured sobs and wracked cries that had followed it had almost broken his heart.

He closed his eyes and kissed her temple. So long as there was breath in his body, she would never again feel alone—or feel the need to hide from her own emotions. That she must *never* do.

And she must play.

He looked at the broken pieces of her cello, scattered all around them. Watching her break it had been both shocking and spectacular. But it was important that she see and feel—and remember—how to play from her heart. Now, while all her wounds were still raw and tender, so that she could play to heal herself, rather than hide from herself.

"Patience." He whispered her name into her hair.

"Yes, Matthew." Her whispered reply didn't quaver.

He cupped her cheek and turned her face up to his. Her eyes and nose were red, her cheeks flushed and her lips swollen, but he found her ever beautiful. "Come with me," he said.

Patience nodded and slipped off his lap and onto the floor.

Getting to his feet, Matthew held out his hand and helped her rise. His heart ached and his cock throbbed as her long, magnificent body unfolded. One of her stockings was still above her knee. The other was around her ankle. But her state of dishabille only served to magnify her sensual beauty. In the sunshine, her skin looked like cream, her nipples like raspberries. She was food—sustenance for his soul.

Keeping hold of her hand, he drew her to the chair beside his cello. Sitting all the way against the straight back, he opened his legs and indicated the portion of open seat before him. "Sit."

Patience's eyes moved from him, to his cello, and back again. She stared into his gaze for a moment. Her look was soft and trusting. Then she turned and sat gingerly before him, scooting her reddened bottom snugly against his erection.

Matthew winced at the contact. Biting back his lust, he let himself kiss her shoulder before reaching for his cello. He brought it in front of her slowly, watching her legs open for it. His instrument was broader than hers, but she adjusted easily. Uncertain how she would react, he moved very carefully to lay it against her shoulder, smoothing his hand over the spot before letting the wood touch her skin. Then, caressing down her arms, he slid his hands over hers.

"Let's touch it together," he murmured, lifting her hands and placing them against the sides of his Montagnana. "Close your eyes," he whispered by her ear, and saw her lashes flutter down.

Keeping his hands over hers, he guided her touch over the curves of the cello's shoulders and into the waist. "Feel how smooth and strong it is." He breathed the smell of her hair and kissed the lobe of her ear.

She shivered.

He moved her hands over the f-holes. "Yet, it will only give as much as you put into it." He brushed kisses along her shoulder.

She sighed and tipped her head against his.

He slid her hands lower, over the belly of his instrument. "Which is why you must give it your whole self." Pressing against her hands, he pulled his cello, and her, tighter. His blood coursed at the sound of her gasp and the feel of her body. "Then you'll know the full measure of joy that it's capable of bringing you."

He drew her left hand up the strings to the fingerboard. "Do you believe me, Patience?"

"Yes, Matthew." Her answer was a breathy sigh, expelled through parted lips. He felt her body tremble. Her hips pressed back against him.

Matthew shuddered as he reached for his bow. He slid the horsehair along her leg and then over her thigh. Her eyes opened. "Take it," he said, softly.

The moment she took the bow, Matthew drew his hands along her arms. "The Montagnana is not easy," he murmured. "She requires strong articulation and vibrato from the left hand. But the more you demand of her, the more she will give, so hold nothing back." He stroked his hands over her shoulders, then down her sides and around her waist. "Now play, Patience; and think of nothing but this moment." He kissed the sweet-smelling spot behind her ear. "I am with you."

She paused. He felt her inhale and exhale. Then, without any preliminaries, the prelude of Bach's Cello Suite Number One—the piece they'd played together at the musicale—began to pour forth, full and potent.

Matthew closed his eyes. She was playing it a count slower than it was typically played. He brushed his lips against her shoulder as he listened. Each note was expressed with depth. She slowed even more in places and quickened in others. He felt the movement of her body, and could anticipate by it the character of the next measure—so beautiful, so full of feeling. He leaned with her into the final notes as they faded.

Then a shiver trembled through him as the low opening notes of Handel's *Sarabande* softly filled the silence. He opened his eyes. Quiet and tentative she began, but then the music grew. It was both strong and fragile—fragile in its strength, and strong in its fragility. It was both things at once, each somehow magnifying the other. It was Patience.

Matthew closed his eyes, for he need no longer look at her to see her. She was in every note, in every rest. She was before him, pressing back against him. But she was also around him. In all her power and vulnerability—in all her beauty and sublimity—in all her perfect imperfection.

As her music filled him—as he held her close, slowly thrusting to meet the gentle rocking of her hips—his love for her overflowed his heart and poured over her in a deluge of want and desire that was as strong, fragile, and palpable as her music.

When had she stopped? When had she turned to look at him, and when had he opened his eyes? Rapt, he stared into her shining green gaze. Tears were on her cheeks. But there was no sorrow in her eyes, only a bright, glistening joy.

"I want to lay with you, Matthew."

His blood surged and his nerves leapt in crawling desire over his body. But he bit back his love and his lust—he bit them back so hard that the effort left him light-headed. He shook his head and his words seemed to blur. "You've been through much today. I want no regrets tomorrow."

She gently set his Montagnana and his bow in the cello stand. Then she turned, her hip pressing his aching erection. He shuddered at the blissful torture.

"It's not like that, Matthew." Her voice was soft and low. "I'm not surrendering because I feel vulnerable. I'm surrendering because I feel strong." She laid her hands against his cheeks and her eyes looked brilliant. "I'm surrendering because I'm in love."

Matthew's mouth went dry and his heart began to pound—too hard and too fast.

Patience leaned toward him. "I love you, Matthew." She pressed her tender lips to his. "I always have." She kissed him again. "And I always will. So have no worries about tomorrow"—she kissed him again—"because I love you forever."

Had his heart stopped beating? He couldn't feel it.

Heaven—every word heaven.

She drew back and smiled—such a smile. "Matthew, I love you."

He drew a gasping breath as he stared into her loving gaze. His heart hadn't stopped. Rather, his heart, his body, and his soul had all become one pulse—one joy.

Love! Elusive love . . .

Patience's love—bestowed upon me.

Patience's pure, passionate love—mine, at last.

"I—" His voice cracked. "I've been waiting my whole life to hear you say those words." His hands trembled as he lifted them to her face. "And now that you've said them, I find they mean even more to me than I had thought." He touched her lips. "Say them again."

Her gaze, eager and earnest, held him. "I love you, Matthew."

He smiled and laughed, only to smile again. Finally, he gave voice to the words he'd spoken over and over in his mind. "I love you, Patience. I love you."

His eyes stung, so he closed them. He closed them and kissed her with all the hungry, fevered passion of love unleashed.

Then, mouths touching, inhaling her love and exhaling his own, he breathed the other words he'd been longing to say. "Marry me."

Marry him!

Patience squeezed her eyes shut against elated tears.

"Marry me, Patience." His forehead still pressed to hers, Matthew clasped her hand and pressed it to his heart. "Give me heart *and* hand. I must have both, even as I must *give* both." He pulled back, and she looked, through her tears, into his shining eyes. "Say yes, Patience. My love for you is too large to live in secret."

Her heart soaring to the Heavens, Patience smiled and cried. "Yes, Matthew. Yes, and yes again!" She threw her arms around him.

His arms clamped around her. "You're mine," he breathed, his fingers clenching in her hair. "You're mine."

"Yes, and you're mine." Patience pressed fervent kisses all over his face. "Forever mine!"

Then his mouth was covering hers.

Patience held him to her and gave him back kiss for hungry kiss. Her heart felt full and whole, and there was so much passion and joy pouring out from her that she tightened her arms around him in the hope of containing all its beautiful bounty within their embrace.

She kissed him and clung to him, even as she felt him stand. Her legs slid down his body. Her arms held him tight, and she balanced on her toes as she grasped his nape and drank desire from his mouth.

She heard him moan, then his hand was on her sore bottom, gripping it and squeezing it hard. Her head spun and she gasped against his lips as he ground his magnificent erection against her. She thrust her hips in answer. Her cunt clenched and her clitoris throbbed.

"I love you," she breathed between kisses. "I love you."

Matthew tore his mouth from hers. His eyes were like black fire. "Never stop saying those words to me," he rasped. "Never believe you've said them enough. Never believe you've said them too much." His hand slipped along her jaw. He touched her lower lip with his thumb. "For those three words, spoken from your lips, mean more to me than anything that will ever be said to me again. So you must say them over and over—for all our lives. And when I am a very old man and can no longer hear, you must keep saying them, so that I can watch your lips and know that you love me still." He was trembling, and his eyes looked like dark glass. "In return, my love, I shall make you weary with my declarations. Morning, noon, and night shall I advise you of my heart's adoration. And should the day come when I can no longer speak, I shall mouth the words so that you may know, even then, that I love you."

Patience felt tears on her cheeks again, and her heart hurt—not from an excess of pain, but from an excess of love and happiness. "I love you, Matthew. I love you." She smiled into his dark eyes. "And so shall I tell you every day—at both daybreak and nightfall, and a thousand times in between."

His arms swept around her and he took her mouth in a kiss that left her shaking and breathless. Then he drew back and took her hand. "Come," he urged.

Patience followed without pause.

Leaving the parlor, he turned them toward his room. His strides were long and fast. Patience hurried to keep up with him. How different this moment was from the first night Matthew had taken her to his room. How different *she* was.

Without slowing, he looked at her. "I love you."

Patience's smile deepened and her heart pounded. "I love you."

A few more steps and he looked at her again, his gaze skimming her body. "Ours will *not* be a long engagement."

"Very well, my love." Exuberant, she almost skipped at his side.

Matthew barely paused as he reached for his chamber door. Swinging it open, he pulled her in with him, and then swung it shut all in one fluid motion. Pulling her across the huge room, his long strides brought them directly to his bedside. Only then did he stop and face her.

Though his breathing was coming fast, everything quieted as he released her hand. His gaze moved over her and his arms lifted toward her, but then he jerked back. Shoving his hand through his hair, he expelled a breath and shut his eyes.

Stepping close, Patience laid her hand on his chest. "What is it, my love?"

His lashes lifted and the dark fire that so often lit his eyes was burning more fiercely than ever. "I've dreamed of this moment," he said softly. "I've imagined it over and over. Every morning, for the ten days we were parted, I came in my sheets thinking about it. I would lie on my stomach and thrust my cock against the mattress while I dreamed of fucking your sweet cunt."

Patience shivered and her clitoris throbbed.

"But now that the moment is upon me," he said, "I don't think I can command my usual control." He lifted his hands, and they were shaking. "I don't have it today, Patience. And I can't say what will happen without it."

"It doesn't matter, my love." Patience smoothed her hands over his chest.

He covered her hands with his and held them against him. "I can't say what will happen without it, Patience, because I've never been without it."

Never?

Patience looked into his burning gaze, and her heart ached with love. "Then we are both virgins of sorts." She pressed onto her toes and kissed him. "I trust you, my love."

Matthew's breathing quickened and his features shifted into lines that were somehow both Plutonian and angelic at the same time—dark lust and bright love. Or was it bright lust and dark love?

It was both. *He* was both.

"I love you," he murmured.

And he was hers—her dark angel.

"I love you," she replied.

His eyes darkened.

Then she gasped as he threw her on the bed.

Chapter Twenty-Three

Consummation of Love

I am my beloved's, and my beloved is mine . . .

Song of Solomon 6:3

Matthew tore off his clothes—throwing cravat, waistcoat, and shirt in all directions.

Patience lay with her red mane fanned around her head and her face flushed with love and desire. Her long pale body, accented by rosy nipples and the bright curls between her legs, looked golden in the late afternoon sunlight.

As Matthew kicked off boots and yanked at socks, she lifted first one lean leg and then the other to remove her high-buttons Both times she drew up a knee, his eye was drawn to the brief show of her feminine flesh.

He ripped at his trousers, a wordless noise escaping him as he shoved them down with his undergarment. Patience slipped off one sagging black stocking. Before she could remove the other he threw himself upon her—pinning her, open legged, beneath him.

Fuck!

Hot, sweet skin and clinging arms and legs.

Grass green eyes and gardenia-scented hair.

Patience—love.

Fuck!

"God, I love you," he groaned. He thrust his tongue into her mouth, his hands into her hair, and the length of his cock against her wet folds—lubricating himself with her body's passion. "I love you and I'm going to fuck you," he breathed against her succulent lips before taking them in another deep kiss.

Drawing on his tongue, Patience moaned and moved—her hips undulating with his in a call to mate that had existed long before speech.

He knew how to answer her.

He burned to answer her.

Reaching between them, he gripped his swollen prick and rubbed the head against her slick opening.

Tearing his lips from hers, he looked into her green eyes—eyes full of love and want. Had Eve had such eyes? Lush with longing, and green as the garden she was born in? "Feel me," he groaned, pushing his knob just inside her. "Feel me."

Patience drew in a breath, and her hips lifted. "Yes, Matthew."

She was so hot and wet. Tightening his grip around the base of his cock, he shook himself hard and fast. His whole heavy length quaked and moved as he inched deeper into his love.

Her lashes fluttering, she moaned, her hips tense and lifted.

"You like that?" he muttered. Tightening his grip, he shook his meat again.

Her eyes squeezed shut and her lips parted. "Yes—yes."

Fuck, she was so tight. He pressed deeper.

And then he felt it—the barrier of her virginity.

Patience's eyes flew open. "Oh, Matthew . . ."

He stared into her gaze, his lust darkening. More blood rushed to his cock, engorging it with the drive to fuck, even as it emptied his mind of any thoughts but those most primal.

He eased his hand from between them and, leveling his weight, settled more firmly, more immovably, against her resistant flesh.

Patience drew in her breath. "Matthew . . ."

"Do you know why I wake every morning with my cock hard?" His voice came from someplace deep inside him. "Because that's how Adam woke from the sleep that gave birth to Eve. Now tell me"—braced on his elbows, he slowly slid his hands beneath her shoulders—"once he saw her, how long do you think Eve remained a virgin? An hour?" He eased his hips forward. Patience gasped. "A minute?" He pressed harder and watched her begin to writhe. "How long, my love?" Staring into her shining eyes, he gritted his teeth. "How long before Adam, hard with desire, broke her to his purpose—fucking her and filling her womb with his seed." He bore down. "How long!"

Patience bit back a cry. "Seconds—now!" Tears sparkled in her eyes. "Take me now!"

Matthew shuddered. "Who and what are you?"

Her body arched beneath him and tears seeped from her eyes. "I am Eve, and I am yours."

"Mine!" Matthew groaned and thrust his body upward. Unbroken, Patience cried out and struggled beneath him, but he felt no pity for her passionate distress. It only enflamed him all the more. For she was his, and this was meant to be. "Mine," he asserted into her tear-filled eyes, and thrust again. Her high mewl was full of yearning, and he moaned as she began to give, adoring submission shining from behind her moist eyes. His heart pounded with love. "Mine," he breathed tenderly.

Then, with a great heave, he sundered her and, bathing in her blood, filled her body with his own thick flesh. "Forever mine."

Forever his.

Pinned and penetrated, her eyes wet with tears, Patience clung to Matthew even as she writhed at the painful pleasure between her legs. It was sharp and raw, and her clitoris was pulsing. Neither bliss nor agony, it was as if she were suspended in some kind of purgatory that promised both, but delivered neither. No matter how she moved, she found no relief. "Please, Matthew . . ."

His eyes glowing, he stared down at her, his powerful body unmoving. "Please what, my love?"

She clasped at him with her arms and legs. "Please, give me more! Move in me!"

Matthew's jaw tensed. "Convince me."

Moaning, Patience pulled him down and opened her mouth under his. She thrust her tongue as she arched against him and stroked her legs along his thighs and calves. His tensely muscled limbs felt large against her own, and she inhaled vetiver as she drank the warm wetness from his mouth. She kissed him and kissed him until they were gasping. Then she finally broke the contact and, tightening her legs around his rugged hips, spoke against his mouth. "I love the weight of your body between my legs, Matthew. I love the feel of your thick cock inside me. I lo the strength of your hands upon me. And I love that you're not afraid to use me well and ride me hard."

He drew back, and his eyes looked like black glass, his features tense with restraint. Patience touched the hair falling against his temple, then pressed her hand against the angles of his cheek. "I feel your power, Matthew, trembling over me." Tightening the fingers of her other hand in the short hair of his nape, she pulled him down and whispered into his ear, "Unleash it upon me."

Matthew groaned. His mouth devouring hers in a scorching kiss, he surged against her, forcing his cock deeper.

Patience drew in his sweet breath and her body tensed, for she hadn't known he had more flesh to give her. But as he continued to kiss her, and to thrust and press, she grew more and more breathless at the size and strength of his penetration. His hard heaviness filled and stretched her, and attending it was the raw pain of her torn virginity.

Tearing her lips from his, she panted and blinked back tears as he thrust again, his powerful body driving her upward.

His hand clasped her breast. Her nipple hardened. "Feel me, Patience," he growled. His jaw was clenched and his eyes were fierce as he drove into her, again and again. "Feel the power of my love."

Patience bit back cries and clawed at his back. It was bliss and agony—the bliss of being filled, the agony of being torn. Two sides of the same coin in a perfect and eternal intercourse, and woven together in the perfect wholeness of love.

And it was unrelenting, for, still, he drove her—thrusting his hard phallus into her virgin flesh, his muscles and limbs straining. "So tight." He groaned. "But I shall make you fit me, Patience." Clenching her hair in one hand, he moved the other to her hip, gripping it. His hold was more perfect than any bonds could ever be, for she felt the weight and force of his intent. His eyes captured hers. "I will fuck you . . ." he said on a harsh whisper, thrusting into her. Her breasts bounced and the severe sound of his voice softened her from the inside out. He thrust deeper. "And fuck you . . ." His deepening voice melted her like wax. His pubic bone slammed against hers. "I will fuck you until you fit." He groaned on an exhale.

Patience sucked in a great, heaving breath. Then, panting short and shallow, she gazed up at him through her tears. He was truly inside her—deep inside her—touching the door to her womb. It was like nothing she'd ever felt—his thickness, filling her cunt and stretching her tightly around the trunklike root of his cock. It was as a glove might feel around a hand, or a corset around a waist. And as she stared into the face of her beloved, she knew that this was both her most base and most divine purpose. To be filled—with man, with seed, with child.

Her body, her heart, and her spirit quivered as one. "Matthew," she breathed, "fuck me, please."

"Yes." He groaned. "Over and over, and again and again." He held her hips immobile, and began rotating his own.

Holding him with her legs, Patience moaned as his prick stirred her, his knob circling the opening to her womb and pressing into her deepest recesses. As always, he touched her where she could not. But she no longer resisted that, for she was his to possess. So she tilted her hips up in offering, and gasped as he reached deeper. "Oh, my love. Yes . . ."

His features hard, he stared down at her. The revolving pressure was constant. Never releasing, never relenting, it heated her with a luscious friction that enraptured her nerves.

Patience trembled and her cunt clenched. She heard Matthew moan, but all she could think was that for the first time she wasn empty. The clenching wasn't a call, it was an answer—a full, potent answer that sent desire surging inward to her womb as muc as outward to her clitoris.

"Oh, God, Matthew!" She stared into his fierce gaze as sh gripped his shoulders.

The more he moved, the tighter he wound her. Everything wa mounting inside her—as if all the blood and fluids of her bod were swirling together and spiraling toward her womb. She shuddered and shrunk inward. Matthew moved faster, cresting the waters of her desire, even as the whirlpool deepened—pulling he and him, into the center of her body until, with a choked gasp, sh was sucked into the whirling eddy of her own primordial lust.

Everything went dark and silent as she spun and spun to t point where life, lust, and love coalesce. And the place was bo so small and so big that she could not fit into it or fill it—

she burst, her nerves exploding. And whirling out into a thousand pieces of bliss, she floated with the waters of her womb, small enough to fit in a thimble, expansive enough to fill a universe.

She lay shattered and weightless. But Matthew was moving—thrusting now. Shifting the tide with his staff, moving the pieces of her back together—thrusting and thrusting. And suddenly she could hear his groans and her own wordless cries. Gripping his buttocks and tilting her hips, she could feel the pain of her torn flesh and, swelling beneath it, a piercing, penetrating pleasure.

She opened her eyes and stared into his, black and blazing.

"I can smell your blood, " he grunted as his body heaved against hers. "Your blood, which is mine. Your blood, which calls me to *come*." His urgent thrusts quickened. "I want you. I love you."

Patience bit into her lip as his cock slammed into her, forcing her desire into a surging wave that grew higher with each thrust. Again and again, and faster and faster he drove her.

Patience wept. She didn't need to hide her face or prevent her tears. So, as Matthew panted and thrust, she let them fall—tears for the pain and the passion. Tears for the emptiness banished at last. Tears for joy, and tears for love—the love christened with blood, and the love that poured from Matthew's eyes as he cried out and filled her, at last, with the fluid of creation.

He was hers.

Forever hers.

He wanted to fuck her again—and again, and again, and again.

Matthew's heart tightened at the incomparably sweet and sensual vision she presented.

They stood in the water closet attached to his dressing room, and she had her foot resting on the edge of the bathtub. Her green eyes regarded him tenderly, her mane of red curls in wild disarray. Long spiral locks fell down her back and around her shoulders, while smaller curls fell over her brow and corkscrewed above her brilliant green eyes. Her lips were swollen from kisses and her cheeks were flushed with the residue of her passion. One black stocking still hugged her left leg, and her pale nudity displayed her still blushing bottom most prettily. God, but he loved her.

He sponged her blood from her thighs—her sweet, virgin blood, her blood that still stained his prick. And as he did so, he gently gripped the underside of her bottom with his free hand. She was so beautiful, and he loved the intimacy of cleansing her—even her delicate folds.

He squeezed out the sponge into the basin and, picking up a thick towel, patted away every last drop of water as he stroked her bottom. Finally, when he couldn't draw the moment out any longer, he pulled back. "All done."

She dropped her leg and, smiling up at him, pressed against his side. "Thank you, my love."

Then, picking up the sponge, she proceeded to wash his cock—very well—too well. By the time she'd fondled his cods and slipped back his foreskin for the sixth or seventh time, he was more than half-hard. "I hope you're prepared to spread your legs again, my love. For much more of this and I will be forced to have another go at you."

Patience smiled and blushed as she wrung out the sponge and reached for the towel. He took it from her and applied it to himself as she watched.

Her tongue slipped out to wet her lips. "Can I help it if you're magnificent?"

Pulling her close, Matthew sucked a moist kiss from her mouth. "Thank you."

"You're welcome." With her arms still around him, she glanced at the pinkish water in the basin and then back at him with a proud smile. "Well, I'm now once and forever fucked."

Matthew threw his head back and laughed. "You're forever fucked, all right. But I assure you, it won't be only once." He trailed his fingers over her hip to the curve of her waist and then the curve of her lovely breast. "In fact, I think you'll find that I shall be availing myself of your tight cunt on a frequent basis." He pinched her nipple, eliciting a gasp from her, and then let his fingers slide down over her delicate navel.

As he stared at her taut stomach, it suddenly occurred to him that he may very well have just given her a baby. His heart skipped and he pressed his palm against her smooth belly.

Patience laid her hand over his. "What is it, my love?"

Matthew looked into her verdant eyes. "I was just thinking that you could be with child."

A flush darkened Patience's cheeks and she looked down at herself. When she looked back at him, her eyes were shiny. "Before you, I didn't think I would be a mother. But now I will be, sooner or later, and I find it extraordinary that I ever thought I *wouldn't* be."

Matthew smiled. "We need to get married very soon. I suggest December."

Patience tilted her head. "But Matthew, December is a rather busy time for a wedding."

"I like December."

"Why?"

He shrugged. "Well, aside from the fact that I promised Aunt Matty we'd be married by Christmas; I like Christmas. And since there's nothing I want more than you, I think Christmas is the perfect time for our wedding."

Patience looked up at him from beneath her brows. "You promised Aunt Matty."

"Yes, I promised Aunt Matty."

Patience looked at him disbelieving. "When?"

"The day after the hunt."

Patience shook her head. "Lord in Heaven, you two really are birds of a feather."

"Well, when it comes to our mutual determination that you marry me, yes, we are. Now, what say you to December?"

Patience let her brows lift then fall. "I say that until you ask my father for his permission to marry me, I can't speak for December."

Matthew took her hands in his, remembering his visit with the Reverend Dare. It hadn't been easy facing the tall, stoic man. He had a formidable presence and the same assessing quality in his eyes as Patience. "I already asked your father, my love."

Patience frowned with shock. "You already—" She cut herself off. "When?"

"When I left Hawkmore House."

Patience looked nonplused. "What did he say? No, wait, what did *you* say?"

"I told him I'd fallen madly and unequivocally in love with you. I told him I couldn't live my life without you, and that, even if it took a lifetime, I would court you and no other." He curved his hand against her soft cheek. "I told him that you give me hope and joy, and that I love just being in your presence. I told him that I admire you for your strength of character, your loyalty and your intellect." He pressed her hand against his heart. "I told him that you make my heart pound and my breath quicken. And I told him that, whenever I am with you, I feel like I have wings."

Patience's eyes glistened. "And what did he say?"

"He said that he didn't quite know how he would get along without you, but that he would never hold you back from your own happiness. Then he was pensive and quiet for a long moment. Finally, he said he loved you. Then, after another moment, he reached over his desk and shook my hand."

"So did he give you his blessing?"

"Actually, he told me good luck. When I asked him if that meant I had his approval, he said that *your* approval would be far more difficult to acquire than his. If, however, I earned your approval, then I could count upon his as well."

Smiling, Patience threw herself into his arms. "Then December it is, my love!"

Matthew held her tightly against him, his heart soaring. "I have something for you," he murmured by her ear.

"Yes." She rocked her hips against his. "I can feel it."

Grinning, Matthew pulled back and drew her into his dressing room. "That isn't exactly what I was referring to, but I would be happy to give you that later." He reached into the top drawer of his dresser and withdrew the black velvet box for which he had paid so dearly. Turning, he laid it in her hands. "For you, Mrs Matthew Morgan Hawkmore."

Patience's brow twisted with surprise and uncertainty. "What's this, Matthew?"

"Open it."

Brushing her hand over the top of the velvet box, she released the catch and slowly drew open the lid.

Her eyes widened on a gasp. "Oh, Matthew! They're beautiful!" She laid the box on his dresser and gently brushed her fingers over the sparkling jewels—necklace, earrings, bracelets ring, belt buckle, and combs. He thought she would try the ring first, but she reached for the combs instead.

Taking them from her hands, he pulled back her heavy curls and placed one comb then the other, before leading her to the long mirror by his armoire. Turning to and fro, she admired them.

He admired *her*. How exceptional she would look at the Millford ball. He couldn't wait to show her off—and to be in public with her as her chosen one.

The diamonds sparkled in her hair like stars, but their brilliance was nothing to her shining eyes when she looked at him through the mirror. "I've never had anything so fine, my love."

Matthew smiled. "I couldn't think of what would suit you better than diamonds."

Patience turned to face him. "I wasn't referring to the jewels, Matthew. I was referring to *you*."

Matthew's heart stopped then started.

"The jewels are magnificent and, as a gift from you, they are all the more valuable to me. Thank you for them. I will wear them with pride." She wrapped her arms around him. "But you are my greatest gift." She tipped onto her toes and touched her lips to his. "Thank you for today—for everything—most especially for your love, but for your wisdom and understanding, too." Her eyes were so soft, so tender. "I love you, Matthew, and I will *never* regret my decision to stay with you. Thank you for giving me the time to make that decision. Thank you for your patience, your trust and your honesty. And thank you for giving me the happiest day of my life."

Matthew held her in his trembling embrace. "Thank *you*, my love. Thank *you*."

Chapter Twenty-Four

Friends

I will rise now, and go about the city in the streets . . .

Song of Solomon 3:2

Gwenellyn

"She seems to be quite popular with your workers," Fitz Roy commented.

Matthew smiled as he watched Patience talking with yet another miner's wife. "She is indeed."

He regarded her proudly. She wore a simple gown of dark gray wool with a black velvet collar and cuffs. A black velvet bonnet covered her bright head. Lined with black lace and tied with a wide scarlet sash beneath her chin, it was a perfect frame for her magnificent face.

"Do you think I will be taking that urchin home with us? She doesn't seem in the least inclined to release her grip on Miss Dare any time soon," Fitz Roy said.

Matthew regarded the small child who had silently accompanied them, via a firm grip on Patience's skirt, through the whole village. The little girl barely took her wide blue eyes from Patience's face, and, even now, moved with Patience into the house of the woman she'd been talking to.

Matthew sighed. "The little thing has probably never seen the likes of Miss Dare."

"Bloody hell," Fitz Roy drawled, "*I've* never seen the likes of Miss Dare."

"No." Matthew adjusted his topper. "Nor have I."

They both sat against a large gray boulder.

Though the day was sunless and cold, they had walked the entire village. As word of their presence had spread, people had come from all directions. But it wasn't for him that they had come—he was already becoming a familiar face. And it wasn't for Fitz Roy's dapper presence. They had come for Patience—for the elegant beauty in the scarlet-trimmed bonnet. But while they came to see the vision she presented, they stayed because she was so much more than that. She spoke to the residents of Gwenellyn with genuine interest and respect. She asked them questions and listened carefully to their answers. She accepted their invitations to step into their dilapidated homes, and she didn't shirk from sitting on the splintered benches or rough chairs that were offered her. She didn't push away a single child, even though they grasped at her skirts with filthy hands. And she smiled at everyone with genuine pleasure.

"She will be a real asset"—Fitz Roy examined his nails—"but I think she will cost you as well. For if I gauge your fiancée and her questions correctly, she is compiling a long list of improvements for your little hamlet."

Matthew tensed. He knew Fitz Roy was right. "When one engages oneself to the daughter of an honorable vicar, one must be prepared to become a philanthropist."

Fitz Roy glanced down the narrow street of ramshackle houses. "No offense, Hawkmore, but it'll take a prodigious lot of philanthropy to turn this place into anything presentable." He crossed his arms over his chest as he sent another appraising look in the other direction. Raising his brows, he turned back to Matthew. "Possibly, more philanthropy than one man can afford."

More philanthropy than *he* could afford. "Possibly," Matthew said, surveying the street himself. It was unpaved and, despite the cold, raggedly dressed children stirred up the dust as they played amidst the ruts and potholes. A retired pit pony hitched to a rickety cart rested on three legs in front of a decaying stable. The fourth leg he held up daintily as if in abhorrence of the rough ground. The houses, small and close together, were in varying stages of disrepair. Like sad old beggars, they seemed to lean into each other for support—their cracked gray walls and thinning thatch testaments to the hard life of their occupants.

Clearly, Benchley hadn't spent any of his prodigious profits to maintain the housing that was offered to the miners with families. And yet—Matthew turned his gaze down the other end of the street—despite the poor condition of the houses, women were sweeping their broken stoops and tending meager little gardens. An old man, assisted by a boy, was attempting to rehang a door on leather straps. Two little girls were picking berries from a brambly hedgerow.

Matthew turned to Fitz Roy. "It could be worse."

Fitz Roy's brows shot up. "It could?" He glanced doubtfully down the street, then shrugged. "If you say so."

Both of them stood as Patience exited the house. She exchanged good-byes with the miner's wife and hurried over, her small appendage still firmly attached. "Oh, Matthew"—she clasped his hand—"thank you for allowing me to come here today. I'm so glad I was able to see this place, and to meet these good people. There is so much that can be done for them, Matthew." She raised her brows. "So much that *needs* to be done."

I can't afford it. Matthew tucked Patience's arm in his and the three of them—or rather, the four of them—strolled toward the main street. "Such as?"

"First, they have no church and no vicar. If any religious service is required, including marriages, baptisms, and funerals, they must travel to Gwenderry for it, which is seven miles away. And as for spiritual guidance—well, needless to say, the people here are far more likely to seek counsel at the pub than they are from the vicar in Gwenderry."

"My love, even if we had a vicar here, the people are more likely to seek counsel at the pub."

"Perhaps," Patience admitted. "But if we had a church, we could also have a church school. Oh, Matthew, many of the older children here remember what it was like to work underground before the reforms were passed. For years, they knew nothing but physical labor and darkness. Don't we owe them some small amount of learning—in recompense, at the very least—for their lost childhoods? And what of the young ones? I began to play the cello when I was five." She laid her hand on the head of the little girl who walked at her side. "Will she ever even see an instrument, let alone play one?"

Matthew looked into Patience's earnest gaze. "We don't even have a church, my love."

"Mrs. Jones—the woman I was last speaking with—told me that there is an old stone building at the end of the main street leading into town."

Matthew nodded. "Yes, there is. It's full of old rail, cracked sledges, and other equipment."

"It's a church," Patience asserted.

Matthew frowned. "How do you know?"

"Mrs. Jones. She says there's a graveyard behind and an old bell hanging from some exposed rafters." Patience smiled as she hugged Matthew's arm close. "Of course, we'd have to renovate it, reinstate it, and build a modest house and outbuildings for whomever would come to tend to the souls here."

I can't afford it.

Her fingers drummed on his arm. "You know, I'm thinking of a particular theology student who studied for a time with my father. He was a big, burly Welshman—and just as comfortable in an alehouse as at an altar. He would have taken his orders by now. I mean, he's likely been assigned to a parish . . . But perhaps, for the sake of these people, he would come."

Fitz Roy actually chuckled. "I told you so," he said wryly.

Shit.

Patience leaned forward to look around Matthew. "You told him what, my lord?"

Fitz Roy raised one black brow. "I told him your aspirations for this place would be expensive."

"My lord, from what I've heard, more money is often laid down upon the gaming table in one evening than it would take to repair, whitewash, and re-thatch all the houses in this village."

Fuck.

Fitz Roy shoved his hands in his coat pockets. "Well, she's got us there, hasn't she?"

Matthew's neck felt stiff. "Indeed she has."

Patience smiled up at him. "I know you've already instituted a raise in wages, Matthew. It's so good of you."

Matthew drew his brows together. "My decision has nothing to do with goodness. I raised the wages because they were below standard. And I did that because I need these miners to *want* to work for me. I need their loyalty, and the best way to get it fast is to buy it."

Patience nodded. Then a moment later, "I hear you've mandated safety lamps for any and all work underground, and that you are supplying these lamps. I also hear you're looking into installing centrifugal fans to ventilate the shafts."

Damn it. Matthew stopped walking and looked into her intelligent eyes. "Patience, I'm doing those things because I can't afford not to. A safe mine is a productive mine. And I *need* a productive mine."

Patience smiled up at him as they continued walking. "You're a very wise businessman, my love. It's no wonder you're so successful."

Matthew frowned and his stomach felt unsettled.

She looked so entirely happy.

"Did you know, my love"—she looked past him at Fitz Roy—"and my lord, that blackberries grow wild all through this region?"

Matthew nodded. "They're quite delicious."

"They are," Patience agreed. "And, apparently, there's an old apple orchard nearby as well. Wouldn't it be wonderful if the residents could learn to cultivate apples and berries? As a community, they could develop and sustain two crops." She sighed as she glanced about. "And don't you think it would beautify the town if we planted trees and flowers? Just think how much cheerier it would look."

Matthew gazed down at her, and his heart tripped in the face of her enthusiastic smile. She wanted so much, for people who had so little. He forced the tension from his body. As soon as he got GWR back up at full steam, he would see that she got what she wanted—her church, her school, her whitewash, and her flowers. "I love you."

Patience blushed and her brilliant eyes softened. "I love you."

God, he wanted to kiss her.

And fuck her.

Her eyes darkened as she bit her full lower lip.

Fitz Roy leaned close, gaining their attention. "Keep looking at him like that, Miss Dare. He'll give you everything you want." Then he trotted up the stairs to the Gwenellyn offices.

Patience smiled saucily at Matthew as they followed. "Is that true?"

"Well, I don't know," he replied. "I am, after all, a very demanding man."

Her smile became flirtatious. "Fortunately, I am prepared to submit to all that you demand."

Fitz Roy held the door for them and as she passed in front of Matthew, the back of her hand brushed his cock.

Matthew tensed then shook his head when Patience winked at him over her shoulder. "I'll make you pay for that later," he said softly.

She looked up at him through her lashes. "Promise?"

Matthew's smile deepened and his heart felt full. "Cheeky girl."

"Here they are!" Aunt Matty announced loudly.

Patience grinned before following the sound of her aunt's voice into the front office.

Matthew and Fitz Roy paused to remove their coats before following as well.

"Come have tea you two." Sitting at a table before the fire with Lord Rivers, Aunt Matty gestured to them. "You're sure to catch your death, milling about on this frigid day."

As Matthew crossed the room, he watched Patience remove her bonnet and gloves. Once she'd put the items on the mantel, she touched the child's shoulder. "Sit and have some tea, Lucy."

With her grimy cheeks, and in her dress with the hem let out and her too-small sweater, the child looked entirely out of place. But Patience and Aunt Matty acted as if there were nothing at all unusual about an unkempt urchin at their tea table.

After seating Patience beside the child, Matthew took the remaining seat beside Fitz Roy. He watched his love. She casually swabbed a moistened napkin over the little girl's cheeks and hands as Aunt Matty poured tea and chattered away about the wonders of the General Store.

"Lord Rivers and I found it extremely well stocked. Didn't we, my lord?" She pushed a cup of tea toward Patience and another in front of the child.

"We did indeed, Mistress Dare," Lord Rivers agreed.

"I daresay it has everything a miner could need," Aunt Matty continued.

Patience nodded with interest as she sugared Lucy's tea and

served her a scone. "What of household items?" she asked her aunt, putting a napkin across the little girl's lap.

"Oh, yes." Aunt Matty poured tea for he and Fitz Roy. "I do believe it has most of the necessary household items. Although, I, for one, simply must have licorice in my house, and there was none to be had—not a single nip."

Matthew exchanged a smile with Patience before Aunt Matty captured his attention.

"Matt dear, I'm afraid I found the store a bit short on sweets altogether."

"Really, Aunt Matty?"

"Mmm, yes—and for a village with so many children . . . Mind you, I would have settled for a lemon drop. But there were none of those either." She sighed. "Only peppermints—which I abhor."

Fitz Roy shifted his pale eyes to Matthew. "You should be writing this down," he drawled. "Licorice and lemon drops—no peppermints."

Matthew shot him a look.

Patience grinned behind her teacup.

"I happen to be quite fond of a good peppermint," Lord Rivers commented.

Aunt Matty drew back. "Really, my lord?"

"Licorice, lemon drops, *and* peppermints," Fitz Roy amended.

Matthew kicked him under the table, which drew a surprisingly startled expression from the unflappable lord.

Patience giggled and Lucy watched her, carefully arranging her hands on her teacup so that she mirrored her.

"Yes, Mistress Dare. In fact"—Lord Rivers reached into hi coat pocket and drew out a small tin—"I always keep a few wit me." He opened the lid. Inside were small red and white candies

Aunt Matty looked at them and then back at Lord Rivers "My lord, I do believe this is the first subject upon which w disagree."

"I hope it won't affect our friendship, Mistress Dare," he sai in his gentle voice.

"Not at all, my lord." Aunt Matty patted his arm. "What's peppermint preference, or the lack thereof, between two matur individuals such as ourselves?"

Lord Rivers smiled as he looked across the table at the child. "What about you, Miss Lucy? Do you like peppermints?"

The little girl didn't say a word.

"Would you like one?" Lord Rivers tried again.

Lucy looked at Patience, but his love only smiled at her, offering no advice.

Finally, the child nodded.

"Why don't you take them all?" Lord Rivers pushed the tin across the table. "There are far too many there for me to eat myself."

Matthew watched as, again, Lucy looked to Patience. Again, Patience only smiled and sipped her tea.

"Perhaps you might share them with your family," Lord Rivers offered.

With one last glance at Patience, Lucy reached for the tin of peppermints.

Once she had it securely in her pocket, she looked again to Patience. This time, Patience gave her a small nod then, leaning down, whispered something by her ear. Lucy looked up at her and basked for a moment in Patience's smile before turning to Lord Rivers and mouthing the words *thank you.*

Lord Rivers mouthed back *you're welcome*, which made the child smile shyly and lean into Patience.

His love offered no consoling touch, but the tender gaze she bent over Lucy's head spoke volumes. And, in that moment, Matthew had a picture of the sort of mother she would be. Understanding and watchful, she would teach by example before word. She wouldn't supply answers unless necessary, and she wouldn't coddle shyness or lack of experience. But she wouldn't be intolerant or impatient either. And in her every touch and smile, her every word and action would be love.

She lifted her soft gaze to his and his heart swelled even as his cock did. He hadn't had her in almost a week, and the need to empty his seed into her womb was riding him hard. He had to have her before she left.

"You certainly know the way to a child's heart, my lord." Aunt Matty's amiable voice forced his attention back to the conversation.

"Thank you, Mistress Dare." Lord Rivers rested one wrinkled

hand over the other on the table before him. "As I age, I am finding I have a renewed appreciation for the honest simplicity of children and childhood."

Fitz Roy's black brows shot up. "Good lord, their 'honest simplicity' is the very thing I find most annoying. One of my young nieces once walked right up to me and declared my waistcoat 'ugly.'"

"Well"—Matthew lifted one brow—"was it?"

Fitz Roy managed to look only moderately outraged. "*Whom* do you think you are addressing?" He made a show of brushing imaginary lint from his arm toward Matthew. "Chartreuse and turquoise checks are most excellent against dark gray."

Matthew smiled, and Patience laughed. He loved to watch her laugh. He loved to watch her do anything.

She shook her head then regarded Lord Rivers with a gentleness in her eyes that was becoming more and more consistent. "My sister Primrose would agree with you, my lord. She has long argued that children see the world with a clarity that adults are incapable of. She maintains that if you really want good advice you should ask a child for it."

"She does say that," Aunt Matty declared. "And she does have such a way with children. Why"—she suddenly fixated on Fit Roy—"if you were to meet her, my lord, you would find her t be the sweetest, most charming young lady. She has the tempera ment of an angel, and her beauty is unmatched, except by that o her sisters, of course."

Fitz Roy leveled his pale eyes upon Aunt Matty. "Mistres Dare, I am the youngest son in a family of ten children, six c whom are boys. This fortunate circumstance means that I hav no obligation, whatsoever, to marry. I am free and I intend to sta that way, so do not waste your matchmaking efforts on me."

Aunt Matty looked pityingly at him. "What of a family of yo own, my lord—children."

"I have twenty-eight nieces and nephews, mistress, all whom seem to suffer, in varying degrees, from either extren verbosity or extreme stickiness. Where it up to me, several wou be sent back."

Undeterred, Aunt Matty smiled. "I know you don't mean th my lord. Besides, a man always has more affection for his ov children than for another man's. Did you know that a male lion will often kill the cubs of another male, but that he is as gentle as a lamb with his own?"

Fitz Roy regarded Aunt Matty askance. "I, alas, am not a lion."

"Oh, really, my lord. Children are a great joy."

As Fitz Roy protested, Matthew leaned his chin in his hand and spoke to Patience. "You know, I think I'm going to miss being the object of her attentions."

Patience smiled warmly at him. "I know. No sooner are we engaged—"

"I heard that, you two," Aunt Matty interjected. "And don't think you're free of me yet. Until you're married, you're not married and . . ."

Her jovial expression faded as her attention was drawn to something behind Matthew. The room quieted. Matthew turned.

A tall, thin man stood in the doorway. Unsmiling, he wore a long black topcoat and carried a briefcase at his side. His topper made him appear even taller and thinner—and more foreboding. "I'm looking for Mr. Matthew Morgan Hawkmore."

"I'm going to London." Matthew stacked several files on his desk. "I'll file a countersuit and make a plea for a quick decision."

"Benchley will try to draw it out," Rivers observed. "Even if the decision goes your way, he will surely appeal."

Fitz Roy, who was leaning against the wainscoting of the front windows, crossed his arms over his chest and remained silent.

Rivers was right. The lawsuit stipulated that Matthew cease and desist from all operations of the Gwenellyn Mine until a decision regarding legal ownership was reached. Benchley didn't even have to win. He just had to keep fighting. In a matter of weeks, GWR would be crippled, and Matthew would be ruined.

Where the hell was Mickey?

He paced behind his desk. "I've got to get the court to lift their production ban. Even if it's for reduced hours, they must allow some operations to continue here. My engines can survive for a time on rations."

He paused by the window behind his desk. In the open

meadow below, Farnsby and Asher were engaged in a game of football with a pack of village boys. As he watched, Farnsby and a tall towheaded lad made a run for the goal together. Passing the ball, they avoided the defenders. And then the boy made a brilliant shot that seemed to arc around the goalkeeper. Farnsby leapt into the air as cheers erupted from the boys on the scoring team. The towheaded lad, seemingly unimpressed by his own skill, took the accolades of his teammates in stride. *The honest simplicity of childhood.*

"What are the people of Gwenellyn supposed to do whilst Benchley and I duel?" he asked out loud. "Winter is coming. How will they survive without work? They'll have to leave—go to other mines." He watched the boys move the ball down the field. "Most of the children in this village were born here. They've lived here their whole lives." He turned to face Rivers and Fitz Roy. "How many will go hungry? How many will be forced into the poorhouses?"

Rivers nodded as he leaned forward in his chair. "That is the argument you must make to the court. Appeal to their humanity and common decency—to their Christian concern for the fate of their fellow man." Rivers got slowly to his feet. "And I shall make known your apprehension for the people of Gwenellyn, for the more public opinion sways to your side, the better." He leaned on his cane. "Most everyone, at some point, has thought to themselves: *There, but for the grace of God, go I.*"

Matthew watched the frail man cross the room. "Thank you my lord," he said as Rivers exited.

The man turned and winked one watery eye. "You're welcome, my boy."

Once he'd left, Matthew flipped open the thin file of legal documents that summarized Benchley's suit. The son of a bitch was contesting ownership of the mine based on the fact that official transfer of ownership documents had not yet been filed for the mine when Danforth gambled it. Never mind that his signature of transfer was on the deed.

"Give me that file." Fitz Roy crossed the room and then held out his hand. "I'll take care of it."

"What do you mean, you'll take care of it?"

"What do you mean, what do I mean? I mean, I'll take care of it," Fitz Roy repeated. When Matthew didn't hand over the file, Fitz Roy dropped his hand and rolled his eyes. "I'll make the argument for the mine to stay open whilst the suit is decided. The interim expenses and profits will fall to the victor."

"You'll make the argument, to whom?"

"To one who has certain power."

Matthew lifted his brows. "It has always been my understanding that the Queen is disinterested in social and economic matters."

"She is. But Prince Albert is *not* disinterested."

Matthew regarded the pale-eyed man before him. Prior to the scandal, he'd never have guessed that Roark Fitz Roy would ever be of any substantive help to him. "Why are you doing this, Fitz Roy? Why are you even here? I can understand the others. Farnsby and Asher—well, they're just jolly fellows who don't seem to care who they associate with. Lord Rivers is near the end of his life and has no son to father. But you—you're the only one of my former circle to return. Why?"

Fitz Roy shoved his hands in his pockets and looked pensive. Finally, he shrugged. "I was bored."

Matthew frowned. "So I'm something to do?"

Fitz Roy met his gaze for a long moment. "Yes, you're something to do—something good and decent. Something worthwhile in my rather un-worthwhile existence." The lazy drawl was still in his voice, but his tone and his pale eyes were serious. "When this thing happened to you, and things went from bad to worse, I didn't think you would survive. But when I spoke to you at the masque, you seemed so determined—so *damn-everyone-to-hell*. I don't know. You awakened some latent, underdeveloped sense of justice in me." He shrugged again. "Maybe it's just the Fitz in me—you know, *brothers in bastardy*, or some such nonsense."

"Nonsense, indeed. You're the descendent of a king. I'm the descendent of a gardener. And therein lies all the difference."

"Yet, you've made more of a mark on the world than I. You built GWR, you've been a member of Parliament, now you own this mine. People can rely on you, Hawkmore, and they do." He paused, his pale eyes assessing. "You're a good man, you see—

always have been. You deserve to defeat this. And if I can help you—well, then maybe that makes me a good man, too." He cocked his brow. "By association at the very least."

Matthew stared at Fitz Roy. They'd known each other for a long time—but never like this. He understood needing to feel worthy of something—of someone.

Picking up the file, he held it out. "Thank you, my friend."

Chapter Twenty-Five

ENEMIES

. . . jealousy is cruel as the grave . . .

SONG OF SOLOMON 8:6

The Millford Ball

"Do you ever feel like the prize pig at the town fair?" Patience asked. "I do."

Matthew smiled at his love as he turned her through the waltz. "Really? You don't look anything like a pig. A prize, yes. A pig, no."

Patience grinned, and Matthew's heart swelled. She *was* a prize—*his* prize. He let his eye move over her for the hundredth time. She was dressed in a gold taffeta gown. It was trimmed across the neckline and shoulders with narrow inverted pleats and a tiny inverted ruffle of gold lace. The ruffle protruded daintily from the inside of her bodice, giving the illusion that it was a bit of revealed undergarment. It made him want to slip his fingers inside. Kid gloves hugged her graceful arms, and her glorious curls were pulled up and back, showing off the diamond necklace, earrings, and combs he'd given her.

She was a vision, and she was his. And, at last, every man in the room knew it, for their engagement had been announced. *He* had won her—he, whom they'd all snubbed. He, whom they'd all assumed, even hoped, would just slink away and crawl into a hole somewhere whilst being robbed of his money and power. He, the bastard.

Gazing into Patience's face, he drew her closer. She didn't care who his father was, or wasn't. "They stare because they've never seen a more beautiful woman than you. What they don't know is that what makes you such a great beauty are things that run deeper than your outward appearance. Your compassion and strength. Your morality and honesty. Your loyalty and passion. Your love."

Patience's gaze was tender. "Must we stay here much longer?"

"Don't you like dancing with me?"

"I *love* dancing with you. It makes me wet. But then that's just another reason to go, isn't it?"

Matthew drew in a breath as his prick pulsed. "You're going to make me hard. And that's very naughty of you."

"Is it?" Her eyes darkened. "But I can't help that dancing with you makes me want to crawl up your body and climb on your cock."

Lust surged through him. He slowly tilted his head. "Naughtier and naughtier."

Patience shivered in his arms and her pulse fluttered above the sparkling diamonds at her throat. "My love . . . ?"

He wanted to take her into the nearest concealed corner and fuck her. But there were no concealed corners for them tonight. Everyone watched them. "I know you feel like you're on display, but this is one party we can't leave early."

"We can't? Why ever not?"

"I told you before—the Benchleys will be here tonight."

"Yes, you told me they would be here. And I respect you for not allowing their presence to dictate what events we attend, my love. But that doesn't tell me why we must stay because of them." She lifted her beautiful brows. "They don't even seem to be here."

Matthew let his eyes flicker around the crowded ballroom. "Oh, they'll be here." He looked back at Patience. She didn't understand because she didn't know everything. He didn't want her to know everything. "It's business, Patience. I need to demonstrate that I can be in the same room with Archibald Benchley. I need to demonstrate that he's meaningless to me."

She tilted her head. "But if we stay, simply to prove that Lord Benchley doesn't matter, aren't we proving that he matters?"

Matthew frowned. On the surface, her point seemed irrefutable, but he wasn't playing a game ruled by truth and logic. "This is about perception, my love. Not ours, but everyone else's."

Patience nodded but then frowned. "But why do we care about these people's perceptions, Matthew? I would think that your integrity and your continued business success would speak louder than standing around in the same room as Lord Benchley. Besides, Gwenellyn is yours. So you've already defeated him."

Just days after Fitz Roy had met with Prince Albert, Matthew had received notification that Gwenellyn was to remain in full operation for the duration of the lawsuit, and that GWR was to maintain its right to purchase coal from Gwenellyn at market rate. Within the week, Benchley had dropped the suit. Matthew was now the undisputed owner of Gwenellyn. Which was why it was perfect timing to face off with Benchley. He welcomed the opportunity.

Patience's elegant shoulders lifted in a small shrug. "Perhaps Lord Benchley won't even come tonight. Then we will have stayed for naught." Her green eyes beseeched him beautifully, and her fingers touched his nape. "Let's go, my love."

Matthew stared into Patience's exquisite eyes, so full of love and sensual promise. Her moist, parted lips begged a kiss, and her body leaned into his.

She breathed, "I love—"

The chatter of the crowd suddenly escalated, drowning out her whispered words. Frowning, Matthew looked up.

From across the dance floor, he stared directly into the arrogant face of Archibald Benchley.

Turning, Patience saw Lord Benchley, Lady Benchley, and Lord Danforth. They stood in a line, the patriarch between his daughter and future son-in-law. Sound seemed to fade and time to stand still as they all assessed each other—Lord Benchley clashing with Matthew, whilst she and Lady Rosalind took each other's measure.

Patience turned away, and in the next moment, sound returned and time rolled forward. The Benchleys and Danforth turned off to the right, whilst Matthew waltzed her off to the left.

The ballroom buzzed like an agitated hive.

A part of her still wanted to leave, but the rest of her was rising to the occasion. She was, after all, not the sort to bow to intimidation—other than from Matthew. Adjusting her shoulders, she smiled at him. "Well, that wasn't so bad."

Though she felt tension in his shoulder, his expression was calm and he returned her smile. "I love you."

She let her smile deepen. "No more than I love you."

Two hours later, Patience was feeling far less resilient. She was accustomed to being looked at, studied even. But this evening was different. Every eye seemed to rest upon them with a kind of expectation. It was more than interest or curiosity. It was as if . . . as if they were the entertainment. And since the Benchleys and Lord Danforth's arrival, the show had definitely begun.

Not that anything dramatic had happened, for both parties seemed to just be continually circling each other—passing through each other's wakes, but never meeting. It made her tense, though, for everyone seemed to be watching avidly, waiting for—no, anticipating—some great drama.

Matthew touched her arm. Having just been on a stroll through the public rooms, they were standing with Aunt Matty outside the ballroom. "I need to go speak with Lord Wollby, my love. Will you and Aunt Matty excuse me?"

"Of course." Patience nodded, even though she didn't like being far from him for too long. But perhaps she could take the opportunity to refresh herself. . . . "Shall we go up to the ladies' retiring room, Aunt Matty?"

"You know I never retire, my dear. Why anyone would ever want to retire—but for tea, of course—I simply don't know. I mean, who knows what excitement one may miss if one is retiring." She flipped open her fan and fanned herself idly. "Retire? Really. One day, I shall have eternity to retire. But until then . . ."

Matthew smiled at her. "Aunt Matty, though I know you don't require any rest yourself, will you do me the favor of accompanying Patience? She needs a brief respite from the press of this crowd."

"Oh! Of course, Matt dearest." Snapping her fan closed, she raised her monocle, which hung from a chain around her neck, and peered at Patience. "Why didn't you just tell me you were exhausted, my dear?"

"Because I'm not exhausted," Patience insisted.

Dropping her monocle, Aunt Matty pulled her arm through hers and patted her hand, "Of course you are. Now come with me to the retiring room. There is no shame in a lady needing to occasionally retire. And just because I have more energy than you is no reason for you to try to hide your own fatigue."

Glancing over her shoulder, Patience exchanged a parting smile with Matthew. She let her eyes linger. He was so incredibly handsome in his evening attire. She luxuriated in his warm, dark gaze. Then Aunt Matty pulled her around a corner, and he disappeared.

God, but she loved him.

"Tell me, my dear, what do you think of this house?" Aunt Matty asked as they climbed the stair to the second story. She was speaking in what was, for her, a discreet tone. "I don't find it nearly so perfectly appointed as Angel's Manor and Hawkmore House. Do you?"

Patience smiled as she nodded to guests they passed on the stair. Her aunt never thought anything was as good as what she or her family had. They could have been at Buckingham Palace and Aunt Matty would surely declare that she didn't find it nearly so comfortable as her own home, and weren't the rugs or the flowers, or the frames on the paintings more perfect at the home of her niece, the Countess of Langley.

Patience glanced up at the magnificent chandelier that glittered over the grand foyer. "I think it's an elegant house, Aunt Matty."

Her aunt shook her head as she glanced up at the same chandelier. "No, I much prefer the chandelier that appoints the foyer at Hawkmore House. And the stair at Angel's Manor is far grander than this one. Even this banister does not feel quite comfortable under my hand."

Patience drew her aunt toward the retiring room and spoke quietly. "Perhaps we should refrain from commenting on these things until we are in the privacy of our coach."

"What? Well, for heaven's sake, Patience, I was whispering," she said out loud. "Gracious, I couldn't even hear myself, so I don't know how anyone else could have heard me. I don't even know how you could have heard me," she asserted loudly as they entered the quiet retiring room.

Only a few, mostly elderly, ladies were in the dimly lit room, but at the sound of Aunt Matty's voice, they all looked over with a start. Patience smiled and nodded graciously as she led her aunt to the far corner of the room.

"Do you want the chaise or the chair, my dear?" Aunt Matty whispered loudly.

Patience glanced through the French doors that led to a private balcony. Due to the cold, no one was there. The chair was closer to it. "I'll take the chair," she whispered back.

"Oh, very well. I'll take the chaise. Though I'm not at all tired. The only reason I'm not insisting you take it is that I have two more dances with Lord Rivers, and I really ought to put up my feet."

"Ssshhhh!" A lady reclining by the fire glared at them.

"Well!" Aunt Matty whispered as loudly as ever, then flounced down on the chaise just as a young girl might.

Patience had to smile as she helped her aunt get situated on her side and covered with a fur throw. Then, taking her hand, Patience sat in the overstuffed chair beside her. In the dim light, her silver hair glinted and all the wrinkles of her face were softened. She looked so tender.

"Do you want to talk?" she whispered more quietly than Patience had ever heard her.

Patience squeezed her aunt's hand gently. "No, thank you."

Aunt Matty nodded and stroked her thumb over the top of Patience's hand. "I just want to tell you that you're doing wonderfully well this evening. You make me proud to be your aunt, Patience."

Patience's heart swelled. "You make me proud to be your niece."

Aunt Matty smiled, then stifled a yawn. "I'm not at all sleepy," she murmured. "But since you want to be quiet, I'm just going to close my eyes for a bit."

"Very well, Aunt Matty." She squeezed her hand again. "I love you."

"I love you, too."

Half a minute later her aunt was snoring softly.

Getting to her feet, Patience carefully extracted her hand from her aunt's and tucked it beneath the fur. Then she kissed the top of her head and, quickly opening and closing the French doors, stepped out onto the blissfully empty balcony.

The cold night air was bracing. She inhaled a deep, cleansing breath. Finally, a moment alone—a moment to reclaim her equilibrium. She released her breath and watched it turn to vapor.

She was grateful for Aunt Matty's praise. She only hoped her aunt's opinion was one generally shared—at least by those who were nice. For while many of the people Matthew had introduced her to were gracious and polite, there were also many who quite openly snubbed them. Not least of all Lady Humphreys, who, followed by a line of gaggling, honking ladies, had rudely cut in front of Aunt Matty and her at the refreshment table.

Rosalind Benchley's arrival had only made things worse. Clearly quite popular with many of the ladies, including Lady Humphreys and her minions, Lady Rosalind's presence had escalated the degree of feminine animosity sent Patience's way. Those who'd been ignoring her earlier in the evening were now sending her obvious glares and disdainful glances. She had patently ignored all malice directed at her, but it had been wearing nonetheless.

Leaning against the railing, she gazed out over the empty garden below and tucked back a loose curl that had slipped over her brow. Thank God for Matthew. His strong, protective presence at her side was like a shield. His confidence was palpable, and not only did the spiteful ladies dare less when he was by her, he also knew who was receptive to an introduction and pleasant conversation. This was, after all, the circle he'd moved in before the scandal. So he knew whom to approach and whom to avoid, and several people had actually approached them.

Stepping back from the rail, she shook out her skirts. It was like being on a seesaw. She wished she could get off, but she accepted that Matthew knew what was best—both for them and for his business.

Smoothing her hands down her bodice, she drew a final cleansing breath. In time, all this nonsense would pass. But for now, she was strong enough to weather the storm.

Turning back toward the doors, Patience started as they suddenly opened and Lady Rosalind stepped onto the balcony.

A shiver prickled beneath Patience's skin as the younger woman closed the doors and then turned to face her.

They stood there for a moment, silent. It was interesting—Lady Rosalind's expression, which had been so sweet and full of laughter below, was drawn into colder, more malignant lines than Patience would have thought her lovely features capable of. She was a beautiful woman, with her dark hair and sparkling eyes—but now, her doll-like face was an unbecoming mask.

"I've come to tell you something that you should know," she hissed.

Using her height, Patience looked down her nose at the shorter woman and said nothing.

Rosalind's scowl twisted, and she took a step closer. "Matt doesn't love you. He loves me." She leaned forward. "He's always loved me. So whatever your public arrangement, *I'm* the one who holds his heart."

Unmoved, Patience shook her head. "Poor girl."

"Poor girl?" Rosalind snarled. "*You* are the poor girl."

Patience sighed then leveled her gaze on Rosalind. "Lady Rosalind, this juvenile behavior does not become you. You abandoned my love in his most dire hour of need, and then you stood by whilst your father continued to slander him. How, in a thousand years, could you ever believe that he would trust you, let alone love you?" She watched Rosalind's angry eyes fill with tears, but the only sympathy she felt was for Matthew and the pain Rosalind had put him through. "You're engaged to Lord Danforth now. Why don't you go back downstairs and begin to show him the loyalty you failed to show Matthew. Perchance, there is hope there for your happiness. Now, if you'll excuse me, my love is waiting." Brushing by Rosalind, she reached for the door.

"We've met secretly."

Patience froze. Self-proclamations were one thing; implicating Matthew was quite another. "I don't believe you."

"At approximately five in the morning on the day of the hunt at Hawkmore House, he came for me. I was staying at Gillyhurst, the neighboring estate. We met at the old mill. It was a young servant by the name of Mickey who brought me to him."

Patience turned back to Rosalind, a tremor of fear moving down her back. That was the morning Matthew had left her early. The morning she'd met Mickey in Matthew's office. But it couldn't be. "I said I don't believe you."

Rosalind's chin was lifted and her eyes were shining. There was no trace of equivocation in her. "He admitted he loved me, and he asked me to go with him to Gretna Green."

Pain pierced Patience's heart. It couldn't be true! Matthew loved *her*. Her knees began to shake. "No."

"When I turned him down, he confessed how jealous he was of my engagement. That's when we agreed to become secret lovers—forever."

Forever. Small white dots began to skitter before Patience's eyes. "No."

"Ask him—ask *your love*," Rosalind sneered, her eyes flashing behind her tears. "You may be engaged to him, but *I'll* always be his first and forever love."

No! "You're a liar," Patience managed, her voice cracking.

"Actually, *he's* the liar for not telling you." Rosalind leaned close. "Of course, I'll forgive him for that." Her head tilted. "But will you?"

"You must admit, she is like some great barge, dragging behind her a flotilla of smaller barges," Fitz Roy commented in reference to Lady Humphreys and her hangers-on. "Each one of them more decorated than next, but none so much as the great vessel at the front."

Matthew laughed. They did rather resemble an armada.

"And who ever told her she could wear ostrich feathers of all things? My God, the woman is an absolute monstrosity."

Matthew laughed again, and several people glanced his way. He didn't care. Let them see him laughing. He felt on top of the world. Despite the Benchleys' presence and a fair number of detractors, he was certain he'd won the evening. Gwenellyn was his and coal was slowly feeding GWR. He and Lord Wollby had spoken, and GWR's second largest shareholder had no intention of selling his shares and was, in fact, interested in investing in the mine. Several of his old crowd had approached him, *almost* as if nothing had ever happened. He had Fitz Roy and Rivers at his back and, to a lesser degree, Farnsby and Asher. And, at his side, he had Patience.

Despite the constant scrutiny and the unrepressed censure of the other side, she'd held up nobly. He'd known she would. But to see her, so elegant and gracious, made him intensely proud. As soon as she returned, they would have a dance or two more, if she wanted, then prepare to leave. He'd accomplished what he needed to, and it was time to give her what *she* wanted—home.

"Will you be ready to go soon?" he asked Fitz Roy.

The man's black brows lifted and his pale eyes rolled. "I am so far past ready to go, that I'm already into tomorrow."

Matthew chuckled and turned toward the stairs. "As soon as Patience and"—his smile faded—"Aunt Matty . . ." He frowned.

Fitz Roy looked up. "Something's wrong."

"Yes." Matthew headed for the stairs. Patience was descending, her gait slow and her chin high, but her eyes were suspiciously shiny and her expression was fixed, almost as if she moved it, she would crack. Aunt Matty, less able to hide her emotions, was frowning with concern and kept glancing worriedly at her niece.

What had happened? If someone had hurt her . . .

Matthew quickened his step and met her before she came off the last stair. He looked almost directly into her eyes as he took her cold hands. "My love, what's wrong? What's happened?"

Patience looked down and turned her shoulder away from the guests milling the foyer. "I need to speak with you privately."

Propriety disallowed them privacy, and they were watched every moment. He needed a public private place.

"The 'tenants nest,' " Fitz Roy offered.

Matthew pulled Patience's arm through his. "Come with us," he said to Fitz Roy and Aunt Matty. Then he led Patience to the high, deep alcove beneath the stairs. Some former earl had carved it out so that when he was required to meet with his tenants, his wife needn't be offended by their rough presence in her immaculate foyer. At balls, it tended to be an oft-occupied wallflowers retreat. But fortunately, a group of matrons was just exiting it.

They all stepped in, but Aunt Matty and Fitz Roy paused by the entrance whilst Matthew pulled Patience to the rear of the space.

"What is it, my love?"

Patience lifted her gaze to his. Her eyes were swimming with tears.

He tensed with anger. "Did someone hurt you?" Pulling out his handkerchief, he pressed it into her hand. "Danforth? Benchley?"

Patience twisted the linen in her hands. "I hope you'll forgive me for this question, but I have to ask it." Her voice was breathless.

A question? "What? Ask me?"

Her lips trembled. "The morning of the hunt, did you meet secretly with Rosalind?"

Ice crept down Matthew's spine.

Patience's face crumbled. "Oh, God!" she gasped. Her tears spilled.

"Patience." He tried to take her hands, but she jerked back.

Her eyes were full of anguish. "You asked her to go to Gretna Green with you?"

Matthew's heart began to pound. "No."

"No?" she breathed, disbelieving. "Your face tells me otherwise."

Fuck! He grabbed her wrist. "I said the words, Patience, but not how or why you think."

Tears rolled down her cheeks. "But you said them, Matthew." She shook her head and tried to peel his fingers from her wrist. "Secret lovers? God, I trusted you. I trusted you! Let me go," she pleaded on a broken gasp.

"No!" Matthew said fiercely. He clasped her other hand. "You've got to listen to me, Patience. None of this is what it seems."

"Seems? What do I care for *seems*?" she choked. "You lied to me!"

"Damn it," he growled, "let me explain!"

"Hawkmore." Farnsby's voice intruded.

"For the love of God, let me go," Patience begged on a whisper.

"Hawkmore!"

Matthew snapped his head toward Farnsby. He was standing between Aunt Matty and Fitz Roy. "Leave us," he hissed.

Farnsby drew back, but he looked completely distraught. He glanced at Patience, then back at Matthew. "Forgive me, but I cannot. Something has happened."

Patience twisted her hands from his and turned.

"Patience, wait!"

She hurried into Aunt Matty's embrace.

"I love you," he said strongly. "*You know* I love you."

Patience looked at him over her shoulder, and his heart tore for the pain in her eyes.

Aunt Matty's face was etched with tortured bewilderment, and Fitz Roy's pale gaze was shadowed.

Matthew looked into the eyes of his love. *Please don't leave me.* "Patience . . ."

His gut twisted as she turned and pulled Aunt Matty with her out of the alcove.

No. She couldn't go. He had to explain. She had to let him explain. "Patience!" He rushed after her.

Fitz Roy and Farnsby both grabbed him.

"Let her go," Fitz Roy said by his ear. "This is not for others to see."

"I don't care," Matthew hissed, shaking them off.

"Wait," Farnsby called.

But Matthew didn't pause until he was in the center of th crowded foyer. There was no sign of Patience's bright heac Where had she gone?

"Hawkmore!" Farnsby said earnestly. He and Fitz Roy ha followed. "I have news."

"Damn it, Farnsby! Not now!" Matthew snapped. Brows sho up. Was everyone staring at him? He didn't care. He had to fin Patience. Once he explained . . .

"There's been an explosion, Hawkmore."

Matthew turned. Hot, prickling pins erupted beneath his sk as he stared at Farnsby. "What?"

"At Gwenellyn." Farnsby shook his head. "The messeng said it's catastrophic—collapse of the main shaft at approx mately three hundred feet, and secondary collapses in two oth tunnels."

"No." Matthew began to shake, and stared at Farnsby throu a haze of growing fury and doom. "How many are lost?"

"It happened between shifts, but there were nine boys down clearing the rails. Only two made it out." Farnsby lowered his eyes. "Another is confirmed dead, and they are not hopeful for the rest."

What was happening? Something wasn't right. Only minutes ago he'd been laughing and victorious. And now . . .

Death.

Disaster.

Ruination.

No! Releasing Farnsby, he made for the door, pushing past people without pardon. How could it be? He'd just supplied the safety lamps. What cruel fate—what evil irony—was at work that boys should die when he was doing everything he could to safeguard them? No sooner was he fully responsible . . .

No sooner was Gwenellyn his . . .

He slowed, then drew up short. Suspicion, hot and insistent, welled up from his gut. No sooner was he winning, than the one thing happened that would defeat him.

Not fate or irony—Benchley!

He whirled back around, searching the foyer. In only a moment he came eye to eye with his enemy. Standing against the far wall, Benchley's cold blue gaze was fixed upon him and, as Matthew stared, the man's lips turned up in a slow, vengeful smile.

"Son of a . . ." Rage roared through Matthew's veins. As he stalked across the foyer, people skittered from his path. With every step he took, Benchley's chin lifted higher.

"Careful," he heard Fitz Roy warn.

But he was done with careful.

He closed in on his enemy.

Careful was completely and entirely *over!*

He cocked his fist and hurled it forward only to be jerked back. Shrieks of alarm echoed around them. Fitz Roy and Farnsby struggled to restrain him. Matthew fought against them.

"Damn it, he will have you arrested for assault," Fitz Roy issed, tightening his hold. "You *do not* want that."

Breathing hard, Matthew jutted forward and stared at Benchey through the hot haze of his wrath. "There were boys in that mine, you son of a bitch! One is dead! And six more are likely ost with him!"

Benchley regarded him, his eyes aloof. "I don't know what you're talking about."

Danforth, who was leaning idly beside his future father-in-law, snickered.

Matthew struggled forward again. Danforth flinched and ladies gasped, but Fitz Roy and Farnsby still held him.

"Now is not the time," Fitz Roy murmured.

Fuck! He slowly eased back as he glared into Benchley's icy blue eyes. "I'll wreck you yet," Matthew snarled.

"You can't," Benchley said, placidly. He leaned close. "For I have wrecked you first."

Chapter Twenty-Six
Paradise Lost

. . . the coals thereof are coals of fire, which hath a most vehement flame.

Song of Solomon 8:6

Patience stood stiffly at the window in Matthew's office. By the light of a waning moon, she watched a fog descend into the center courtyard of Angel's Manor. Curling tendrils of the white mist rolled over the manicured topiaries and stealthily approached the house. The clock on the mantel chimed midnight.

"Thank you for coming down," Matthew said. "Won't you even look at me?"

Patience closed her eyes. They hurt from crying. Despite Lord Asher's presence in the coach, she hadn't been able to hold back tears. She had cried quietly, clasping Aunt Matty's hand for almost the whole ride back. Matthew must have left the ball right after them, for she'd only just sat down with Aunt Matty in the privacy of her room when the maid had delivered Matthew's summons. "It hurts to look at you."

"Please, Patience. I need to explain."

Opening her eyes, she watched the fog creep up the window before turning to face Matthew. His jacket removed, he was standing by the fire, his dark gaze both tense and somber. His hair was parted and forward against his temples. Her heart constricted, for she loved him so much—yet, he had lied to her, betrayed her. Her sore eyes welled so she lifted her chin to keep her tears from falling.

But she couldn't quite. A few escaped.

Matthew's face softened and he stepped toward her. "My love—"

"No!" she warned, jumping back.

His jaw clenched, but he stopped.

Thank God. Despite her wounded heart, her body and soul yearned for him still. She swallowed more tears, for the realization only increased her misery. "Say what you have to say," she urged.

"Patience . . ." Matthew regarded her for a silent moment. "Archibald Benchley is trying to destroy me." Anger was in his eyes and there was a hard edge to his voice. "The morning of the hunt, I met with Rosalind to obtain information. She'd sent me a note, implying she wanted to reunite with me. So I used it as the reason for our meeting. I did not go because I love her. I did not go because I wanted to run away with her to Gretna Green. And I most certainly did not go because I had, or have, any intention of becoming her secret lover."

Patience regarded him. Something was boiling beneath his skin—she could feel his tension. In fact, she'd felt it the moment she'd walked in the room. She frowned. "But how could you say those things?"

Matthew began to pace before the fire. "I said what I had to say, Patience. And for the record, I *never* told her I loved her, *or* that I would be her bloody secret lover." He spat into the hearth. "The thought sickens me."

"Yes, me as well." He stopped pacing to look at her. She crossed her arms. "But, for the record, you did ask her to go with you to Gretna Green."

Matthew frowned and rested his hands on his hips. "*For the record,* no, I didn't *ask* her. I said we could go there. And I said it simply to mortify her, which it *did.* She couldn't refuse me fast enough." Turning toward the fire, he rubbed his brow as if it ached. "Damn it, Patience, the whole time I was with her, was thinking of you. Before she came, I was thinking of you. didn't want to be there. I only stayed for the chance that I would get some information from her." He turned back to her, his brow twisted with regret. "And, after, I felt sullied—sullied for not telling her exactly what I think of her, and sullied for even meeting with her, when my heart, my body, and my soul already belonged to you." His dark eyes held her. "She has written to me since, Patience. I've thrown every note away unopened—as I should have done with the first one." His mouth was a hard line. "At th masque, I told you that you were the only woman I wanted. It was true then. It's true now. It will always be true." He paused. "I love you, Patience. Forgive me."

Could she? Just like that?

Patience took a long slow breath and considered. She did believe him, but she'd cried a cupful of tears and she still hurt—though, perhaps, not quite as much.

He had so much more to tell her—and not very much time. "Perhaps, if you knew the extent of Benchley's malice, you would better understand why I met with Rosalind."

"Perhaps," Patience conceded. "For that *is* a large part of what still troubles me about this, Matthew." She shook her head. "That there was some necessity to meet with your former fiancée in secret, for the purposes of extracting information about her father?"

Matthew frowned and his fury, so near the surface, rose. "You make it sound so nefarious, but it isn't I who began this. It is Archibald Benchley who is the immoral one—the despicable one." He spat the word. "I have only defended myself, as any man has the right to do, be he bastard or no!"

Patience's frown had deepened and now it was shaded with concern. "Matthew, what exactly is going on?"

A scoffing exhale escaping him, he shoved his hand through his hair. Where should he begin—at the beginning or at the horrific end?

"I've heard some gossip, Matthew. But I thought it was just that—gossip."

He looked at her sardonically. "There's usually some root of truth in gossip, Patience. That's why it's so pernicious—the foundation of truth lends unwilling support to the lies that sprout from it, lies seeded by wicked people who seek to elevate themselves at the expense of others."

"I know all that, Matthew. That's why gossip should be ignored."

"Yes, but here's the problem with that, Patience." He began to pace. "Ignoring it doesn't make it go away. In fact, it makes it worse. For people take silence as an admission of guilt."

"Perhaps. But the truth will be out eventually, Matthew. One must have patience."

He stopped pacing to look at her. "*Patience*, Patience?" *By God!* "I *was* patient." He crossed to her. "I was entirely patient while Benchley went around feeding the truth of my illegitimacy with the lie that I knew about it all along." He began to pace again. "I remained patient as people snubbed me and gave me the cut directly in the street. I was patient still as those who I'd called friends fell away. And whilst I was implementing all this 'patience,' do you know what happened, Patience?" He stopped and jammed his hands against his hips. "Benchley's malice against me escalated. And his lies fueled a growing wave of ill will toward me, until, I believe, even those people who might have been inclined toward my favor were swept up by Benchley's malevolent tide. And this is where things go from bad to worse in my little parable of patience. With a consortium of disdain against me, Benchley now used his loathsome influence to infect my business associates. In very short order, I find that I'm losing massive amounts of money."

Her frown etched deeply into her brow, Patience stood silent.

But he was hardly finished. "Let's segue here to my 'secret' meeting with Rosalind, where I 'extract' the information that Benchley wants far more than my ruination—he also wants my company. And why not? While I'm going along trying to live life like nothing's happened—being 'patient' and 'ignoring' the gossip—he's taking action. Before I know it, he and all his colliery cronies are either refusing to sell to me, or are overcharging me. And what they do agree to sell me, is suddenly running late, or short, or is even 'lost in the shuffle.' How do you lose ten *fucking* tons of coal, Patience?" He waited for her answer.

Patience stood silent, the only sign of her agitation the rapid rise and fall of her chest. The diamonds at her throat sparkled.

Matthew whirled to the hearth and kicked at the heavy grate. The logs shifted and sparks flew toward him. Gripping the mantel with both hands, he stared into the flames that mirrored his anger. Then, forcing the decibel of his voice down, he continued. "When I won the mine from Danforth, I thought my problems were solved. I would mine my own coal, feed GWR's engines, and ship to the customers we'd been unable to service. It was perfect.

But Benchley couldn't allow me to get away with that—it would ruin his plans for my ruination, and make it impossible for him to steal my company. So he contested my ownership, in the hopes a decision would take long enough to bankrupt me. And when that didn't work, he took the ultimate, seemingly undefeatable action." Matthew turned to Patience. "He blew up the mine."

Patience sucked in her breath and her eyes widened with horrified alarm. She took a faltering step forward. "When?"

"This very night—eight twenty-six, to be exact."

"Was anyone—" She pressed her hand to her breast. "Was anyone hurt?"

"Nine boys were down the pit. Two made it out. One is dead. Six are missing."

"It there hope for the missing?"

"Not much."

Patience's eyes welled and, lowering her head, she covered her mouth with her hand.

Despite his own wrath and pain, his heart ached for her obvious sorrow. Crossing to her, he took her in his embrace. "I'll know more tomorrow, once I assess the situation for myself. Obviously, I will ensure that every effort is made to find them." *Dead or alive.*

She nodded against his chest and, after a moment, lifted her wet eyes to his. "You said Benchley did this, Matthew?"

He nodded. "If only I'd acted against him sooner. I might have prevented this."

"No." Patience gripped his arms. "Don't do that. This is *not* your fault, and there is no way you can predict what would have happened had you acted differently. Something worse might have happened."

"Or something wonderful might have happened."

"Or something worse might have happened," she repeated, holding him in her unwavering gaze. "I know you feel responsible for the people of Gwenellyn, my love, but we can only deal with what is, not what might have been."

Matthew nodded. "Very well." He knew she was right, but it didn't make him feel any better. "You should have seen him when I confronted him tonight—so proud of his handiwork"—he clenched his jaw—"and Danforth, preening at his side."

"We must go to the authorities."

"The authorities?" Matthew scoffed. "There will be a formal investigation, Patience, but I have no proof against him. Even if Fitz Roy, Farnsby, and I were to testify to Benchley's words and demeanor tonight—to his implied responsibility—he would simply deny it."

"It must be done anyway, Matthew. The people of Gwenellyn deserve justice. You deserve justice."

"Oh, *I'll* have justice." Where the *fuck* was Mickey?

Patience pulled back. "What do you mean? Why do you say it like that?"

Matthew looked at her. "I mean just what I said, Patience." He turned and walked to his desk.

"You're too close to this, Matthew. There is a reason justice is blind," she said, following him.

"Really?" He braced his fists on his desk. "What *is* the reason—because I don't really believe its impartiality? That's superb in theory, but patently impossible in reality. Do you know what I think the reason is, Patience? I think justice is blind so that she needn't see how *massively* ineffectual she is."

"Oh, and you can do better? I don't believe that, Matthew. I said it in the gallery and I'll say it again: *revenge is never free*. There is always a cost, Matthew—*always*. And you will never know what it is, until it's too late."

"And I said to you in the gallery that I'm not Saint Matthew."

A tense silence fell between them and then, as if on cue, a knock sounded at the door.

Matthew kneed closed one of the drawers of his desk. "Don't worry, Patience. Unlike Benchley, I have a care for human life." He moved to the door. "My 'justice' is trivial compared to his crimes."

"Revenge is never trivial."

Damn it! Grabbing the doorknob, Matthew jerked it open and found Mickey Wilkes. *Now this is timing!* "Tell me you have the proof."

Mickey pulled a thick stack of letters from his coat pocket and handed them over.

Matthew stood back for Mickey to enter while he stared down at them.

The boy sauntered in. "Wha's e'eryone doin' awake, Mr. 'Awkmore? Thought fer sure the 'ole 'ouse 'old would be sleepin'." He immediately drew up straighter when he saw Patience. "Good ev'nin', Miss Dare!" Mickey's eyes moved over her avidly. "Ya look like a princess." He bent a little at the waist. "I feels like I should bow down t' ya."

Patience gave him a small, strained smile. "Thank you, Mr. Wilkes. But I am the same plain miss as always."

Matthew let the door swing closed and walked back to his desk. "The house is awake, Mr. Wilkes, because there's been an explosion at the Gwenellyn Mine. We are all in despair over it, and"—he glanced at Patience—"things have come out."

"Oh." Mickey nodded. "Were anyone hurt?"

"Yes." Matthew's chest constricted every time he had to say it. "A boy has died and six more are missing."

Mickey paled. "Oh." He frowned. "This were Benchley's work?"

"Yes." Matthew looked at Patience.

She looked at the letters. "What have you there?"

Matthew ran his thumb over the faded red ribbon that bound the letters. "The proof that Rosalind Benchley is a bastard."

Patience gasped.

Mickey shook his head. "It isn't Rosalind."

Matthew's shoulders tensed. "It isn't Ros—? Who the hell is it, then?"

Mickey looked at him and there was anger in his eyes. "It be Benchley his self."

Red spots flashed before Matthew's eyes. "What!"

"Yeah. E'rything Biddlewick said 'ad t' do wit' Benchley, no his daugh'er. I knew somethin' were off soon as I saw MacQuarrie, fer 'ees an ole bloke. Then af'er I go' to know 'im a lit'le an' go' 'im to talkin', 'ee tol' me all 'bout 'ow 'ee 'ad a son. Said the son were an important man, only the man what raised 'im 'ated ''im fer no' bein' 'is own."

A muscle pulled painfully in Matthew's neck. "Well this explains much," he growled.

"Yeah." Mickey nodded. "MacQuarrie tol' me 'ow it broke 'is 'eart that 'is son were bru'ilized fer bein' what 'ee were. But 'ee didn't think there were nothin' 'ee could do 'bout it."

Matthew looked at Patience. He was shaking with fury and it calmed him a little to look at her.

"Because his father knew and punished him, Benchley couldn't believe that your father could know and *not* punish you, let alone keep it a secret from you," she offered.

"It doesn't matter," Matthew said tightly. "Soon everyone will know what a hypocrite he is."

Patience frowned. "What are you planning to do?"

Matthew faced her. "I'm going to publish these letters. I'm going to destroy Archibald Benchley before he can completely destroy me."

"So you're going to do to him what was done to you?" Patience shook her head. "You can't do that, Matthew."

He felt as if his blood were becoming liquid fury. "I beg your pardon?"

"I said, you can't do that."

Matthew looked at Mickey. "Out."

With his head lowered, the boy left, slump-shouldered, and pulled the door closed behind him.

Matthew turned back to Patience. "And why is it that I can't do that?"

"Because it would be dishonorable, Matthew. You had Mickey steal those letters. They don't even belong to you. And, tell me, what will become of Rosalind once you expose her father?"

"What do I care for Rosalind? What do *you* care for Rosalind? Earlier this evening, she was spewing venom all over you. Now you want to save her from scandal?"

"I want to save *you* from scandal—from dishonor."

"Dishonor?" His laugh was a harsh bark that hurt his throat. "Benchley is the dishonorable one! He is the one who spread lies about me. He is the one who tried to bankrupt my company and then steal it from me." He pounded his fist on the desk. "He is the one who blew up the mine and brought death! And you speak to *me* of dishonor? You are misguided, Patience!"

She lifted her chin. "No, I'm not. And I'm not comparing you to Benchley. His actions have been more than dishonorable, they've been criminal. But that is all the more reason to seek justice through the law."

"All right." Matthew tossed the letters on his desk. "Tell me what you would have me do then, Patience. What's your plan?"

She crossed her arms over her chest. "I don't pretend to have all the answers, Matthew. But it is when wrongdoing seems most justified that we must most resist it." Stepping closer to him, she clasped his hands. "I know nothing in this seems easy, Matthew, or certain. But, together, we can find the answers. I have faith in righteousness."

"That's your plan? Have faith in righteousness?" Matthew shook his head. "Here's what I'm going to do, Patience. I'm going to expose Benchley for being a hypocritical bastard. Once I do that, the tide of public opinion will turn in our favor. And once the tide turns, the other mine owners will return to doing business with me. GWR will be saved and, slowly but surely, it will return to its former stature."

Patience folded her arms back over her chest. "And what about Gwenellyn? How does it fit into your plan?"

Matthew's chest tightened again. "It doesn't. I can't save Gwenellyn. If the report is even only half accurate, I can't save it. I have to focus on GWR now. That's our only hope for financial and social survival."

Patience looked at him like he'd lost his mind. "How can you abandon them? Without the mine, there is no village. What are they to do?"

"They will have to seek employment elsewhere."

"I can't believe you're not going to help them.

Fuck! "*I* can't believe you don't understand the situation. I have almost nothing left, Patience! Shall I spend my last pound note on Gwenellyn? What for?" Flipping open his ledger, he spun it around for her to see. "What I have isn't enough to make a difference. And we need that money to live. Everything costs, Patience—this house, those jewels you love so much. Let's face it, I can hardly imagine you keeping house in one of the shacks at Gwenellyn."

Patience raised her eyes to him and they were full of anger and hurt. She pointed to the ledger. "What's this?"

Matthew looked and his gut turned as he stared at the entry for Cavalli. He was silent for a moment. Then, "Patience, I—"

"I do believe that date was the night of the musicale," she interrupted. Her eyes were furious and shiny. "Why were you sending Cavalli five hundred pounds on the night of the musicale?"

I was afraid. "I didn't want you to go."

"That was *my* decision, Matthew! You had no business usurping my will! God, I see where your money goes." Reaching behind her neck, she unclasped her necklace and then removed her earrings. She slammed them on top of the ledger, then pulled out her combs. She looked at them longingly for a moment before laying them with the other pieces. "I loved these jewels 'so much' because you gave them to me. I would have worn glass beads with equal pride. And as for this house"—she looked around the room—"I don't even like it. I never have." Her eyes swam with tears. "And I don't see why it's called Angel's Manor, because there are *no* angels here."

"Patience . . ."

Turning on her heel, she strode toward the door.

"Patience!"

She reached for the doorknob and opened it.

"Patience, stay!" Matthew roared.

She froze then slowly turned.

She looked at him across the space that divided them, and raised her chin high. Her cheeks were wet and he'd never seen her look so cold and yet defiant. "No, Matthew," she said, "I cannot oblige you at this time."

Matthew's breath left him with a groan.

She turned and left.

Shaking uncontrollably, he picked up the small oil lamp from his desk and heaved it into the fire. It crashed then exploded against the back in a burst of flame . . .

Leaving him standing in a dark world, lit only by fire.

Chapter Twenty-Seven

Pluto Without Persephone

My beloved is gone . . .

Song of Solomon 5:6

Matthew stared at the seven mounds of earth as he listened to Father Dafydd speak the words of the twenty-third Psalm. The day was cold and the air was filled with the breath of the town, as every resident of Gwenellyn had come to the old graveyard in order to honor the fallen boys.

Father Dafydd's rich baritone was reassuring, and Matthew was grateful he'd been willing to come to do the burial services, for his presence seemed to be a great comfort to the people of Gwenellyn.

Patience had been right about him. He would have been perfect for these strong, stalwart people.

So, too, would she have been. Why hadn't she returned to him?

When would she return to him? Matthew stared out his office window. Mark joined him. "I told you not to hurt my wife, Matt. Passion is upset and worried—about both of you." He grasped Matthew's shoulder. "And so am I. Whatever happened between you and Patience, put it aside, make amends, do whatever you must, but don't let her go."

Do whatever he must?

What was that? He didn't even know.

He'd been sure she would return to him—once she thought about it, once she considered all the ramifications. Besides, no one could give her what he gave her.

He sighed as he watched the tennis ball pass between Farnsby and Ashers' rackets. Mark, Fitz Roy, and Rivers all looked as bored as he felt. Even Farnsby and Asher were not their usual jovial selves.

Really, it was too cold to play tennis.

Winter was falling.

Matthew let his hand fall over the scroll of his Montagnana. Closing his eyes, he called up the memory of Patience playing as she leaned against him. His heart skittered crazily for a moment, then settled.

Sitting, he drew his instrument between his legs. He caressed it as he'd taught her to do. Then he played the Sarabande—slowly.

When he finished, his eyes were stinging. He looked around the empty room and then gazed down at his cello. He put his arms around her.

If all of Angel's Manor were ablaze, it was only her he would save. She and the silky black stocking Patience had left in his room on the happiest day of their lives.

"You look unhappy, Mr. Wilkes." Matthew sat beside the boy on the bench situated right in the middle of the center courtyard of Angel's Manor. The house surrounded them.

Mickey looked at him. "I jus' keep thinkin' that if I'd go' 'ere faster wit' the let'ers, that you could 'ave done somethin'. Ya know, 'fore the 'xplotion." His eyes filled with tears. "Is jus' that I cain't read—so I 'ad to take the let'ers to a friend o' mine. Ya know, cuz wha' if there weren't nothin' in 'em." He dropped his head in his hands. "I's so stupid!"

"No. No, you're not." Matthew's chest felt tight. He knew what Mickey was feeling. "Don't do this to yourself. The explosion was *not* your fault. And you can't know what might have happened if anything had gone differently."

He pictured Patience's earnest face then looked at Mickey. "We can only deal with what is, Mr. Wilkes, not what might have been."

Mickey nodded.

Matthew patted his shoulder. "Those words might not help right now, but they will."

He stood up and looked around the massive walls of Angel's Manor—all facing inward and with their plate glass windows reflecting off one another. How confining they were.

Was this really who he was? A man with such a huge part of himself always facing inward, yet not really seeing?

He ran for the house.

He didn't stop running until he reached his dressing room. There, he stood, panting, in front of his long mirror. Gripping the sides, he stepped closer, so that he could see only himself. For he suddenly wasn't certain what he looked like without a background. Who was he all on his own—with nothing behind him?

He searched himself with his own dark gaze.

Who and what are you, Matthew Morgan Hawkmore?

Paint your own background.

He suddenly had a vision from his childhood. He was standing in front of a long mirror and he was carefully mimicking the man behind him, who was shaving himself. George Hawkmore always shaved himself. The tall man would stand there with his blade and quietly make amusing and exaggerated faces, all of which Matthew would imitate. They never spoke, only shaved.

We can only deal with what is, not what might have been.

He was a bastard, yes. But not like Benchley who'd been castigated for it from birth. No, from George Hawkmore he'd received praise and affection. While the man may not have made him, he'd helped form him.

Matthew watched his own tears fall down his face. He didn't brush them away or try to prevent them, for they were in gratitude for *what was*, not what might have been.

And suddenly everything was simple and clear. His heart surged with happiness and his spirit felt light.

He knew what to do.

For he knew who and what he was.

He was George Hawkmore's *son*, and he was an honorable man.

Chapter Twenty-Eight
Paradise Reclaimed

Many waters cannot quench love, neither can the floods drown it . . .

Song of Solomon 8:7

One month later ~

"Shall we go in soon and have a little tea?" Prim asked.

Patience folded the letter from Passion that she'd been reading before looking up at her younger sister. Prim was reclining against a broad tree stump, and Patience was reclining, on her side, against her. The day was unseasonably warm, so they'd come to the large pond that had been their retreat since childhood and laid a blanket on the shore. "Must we?"

"No." Prim smiled and continued to stroke her fingers through Patience's curls. "We can stay here as long as you like."

Patience sighed and snuggled against her younger sister—something she'd never let herself do before. She'd held Prim often, but only to *give* comfort, never to *take* it.

She was a different woman now.

Closing her eyes, she let the warmth of her sister's body anc the slight warmth of the winter sun comfort her. And as always the moment her eyes closed memories of Matthew filled he head—and heart.

"My beauty."

"Yes, Matthew?"

She felt his lips touch hers. "Wake."

She opened her eyes and stared into his dark gaze. Sunshin streamed through a bay of mullioned windows, illuminating hi gold-tipped hair. He smiled then turned toward the light. His back was smooth and perfect. His wings fanned the air.

"Matthew," she called.

He looked over his shoulder. "Wake, my love."

"Wake, Patience. Wake."

Patience felt Prim squeeze her shoulder. She forced her eyes open. "What is it?"

Prim smiled softly. "Someone is here to see you."

"What?" Patience frowned sleepily as she sat up. "Who?" Turning, she squinted as the sunlight reflected off the pond. Lifting her hand, she shaded her eyes.

Matthew!

"Oh, God." Her back straightened and her heart began to pound.

His attention was fixed on them as he walked the path that led around the pond. She feasted on the sight of him, tall and graceful. He carried his jacket slung over his shoulder and his fitted waistcoat emphasized the breadth of his shoulders and the leanness of his waist. He wore no hat, and the longer strands of his gold-tipped hair had fallen against his temples in the way that she loved.

Prim got to her feet. It took Patience a moment longer, for her legs were shaking. And as Matthew neared, his beautiful eyes fixed upon her, her whole body began to tremble.

Prim stepped forward with a smile. "Hello, Matthew." She gave him a brief hug and a kiss on the cheek, as if she greeted him all the time. "It's so good to see you."

His mouth turned up. "Hello, Primrose. Thank you." He lifted his gaze back to Patience. "It's good to be here."

Prim turned and picked up her bonnet from the blanket. She paused by Patience and gave her hand a gentle squeeze. "I think I'll go see to that tea now."

Patience nodded as Prim kissed her cheek. Then her sister walked off toward the path, giving Matthew a farewell smile as she left.

Separated by five or six paces, they stood there quietly. Matthew's eyes seemed to move over every inch of her, and she drank her fill of him as well. But finally, Patience lowered her gaze; for the more she looked at him, the harder it was not to cry. All she could think of was the hope and happiness that they had shared—and the love. But that was broken.

"God, but I've missed you," he said, longingly.

Patience drew a steadying breath before lifting her gaze back to his. "I've missed you, too," she managed calmly.

His eyes were shining. "Have you been playing?"

Back at Angel's Manor, he'd given her his Guiseppe Guarneri—the golden red orange instrument she'd seen at Gwyn Hall. When she'd left him, she left the instrument as well. But he had sent it, with a note saying: *This is yours*. She loved playing it. "Yes, I adore the Guarneri. Thank you for sending it. I play it every day." She pressed her hands against her skirts. "You?"

He shook his head. "I'm afraid the Montagnana has been silent of late. I've been very busy."

Patience raised her brows. "Have you been?"

"Yes." His eyes moved slowly over her features. "That's why I couldn't come to you sooner."

Patience nodded as she folded her arms over her chest. "And how is your scheme progressing? I've yet to see any of the letters in the paper."

"I had Mickey return the letters, Patience."

She slowly unfolded her arms. "You did?"

Matthew nodded. "Yes, all of them."

Happy shock shivered down her spine. "But what of GWR How will you hold it without destroying Benchley?"

"I won't. I sold all my shares in GWR to Lord Wollby."

Patience shook her head to clear it. Had he really just said he' sold his shares? "I—I don't understand."

A smile flickered at the corner of Matthew's mouth as h shoved his hands in his pockets. "I informed Lord Wollby Benchley's plan to take over GWR, so that he could impleme a plan of his own, and then I resigned from the board. Gra West Railway is no longer my concern." Matthew shrugge "And with me out of the picture, Benchley will have a diffic time convincing the other mine owners to keep standing by hi Refusing to sell to the bastard son of a gardener is one thin Refusing to sell to one of the most powerful lords of the rea is quite another."

Patience tried to calm her racing heart. "But I thought GWR meant everything to you."

"So did I." Matthew held her in his gaze, and it was so tender. "But as it turns out, it doesn't even run a close second to what means everything to me." He took a step closer to her and then another. His lashes fluttered. "Shall I tell you what means everything?"

Patience drew shallow breaths as hope filled her and pressed against her lungs. "Yes."

"Being worthy of you."

Patience drew a shuddering breath.

Matthew took another step toward her. "And being worthy of myself."

Patience's eyes filled. She wanted to throw herself into his arms, but she couldn't seem to move. She was afraid if she did, that the spell would be broken—that she'd wake from the dream this must surely be.

He covered her hand with his. "I sold Angel's Manor, Patience—the furnishings, the art, everything. I've convinced Mark, Fitz Roy, and Rivers to invest in Gwenellyn with me. We're going to dig out from the explosion. It'll take months, but once we get it back up, it should begin to turn a profit fairly quickly."

Patience's tears slipped down her cheeks as she stared into his dove's eyes.

Lifting her hand, he touched her fingers gently. "Your Father Dafydd has agreed to stay. He and Mickey Wilkes have already emptied the old church. Mickey's working in exchange for learning to read, which, it turns out, he's always wanted to do. Farnsby and Asher are funding our school. Apparently, all those bets they place with each other are real. They've been putting the money away since childhood, so we should be able to build a separate school, rather than use the church. And, finally, I want you to tell Aunt Matty that the general store is stocked with a full assortment of candies—particularly licorice and lemon drops. So she must come and have some. Oh, and I bought Gwyn Hall from Mark, Patience."

Patience began to sob.

Matthew pressed his handkerchief into her hand and then dropped onto his knees. "Miss Patience Emmalina Dare. I am madly and unequivocally in love with you. I cannot live my life without you, and even if it takes a lifetime, I will court you and no other." He pulled her hand to his cheek. "You give me hope and joy, and I love just being in your presence. I admire you for your strength of character, your loyalty and your intellect." He kissed her fingers. "You make my heart pound and my breath quicken. And when I am with you, I feel like I have wings."

His eyes were swimming with tears. "Marry me, Patience. I have much less to offer you materially. But I offer you a good man. An honorable man. A man who will love you forever."

With a sob, Patience dropped onto her knees and threw herself into his arms. "Yes! Yes! Yes, my love!" The feel of his body against hers, the woodsy vetiver against the smell of his skin, and the softness of his hair under her hand all made her shake with need.

He kissed her urgently and deeply, then pulled back. "I have something for you," he murmured against her lips.

He pulled a small box and an envelope from his coat pocket and placed both in her hand. "For you, Mrs. Matthew Morgan Hawkmore."

Patience opened the box. Inside were her diamond combs wrapped in a cream-colored satin ribbon. Her heart lurched and she didn't think she had more tears or more happiness.

"I sold the rest of the jewelry, Patience. The money is there in the envelope."

Patience looked inside. It was several hundred pounds.

"That's the money for your thatch, your whitewash, and your trees and flowers."

Patience clutched the box and the envelope to her breast. Then she curved her hand against his cheek. "What took you so long, my love? I've been waiting for you."

Matthew stared into her eyes and his own were wet. "I'm here now." He slipped his hand into her hair and she felt it trembling. "Are you prepared to give me what I want?"

She smiled. "What is it you want?"

His tears fell, but the dominant light was in his eyes. "I wan you, Patience, for you have lit my dark world."

Patience leaned close and kissed his tears. "Then steal m away and hide me in your shadow, my love. Chain me to you side and demand my submission." She kissed his sweet mouth. "Take everything from me and, in the doing, give me *everything* I desire."

Matthew crushed her in his embrace. "Forever, my love—forever!"

Epilogue

January 16, 1852

My Dear Henrietta,

I told you to stay in England for the winter! Did I not? Did I not say, 'Henrietta, stay in merry old England where you belong'? But did you listen? No! Honestly, in a thousand years I could not have invented a story so shocking as the truth that is unfolding.

I would ask you to guess at what that truth might be, but you never shall (guess), so I will tell you everything. Do be sure to have a cup of strong tea nearby in order to fortify yourself, for once you hear . . .

Well, this is it then: Lord Benchley has been arrested upon suspicion of conspiracy and murder!

It's true, my dear! It's really true! You remember the horrible accident at Mr. Hawkmore's coal mine—the one in which poor young boys were killed? Well, it wasn't an accident at all! It turns out Lord Benchley hired some villains to blow up the mine so that Mr. Hawkmore, without a source of coal for GWR, would be forced into bankruptcy and utter ruination. Apparently, Lord Benchley even intended on taking over GWR once he'd driven it completely into the gutter. Can you imagine such despicable machinations?

Of course, revenge is never a straight arrow, is it, my dear?

Lord Benchley couldn't have known his scheme would take the life of innocents. But he must have known that it was horribly dangerous—that someone could have been hurt, or killed. And what of all the poor people who depended upon that mine for their livelihoods? I tell you, Henrietta, we had a serpent in our midst in Lord Benchley.

By the way, you must be wondering how all this came to light. It seems Benchley admitted everything to his new son-in-law, Lord Danforth, who, unable to live with the thought of keeping such a villainous secret, went to the authorities. Alas, if only he'd known of it before it happened, he might have prevented the death of the boys. But at least he was able to provide certain details and even some of the names of the actual perpetrators hired by Benchley (who have also been arrested).

Though Lord Danforth is, of course, shocked and dismayed to find himself wed into a family tainted with such wickedness, it is opportune that, as Lady Rosalind's husband, he is able to take over the administration of the Benchley estate and financial interests which now pass entirely into his control. Though, just between us, Henrietta, I can't help but think it won't be long before the Benchley fortune is greatly reduced by Lord Danforth's regrettable tendency to gamble—and spend. Since Benchley's arrest, he has already made all number of extravagant purchases, and the Lady Rosalind seems to be caught up in the same fervor. Just the other day, I heard tell she is sporting a whole new wardrobe, and that she is planning a sumptuous weeklong gala that is to be held at Benchley Hall this coming summer. Lord Tuttleworth and I are uncertain if we shall attend.

But enough about Lord and Lady Danforth. The exciting couple of the moment continues to be Mr. and Mrs. Matthew Morgan Hawkmore. I told you I would procure the details of their very private wedding, and so I have—and from none other than the aunt of the bride! Yes, Henrietta, I met her entirely by chance when I happened to run into Lord Rivers and her at the tea parlor in St. James. So here you are, my dear, practically a firsthand account ~

The couple was married in the tiny chapel of their new

home at Gwyn Hall. The day was gray and cold, and only family and close friends were in attendance.

As with the Earl of Langley's wedding, the father of the bride performed the ceremony under special dispensation. The younger sister of the bride sang (yes, apparently there is one more of these Dare sisters), and the Earl and Countess of Langley stood in attendance to their respective siblings.

The bride (who is a great beauty, I can tell you) wore a simple gown of cream-colored silk faille. Over it, she wore a fitted jacket with long sleeves and a deep hood, which she wore in place of a veil. She carried a bouquet of leaves and pomegranate flowers that, apparently, look something like peonies and were the very color of the bride's bright red hair. The groom, as you know, is darkly handsome and by all accounts could not take his eyes from his bride as she recited her vows—to love, cherish, and obey.

After the ceremony, a light snow fell on the couple and their guests as they walked to the house (isn't that romantic?). Oh, and the bride removed her jacket for the wedding feast and displayed an elegant off-the-shoulder bodice. It had a pointed waist and pleated layer of lace shot with gold threads and pearls around the neckline. Her only other adornment was a cream-colored ribbon round her neck and diamond combs in her hair.

The wedding feast was made up of hearty winter fare, and served in the dining room with all being seated around the table. The wedding cake was flavored with spices and Madeira (I'm trying to procure the recipe).

Finally, the bride and groom danced, along with some of the other family and guests, to the accompaniment of Lord Fitz Roy on the piano. Apparently he is very good, yet no one I ask has ever heard him play. And then the evening finished with everyone singing Christmas carols.

Doesn't that sound like the loveliest wedding, Henrietta? Everyone who hears of it thinks so. Certainly it's a very stark contrast to the grand and sumptuous nuptials of Lord and Lady Danforth, which you and I were privileged to attend. But do you know, Henrietta, despite the magnificence of that occasion, I think I would rather have attended the little wedding in the woods.

Ah, well . . .

Some are saying the Hawkmore wedding will start a new trend. Indeed, it seems the Hawkmores may influence many new trends, including a renewed interest in reform, and the notion of good works being good business. I tell you, Henrietta, no one can believe that Matthew Hawkmore walked away from GWR and sold practically everything he owned in order to save the Gwenellyn Mine.

But even those who don't understand or agree with his decision admire him for it. And he already seems to be making progress with the venture. A temporary shaft is being dug, and he has taken on investors. Meanwhile, Mrs. Hawkmore is seeing to the improvement of the town, and even reinstated a church there. She's also succeeded in raising money for the establishment of musical and educational scholarships for the children of the village. Truly, Henrietta, they have thrown all their efforts and personal resources toward the salvation and betterment of this seemingly small, inconsequential village—when all common sense dictated they walk away. I, for one, hope they will be rewarded both financially and otherwise. And I'm not the only one who is for them.

Mr. and Mrs. Hawkmore had already been put on several important guest lists—and, now, since Benchley's arrest, the social tide has turned completely in their favor. Everyone wants them. The only problem is that the new couple decline more invitations then they accept, and they seem to be very selective about their friends—which is only making them even more sought after.

And then there are the dinner parties they hold, which are said to be lively and informal affairs. Henrietta, the Queen and the Prince have been guests in their home! It was completely impromptu, and they came with Lord Fitz Roy. But word has it that they had such a lovely time, that they have decided to purchase an out-of-the-way house in the woods as well—Balmoral, which they have oft visited.

So, there you have it all, my dear. Who could have guessed, just months ago, that things would end so well for Matthew Morgan Hawkmore? Then, he seemed doomed to a dark world.

But now . . .

Well . . . Now, you're considered fortunate if you're invited to tea or to dinner at the old Tudor house in the forest. The party will be small, but the friends are close. And, most importantly of all, the host and hostess are people of the noblest quality and character. . . .

Yours,
Augusta

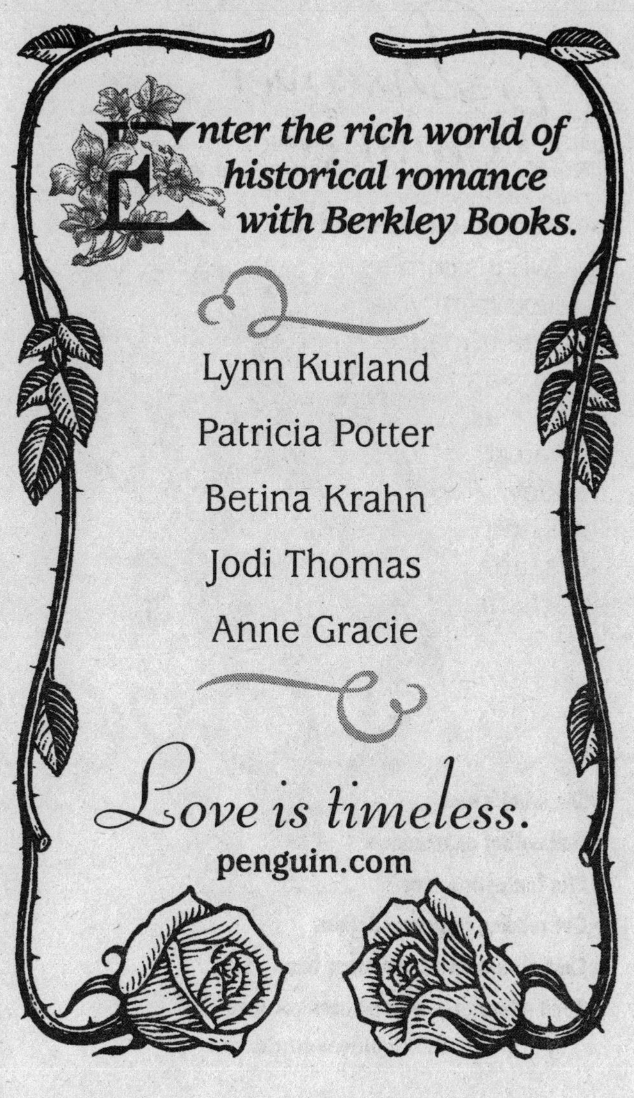
Enter the rich world of historical romance with Berkley Books.
Lynn Kurland
Patricia Potter
Betina Krahn
Jodi Thomas
Anne Gracie
Love is timeless.
penguin.com